SILVERCREST ACADEMY

UNCHAINED SHADOWS

KC KEAN

To Michael,

This is the third book dedicated to you. Could you stop being so nice, caring, and selfless, please? You're making me look all mushy and shit.

For real, thank you for being you, and for always dedicating yourself to our family.

In times when I am lost, you're still my lighthouse waiting at the shore, guiding me home.

I love you.

ELIVEN REALM
AMBERGLEN
SHADOWMOOR

HAVEN COURT
CREST
EMY
PINEBROOK
DALE
WASTELANDS
LICA REALM

How am I supposed to be enough for her right now? I'm not even enough for myself.

– Brax

ONE

Raven

I'm frozen in place, my breathing labored and my heart beating so fast my rib cage rattles.

Everything is too much and not enough all at once.

I can hear the sound of dripping water echoing in my ears over the insistent ringing of my pulse, but I can't turn to look. I can feel the floor beneath my feet rumbling slightly, but I'm still glued to the spot.

Brax squeezes my shoulder, my name on his lips, but it's not penetrating my mind deep enough to get a response from me.

I can't.

I can't take my eyes off them.

I can't bring myself to blink.

I can't.

My world is divided. Split by a barrier that refuses to

budge. Everything I know is crumbling around me as I gape helplessly while it continues to unfold.

"Raven," Brax repeats, and I shake my head slightly. Doesn't he see? Can't he understand? He knows what's happening right now just as well as I do.

"Raven!" My name is called again, but this time, it comes from Zane. He can't reach out and squeeze my shoulder, hold my hand, or even kiss my forehead.

No.

He can't do any of those things.

Neither can Eldon or Creed, who flank his sides.

"Raven, you need to go," Eldon declares, a solemn look in his eyes that burns my soul, threatening to melt me on the spot.

"Go where?" I rasp, my voice hoarse as my whole body pulses with pent-up adrenaline.

"Anywhere but here, Little Bird," he replies, my nickname warming my heart a whole degree before I remember what he's saying.

If I leave, they can't come with me. Not if they're still standing on the other side of the gateway, which leads to the Realm of Shadows. That won't be possible, and it's certainly not on my agenda.

"I'm not going anywhere without you. *Any* of you," I clarify, looking from Eldon to Zane, then taking in Creed.

Too much has happened too fast, and once again, I'm

left gaping in horror at my reality. I need time, a moment to fucking think, a damn time machine so we never step through the gate to begin with.

Fuck.

"Raven, right now, you don't really have a choice," Creed mutters. I almost don't hear him, but my brain picks up on every painful syllable that parts his lips.

"How can you say that? How can you just ask me to leave?" I snap, my anger not actually aimed at him, but he takes the brunt of it anyway. Creed doesn't reply at first. His gaze drifts to my left, and I know he's turning to Brax to take control of the situation. Fuck that. "We haven't even tried to find a way through. We haven't attempted a damn thing. First, we do that, then, if there's no option, we'll come back in there to you."

My nostrils flare as my spine stiffens, ready for any kind of argument they may throw back at me, but to my surprise, none of them seem ready to reach my level of anger quite yet.

"Dove," Zane starts, and I instantly give him a pointed look. He better have some kind of positivity to add to the situation or he's going on my shit list too. "I'm not sure what we can try. The veil that hangs between the arches of this door isn't moving a single inch." He lifts his hands and presses with all his might, even turning his arm invisible to see if it will make a difference, but it doesn't.

"Fire," I mumble, glancing at Eldon as my body still trembles. Thankfully, my fireball appeases me and lifts a ball of flames to the veil hanging between us, but it's not a surprise when nothing happens. "Where's Brax's mother? Please, ask her," I beg, taking the smallest step toward them before I'm quickly stopped by the invisible barrier separating us. "Why can't I get back in?" I snap, anger burning through me as I wave my hand through the air, only to be met with a solid wall of nothing.

"There must be people nearby who aren't permitted entry." I turn to Brax's mother, who appears a step behind my men, a deep frown settling between her eyes.

"What does that mean? It shouldn't have let Zane, Creed, and Eldon through to begin with," Brax grunts, looming from behind me as he stares at his mother.

She shakes her head softly, her gaze dropping to the floor for a moment before she seeks out her son once again. "Brax, I wish all of this was as easy as that, but it's not."

"Then explain it to us. Please," I beg, tucking a loose tendril of hair behind my ear.

"I don't know where to even begin," she replies, the weight of the words tightening my chest.

"Anywhere, please, just help us."

She glances to her side, presumably looking at Brax's

father for reassurance, but I can't quite see him. "The gate only opens to those it deems worthy. It touches the magic of all those in its vicinity, and if it doesn't like what it senses, it will tighten the veil or disappear entirely."

"How does it exist?" Brax asks as I simply gape at his mother.

"I'm not sure of its exact origins, but there's so much to this life I don't have the answers to, son, and I've been searching for a long time."

"What does that mean?" he snaps back, his eyebrows furrowing as he plants a hand on my waist, pinning me to him in a protective stance.

"That's what our assignment has always been at The Monarchy, Brax. Even now, on the other side of the veil, hidden in the Realm of Shadows. There's information everywhere, and we are researchers."

Something in her words makes me pause.

"Researchers?" I blurt, staring into her eyes.

"I'm sorry?"

"You said you *are* researchers, not past tense, not previously: *are*. What are we missing? What aren't you saying?" I feel Brax stiffen behind me, tension building to new heights as his mother once again looks to her husband for reassurance.

"We were researching the gateway to the Realm of Shadows."

Her words hang in the air, dancing over my body like the feel of the sun beating down on me while a light drizzle peppers my skin, but I know this time there's no rainbow coming.

"You're not dead. You're trapped too."

Her gaze drops to the floor, and to my surprise, Zane turns to look at her, rubbing a hand between her shoulder blades in comfort as reality continues to set in.

"Mother," Brax whispers, completely breathless, and my heart aches for him.

"We've been trapped in here this entire time, trying to find a way back to you," she admits, her voice cracking at the end as her emotions get the better of her.

"Fuck," Brax rasps, and I blindly grab his hand as he remains behind me. I squeeze as tight as I can, letting him know that I'm here, sure that this is hard for him to swallow right now.

A long time has passed. A long time without his parents, and I can't bear to think about the possibility of being away from Creed, Eldon, and Zane for that long.

"So, they can't get back in here because the magic in the veil senses something in its surroundings that it doesn't like," Zane reiterates, and Brax's mother nods, confirming another painful truth.

"Why were they able to pass back through then?" Eldon asks, while I glance around Brax to check if anyone is with us, but there's nothing but shimmering rubies and dripping water in the depths of the Ashdale caves.

"Brax has been before, as if he died and…" His mother slaps a hand over her mouth, choking on the reality of what she just said.

"I did," Brax murmurs, digging his fingers deeper into my waist. "I died and Raven brought me back."

Her eyes widen in surprise before she nods in understanding. "That explains it then," she manages, swiping at the tears tracking down her face. "If Raven is a necromancer, then her connection with the shadows is strong, and the fact that you've crossed the veil before makes it easier for you, too," she adds.

My instant thought guts me as I consider how much easier life would be in this very moment if all four of my men had fallen at some point leading up to now, then I could have brought them all back. This would no longer be an issue then.

"Can she come to revive us on this side?" Eldon asks, taking my thoughts to the next level. We all spin in unison to look at Brax's mother, but the solemn look on her face already gives us our answer.

"We've tried a thousand different ways to find death on this side, but it's impossible. Besides, she can't get back through again right now. The veil isn't safe."

The ground beneath my feet rumbles at her words and

murmurs in the distance mix with footsteps that begin to get louder as they head our way.

"They're coming," Brax states, and I follow his line of sight. I still come up empty-handed, but he's right; we're not going to be alone for much longer.

"You need to leave, Dove. Now," Zane states, firmer this time, as my heart tightens in my chest.

I know I have to, I know I do, but fuck… saying it and doing it are two completely different things. I don't know if I'm capable of it.

"Raven, we need to move," Brax declares, like it wasn't already hard enough to hear the words come from Zane.

My eyes fall closed, the world drifting to darkness around me as my soul bleeds out where I stand. Searching deep for strength that I know I don't have right now hurts, but I find a semblance of something and I tug at it with all of my abilities.

I have to go. I have to say goodbye. Only for now. Not for forever. Never for forever.

Blinking my eyes open, I scan over my three men who are just out of arm's reach.

"It's going to be okay, Dove. We're going to figure this all out," Zane murmurs, warming my heart, and I nod.

"I need you to keep each other safe and keep a tally

going for every time he's an asshole so I can pay him back eventually," Eldon states, wagging his finger between Brax and me, and the corner of my mouth tips up.

"Be strong, Raven. Be who you are, and we will work from both ends to try and figure this out as quickly as possible," Creed adds, and as much as my heart breaks at the distance between us, I take the strength they're offering and bask in it.

With a nod, I relax my shoulders and take a step back with Brax, who moves to my side. The words that have burned the tip of my tongue for so long need to be known, need to be heard, need to be tasted.

My lips part. "I—"

Movement flickers and green swoops before my very eyes before I find myself staring at the cave wall. It takes a second for me to realize the doorway has closed between us. My men are gone. I reach for the handle, just like last time, but it's no longer there. All that greets my palm is the stone wall of the cold, damp cave.

No green. No shimmering emeralds. No glimpse of hope.

Ripped away in an instant, my heart shatters into a million pieces as my knees give out and I fall to the floor. I don't meet the ground, though, not on Brax's watch. His arm bands around my waist, holding me off the dirt in one swift move.

I curl into his hold as he turns me so I can tuck my face into his neck, but it doesn't stop the sound of others approaching.

I need to pull myself together and quickly. I can't give anything away. But I'm sure the absence of Eldon, Zane, and Creed will be noted instantly.

Fuck.

"I don't know how I'm going to do this," I rasp, clinging to Brax like my life depends on it.

"Of course you do, Shadow. You're the glue holding everything together, even now. Your strength is incomparable, and for Eldon, Creed, and Zane, I know you will do everything in your power to keep them safe."

"And you," I breathe, leaning back to meet his gaze. One brown. One green. One smile.

"And me," he repeats, lowering me to the ground when he's certain I'm not going to fall again.

The moment the soles of my shoes hit the floor, noise erupts around us. Erikel and his men appear through a darkened tunnel that forms in midair. I gape in surprise at the fact that they're bypassing the way we got in here and manipulating everything around them.

My anger is instantly at the forefront of my mind again, desperate to be unleashed on this motherfucker and his damn followers. His dark eyes settle on me and I force myself to remain as calm and collected as possible.

"Where is it?" he snaps, wagging a finger in my direction as he prowls toward me, his fur cloak dragging behind him.

"Where's what?"

"Don't play games with me, Raven." My eyebrows pinch in confusion as I try to understand what game he's referring to. "Where. Is. It?" he repeats, coming to a stop a few yards away. Brax adjusts his stance slightly so he's in front of me without blocking my view of the enemy.

"You're really going to have to spit it out, Erikel. I don't know what you're talking about."

"The Potens Ruby. I want it. Now."

Understanding washes over me. The mention of what we were actually summoned here for comes flooding back to me.

The Potens Ruby.

We found it, and now he wants it. Yet... I don't have it, and neither does Brax.

Eldon does.

"I haven't found it," I grumble, wetting my bottom lip as I watch Erikel's gaze darken further. "Search me if you have to," I goad, and Brax scoffs.

"Like fuck will any of these men search you to find out." The cords in his arms coil tight, his veins protruding as he stares every single one of Erikel's men down. Including the big guy himself.

My heart races as a part of me pleads for Erikel to make a move and give me a final excuse to let off some steam, but despite my hopes, he turns his back on me with a shake of his head and a wave of his arm.

"Keep searching, men. There's nothing of use to me here right now."

23

TWO
Brax

A constant tremble runs through my body, refusing to relent. I'm so caught up in my own thoughts, freaking out, it's leaving me incapable of grasping everything happening around me. I don't know which way is up, where to turn, or how to proceed. This is more than I think I can handle.

Us.

It's me and Raven.

Just me and Raven.

My friends, my brothers… fuck.

I haven't had to function without Eldon for longer than I can remember. Now, with Creed and Zane gone, too, I don't know how to think. They're just as much a part of me as I am them.

There's a reason I've always been open to sharing

a girl with them. I can't handle the duty of making her happy, keeping her safe, and everything else that comes along with providing for the woman you want by myself.

Now here I am.

Fuck. Fuck. Fuck.

How am I supposed to be enough for her right now? I'm not even enough for myself.

Glancing down at Raven, my chest tightens. She needs me. Technically, she needs all of us, but she's stuck with me as her only option, so we're both going to have to compromise. It won't be for long. I swear it.

"Follow me, Soul Dancer," Erikel calls out without looking our way. I remember the last time he used that nickname for Raven and I fucking hate it.

Her lips pinch as her nostrils flare. With narrowed eyes, she puts one foot in front of the other, following his order, but not before reaching for my hand to keep me at her side.

We trail after him and his men, stepping through the gateway they created instead of taking the narrow entrance we originally used to get in here. We appear outside a moment later. The sun has set, leaving only the moon to glow down upon us.

I'm surprised by how many students are already out here. Gathered in small groups, everyone looks uncertain, defeated, and exhausted. If that's what everyone else looks like, I dread to think of what they see when they look at me. I'm trying my hardest to hold myself together, but it's easier said than done.

Raven points to the left and I follow her line of sight to find Leila and Grave huddled together on a boulder. They're sitting side by side, their thighs pressed against one another as they quietly talk.

I squeeze Raven's hand, indicating for us to head that way, but Erikel suddenly whirls around to face us. His brows are knitted together as he looks down his nose at us.

"Where are the others?"

"Who?" I grunt, hating how tight Raven clings to my hand, her emotions pouring into me. I want to take them all away, every last one, but I can't, and that's a hard pill to swallow.

"Don't play dumb with me, boy. The rest of the necromancer's brothel," Erikel snarks, and my whole body goes rigid with anger. My teeth grind together as I try to breathe through it, but I just want to lash out and take this fucker down.

"We split up inside, trying to find what you wanted," Raven answers, and his gaze quickly shifts to her as he assesses the truth of her words.

His eyes narrow but he seemingly accepts it, spinning away again as he quietly talks with his henchmen.

Raven exhales heavily, her eyelids closing briefly, and I instantly wish Zane or Creed were here. They'd know exactly what to do to make her feel better.

"This is so fucked up," she breathes as we move through the gathered students to where Leila sits.

"I know, but we need to wait until we're safe to even think about it," I admit, and the desperation on her face is evident.

"It's gone, Brax. The gate is gone," she mouths, her knuckles turning white as she holds on to me tightly.

Fuck.

"I know, Shadow. I know."

She stops suddenly, wiping her free hand down her face before tilting her head back to look up at the sky, all while I stand helplessly beside her with no clue how to fix it.

My parents, my brothers; everything is fucked. Fucked so hard. I'm ready to sink into my own mess of thoughts, but I can't focus on that when I can see how shattered she is, too.

"It's just the two of us for now, Shadow, but we'll figure this out. Fuck knows how but we won't accept anything less than resolving all of this."

She peers at me, the smallest and softest smile ghosting her lips for the briefest moment. "We'll get through this."

"We will," I agree, and I notice her body relax a little, but the tension still radiates between us.

"Well, you might," she reiterates, moving again, and I'm a sucker to stay at her side.

"What's that supposed to mean?"

She shakes her head, a grin appearing on her lips once again as her tongue peeks out, touching her bottom lip for the briefest moment before disappearing again.

"Well, you swore not to get me off until Sebastian was dead. Because he's clearly under their magical control, it doesn't look like it will be happening any time soon. At least the others weren't so hell-bent on being an asshole."

I gape at her, lips parted more than I wish, as she comes to a stop in front of Leila, effectively dismissing any further conversation.

"Hey, I was starting to wonder where you guys were," Leila says, standing before us while Grave stays where he is. She frowns almost instantly, glancing around us. "Where are the others?"

Raven peers at her friend but not a single word comes, and I have to quickly catch up instead of remaining focused on the final statement she gave me before we were interrupted.

"Gather around," Erikel snaps, pulling everyone's attention to him.

Raven shakes her head at Leila, turning to face our self-elected leader with the rest of the student body out here.

He stands on a boulder, the golden warrior to his left, Fitch to his right, with the students from Shadowgrim Insitute crowding closer to him while the rest of us keep as much distance as possible.

Once he's certain he has everyone's attention, his eyes cut to Raven. "I want the location of Creed Wylder, Zane Denver, and Eldon Rhodes."

Fuck. We should have known he wasn't going to let it drop as easily as that.

The golden warrior's attention perks up and he glances from Erikel to Raven and back. Fuck him, though. We wouldn't be here if he hadn't delved deep into his son's mind against his will. We wouldn't be parted from my brothers with the weight of the realm firmly on our shoulders.

"I don't know where they are," Raven states, making Erikel bare his teeth in anger. I don't think we're going to get away with saying nothing at this rate.

"Don't lie to me. You know where they are, and my Potens Ruby," he snaps, sweeping his hand in our direction, and the golden warrior instantly starts to move toward us.

Nobody says a word as we all watch his movements. His onyx eyes, which are usually blacker than black and void of anything at all, swirl with unspoken questions that he sure as hell isn't getting the answers to.

"I can read your pretty little mind," he warns as he comes to a stop in front of us, hand lifted and palm turned up in warning.

Over my dead fucking body.

I take a step forward, ready to put this asshole in his place, but Raven beats me to it. She reaches out, grasping onto thin air as her jaw tics. "And I can read yours."

Laughter echoes around us, booming from Erikel with a gulp of excitement while the rest of the onlookers remain as confused as ever.

"Ah, mirror magic. How fun, you're going to quickly learn you're no match for me," the warrior promises, the two of them at an impasse, refusing to back down.

I need to do something, but the reality is I'm the brute force. Raven is more powerful than me in every sense of the word. We already know my strength means nothing against Creed's father, not in that armor.

"Help! Help!"

Panic swarms the air as hurried footsteps approach, interrupting another intense moment, but I'm thankful for it this time.

Gasps distract me, pulling my attention to Sebastian, who continues to approach, calling for help. He doesn't stop until he's standing directly in front of Erikel, where he drops to his knees and places something on the floor.

The golden warrior finally relents, turning to see for himself what all of the commotion is about, and that's when I see what has everyone worked up.

Fuck.

"It's Genie… she's dead," Leila whispers in shock as

murmurs travel through the crowd around us.

Her limp body lies between Sebastian and Erikel. The latter stares with wide eyes as Sebastian kneels with his head in his hands.

Does he really care, or is this the magic? Either way, it doesn't really matter in the grand scheme of things. As much as Raven has a sudden soft spot for him and his situation, I still can't see past the shit he's done, and seeing him full of despair is barely a drop in the bucket of what he deserves. If he's that sad about the loss of Genie, I can sure as fuck help him join her if he wants.

"Who did this?" Erikel bites, darkness wrapping around us as silence quickly greets him. His eyes snap to Raven and I know what's going to come next before he even opens his mouth. "Bring her back. Now."

She assesses him while I fight to keep my mouth shut. I want to demand that she stay away and cut her magic off from them, but I know she has her own mind. This is her decision, and we both know she'll have a better game plan at this moment than me.

I'd probably wind up dead, and she probably doesn't need the added stress of that right now.

It's no surprise when she starts to move. I grip *her* hand tight this time, pinning myself to her side as she swoops past the golden warrior and through the parting crowd to where Erikel stands.

The closer we get, the more noticeable his tremble becomes.

He's mad. *Mad* mad.

Raven tries to release my hand and I frown down at her. She gives me a pointed look and I reluctantly relent, instantly hating the loss of contact as she drops to her knees beside Genie. Sebastian doesn't move an inch, seemingly happy to keep his face in his hands.

"Now," Erikel barks, and I don't miss the eye roll my woman gives him even though he can't see.

I inch closer, acutely aware of everything around us as I stand guard.

A few moments pass, Raven's hands hovering over Genie's body without actually touching her until she shakes her head. "I can't."

"Try. Harder."

Raven rolls her shoulders back, moving her hands to Genie's chest, but quickly shakes her head again. "I can't. It's too late."

Her voice cracks ever so slightly at the end. The reality of what happened is washing over her, and I swiftly reach down and pull her to her feet. She spins in my hold, pressing her face into my chest, and I shield her from the world.

She's not crying, shaking, or disheveled beyond words, but it helps turn her away from Erikel, who lets out an almighty roar of rage before falling to his knees beside

Genie's lifeless body. His fur cloak drapes around him, providing a blanket between him and the gathered crowd, who stand in complete shock.

He may be slightly hidden, but the words that part his lips remain etched into my mind.

"You won't have died in vain, my darling. I'll take this realm and the next for your mother, and now for you."

35

THREE

Eldon

One moment, the love of my life is standing before me, an invisible barrier between us, and the next, she s gone.

Gone.

Like a soft laugh drifting in the breeze, never to be heard again.

My heart aches, my soul burns, and my life feels like it hangs in the balance.

The second she's ripped away from me, I'm overcome with the need to feel her skin against mine, hear her voice soothe me, and breathe in her scent. It's an instant, unwavering craving that I can't shake as it grows, burning through my veins as I stand helplessly in the Realm of Shadows.

One glance at Zane and Creed reveals the same pain

in their eyes. Helplessness clings to the air, claiming us as its victim as life seemingly continues on the other side of the gate.

I give myself a moment to dwell, to break, to sink deep into the depths of despair, but that's it. Not a second longer. We need to be positive and focused if we plan to find a way out of here.

"Come," Brax's father murmurs, waving for us to follow after him. Brax's mother hurries to his side and I watch them for a moment, the way he sweeps his arm around her shoulders, pulling her in close as he presses a kiss to her head.

We're not the only ones hurting here, and they've been lost to this pain far longer than we have.

Fuck.

"Let's go," Zane mutters, patting me on the arm, and the three of us follow after them.

It's the strangest feeling to walk among… nothing. Not a bird chirping, no rustle of a breeze over leaves, or even the waves crashing in the distance that have offered us comfort at the academy.

Instead, we're surrounded by an off-white that seems to go on forever. The only thing present is the home before us. I'm sure it would look sweet and comforting in any other setting, but it looks eerie as hell right now.

A white wrap-around porch lures us closer before we

step inside the house.

"How is there even a home here?" Zane asks, and I shrug, just as bewildered as him.

"It's a replica of our home in the outside world. Come, we'll explain what we can over a drink," Brax's mother states, leading the way into a large open kitchen. White wooden cupboards and granite countertops greet us. Small green plants are dotted around the space. The lush colors and added life catches me by surprise, but I keep my thoughts to myself as I take a seat at the dining table with Zane, Creed, and Brax's father.

We sit in silence, each lost in our thoughts, until Brax's mother approaches with a tray of steaming mugs, placing one in front of each of us before taking the seat beside her husband.

"Thank you." I have no idea what it is, and as much as my stomach is in knots, I bring the mug to my lips and take a sip.

Hot cocoa.

Damn, it's been forever since I've had this. My mother used to make it all the time for me when I was small. I smile fleetingly at the memory, a time of calmness and no stress grounding me and giving me the boost of hope I need before reality settles back in.

"Do you want anything to eat?" Brax's father asks, and I shake my head while Creed and Zane decline too.

"What do we need to know about this place?" Creed asks, cutting straight to the point, and my attention swings to Brax's parents, desperate for details.

"Well, first, I'm Marieta and this is my husband Peta. Just in case you don't remember from when you were young. To wager a guess, I'm going to assume that you're Zane Denver, Creed Wylder, and Eldon Rhodes," she lists off, pointing at each of us respectively.

"How do you know that?" Zane asks, his smile not quite reaching his eyes as he assesses them.

Marieta smiles softly, taking a sip of her drink before responding. "Creed is the double of his father. I've never met anyone as calm and collected as Rosa Rhodes, and the way you hold your shoulders reminds me of Rhys." She points at Creed with the latter, making a smile appear on his face for a split second.

My eyebrows are almost in my hairline as I gape at her in surprise. I know she knew my mother, that's how we came to take Brax in when we were younger, but she knows all of our parents? Deep down, that doesn't surprise me, but it still catches my attention.

"How did you end up here, Marieta?" Creed asks, his jaw tight. I'm sure the reminder of looking like his father isn't helping him.

Peta places his hand on top of Marieta's as he addresses my friend. "We were working on an assignment for The

Monarchy. After leaving Silvercrest Academy, we were enrolled as researchers in Haven Court," he explains, and Marieta offers a soft, sad smile.

"A lot of our research revolved around the Basilica Realm, which meant we were involved in battles more than achieving any research most of the time," she adds, shaking her head, her eyes glazed over as if a memory is playing in her mind.

"We were perfect in battle, darling," Peta murmurs, making her smile grow wider.

"We were, but we're getting off track," she whispers back, swiping a hand at her cheeks before turning back to us. "We were trying to gather intel on magical artifacts that we knew other realms were searching for. The emerald gate being one of them."

"Why would someone be searching for access into the Realm of Shadows?" Creed asks, leaning back in his seat with his arms folded over his chest.

"Imagine being led by darkness, desperate to hold reign over all of the realms, all while desiring the magical abilities of a necromancer without the power to control the shadows yourself."

Her words hit hard. Not because they don't make sense, but because they do. It definitely makes sense for someone like Erikel. But why use Raven's necromancer abilities to bring people back from the dead and not force her to control the shadows? Why continue to search for artifacts?

"Clearly, controlling someone to orchestrate the shadows still isn't enough. Erikel must want the power for himself," Zane states, answering my thoughts.

I nod mindlessly. I'm never going to understand Erikel and his thought process.

"That's what they don't understand about the emerald gate. If it senses ill intent, it will never appear," Peta explains, repeating what Marieta said when Brax and Raven were standing on the other side of the gate.

"But it showed itself to you." I glance between them as they nod in agreement.

"It did, which feels like a cruel joke at this stage. Our intention was to understand it and protect it," Marieta murmurs with a hollow chuckle.

"That's exactly what it's allowed you to do, unfortunately, from in here instead of out there," Creed says with a shrug, gaining Brax's parent's attention as they stare at him in surprise.

"Have you kept track of how you've tried to escape?" Zane asks, redirecting the conversation, and they both nod.

"Good. We're going to need to take a look at that," I add, and Marieta exhales softly, a smile touching her lips.

"That sounds perfect. We definitely need another set of eyes to take a look over everything. But it's not just a file or scrap of paper. It's a whole room. Once you've finished with your hot cocoa, we can show you." I take a deep breath, relief and hope desperate to blossom in my soul. "How is your mother?" she asks, glancing over the top of her mug at me.

"She's good. I haven't been able to hear from her in a few weeks with all of the mess at the academy, but she's as amazing as ever," I explain. "Although, I definitely use her as a weapon against Brax when he's being quiet. She always helps bring out his softer side," I add. I don't know why until I see the happiness shimmering in her eyes. She needed to hear that.

"Thank you," Peta mutters, comforting his wife, who clears her throat and turns to look at Zane.

"And how is Rhys?"

Zane scrubs the back of his neck. "He's keeping his head above water while everything is coming to a head at The Monarchy."

"And putting you guys first, I assume? His love for you and your sister, as well as your mother, is unparalleled," she states, making Zane smile as he nods.

"And your father?" Peta asks, turning to look at Creed.

"Mine?" he retorts with a frown, confusing Peta, who nods slowly.

"Yeah, of course. Zeek is my best friend. Always. I'm going to have to have words with him if I ever get to see him again if he hasn't told you that, too," Peta insists, leaving Creed to gape at him before he quickly clears his throat and sits up in his seat.

"We believed he was killed in battle in the Basilica Realm," he breathes, making Peta's eyes widen in horror.

"No. I'm so sor—"

"Until he reappeared a few weeks ago under their control," Creed interjects, and I'm certain Peta is going to pass out with the information.

"Under their control as in…" It's Marieta's turn to comfort her husband this time, desperate to clarify what Creed means as she rubs her hand down Peta's back.

"As in, he's the leader's guard. Dressed in golden armor stained with blood and merciless when following his orders." Creed's voice grows hoarse as he spits the words out, and Peta's head falls into his hands.

"I'm so sorry, Creed. I can't imagine how any of this feels for you, but I can tell you with certainty that your father is one of the best men I know," Marieta insists. Creed nods, looking away.

I have no clue what time it is right now, but earlier, when we were still at the academy, we learned that Erikel knew The Monarchy was coming to help us because Creed's father managed to find the information for him. At the same time, he managed to hide other facts from Erikel, so once again, we're left with a very unclear picture of his intentions.

"So, it's officially all gone to shit out there then," Peta states, and I laugh.

"To summarize, yeah."

"I thought it would have happened sooner than this, if I'm honest." He says nothing else as he finishes his drink and takes his mug to the sink.

"And Brax?" Marieta murmurs. "How did he die?" The memory floods my mind, and my hands clench involuntarily at the pain. "The first time he arrived, he left just as quickly," she adds, and my chest clenches. Knowing he made it all the way to the Realm of Shadows before finding his way back to us makes it all the more real.

"It was during an attack at the Shadowmoor outpost," Zane states. "We were ambushed by the Amayans and one of them managed to get to him, then Raven's abilities finally came to her."

"Came to her?" Peta asks, standing behind his chair now.

"Yeah, that's a story for another time, but she didn't know she was a necromancer until she was a wreck hovering over Brax's body. Her cry was… gut-wrenching, and a moment later, his eyes were open again."

"She's not like any necromancer I've heard of before," Marieta whispers, dabbing at the corner of her eyes again.

"She's not like anyone we've ever seen before," Creed reiterates, swiping a hand down his face.

"Let's take a look at the room, shall we?" Peta offers, and we all nod in agreement.

He leads the way back into the hallway, turning us toward the end of the hall. I don't know what I expect to see on the other side of the door, but it's not this.

Paper litters the entire wall, words scribbled everywhere. Items littered around every surface seem just organized enough to be considered categorized. There seems to be some kind of color coding going on: yellows, blues, pinks, and greens.

"This is everything we've tried so far, and these are options we're trying to put together," Peta states, waving his arm around the room.

Fuck.

"We're stranded and helpless," Creed grunts, and I take a deep breath, refusing to let that be the truth.

"That's what we've been for all these years. I don't want to give you false hope because I sure as hell don't have any," Marieta states, running her fingers mindlessly over the papers on the wall.

"You best start believing in it." Her eyes widen in my direction as I stand tall.

"You can't be sure."

"No disrespect, Marieta. Brax may be your son, but you don't know him as well as we do. He won't rest until we're all together. For his sake, for yours, ours, but most importantly, for Raven's." My words hang in the air for a few beats and I'm certain she's going to brush me off, but to my surprise, she takes a deep breath, standing taller as she nods.

"I hope so."

"I know so," Zane clarifies, making her smile.

"So, what's going on out there?" Peta asks, and I realize they've caught us up to date on things in here, but they have no clue what's happening in the real world.

Where to even begin?

Planting my hands on my hips, I exhale. "Everything seemed to be okay from our perspective until Erikel arrived. There were a few attacks we were made aware of, and we were on a visit to Shadowmoor outpost when it was attacked, but everything really did go to shit when he showed up."

"Erikel?" Marieta frowns, knitting her hands together.

"He's from the Basilica Realm," Zane explains, and she gulps, turning to look at Peta.

"I thought he was dead," she breathes. "I watched you kill him," she adds to her husband, who looks as defeated as she does.

"So did I." Peta looks our way. "Are you certain it's him?"

I shrug. "I didn't know this man existed until he appeared at the academy. I have no idea."

"It has to be him, though, right? Who else could it be?" Zane asks, his brows knitted as tension ripples through me.

"Do you know what Erikel's magical abilities are?" I glance back to Marieta, who nods.

"He had the strongest telekinesis abilities I've ever seen."

"Anything else?" I push, my heart starting to gallop.

"No… why?" Peta answers, casting his gaze over each of us.

I gulp, turning to look at Creed and Zane, who both look at me with the same uncertainty in their eyes that I feel deep down in my soul.

"We have witnessed an ability from him that we believe he keeps secret, but we also haven't seen him use any telekinesis," I breathe, and Peta scoffs.

"Impossible, that man used his abilities every second of every moment," he insists. "What have you seen him do?"

I wet my lips, looking down at the scattered sheets on the floor before returning to them. "We've witnessed him skinwalking."

Peta goes still, his jaw slack as Marieta lifts a hand to her chest, shaking her head softly.

"That's inconceivable. He… there's only ever been one skinwalker. If Erikel had been one, he would have been captured by The Monarchy instead of slaughtered."

"It doesn't make any sense. We've seen him shift before our very eyes. He can do it," Zane insists, and Peta finally moves again.

"Or the person doing the skinwalking was doing it."

If I thought all of this skinwalking bullshit was too much before, it just went to a whole other level. Fuck. No wonder my head is pounding.

"Who was the only known skinwalker?" Creed asks. Marieta and Peta look at each other for the longest moment, like they're trying to piece it together, but it doesn't seem possible to them.

"Tiran, Tiran Burton."

FOUR

Raven

We're filtered through the gateways like cattle, reappearing at Silvercrest Academy as if we never left, as if my life hasn't altered, everything tipped upside down and burning my soul with raw purpose.

The atmosphere is solemn. Not from the loss of Genie, who has been left in the sand at Ashdale, as you would expect. It seems to be more from the fact that we don't have a single freaking clue about what is actually going on around us.

Not me.

Not Brax.

Not anyone.

There's no way to predict what is to come, what Erikel will throw at us next. We're simply expected to follow our new leader blindly, just like the students from

Shadowgrim Institute.

How they're handling the situation right now is what sets us apart. We could all be in the same clothing and their calmness would identify them clearly. They're not floundering, etched with concern, and fighting to keep their heads above water. They're used to it. Probably enjoying the excitement of the unknown at this point.

It's not for me.

Not one bit.

Standing with the growing crowd of students, we all reluctantly await our next direction, but to my surprise, Erikel waves his hand in the air. "Men, assemble. The Monarchy attack is imminent. We must prepare," he orders, sauntering off without a backward glance.

The students from Shadowgrim follow after him with ease while the rest of us remain in place. I don't know what he's planning for. The Monarchy's plan wasn't to ambush them. It was all about our extraction, at least for the time being. If he thinks I'm going to help prepare to take down our only hope, he's delusional.

"The rest of you head back to your houses. Tomorrow will proceed as normal," Fitch declares, effectively dismissing us before his gaze zeros in on Leila. One wave of his hand and she shuffles from foot to foot beside me.

"If you don't want to, you don't have to," I hear myself say, despite the fact that we still need to act as normal as possible. But more and more, we're seeing what he can achieve, how there's more to him than we know. Forced by magic or not, Fitch can't be trusted.

She turns her gaze to me, the panic in her eyes clear, but despite the shimmer of doubt, she shakes her head. "I'm good."

Grave lets her go without complaint, but I don't miss the way he watches her go, scrubbing nervously at the back of his neck. If he knew what we know about Fitch, would he defend her, protect her, or feed her to the lions?

"Let's get out of here," Brax murmurs, splaying his fingers at the base of my spine as he pulls me from the thinning crowd. Instead of taking to the pathway like everyone else, he slips behind the shrubs and trees for some privacy before he attempts to generate a gateway.

Three tries and no luck. The glare on his face practically vibrates from him.

"They must still have the wards in place, or something from the drill earlier is still suppressing the transportation magic," I recall, remembering the moment when we were in Figgins's office, ready to go and see Ari, before everything went to Hell. "It's okay, though. Maybe the walk will do us some good," I offer, but it does nothing to relax the tension building in his shoulders.

He doesn't utter a word in acknowledgment as he takes off, leaving me to hurry after him. We rejoin the path, my grumpy gargoyle leading the way as usual, when he suddenly stops, turning to face me with his eyebrows furrowed in confusion. His gaze travels around us, noting every student that passes as we stand in the center of the walkway.

It takes a moment for me to piece it together, but once I do, it all makes sense.

He's used to walking ahead, living in his thoughts while I walk with the others. Now, if he takes the lead, there's no one to protect me from behind or at my sides. If I thought it once, I'd have thought it a thousand times since the emerald gate shut before us.

It's just the two of us.

Brax and me.

For now, at least.

I don't know what words of comfort to offer him. I know none will make it easier. His eyes track between mine, searching for something I can't quite put my finger on before he reaches his hand out, palm face up, and I don't waste a second before placing my hand in his.

We walk in comfortable silence, side by side, hand in hand, as we get lost in our own minds in the presence of one another. I want to give him a moment to get a grasp on exactly what we're sinking in, but I can't help but fixate on the small dead weight inside of me.

Not from the guys. I'm clinging to hope when it comes

to them. It's because of Genie. Well, not her specifically, but more the fact that for the first time since I was forced to bring someone back I… couldn't. It felt like a deeper loss than on the surface. As much as I didn't want Genie's death on my hands, it doesn't pain me like I thought it might, but my soul, the core of my magic, that hurts. Maybe from the pent-up energy brought to the surface, ready to work to no avail. Now it sits heavy in my gut with nowhere to go.

Before I know it, we're back at the house, the door closing behind us with a thud, and the silence screams in my ears.

Fuck.

The quiet is too much. The walls are used to handling the thoughts and voices of five, and now there are only two. I can't wrap my head around it. It hurts too much.

Releasing Brax's hand, I head for my room, my gut twisting even tighter as I take in the huge bed. The bed meant for all of us. The bed that looks too big, too empty, too… sad.

My heart aches, but I feel Brax's presence behind me, his body heat wrapping around me even though we're not touching as he sighs, feeling the weight of the silence as much as I am.

"Let's shower."

He walks around me, heading for the bathroom, and I follow after him, a numbness creeping down my spine as longing claims me. The shower turns on with his magic, but he takes the effort to strip out of his clothes one layer at a time. I roll with it, taking my time with each item of clothing I have on, letting the process ground me as I run through the mundane task.

Brax steps under the spray first, and I keep a step behind him, drawn to him like a moth to the flame. He's my grounding rock right now. The reason I can still see straight. The one wading through the fog that clouds my mind. Not that I could tell him any of that, not when he's sinking too. The last thing my gargoyle needs is to feel any more responsibility for me than he already does. Not when he's helping me. I can see the effort in every move, every breath, without a single grumble about it.

The spray from the shower warms my skin, making me shiver as I tip my head back. Every drop of water eases the tension in my muscles and my shoulders sag with relief. My eyes drift close as I breathe slowly, just letting the steady stream beat down on me.

I startle when hands wrap around my waist, followed quickly by a cloth a moment later. Blinking, I find Brax running the fabric over my damp body and lathering soap onto my skin. Once he's satisfied with my top half, he drops to his knees, proceeding with the same attention and care as he cleans my legs, ass, and finally, the apex of my thighs.

He doesn't linger, quickly getting back up on his feet and reaching for the shampoo. As he takes the time to wash my hair, emotions bubble to the surface. His delicate touch, the unspoken consideration of my needs, all of it, blossoms wildly in my chest.

Once he's done, I'm left panting, gaping at him in awe before I finally find the ability to move. This time, I reach for the cloth, not caring if the body wash is fruity as I work it into his skin.

I enjoy tracing his collarbone, down between his pecs, and over every ridge of his six-pack. The feel of the raised cords in his arms reminds me of the strength this man holds. I'm still fixated on it when I drop to my knees, starting at his feet before I make my way up to his knees and reach his waist.

His cock stands stiff and aimed in my direction. Looking up at him, I find him staring at me, chest heaving with every breath as he takes me in. I can see the conflict in his eyes.

Any other time there would be no question whether I would take him in my mouth, desperate for it, but because Zane, Creed, and Eldon are fuck knows where, it feels… inconsiderate? Fuck, I don't know.

His eyes darken. One brown. One green.

The world stands still around us for the briefest moment, and before I can think more of it, talk myself out of something I need more than my next breath, I inch forward, taking his long, thick length between my lips.

My gaze remains locked on his as my tongue swirls around the tip. His jaw ticks, and his neck muscles clench, but he doesn't push me away or tell me to stop. Bracing my hands on his thighs, I swallow him to the back of my throat, humming at the salty taste of him against my tongue.

Damn.

One taste, and I'm practically feverish for more. I feel the weight of his hand in my hair, but he doesn't move me along. He doesn't need to. I'm in a frenzy. He hits the back of my throat and I retreat, repeating the motion faster and needier with every pass as I hollow out my cheeks, tightening my suction.

"Fuck, Raven," he rasps, his eyelids falling to half-mast as I feel him grow in my mouth. Hotter, longer, wider, it stuns us both when he fists my hair and lets out a low groan, spilling his cum down my throat.

He slumps back against the tiled wall and I jerk in surprise from the water that hits my face. I hadn't realized he was shielding me from the shower.

Releasing his cock from my mouth, I lean back, a satisfied sigh parting my lips before I stand. He eyes me with a sense of bewilderment I've never seen from him before, and I instantly worry he's expecting me to demand something in return. That's not what this is about, so I quickly step out of the shower and wrap a fluffy towel around my body.

Reality begins to creep in again, the small reprieve from the actuality that we're drenched in making its way back to the surface. I turn to face him, offering him a soft smile as I hand him a towel. No words are needed, and no regret bubbles to the surface. He needed the pause from the crazy just as much as I did.

I hold the towel tight around my chest, clinging to the warmth as I step back into the room. I don't want to look at the bed, but it's impossible not to. I'm sure it's going to break me down this time, but before I can exhale a pained breath, a sound catches my attention.

My ears perk as I stand tall, trying to follow where it's coming from. Brax's gaze catches mine, and he frowns for a moment before understanding washes over his face.

"It's Zane's shell," he mutters.

Shell? Oh, shit. The device he has to speak with his father? I stare down at it, confused with why the fuck it's going off right now. "Weren't these things broken after Captain Bag of Dicks arrived? Isn't that why we spent all that time in Lyra's little pocket dimension?"

Brax shakes his head. "No, he was using it, his father was just unable to answer, which is why he had to take the more open communication route."

I nod like it makes sense, but it really doesn't. I don't

have time to process it. My eyes widen and I quickly use my magic to lose the towel, replacing it with a pair of leggings and a sweater, leaving my damp hair to fall over my shoulders.

Whirling around to Brax, I find him dressed in a pair of black jeans and a black fitted tee with a peach-colored shell filling his hand. He cocks a brow at me, seeking my confirmation that I'm ready, and I nod.

A moment later, the space between us is filled by a projection of Rhys Denver.

"Hey, son, I just wanted to—" Rhys goes quiet as he slowly glances from Brax to me and back again, a deep crease forming between his eyes. "Where's Zane?" I gape at him momentarily, at a complete loss of where to begin. "Brax?" he encourages after he's greeted with more silence from the pair of us, and all Brax can do is grunt in response.

Fuck.

Shifting, I take a seat at the foot of the bed before I lock eyes with the glimmer of hope that's been keeping us going. I take a deep breath but it does nothing to calm my racing heart. "I don't know where to start," I offer hoarsely, the concern on Rhys's face deepening as he moves around the space as if he's here in the flesh, taking the spot beside me.

"At the beginning."

I don't even know where that is.

"Erikel learned you were coming to rescue us tomorrow."

"Tomorrow?" Rhys questions. "You mean in a few hours?"

I shrug. I have no idea what time it is, and it feels like I've lived a whole lifetime since I last spoke with him. "I don't know. All I know is he learned the truth and insisted we go on a mission to the caves in Ashdale." My gaze drifts to my hands, knitted together in my lap as my lips dry. Thankfully, he doesn't push, giving me a moment to process. "Everyone was searching for the Potens Ruby, but we actually found it." I force my gaze back to his, and even though he seems surprised, I can still see the uncertainty in his eyes, waiting for the part where we explain where Zane is. I want to cut to the chase and give him the details he needs, but explaining it all out loud from the beginning is helping me understand better. Breaking everything down is almost cathartic.

"Do you have it with you now?"

I shake my head. "No. Eldon has it."

"Is he with Zane?" he pushes, a storm swarming in his eyes as he tries to show me as much patience as possible.

Nodding, I see a pinch of relief in his eyes, but not enough. "After we found it, we also found the emerald gate to the Realm of Shadows."

His eyes widen but he doesn't utter a single word.

Brax clears his throat, pulling both of our gazes to him as he nervously scrubs at the back of his neck. "It's my fault, Monarch Denver. Ever since…" His eyes drift to me before resettling back on Rhys. "I've been having vivid dreams of visiting my parents in the Realm of Shadows. I had researched the emerald gate when we were trying to learn more on the Potens Ruby." He glances down at his feet, defeat getting the better of him. "If I had kept my curiosity to myself, Rhys, the burning desire to… seek more, we would all be here together."

"Is Zane in the Realm of Shadows?" The question hangs heavy in the air, forcing a pained squeak from my throat as I nod, unable to say the words out loud. "Creed and Eldon too?" I nod again, and he exhales slowly. "Are Marieta and Peta with them?" I frown, unsure who he means, but Brax nods this time, answering for us.

His parents.

"Yes, sir."

"Brax, this isn't your fault. I need you to know that," Rhys breathes, swiping a hand down his face. "They may be in the Realm of Shadows, but it's not because they're dead. I've spent a long time trying to bring your parents back. I haven't been successful, but I've never had a necromancer on my side either," he states, turning to glance at me.

"You knew they were there?" Brax's voice is raspy as he glares at Zane's father, who hangs his head in defeat for a moment before he looks back at him.

"Not the whole time, but things didn't add up when I continued to pursue their research in honor of them. About six years ago, I learned of their existence, but I didn't want to stoke hope in a situation I may have never been able to resolve. I'm sorry for that, Brax. Truly. We've never had anyone travel through the gate before, the risks were unknown. Technically, they still are."

Brax glares at him, nodding once, sharp, harsh, not yet forgiving, and Rhys doesn't push him any further.

"The gate disappeared, Rhys. We don't know where they are," I murmur, my chest clenching so tight I'm sure I'm going to pass out.

"Yeah, it does that," he replies with a half smile.

"We need your help. Now more than ever." It's obvious, it always is. He's helped us every step of the way, but things are different now. I'm being torn apart at the seams and need someone to hold the stitching together. That's Brax. But at the same time, we need someone to help us complete the pattern ingrained into my soul. A pattern that can only be fixed with Creed, Eldon, and Zane present too.

"You have it. Always." I take a deep breath, relieved at his promise. "Is Erikel awaiting our arrival now?" he asks, already seeing the big picture and guiding us.

"Yes. He's already called the students from Shadowgrim Institute into action. I'm sure he's banking on your arrival at this stage. As much as I want you to come to save us, I don't think now is the time," I admit, and he nods in agreement.

"Let me reassess, but don't utter a word of this to anyone else. I'll keep it to myself here too. If you have any emergencies, use the shell. Otherwise, keep it close. I'll call when I can."

I nod and he turns to Brax, waiting for the same acceptance from him too. It takes a moment, but once he has it, he disappears. The room goes quiet. The two of us are alone again, staring at one another with more questions and fewer answers fluttering between us.

The clock is ticking, time is running out, and I fear the end in sight is far from the one we wish for.

FIVE

Raven

Soft sunlight, the warmth of it euphoric, dancing along my eyelids, stirs me awake as I stretch out my aching limbs. I can't remember when it ever felt this good before and it takes a moment for my eyes to focus as I take in my room.

It lasts for the shortest moment before I remember the current state of my life, the pain determined to follow me around, and my bones run cold. Clutching the sheets to my chest, I roll to my side, lifting my knees as I curl in on myself.

Eternity came and went last night. The ability to fall asleep continued to evade me until the early hours. I wasn't alone, though. Brax seemed to be struggling just as much as me. The call with Rhys last night helped somewhat, but it only added further questions to my over-wired brain, making it impossible for me to shut it off.

Another day. Another overwhelming pang of the unknown.

How are we supposed to figure out how to get back to Zane, Eldon, and Creed when we have to be present here? More than that, how are we going to explain their absence?

Shaking my head, I force the thoughts to the back of my mind, storing them for later. They've run on a loop, keeping me awake most of the night, but I can't allow them to take my focus from the day too.

I give myself an extra ten seconds curled up in a ball before I force myself to my back, staring up at the ceiling helplessly.

Grunts rumble through the room, dragging me to the present and leaving me confused as I glance around, unable to see the source of the sound.

Despite the desire to fall back asleep or simply lay here feeling sorry for myself, I follow the sound, crawling to the foot of the bed where I find Brax. I catch him dropping down into a push-up, the grunt slipping from his lips as he repeats the process again and again.

Hot.

Too hot.

What I would do to hear those sounds with him dipping low to thrust his cock inside me instead. The thought makes my cheeks heat and my thighs clench. A tiny squeak tickles my throat and I find wide eyes staring up at me in the next breath.

Startled, Brax drops to his knees, reaching for the bottle of water beside him. His gaze remains locked on mine as he downs most of the bottle in one gulp. The darkness in his pretty eyes is like a shot to the heart, reminding me of life as we currently know it.

The bed sheets instantly feel cold against my skin. The bed empty. My heart aches.

"Sorry," he grunts. "I didn't mean to wake you, but I needed to work out and leaving you in here alone wasn't an option."

I shift, adjusting to sit cross-legged on the bed as I frown at him. "Why?"

He shrugs, glancing away from me, and I understand instantly.

Folding my arms around myself, I wet my dry lips as I try to find the calmest words. "Just because the guys aren't here doesn't mean you have to change your routine. Certainly not for me. You can't be by my side all of the time. I know that."

"Yes, I can." He shakes his head as he scoffs at me, making me sigh.

"You really don—"

"I want to," he interjects, cutting off my words and rendering me speechless.

Fuck.

He pushes up off the floor, hovering above me with the storm still swirling in his eyes as he grabs my chin, tilting my head back even farther. His lips crush against mine in the next breath, claiming me with the most blissfully perfect bruising kiss that ever existed.

It doesn't last long enough. It never would have. All too soon, he's releasing me and taking a step back.

"Get dressed, Shadow. I'm going to shower. Then we can figure out some food before seeing what shit show this day has in store for us."

I nod, offering him a soft smile as he moves toward the bathroom. I instantly hate the distance between us. Watching every inch of him, I notice the cords in his neck are tight, his muscles bunched together more than usual.

"Brax, are you okay?" I call out. I don't know what feels different, and I know we're dealing with a lot of crap right now, but I feel like I'm missing something. He turns to look at me, his eyebrow raised in question, and I roll my eyes at him. "Apart from the obvious, of course."

Fucker.

He sighs, hanging his head for a brief second as his eyelids fall closed. I wait. I don't want to push him for answers that I don't even know the question to. Thankfully, he takes a deep breath and tilts his head to look at me.

"My dreams took me to the Realm of Shadows again

last night."

Fuck. I hadn't considered that it may have even been an option.

"They did?" I croak, wishing like hell I could do that too.

He nods, but he doesn't seem happy. "I saw the house, my parents, the guys… all in the distance. I woke before I could get close enough."

My academy-issued blazer sits perfectly on my shoulders, my skirt falling mid-thigh as I look every inch the excellent student while begrudging every step I take toward the main building. Zane's shell is tucked in my backpack, on hand should anything come up, and my fingers are linked with Brax's. His grip is deathly tight, but it fills me with the strength I didn't know I needed.

As we take the pathway, more and more students join us, and one thing is for certain: there's a new level of uncertainty looming over everyone. It's solemn. Everyone's movements are sluggish and paced, no one wanting to approach today just like any other.

Maybe it's the anticipation of The Monarchy coming and Erikel's preparation for it, but we know it won't happen. Not now that Rhys is up to date. Nobody else knows that though, and I don't plan on telling them. Not that we did the last time, either. Which reminds me to keep the golden warrior as far away from us as possible.

I still don't see Leila as the double doors leading inside come into view and it stirs my gut. I hope everything was okay with her father last night.

The worry is paused when I see Professor Figgins hovering by the entrance. I stand taller, my pace quickening, and Brax keeps at my side, despite having no clue what I'm doing. The fact only makes my heart grow warmer for him. He'd follow me into the pits of Hell, just as I would him.

I've tried a few times since I got back from Ashdale to reach out to Ari, but it's not working. I need to know why or come up with a plan to head out there to see him.

Her eyes lock on mine, her shoulders sagging with relief as she subtly nods us closer.

Before I reach her, my path is blocked by four men. The alternative uniform to my own immediately identifies them as Erikel's students from the Shadowgrim Institute. If that didn't, the sneers on their faces would solidify it.

I have no energy to deal with their bullshit on top of everything else today.

"It's the little soul dancer," one of them says, taking a step forward. It's Ruben, I think. He seems to think he's a leader among the rest of us, but he's most definitely wrong.

With my current head space being filled with fight or flight, I would love nothing more than to bring this asshole to his knees and put him in his place.

Brax's hold on my hand tightens somehow, spiking my own annoyance even more. When I don't instantly respond to Ruben, he takes a step forward, running his eyes over me from head to toe and back again. Brax inches forward, too, blocking me slightly from the fucker's view, but I'm intrigued with what else he's going to say. Right now, he's fueling the rage burning so easily inside of me, and I want as many reasons as possible to beat his ass.

"Where are the rest of your fuckboys?" he asks, eyes drilling into mine as he tilts his head.

I should have known that question was coming. I don't want to answer him, but I know that will only make the situation worse.

"I don't know what you're talking about," I grumble, dramatically rolling my eyes at him.

"Don't play dumb," he sneers as one of the others mutters the word bitch under his breath. Nice. *Real* nice. "Where are they?" he repeats, rolling his shoulders back as his gaze briefly shifts to Brax for a moment before settling back on me.

Biting back another sigh, I stiffen with irritation. "I. Don't. Know. Why don't you tell me? We all left for the caves together, and they haven't made it back. I want to know where they are more than anyone else." My voice is louder than necessary, but I can't control the emotion consuming me.

Ruben's eyes narrow, assessing me when one of his friends pats him on the shoulder, snickering before he even speaks. "Be real, Ruben. They probably got sick of sharing her loose cunt and didn't—"

Brax slams his fist into the fucker's face, cutting off whatever else he was about to say. Ruben is quick to jump to his friend's defense, but his punch is greeted by Brax's gargoyle form and the asshole howls in pain, dropping to the ground.

I'm rooted to the spot, aware of the crowd watching as Brax knocks down the final two Shadowgrim students until they're all flat out on their backs. He leaves them groaning in agony while he stands tall over them, flexing his hands as they go from stone to flesh and bone.

"That's enough," Figgins hollers, moving closer, but her steps are tentative, with very little authority in her tone as she steps in too late to deescalate the situation.

"Go back to your fucking perch," Brax growls, waving his hand toward where she was standing a few minutes ago. "You should have interjected when they first came at Raven. You didn't. So I had to take matters into my own hands."

She cocks a brow at him before turning her attention

to me.

Shit.

Cutting the distance between Brax and me, I gently place my hand on his arm before stepping in closer. "She's on our side, Brax," I breathe, keeping my voice low as he frowns at me.

She was simply saying what is expected of her as a professor on academy grounds. She didn't seem all that fussed about Brax beating the fuck out of them. He does have a point though, she didn't interrupt the scene they created.

Brax drags a hand down his face, still watching the assholes on the ground in case they try to retaliate with their own magic, but they seem content to roll around, spitting insults as everyone else watches in amusement.

We haven't stepped foot inside the academy yet and I'm ready for the day to be over. We really don't have the time to deal with this. It's exactly what has me stressed. I would rather be holed up at the house, on the shell with Rhys as we hash out a solid plan.

"Raven Hendrix." I still at the sound of my name, turning to find Professor Fitch standing in the entryway. His hands are braced behind his back, his gaze narrowed as he looks down his nose at all of us. It's strange to think I trusted this man more than most when I first arrived, but now… I hold him with more suspicion than anyone else.

"Your parents are here for a visit," he states, sending a shiver down my spine.

That can't be possible. Rhys mentioned the issues they're having with my father. That wouldn't have changed overnight, surely. I can't say that, though. I can't confirm that I'm in contact with Rhys.

Instead, I peer at Brax, trying to silently convey my uncertainty, and I see the same understanding in his eyes without having to utter a single word. It doesn't seem like Fitch sees it, though, as he gives his order.

"Follow me."

SIX

Zane

It doesn't make sense. Erikel could have killed Burton and assumed his position as him afterward, but for Burton to have been Erikel this entire time… it's impossible.

The thought has kept me awake for hours. Staring into the abyss as I lie fuck knows how far away from Raven for the first time since she waltzed into my life. My heart aches and my mind reels with every what-if that plagues us.

Marieta offered us Brax's room, but it felt too intrusive on our part, so we decided to set up camp in their living room. Eldon is on the sofa directly above my spot on the floor, while Creed fills the one that sits parallel to us. Both lay still and quiet. I'm not sure if they're asleep or not, but the silence in the room only makes my thoughts louder.

Kicking the sheets off, I sit. The bite of the rug presses

into my palms as I push up onto my feet. I need a minute. Somewhere to breathe and distract me from my thoughts.

I edge my way to the door as Creed and Eldon remain still. Pulling it closed behind me, I head for the messy room scattered with all the details of Marieta and Peta's attempts at escaping. There's enough in there to keep me busy for a while.

Flicking the light on, I stand and cast my gaze over every inch of the room. It's overwhelming at first; it was earlier, too. As much as it's all organized, I have no idea where to begin, but I need to figure it out if we're going to find our way back to Raven and Brax.

Marieta and Peta have given us the basics, but I need a deep dive into every single detail if we're going to find a way out of here. The facts laid before me will give me much more intel, which is exactly what we need if we want to be able to find a way out.

Raking a hand through my hair, I shuffle to the far left of the room and decide to start at the first piece of material I come across. It might not be the best plan of action, but it's the best I've got to focus my chaotic thoughts.

Will I ever regret stepping through the emerald gate that led us here? No. I'm certain of it. But that doesn't stop me from hating my current reality.

I want to be wherever Raven is. Always. And this isn't there.

Sighing, I reach for a piece of paper taped to the wall. The handwriting is scratchy and rushed, making the words difficult to make out, but it seems to allude to a list of items, which may have been needed in one of their attempts to escape. Sticking the paper back on the wall, I move farther along, ghosting my fingertips over the labeled cabinets.

I crouch down, but the second I balance on my haunches, the room shakes and a soft beeping rings out.

Rushing to the door, I step out into the hallway at the same time Eldon peeks his head out of the living room. Hurried footsteps race down the stairs and both Marieta and Peta appear at the bottom of the staircase a moment later.

"Someone is here," Marieta murmurs, tying a bathrobe around her waist as she ushers Peta to the door. There's a glint of silver in his hand and it takes me a second to note that it's a blade, but within two seconds of them opening the door, it's discreetly placed in his sheath. "Brax."

One word and I'm darting down the hallway to the open door. Creed and Eldon beat me to it, following Brax's parents out onto the deck. The familiar sight of my brother settles a storm in my soul, but when it's clear Raven's not with him, my chest threatens to cave with anguish.

Hold it together, Zane. Hold it the fuck together.

Brax's eyes widen when he takes in all of us, a hint of relief washing over his features as he moves faster, hurrying toward us. Eldon cuts between Marieta and Peta, desperate to get to the guy who has been by his side longer than anyone else, but before he reaches him, Brax disappears before our eyes.

My chest heaves with every breath as I wait for something else to happen, but nothing does. It's just the five of us standing around the porch, frozen in place as a dark gray hue glows around us.

"He must have woken up," Peta finally says after what feels like an eternity.

"Woken?" Creed echoes, his voice groggy.

"Yeah. Apart from last night, he only appears in his sleep, and it's always a brief visit. Not usually as brief as that, but…" Marieta's words trail off as she wraps her arms around herself. Peta steps into her side, wrapping his arm around her, the pair of them propping each other up as sadness seeps from them.

It's not lost on me that Marieta swung the door open in a bathrobe while her husband wielded a blade. With the hopes of Brax coming again, all of their cares went out of the window, their safety suddenly a negligible indifference.

"Let's head back inside," Peta offers, waving to the door as he guides Marieta.

The door falls closed with a disappointing thud and I glance at Creed and Eldon, who have the same bewildered expression in their eyes that I feel. We're out of our element. Now more than ever. The fact that we don't have a familiarity or stronger understanding of everything in the Realm of Shadows only makes it even more daunting.

To my surprise, Marieta and Peta don't instantly head upstairs. Instead, they step into the kitchen. "Do you boys want a drink?" Marieta asks, inviting us to join them.

I murmur my appreciation as we take the same spots at the table as we did earlier. Peta helps his wife this time while the three of us sit in silence, at a loss for words.

I'm already sick of feeling like this. It's frustrating as fuck. I've never been helpless, and I refuse to start now.

Taking a deep breath, I tilt my head to look toward Peta, but Creed breaks the silence before I get the chance.

"Does Raven ever come with him?"

Marieta looks at him with a sad smile as she shakes her head. "No. I met her for the first time yesterday, but I get the feeling she's the reason the shadows have become more animated."

"More animated?" I ask, leaning back in my seat. It's weird for her to say that when we're in the Realm of Shadows, and I haven't actually seen a single shadow yet. That might have something to do with being in here the entire time, but still.

"Oh, you can't see them," Peta interjects. "We'll help with that in the morning. Or when I've managed enough sleep to be able to focus," he adds, and Marieta strokes his arm in comfort.

"What he means is, the shadows aren't visible to those who aren't dead. Your soul has never officially crossed over to the other side, so it can't naturally see the others around you. It took us some time, but we figured out a way to be able to actually know our surroundings. That being said, we have wards in place to protect the house, so you won't see anything unless we're outside."

I nod in understanding. It's weird as fuck how blind I feel because I'm not dead. I consider if it would be worth it to truly know the world around me.

"I've been thinking a lot about what you said last night about Burton and Erikel," I state, aware they're in no fit state to help with our visual abilities but hoping they have enough brain power left to help my thoughts.

"Is that why you haven't slept?" Marieta asks with a raised eyebrow, and I shrug. There's no point in denying it.

"It can't be possible," I continue, noting the confusion in her eyes. "Burton can't have been Erikel this whole time. It's impossible," I clarify. Brax's parents share a look like I'm a child, one that can't piece everything together, but I know what I know. "We've seen them both in the same place at the same time."

"Holy shit, yeah. We have," Eldon murmurs, pointing his finger at me with wide eyes as he realizes the same.

"It could make sense for Erikel to be Burton once he

killed him, but the other way around? How is that possible? We even watched Erikel stab Burton before our very eyes. That's how they learned Raven was a necromancer. They made her bring him back to life in front of everyone. Otherwise, they were going to kill Creed," I ramble, probably oversharing, but now that my lips are moving, they just can't seem to stop.

"And multiple times when he first arrived. When he was introduced to us for one. They were both there. Side by side," Creed adds, backing my thoughts.

"It doesn't make sense," Peta says with a sigh, swiping a hand down his tired face.

"None of this makes sense," I agree. "It hasn't since it began."

That's the truth.

I've never known life to be as fucked as this, but here we are. I can't keep drowning in it. We need to learn how to navigate these waters. We can't succumb to it, and we can't do just enough to survive. I'm through with just staying afloat, barely managing to tread water. We need to take action and we need to do it now.

Glancing around the room, I'm reminded that my location doesn't make that as possible as I would like, but as the doubt tries to cling to my thoughts once again, I shove it to the back of my mind.

"Burton could have projected himself as Erikel while

standing in the room. Again, I'm not certain, but as insane as it sounds, it's possible," Marieta offers, making my eyebrows pinch in surprise.

"That sounds like a lot of magic all at once." My magic thrums through my veins in agreement.

"Burton is a powerful man, Zane. They don't give the role of head professor at Silvercrest Academy to just anyone," she replies gently, the words much heavier than her tone.

"That still seems like a lot," Creed states, agreeing with me, but the way Peta shakes his head makes me pause. "And if Raven brought him back from the dead, wouldn't that allow Burton to travel to the Realm of Shadows too?"

My eyebrows rise at Creed's realization.

Fuck.

"That could have been his plan all along, yes," Marieta murmurs, flooding my veins with a nervous tingle.

"When you're a man on a mission, fueled by the hunger for power, anything is attainable. I'm not saying you're wrong, but things really are as crazy as they seem sometimes. We will get a better understanding of this, I swear it." He brushes a kiss to Marieta's temple before turning back to me. "Go and get some rest, love. I think I'll spend some time in the room with these guys. Hopefully, we'll get information overload and pass out." He chuckles, making Marieta smile as she rises from her seat.

"Goodnight, boys. Please do try and sleep, though. You're going to need it."

She slips from the room without a backward glance, and it's only when her footsteps echo from above that Peta moves. He doesn't speak, waving his hand for us to follow him. If Creed and Eldon are unhappy with the delayed bedtime, they don't utter a word of complaint.

Stepping back into the room filled with the proof of their adventures, I let Peta take the lead. He doesn't go to a drawer or pull a scrap of paper from anywhere. Instead, he moves to the words practically carved into the wall to our right.

His fingers run over each letter, obstructing my view of what has his attention. After a moment of shuffling from foot to foot, I'm ready to nudge him to the side, but he turns to face us before I can overreact.

"I never understood what these words may mean, but now I think I do." He takes a step back, and the three of us fill the spot the moment he vacates it, eyes scanning each word. The first pass-over turns to garble in my mind, and the second helps me focus a little, but it's the third pass that has the words settling in my soul.

Follow your heart, find solace in the shadows, and take down the dawn.

SEVEN

Raven

Fitch parts the sea of students remaining, not bothering to glance back to see if I'm following. He knows I will, even though I know with certainty that my parents aren't awaiting me.

I don't have to say a word to Brax. He's at my side, so pretending to want to face whatever awaits me alone is pointless. He's never going to leave my side. This morning proved that.

He slugged those fuckers effortlessly, and I'm not embarrassed by the fact that I'd much rather be back at the house, on my knees, licking at his scuffed knuckles before I get another taste of his cock, showing my appreciation in the best way I know.

That will have to wait for now. Instead, we have the joy of discovering whatever bullshit awaits us.

I use my mind to call out to Ari, praying to hear his voice again, but nothing comes. I feel him in my gut, though. Our connection is still there, which is a relief, but I'm confused as hell with what's changed overnight. I was hoping to ask Figgins, but she disappeared with the students when Fitch made his public declaration.

"Where are we going?" I ask, speaking a little louder than necessary, but it's clear he's not waiting around and I would like to pepper him with questions on our way.

He doesn't offer a response, which pisses me off. A quick glance out of the corner of my eye at Brax reveals that he looks even more irritated than me. He grips my hand like a vice, storming toward Fitch, forcing me into a jog as I work to keep up with him.

We don't slow until we're in front of Fitch, and even then, he doesn't stop, but it's a little easier to keep in step with him.

"Where are her parents?" Brax grunts, and Fitch rolls his eyes, distaste wafting from him.

"They're waiting in Erikel's office," he bites back, clearly not wanting to offer us any kind of insight.

Asshole.

"Why?" I push, refusing to relent.

"Because."

"Because, what?" I grind out, nostrils flaring.

"I. Don't. Know. But I'm sure you'll find out once

we're there," he grinds, hands clenching at his sides.

It's no secret that Professor Fitch can be an epic ass, but this isn't his usual approach with me or the tone he uses. It either leads back to Erikel or Leila. Thinking of the latter, I redirect my questions. He's going to lead me to my impending doom whether I like it or not, so I may as well try to get what I can out of it.

"Where's Leila?"

His steps falter a little as he glances at me out of the corner of his eye. "My daughter's whereabouts are not of your concern."

"Your daughter is my friend. I think we can both agree that the academy isn't the safest place to be at the moment, and her welfare is important to me." I want to add that I know he's a scheming asshole. With or without Erikel's magic putting him under his command, there's more to this man than meets the eye.

He stops suddenly, forcing us to do the same as he glares at me. "My daughter has been made more than aware that she needs to avoid falling under your spell at all costs, Miss Hendrix."

What the fuck does that mean?

"What have you done to her?" Every word vibrates in my chest as I stare deep into his storming eyes.

His chest rises and falls harshly with every breath he takes, glaring down at me like the lowly peasant from

Shadowmoor I am. He parts his lips, fire raging in his eyes, ready to attempt to put me in my place, but he's interrupted by the door beside us swinging open.

"Raven, honey."

I freeze. I would know that voice anywhere. But how?

Turning slowly, my eyes widen when I find my father standing in the open doorway. I glance around him, startled that we are, in fact, outside of Erikel's office, or Burton's old office, whichever way we look at it.

The usual navy Monarchy-issued attire fits my father as perfectly as ever. Polished brown shoes don his feet and his peppered hair is swept back off his face. His eyes glisten, his smile reaching wide across his face.

"It's been too long. Come."

I peer up at Brax for a moment, trying to get his read on the man before us, but he gives nothing away, waiting for me to take the lead. I glare at Fitch before I step through the doorway, my back stiffening when the door closes behind us with a hard thud.

My father takes a seat on the long brown leather sofa and I take a tentative seat in the chair across from him. Brax sits beside me, dragging the chair closer to me, refusing to let go of my hand as my father leans forward, bracing his arms on his knees.

Clearing my throat, I falter under his intense stare. "Where's Mama?"

He waves his hand, smiling even wider as he maintains eye contact.

I'm certain with all that I am that it's Erikel beneath the façade. It's a good one, I'll give him that, but as much as he can look every inch of the man my father is, the mannerisms are off. Especially his attempt at using a term of endearment with me. My father has never called me *honey* a day in my life.

"We can talk without her for once, can't we?" he muses, making my muscles bunch even more. We've talked a lot without my mother's presence these past few months. It's the whole reason I'm here.

I rub my lips together, unsure how to proceed. I can't reveal the fact that I know it's not my father, that it is, in fact, Erikel, because it's too soon to expose him yet. A part of me also wants to know what he thinks he's going to achieve with this little meeting.

Squeezing Brax's hand, I steel my spine and take a seat across from the imposter before me. Brax is reluctant to release my hand, but he eventually does, dropping into the spot beside me.

"We don't need an audience," my father says, peering at Brax, who grunts in response as he nestles further into his seat, ignoring the dismissal.

"He stays. You know he always waits with me," I offer, forcing a smile to my lips as my father nods, but the distaste remains. Definitely not my father. He's met Brax once before, and it wasn't in this kind of setting. "What brings you here without Mama?" I ask, crossing my legs as I assess him.

My heart races, but I bite it back, acting as normal as my nerve will allow.

He clears his throat, adjusting the lapels of his suit jacket. "I managed to call in a favor. I know there's been a blocker between students and parents and I wanted to check in on you and make sure you're alright under the circumstances."

I can't decide whether to try to ruffle his feathers by bad-mouthing the fuck out of Erikel to see his reaction or fall pliant like I'm sure he hopes.

"How do you think she's coping? She's trying to come to terms with her abilities. Abilities you subdued for so long, and before she can get a handle on them, she's used as a tool in somebody else's war." Brax's jaw tenses as he grunts his disapproval, unknowingly choosing the direction we're going to take the situation.

My father runs his tongue over his teeth, adjusting in his seat as he glares at my gargoyle. "I did what I felt was necessary to protect my daughter. Maybe if she hadn't grown a soft spot for you and your friends, then she would never have allowed such a wise man as Erikel to use that Wylder boy as leverage over her."

Fucker.

Wise man, my ass.

Nobody can toot their own trumpet like Erikel. That's not going to change now under someone else's form.

I feel Brax's irritation rise, pulsing around him in waves. As much as I would love to see him take this fucker to town, I know I need to take control before things go sideways.

"Well, you've seen I'm fine with your own eyes, Papa." The name for him burns my tongue, but if I'm pretending, I may as well be as committed as possible. "Was there anything else you needed?"

"Raven, you haven't answered my question." He taps at his chin as he looks me over from head to toe. "Are you okay here?"

The brazenness of this man. He clearly wants to know my thoughts on him, like a fly on a wall in a restricted room. He's a damn leech that won't relent. I shrug. "I'm fine. Surviving. Just as I always have. Now is no different. With or without you, I'll figure it out. I always do."

I see the sparkle in his eyes, the unspoken challenge. It's a real glimpse into the cynical eyes of our unwanted leader.

He nods, pursing his lips as he makes no effort to move. "Where is the Wylder boy? I expected to see him as well."

Ah.

That's what this is about.

He wants to know the whereabouts of Zane, Creed, and Eldon.

Fuck.

I should have known. He couldn't get the information from me, so he's willing to take the forms of others to get it. What a rookie mistake. Of all the people to glean that information from me, my father sure as shit wouldn't be one of them.

The reality is, I have to give him something, and I only have a split second to decide.

My face falls to my open palms, shielding away from the man opposite me as I take a deep breath. A cry bursts from my mouth, croaking into a sob as I slip from my seat and crumble to my knees.

My lip wobbles, my show becoming a reality as my emotions rush to the surface. "Papa, I can't…I can't…you need to help me. Help us. I-I d-don't know where they are." I drop my hands to my lap, tilting my face up to the man posing as my father, watching as he traces the tears tracking down my face. "Erikel took us to Ashdale to… find the Potens Ruby. We separated in hopes of finding it more quickly, but they never reappeared and he made us leave before we could find them."

My nostrils flare, willing the raw pain and tears to retract, but it's impossible.

I'm raw. I'm vulnerable. I'm theirs. And if that means acting like this as a distraction in front of the enemy, then so be it.

My father shifts uncomfortably in his seat, toying with the tie around his neck as he frowns. "What do you mean? Everyone should have been accounted for."

I shake my head. "They weren't, Papa. Now I don't know what to do. I can't sleep. Worry plagues me. I'm sinking in a world that I'm not ready for." I almost cringe at myself. My tears may be real, but the words coming from my mouth aren't, and I worry I'm working it too hard.

"Raven, come," Brax murmurs, reaching for my hand and pulling me to his side. I take the seat beside him once more, looking down at my lap. "Can you help us or not?" he adds, talking to the imposter, who doesn't instantly respond.

I take a deep breath, and another, and another, before looking up through my lashes at him. I find my father's eyes locked on me, his eyebrows furrowed and lips drawn tight.

Finally, he clears his throat, rising to his feet. "I'll demand Erikel take another look around the caves," he states, stunning me. If he hadn't outed himself already, he did then because I only said Ashdale. I didn't mention any caves.

Hiding the realization from my face, I swipe at my

tears and stand. "Thank you, Papa. Thank you."

He nods once. Sharp and short before storming from the room without a backward glance.

Goodbye to you too.

"What the fuck was that about?" Brax murmurs, but I shake my head, not wanting to talk in here in case we're being watched in any way.

Turning to look at him, I squeeze my arms around his waist. His arms drape around me, holding me close as he breathes me in. "Please get me the fuck out here," I whisper against his ear as I brace on my tiptoes.

Wordlessly, he grabs my hand and tugs me toward the door.

Back out in the corridor, we still don't speak, putting as much distance between us and Burton's old office as possible. When we come to a stop in front of the classroom we're supposed to be in, I consider whether it's worth even joining now.

As if sensing my indecision, chairs scrape across the floor and students begin to disperse and I realize the day's first class is already over.

We weren't gone that long, were we?

Instinctively taking a step back, we let everyone filter around us until Leila comes into view.

"Hey, where were you guys?" she asks, hooking her backpack over her shoulder. Her gaze flickers between the two of us, neither of us having an answer for her. Is she herself or another imposter? "What?" Shaking my head, I start down the corridor, Brax at my side as Leila hurries to keep up with us. "What am I missing?"

I rub my lips with uncertainty and Brax takes the lead instead. "When we were in Silvercrest High, what house were you in?"

I frown, but keep my mouth shut.

"What house?"

"Yeah, your team. Red, yellow, blue, or green? Which was yours?"

She rears her head back, clearly as confused as I am. "I was yellow, just like you. Why is that relevant right now?"

"Who was our head professor?"

Uncertainty continues to dance in her eyes as she glances at me, but I have nothing to offer, so she returns to Brax.

"Professor Wallace."

Brax exhales, turning his attention to me. "You're good. She's…her."

Bewilderment morphs into surprise as understanding washes over me.

"What does that mean?"

I wince as I turn to Leila. "It means he was making sure you weren't someone pretending to be you."

"Why would somebody do that?" Her steps slow, but I

quickly reach out, hooking her arm with mine as I pull her along with us.

"Because that's why we weren't here."

"Fuck. Are you guys okay?"

I nod, despite the swirling panic inside of me confirming that, in fact, I'm not. But that's something for me to break down later. Not in the presence of others. I've already released some of my vulnerability in front of someone I didn't want to this morning. That's my limit and I've already surpassed my comfort with it.

"I'm good. Let's get to the next class, shall we?" I offer, and even though I can see the indecision on her face, she agrees.

"Was my father okay with you?" she asks, and my nose crinkles.

"As okay as possible." I'm quickly reminded of what he said on the way to seeing my father about how Leila now knew to keep me at arm's length. Maybe I should still be cautious with what I divulge until I know what he meant by that. "Are you free tonight?"

"Uh, I kind of had plans with Grave, but—"

"No, no. You're good. Tomorrow?"

"Tomorrow is clear. Are you sure you don't mind?"

"Of course. Is your father okay with that?" I know he's made his feelings known. That's why she was so sullen in the courtyard the day I pointed fingers at her, thinking it was her who revealed that The Monarchy was coming, when it was, in fact, Creed and his father.

A flash of gold passes in front of my face, as if thinking the thought made him appear. Looking up, I'm not surprised to find the crimson-stained gold armor blocking my path.

As if I need anything else today.

The three of us come to a stop, letting the other students walk around us as the golden warrior glares down at me. The sight of his eyes makes me want to scream, the familiarity of their deep color making the distance between Creed and me more and more noticeable.

"Follow me." His grunt is an order, but Brax doesn't move an inch, squeezing my hand tighter.

"No." Brax sounds bored as he stares pointedly at Creed's father.

"I'm not asking. You can continue to class," he adds, pointing at Leila, who gapes at him like a fish out of water for a moment before turning to me.

Sighing, I smile at her. "You're good. I'll meet you there, okay?"

She purses her lips, searching my eyes for something. I don't know what, but she seems to find it as she nods, joining the other students down the hallway.

The golden warrior turns for the closest exit, not glancing back to see if we're following or not.

"Is today over yet?" Brax grunts, reluctantly following

after the asshole, and I hum.

"I wish."

We follow him outside, where it quiets, watching as he continues to the left, hovering by a shallow archway. I release Brax's hand, folding my arms over my chest as I come to stand face to face with Creed's father.

"Where is he?"

I roll my eyes. I've already been through this once today. If Erikel thought sending this fool to try and get any further details from me, he's mistaken. Yet again, the issue is that they don't know that we fucking know.

"Well? I said where is he?" he snaps, and Brax instantly growls.

"Watch your fucking tone."

The two of them stare each other down, the air around us quickly becoming volatile. Sighing, I cut to the chase. "We haven't seen him since the caves. I just told my Papa the same thing and he promised to encourage Erikel to go back and search for them." The panic in my voice isn't as forced this time, and I slam my lips shut, hating the way vulnerability seeps from me so easily.

His brows gather as he stares down at me. "I don't believe you."

"I don't care if you do or don't. I want him home; I want all of them home. I would never willingly choose to leave him or the others anywhere. You know that. You saw what I was willing to sacrifice for him before, don't try me now," I grunt, beyond irritated that it's not even lunchtime and my day is spiraling so epically.

He takes a step toward me, eradicating any remaining distance between us, but Brax manages to slip between us without touching the warrior.

"Lay a hand on her and I'll snap your fucking fingers," he seethes.

A slight grin of amusement drags across his face as he assesses Brax. I'm expecting him to throw his weight around and take the information from me without care, but to my surprise, he takes a step back, dragging a hand down his face instead.

"I love my son. More than anything else in this world. More than he loves you or you him. I don't care about any of that. Just him. I'll do whatever it takes to keep him safe. Even from you. If I find him in any harm because of you, I'll bury you myself."

EIGHT
Raven

"**C**ome on, Raven. You've got this."

"I really don't think I do," I grumble, my limbs aching as I consider stopping, but the glint in Brax's eyes tells me that's not an option. I know it isn't, but that doesn't stop me from dreaming of it.

"You're literally up to the shoulders. Just a little more and you'll be complete."

"Completely made of stone, Brax. Finish your sentence," I snap, wincing at my own tone, but I'm irritated, and…a little panicked.

"You're going to make the prettiest gargoyle I've ever seen, Shadow. Show me."

I glare at him, but he doesn't flinch under my intense stare.

The moment classes were done, we got the hell out

of there and headed home. We came out here to distract me with some mirror magic training. Brax is taking this to another level tonight, though, insisting I can handle it, but I'm not sure I can.

The thought of being completely stone, eyes and mouth included, frightens the hell out of me. I can't deny it, and he knows it.

"Can we do something else today?" I ask, my voice softer than usual, revealing yet another vulnerability for the day. The only difference now is that I don't care if Brax sees this side of me. If anything, I want him to. Being my true self with him soothes my soul instead of leaving me embarrassed.

"Raven, take a deep breath. I promise you, it's not going to feel as restrictive as you imagine." I purse my lips at his promise, but the words do nothing to ease the tension rattling my bones. "Your head is locked on everything going on in your life right now, which is only enhancing your worry over this. Try to let the rest fall away." I glare at him, hating that he's probably right. I inhale slowly, dragging out the exhale, but it doesn't ease me much. "We can stop, and you can tell me everything on your mind. Apart from the obvious, of course."

Fuck.

That doesn't really sound any better.

Pull it together, Raven.

With my very lacking pep talk, I relax my shoulders back, noting how the movement doesn't feel as heavy as I would initially have assumed, before I fuck it all to Hell and let the rest of Brax's magic wash over me.

I gulp as my throat stiffens, the feeling creeping up my jaw, over my cheeks, my eyes and ears, and finally, my head. Remembering what Brax said, I focus all of my attention on my breathing as I become accustomed to the shift.

It's the weirdest feeling I think I've ever experienced in my whole life. My movements feel like they're lagging at first, the weight not as bad as I assumed it would be, but the craziest thing is blinking. I can hear the sound of stone rubbing on stone and it makes me cringe, but the feeling doesn't match the noise. It feels like…normal.

"That's my woman. Smile for me, Shadow."

I tilt my gaze up to look at Brax, who grins down at me. It's a rare sight, an even rarer one to see pride in his stunning eyes. One brown. One green. I'm ninety-nine percent sure he's softer and gentler with me right now to compensate for the fact that the others aren't here. It's a side of him I thought I would never witness, a side I'm sure won't stay around forever, a side that makes me want to push him. To see his bite, his growl, his rugged side.

I'm getting distracted. Again.

Releasing my hold on his magic, the stone drifts from

my skin effortlessly, and I'm pulled off my feet without warning a moment later. Soft-yet-firm lips press against my jaw as arms band around my waist.

"You love being a good fucking girl, don't you, Raven." It's not a question. Not really, and he fucking knows it. "But that doesn't mean you can't unload on me. Tell me what's going on in the pretty head of yours and I'll reward you."

My thighs clench. He can't mean…could he?

Whether he does or not, I need to be open with him. If we're going to get through this together and find the rest of our family, we need to be transparent with one another.

Taking a deep breath, he must sense the change in me because he slowly lowers me to my feet, but he doesn't lean back or put any distance between us.

"Apart from the fact that my heart is tearing into pieces because I don't technically know where the guys are, I've been trying to reach out to Ari with no luck. The confusion and worry of it is starting to weigh heavily on me. Everything was fine before the drill that interrupted us going to see him. I can feel his presence, which isn't drenched in pain or anything, but it still leaves me unsteady. I can't really explain it, but there's been a shift and I don't like it."

Pressing a small kiss on my forehead, he takes a single step back and focuses to his left. He wets his lips, and after a few moments, he turns back to me with a sigh. "I still can't make a gateway."

My heart swells with appreciation that he would even try. "Do you think the drill could have affected my communication with him? I mean, I technically spoke with him on the way to the courtyard that day after the sound echoed through the halls, but…I don't know. I'm pulling at straws trying to understand."

"Maybe. I think it's important for us to visit Lyra and Figgins tomorrow," he states, scrubbing at the back of his neck, and I nod in agreement.

"Thank you."

The corner of his mouth tips up. "What else?"

"Hmm?"

"What else has you worked up?"

I frown, not really able to explain it. "It's not anything in particular. I'm just angry. Frustrated. Mad. I want to beat the shit out of something, everything. I just want all of my guys here together, with me. That's selfish as fuck, I know, but…"

"It's not selfish, Raven. I want them here too. And if I was there instead of by your side…" His eyes stare deep into my soul. "I would be going insane. There would be no doubt about it." Tingles zip through my blood, but I quickly pout when he takes another step back. "I know I'm not the calm one, or the deep, understanding one, and I'm not funny at all. I can't offer you anything the others can, but there is something I *can* do."

I want to tell him I don't want or need any of those things from him, but I know they're wasted words on him. "What can you do?" I ask, intrigued.

"Let you beat the shit out of me."

I laugh, but the pointed stare I get tells me he's deadly serious. "No." I shake my head, but he captures my chin, holding me in place.

"Why? I can handle it."

I giggle this time. "It's not you I'm worried about. It's me. Your muscles have fucking muscles. That will hurt like hell."

He smirks, too pleased with himself. Fucker.

"Come on, Raven. Show me a good time. Don't think I didn't notice the fighting pits when you took us to Shadowmoor. You were familiar with them, even if you hadn't stepped foot in one. Show me what you're made of."

He's goading me and it's working.

Worst of all, he knows it.

He doesn't bother waiting for my agreement. He knows he already has it.

Turning to face him, I tuck a tendril of hair behind my ear. "Maybe we should be focusing our efforts on trying to locate the emerald gate," I murmur, my gut twisting with guilt. I can't be working on my own issues when the guys are out there somewhere.

Brax frowns. "Our best bet of connecting with them is in my sleep, Shadow. We have no fucking clue where the emerald gate could be now. Hopefully, tonight, I'll get closer to them, but for now, we're doing this because if the guys find out I haven't tended to your needs, it will be me in the Realm of Shadows, and not in the way they are. The dead way."

I roll my eyes at his dramatics. "I would bring you back."

"Not if they didn't let you," he retorts, cocking a brow at me in challenge.

Definitely dramatic.

Using magic, I change out of my uniform into a loose tee and shorts, sneakers and fresh socks on my feet. Brax eyes me for a moment, and I expect him to do the same, but instead, he makes a show of loosening his tie. The material flutters to the grass, quickly followed by his blazer, before he starts to unbutton his shirt.

My tongue peeks out, failing to moisten my drying lips as his shirt is discarded without care. Once he kicks his shoes and socks off, he turns to face me head-on; knees shoulder-width apart and slightly bent.

Fuck.

This man is going to fight me in just his academy pants.

How am I supposed to focus when his muscles flex before my very eyes? I get the overwhelming desire to step forward and bite his pebbled nipple, but I refrain, refusing to give in to his teasing.

"Let's go, Shadow." He cracks his neck from side to side, lifting his arms to protect his chest.

Relaxing my shoulders back, I tighten my core and soften my knees, taking up my familiar fighting stance. He was right. I never stood in the Shadowmoor fighting pits, but that didn't stop me from training. At least that way, I was always able to protect myself. It was a necessity.

My curled knuckles catch my attention and I note that it's been a long time since they were busted and bruised, just like they were when I first arrived here. It feels like a lifetime ago, but the familiar stance brings everything back to me.

Inching closer to Brax, I keep my arms high, eyeing him from head to toe, trying to assess where he might have an opening, but it doesn't come as a surprise when I don't see one. I'm just going to have to make a move and let the rest happen. Dancing around him, he spins to follow me and I tap out with my left arm first, testing my reach and his defense. My fist meets his bicep with the briefest tap before I retract.

A grin touches the corner of his lips and I can see the snarky comment on the tip of his tongue that's about to come. Before he gets a chance to utter a single word, I repeat the motion, only this time, I follow it up with a firmer hit from my right hand.

I still meet his arm with both touches, but I don't miss his eyes widening with the firmer hit from the second touch.

"Am I playing around with a punching bag, or are you actually going to move?" I ask, bouncing from foot to foot, very aware I'm the one doing the goading now.

"I just wanted to see what you may have to offer. Not much, it seems." He shrugs, quickly gaining the upper hand again.

Fucker.

Despite his words, his arms loosen and I see the flutter of his muscles a split second before his arm extends. I twist, taking the blow to my arm. His touch is hard, but nothing compared to what it would be if he were in gargoyle form, and I love it. Any of my other guys would be going easy on me. Not him, though. Not Brax.

He knows just how to extract every piece of effort from me. He tears at my rage and my pent-up frustrations, giving me an outlet to exert them. This is just like when he told me to run, only this time, I'm already in his grasp.

I duck down quickly, his arm not fully retracted as I kick out, the top of my foot connecting with his thigh. He doesn't stumble, not even a little, but that wasn't my intention. A smirk is on his face, just as I expect, his arms angled down slightly as if he's about to retaliate, but as I plant my foot back on the ground, I shift to the right, dodging his move as I connect my fist with his stomach.

A whoosh leaves his lips, the surprise in his eyes heating as he stares down at me. My hand aches from the tight bundle of muscles I hit, but I don't dare shake it out. Instead, I focus on stepping back as I reach my full height again.

My chest rises and falls, heavy with every breath, but to my surprise, Brax's is the same.

His arms drop, swinging at his sides as he assesses me. I don't know what game he's going for here, but I refuse to let my guard down. My hands flex, my knuckles whitening as I try like hell to keep my body as relaxed as possible, but the longer he stands there, the louder my pulse thumps in my ears.

It's on the tip of my tongue, ready to call him out on whatever game plan he has, but he speaks first.

"You've got from the count of three, Shadow." His voice is croaky, the husky tone and words themselves render me speechless as I gape at him.

Wait, what?

My lips part, but nothing comes out.

"Three…"

Three? What the… "For what?" I manage to blurt,

but he shakes his head, taking a step toward me, and I instinctively take a step back. The heat in his eyes grows brighter with the simple move.

"Two…"

"Brax." His name is a yelp on my lips as I involuntarily back up another step, even though he doesn't move.

"One."

I'm rushing for the house before he finishes that one single syllable. I spring the door open, chancing a sneaky glance over my shoulder, and I know I made an error immediately.

His hands grab my waist, hoisting me into the air as I squeak like a damn fool. Instead of continuing to march into the house, he spins us around, heading in the opposite direction as my stomach hits his shoulder.

I'm panting, helpless, and filled with adrenaline.

"You should have started running sooner, Shadow," he states, striding across the grass so casually it feels surreal.

"You could have given me longer," I grunt, wiggling in his hold, but I don't move an inch.

"That's it, Raven. Fight me. Just how I like it."

I still.

Fuck.

My eyes fall closed, my core clenching at the tinge of promise in his words.

I don't want to fight, I want to succumb to him, but

once again, I'm reminded of the Brax that chased me through the academy grounds, smashing the glass to get into the house so he could fuck me into the sofa.

That version of him is like throwing air magic at my already burning flames.

Wetting my lips, I slam my hands against his ass, trying to lift up, but I don't get far. "Put me down," I demand, my voice raspy as he chuckles, his back rumbling with the movement.

"You're going to have to be louder than that, Shadow."

This time I slam my fists into his ass, swinging my legs around as I fight against his hold. The adrenaline pours through me, ignited by the pushback as Brax's hold tightens, encouraging me more.

He continues to move us, relishing in my fight that he manages to contain. He doesn't falter, even when I become more frantic and sporadic with my swings, both arms and legs, until I'm suddenly floating through the air.

I hit the ground in the next breath, the wind leaving my lungs as I gape up at him. A pleased smile spreads across his face as he looks down at me through hooded eyes.

The blades of grass tickle my skin as I press my palms into the ground. I'm still trying to catch my breath when he reaches down, grabbing the neckline of my tee with his bare hands and tearing at the fabric. It parts effortlessly at his touch, goosebumps rippling over my chest and stomach as the breeze dances over my skin.

When I grab his wrists, he doesn't even look up at me as he smirks, snapping my bra in two. "I don't know why anyone uses magic to remove clothing when it's so much sweeter like this," he murmurs, his gaze traveling over my exposed breasts as his hands continue lower.

I dig my nails into his skin, but he doesn't even flinch as he tugs at my shorts. I try to swing my legs at him, eager to give him the fight he's so desperate for, but he quickly drops to his knees, pinning my thighs to the ground as he discards my shorts to reveal the lace panties underneath.

"Did you wear these for me?" His gaze finally meets mine, desire swirling with promise.

"No."

His eyes narrow, his jaw ticking as he trails a finger over the delicate material.

"That makes sense. If it were for me, you wouldn't be wearing anything at all," he remarks, and a second later, the sound of tearing fabric echoes in my ears.

His legs press into my thighs, holding me in position as I release my pointless hold on his arms. His eyes trail over me slowly, from head to core and back again. I'm bare and spread out on the ground for him.

Anyone could walk around the back of the house and see us like this, but he doesn't seem to care and neither do I.

My skin is hot with need, but I want to see him fall to his knees first. "You have me right where you want me. What now?"

"It's cute that you think you need to know that information in advance," he says with the sexiest grin turning up the corner of his mouth.

Ass.

"I deserve that information, Brax. I'm not playing this game with you where you get me all worked up again and leave me needy because you made a dumb promise," I snap, my body tensing. I'm not lying. I can't play around like he did in the cave. Not right now. I can't handle it.

He frowns, staring at me for what feels like forever until his fist slams into the ground beside my head. "Do you have any idea what you do to me?" he bites, leaning closer so his face hovers over mine. I'm taken aback by the tightness in his tone, confused with where the fuck it comes from, but I don't back down.

"I have an idea," I mutter, very aware of what all four of my guys do to me, including this angry asshole.

He shakes his head as he grumbles, "No, you fucking don't." His eyes stare deeper into mine as his nostrils flare.

"How so?"

"You set me on fire, Raven. Make me question my entire being. Leave me confused as fuck. Desperate to go against my own word. Something I've never, *ever* done.

Yet for you, I would do anything."

I feel like I can't breathe, yet I get the overwhelming urge to express how I feel as well.

"I have never let anyone close to me. Not even a friend. Then the four of you came along and broke through every wall I've spent so long perfecting, strengthening. Piece by piece, you break me down and leave me bare. I'm lying here physically naked, but I'm emotionally exposed too. You make me...*feel*. The numbness fades and there's so much emotion beneath the surface that I've never felt before. I don't know what to do with it."

His jaw tics. I can practically hear his thoughts. Trying to find the right words to express that this is harder for him to accept than me, but it's not a battle I want. Not when my heart breaks and melts for them all at once.

I want to scream with the pain of the separation from Eldon, Zane, and Creed, but it mellows when I let the truth settle over me.

I've known it. I've known it for a while now. I wanted to find a way for them all to hear it at the same time, but now that I'm lying here, exposed and vulnerable once again, instead of the words feeling like lead on my tongue, they're bursting to part my lips.

"I love you." I exhale, the feeling of contentment washing over me as I accept the words. "I love you all." The words make tears prick my eyes and a ghost of a smile touch my lips. "But I love *you* because you don't treat me like a delicate flower. You see past everything, looking deep at my soul. The good, the bad, the ugly, and you accept it all. You accept *me*. You make vows like killing my brother and refusing to touch me until it's done because you believe so strongly in righting the world for me. You protect, you demand, you snap, and you order, all of it with love, and I feel it in my fucking bones. You've never promised to be a good man, a nice guy, but you've given me every inch of yourself instead. And on top of it all, when the two of us lie here in this moment, you know you have gone above and beyond for me since we left Ashdale, fighting to be a version of Creed, Zane, and Eldon too. Not for you, not for them, but for me. I didn't know how to accept that, someone's dedication, undoubted loyalty and trust, and you didn't give me the option, feeding me drips of a life I breathe for." My bottom lip trembles, effectively cutting off my rambling, but now that the dam has been opened, I'm powerless to stop it.

His eyes drill into mine, the muscles in his neck bunching as he holds his position over me. I sink my teeth into my bottom lip, awaiting the taste of copper on my tongue, fighting back all of the emotions bubbling to the surface as the truth spills from my mouth.

"You make me whole, Raven. Whole," he rasps, shifting his legs so he's no longer pinning me to the ground, but I don't move, too enraptured in his eyes. One brown. One green. His tongue peeks out and his pants disappear from his legs, revealing his long, stiff cock jutting in my direction. "Magic can be useful sometimes," he muses, making me grin, and he uses that moment to grab my thighs, lifting them to my chest as he aligns his length with my core.

I gasp as he inches inside of me, my desire easing the friction as he stretches my pussy.

"Fuck," he grunts when he's fully seated inside of me.

I grasp the blades of grass beneath me but they offer me no support. Pressing my palms into the ground instead, I try to lift to my elbows. Brax stops me before I'm up, hand draping around my neck as he lowers me.

His fingers flex, tightening just right around my throat as I gulp.

"Just because I love you too doesn't mean I'm going to go easy on you," he rasps, snapping his cock in and out at an unbelievable pace, forcing a moan from my lips. My heart feels like it's going to explode from the slip of his tongue, but I don't get a chance to process it as he repeats the move again. "You're making me break my vow, Shadow. That has to come with a punishment, too," he adds, tightening his hold on my throat, cutting off my airway, and my senses instantly heighten.

My face heats, my pulse pounding as my brain pleads

for oxygen, but his hold doesn't relent as he thrusts into me harder, faster. Gripping his wrists, I know how useless it is, but I fight against him anyway. I dig my fingers into his flesh, my mouth parting on silent cries as my body plays to his rhythm perfectly.

On his next thrust, he takes me over the edge. No warning, no build-up, just pure pleasure claiming my body, tingling through my veins as ecstasy turns me into a puddle in his grasp.

He broke his vow.

"We're not done yet, Shadow," he grunts, releasing his hold on my throat as he grabs my waist, spinning me beneath him.

I'm beyond disoriented as he pulls me around like a rag doll. Palms pushing into the ground, ass in the air, knees in the dirt, parted and waiting for him. He fills me again in the next breath, filling me deeper as he spreads my ass cheeks. His fingers are bruising, each slam of his cock punishing, but all it does is send tingles through my veins again.

"Fuck. How is it supposed to be a punishment when everything I do makes your pussy drip?"

I grin, glancing back over my shoulder at him. "Say it again." He frowns, confused by what I'm asking for, but his pace doesn't falter. "Say it again, Brax."

A flicker of understanding crosses his eyes, but he quickly tamps it down, pushing a hand between my shoulder blades. I lower my chest to the ground, my hands still clutching at the grass as his hand moves from my back to my head, pressing my face into the ground.

I startle when I realize how close we are to the cliff edge. If I reach my left arm out it would drape over the side. It's freeing, almost as much as speaking the truth to him was.

"Say it," I push again, my lids falling closed as he claims my body with every pounding of his hips. His fingers tangle in my hair, pinning me more harshly against the ground as he fucks me with raw abandon.

"Come for me, Shadow," he orders, his voice raspier now.

"Say it," I repeat again. He grunts, not wanting to give me what I want, but saying it is fucking beautiful, and hearing it… wow. "I love you, Brax."

He stutters, his hips faltering before suddenly quickening to a pace I didn't believe possible. I feel his heat along my back before his whisper against my ear. "I love you."

My pussy clenches around his cock as my world flips. The words start a chain reaction, tingling from my toes, rippling through my core before zapping through my fingertips. My pulse echoes in my ears as I succumb to the orgasm.

Brax's thrusts become sporadic as he finds his release,

and it's only when my pulse quiets in my ears that I hear the chant falling from my lips.

"I love you. I love you. I love you."

He collapses above me, his breath brushing over my neck as I come down from the greatest high.

I have no idea how much time passes before I blink my eyes open to see the last tendrils of light disappear from the sky, casting pretty shadows over the mountain range in the distance.

A shiver runs through me as the chill in the air brings me back to the present.

In this moment, when pain mixes with pleasure, love, and abundance, the reminder of the guys missing from my presence clings to me.

I refuse to let it be my downfall, though. No. It's my focus, my promise, my vow.

I'm going to tell them I love them.

No matter the cost, no matter the sacrifice. My future is worth it all.

NINE
Raven

Sleep eludes me. A familiar feeling at this stage. My eyes are glossed over, not really seeing as I blink into the darkness. Brax's arm is draped over my stomach, holding me close as his steady breathing offers comfort.

Caught between drowning in numbness, crying until the sobs make me pass out, and the desperate need to do… something, anything, leaves me paralyzed beneath the sheets. My mind is unrelenting, circulating on every worry I have, playing on repeat as they keep me awake.

Once upon a time, the thoughts that kept me up at night were warped with worry over what the next day would look like if the bruises from the prior night's attack would be noticeable and sore. Who would I be as a Void? What future would I even have? One even worth living?

Now… as dark as my mind once went, it doesn't

compare to this.

Where are Creed, Eldon, and Zane?

Are they safe?

Is there hope?

Where is the emerald gate?

How can we find it?

Is there another way?

How can I hop in on Brax's dreams that seem to take him there?

Is he there now?

I glance over my shoulder to see him sleeping contently, giving nothing away, and I sigh, curling back in on myself.

What did Rhys mean when he warned me something wasn't okay with my father?

Do I care?

Is Ari safe?

Why isn't he hearing me?

Why can't I go and see him?

What could be happening at the compound?

How do I get there without a gateway or my familiar's aid?

My eyes squeeze tightly closed, trying to strengthen a connection with him. I feel the pool of warmth in my gut that I've come to associate with him, but otherwise, there's nothing.

What will it take to bring Erikel down once and for all?

Can we truly rely on The Monarchy to do it?

I know the answer to that already. The truth floods through my veins and I hate the reality of it. If I want to see this all come to an end, then I'm going to have to do something about it. What was it that Eldon said when I first got here? A murmur of a prophecy. I remember the conversation like it was yesterday.

"I get them sometimes, but they're hard to decipher. It could be nothing."

"It was a raven."

"It had pink feathers."

"There was a map, and the raven's claw was placed on Shadowmoor."

"What else?"

"Nothing." I can see the denial in his eyes.

"What else, Eldon? What else did the raven have or do that could possibly make you think it was me?"

"I don't know. I just know that in my vision, a war was coming, a war across realms, threatening all of existence. And the raven... she saved us all."

Saved us all?

It felt extreme at the time. Shit, it still does now, but is this what he meant? Erikel?

Scrubbing a hand down my face, I shift beneath Brax's arm so I can lie on my back, letting his hand rest against my stomach as I stare up at the ceiling.

No matter how much I try to rid it from my existence, helplessness clings to me like a second skin.

The first shadow that shimmies across the far wall catches me by surprise, but by the fourth, my eyes aren't as wide. I'm used to waking up and being surrounded by them. This is the first time I'm catching them as they begin to appear. It's captivating.

Four grows to ten, and I stop counting by the time I reach twenty. There are too many for me to keep on top of, and it doesn't seem to be as though they're done coming. I lie silently, watching, following, trailing their every move, until one pauses on the far wall, the silhouette turning as though it faces me, and my heart lurches in my chest.

Just like the other time, it begins to grow, consuming more and more of the wall as its shadow takes hold of the entire room. It inches closer, dominating my attention as everything else around me fades into the background.

My spine stiffens when I sense a rasp echo around the room. I glance at Brax, but he's as still as he was before, fast asleep. I know it's not him, though. It's the shadow peering down at me. The sound comes again, making me frown as I try to decipher what the hell it's trying to say.

"Sleep. Sleep, Raven."

I gape as the words register. I want to tell them I've fucking tried. That it's impossible. My eyes refuse to give and my brain point-blank declines the order to shut off and sleep. But I don't have a choice because the room goes dark around me.

Free falling in the darkness, nausea churns in my gut as the weightless feeling leaves me breathless. Everything stops with a thump and I glance around, disoriented, to find misty white and pale gray surrounding me.

I scramble to my feet, gaping down at the oversized tee that falls mid-thigh on me. A creak squeaks behind me, making me whirl around in panic to find a familiar wrap-around porch just a few steps away.

"Raven?" My eyes widen and my heart feels close to exploding when my eyes lock with Zane's. "Raven," he repeats, the disbelief in his voice real as my face falls into my hands.

Is this what sleep has become? Hauntings of what I desire most?

Maybe I should have stayed awake. Maybe I shouldn't have let the silhouette get so close to do… whatever the hell it did to me.

Fuck.

"Dove?" The nickname on his lips makes my throat bob and my fingers tremble. A moment later, hands run down my arms in the softest touch, evoking a gasp from my lips that mirrors the noise coming from Zane. "You're here. You're really here."

My hands slowly fall away from my face as I look up

into his hazel eyes in awe.

"Zane?"

"Oh, thank fuck, Dove," he rasps, lifting me in the air as he pins me to his chest, twirling us in a circle.

I can't truly process what's happening as he places me back on the ground, but all too quickly, I'm launched into the air again, only this time, it's at the hands of Eldon.

"Fuck, Little Bird. Fuck. Fuck. Fuck." He clings to me like his life depends on it, and I squeeze back just as tight. His fingers tangle in my hair and his other arm is banded so firmly around my waist that I'm sure I'm going to pass out.

When my bare feet make it back to the ground again, my forehead is pressed against his chest, my mind still delirious with disbelief as soft kisses pepper all over my head.

Just as I lean back to peer up at him, he's ripped from me, my eyes widening as I remain startled, only to have Creed replace the very spot Eldon was in moments earlier. Tired and pained onyx eyes find mine as he simply stands and stares at me for what feels like an eternity.

He's not like Eldon and Zane, tossing me in the air all carefree and excited; he's calculated, restrained, and controlled. He's my Creed.

I eliminate the distance remaining between us. Gripping his black top in my hands, I press myself against him. Chest to chest, his arms descend around me, engulfing me in his warmth, and I sag in his embrace.

"It worked. It actually fucking worked."

I frown at Zane's words, acutely aware that he still lingers close by. Tilting my head, I turn to face him, but Creed grips my chin, pausing me as his eyes pierce into mine. His lips descend, cutting off my next breath.

His tongue pries my lips open before dancing along mine. My hands lift to cling to his shoulders, completely distracting me until he rips his lips away, our short, sharp breaths mingling between us.

"What worked?" I ask hoarsely, still confused about my surroundings and how real they are.

Before he answers, Creed takes a step back, reaching for my hand and turning me to face the house. Brax is standing on the porch with his parents flanking him, and there's a softness to his shoulders that I've never seen before.

"The five of us have spent all day going over everything that has been tried and failed before so we can see what fresh options we may have of getting out of here. I'm not going to lie, Raven, nothing was working. I was certain it was completely going to shit." He glances away from me, the frustration getting the better of him, but he quickly regathers himself. "That is, until Brax arrived."

My gaze flickers to my hotheaded gargoyle, who was sleeping soundly beside me just moments ago.

"What changed?" I ask, following Creed's lead as he moves toward the porch steps.

"Not to give him an even bigger ego than he already has, but he really did show up and see everything from a different perspective," Eldon states from my right, Zane a step beside him.

"I made them see that we can use the shadows here to draw you in too. Then, we can see this through together. As a team. Like we always do."

I gulp, nodding in agreement at Brax as a soft smile takes over my lips. The silhouettes can aid them pulling me through to the Realm of Shadows? Hope consumes me. "We're really here? Together?"

"We're in our dreams, so not quite the same, but it's more than what we had," Brax offers, and his mother strokes a comforting hand down his spine before turning to me.

"We'll give you guys a few minutes to chat, then I think we have a lot to go over together when you're ready." Her smile reaches from ear to ear as she glances over each of us before stepping inside, her husband right behind her as the five of us stand together.

It feels surreal, overwhelming, and joyous. So fucking joyous.

As if sensing the emotions rippling through me, each one of my guys inches closer. Creed's fingers tighten around mine. Eldon's hand finds the small of my back. Zane circles behind me, grabbing my waist as he presses a kiss at the nape of my neck, while Brax moves to stand before me, towering down like the strong gargoyle he is, tipping my chin back to look up at him.

With each of them touching me, my heart feels whole. Relief floats off me in waves. It feels so strong. I'm certain I'm going to see it cascade around me.

"How are we touching?" The question falls from my lips without thought.

"I don't know, but I don't care either," Eldon murmurs, making me smile.

"What I want to know is if I can fuck you right now, Dove. Prove you're real," Zane whispers against my ear, making me shiver.

"Maybe next time, asshole. We really do have a lot to discuss. Remember?" Creed grumbles, putting a stop to the idea immediately.

"Fucker," Zane utters under his breath, and I snicker, the same taunt running through my mind too. But there must be things I need to know if how I got here is anything to go by.

"If you're cock blocking, Creed, you better lead the way," I state, earning a grin from Eldon at my other side.

Without another word, the five of us head inside, happy to bask in each other's proximity as they lead me to the kitchen. Steaming mugs of hot cocoa are waiting on the dining table. Much to Zane's disappointment, I take the seat between Creed and Eldon and wrap my hands around the warm mug.

"Thank you," I breathe, my gaze traveling to Brax's mother, who smiles back at me in response. "It feels like forever since I've seen you all," I murmur before taking a sip.

"The longest period of time in my life, Dove," Zane declares from his spot on the other side of Eldon, wedged between him and Brax.

"How did you get me here like that?" I ask, aware that we clearly have things to catch up on, but I need to understand this first.

"It was Brax's idea," his father explains. "Depending on how you look at it, fortunately or not, Eldon, Creed, and Zane can't see the shadows. Just like we can't unless we use a special apparatus that we built, but for Brax, it's different." He waves a hand at his son and I follow the movement with my eyes.

"Communicating with the shadows is… weird, but easy enough." My eyes widen. Easy? How? I haven't communicated with them at all, and I feel like I'm constantly surrounded by them. "Once I appeared here in my dream and thought about it, I created a safe zone in the yard out back, generating energy that lured them closer. Mention of a pretty pink-haired necromancer was an easy enough discussion. It seems you hold a lot of hope for more than just us, Shadow," Brax states, making me frown in confusion.

"Wha—"

He waves his hand, interrupting my question before I can jump ahead.

"They were happy to help. Even the shadows can feel your pureness. Your strength, resilience, all of it. They know you're not here to wield your magic to use them at your will."

"Why would I do that?" My nose crinkles in distaste at the thought.

"Exactly. You're the piece of the puzzle that fixes all of this, we just don't know what that looks like or how we're going to do it, but we're all here together. Ready to fight. Not for the next generation or for the Elevin Realm. Not even for Silvercrest Academy. We're all ready to fight for you."

I gape at Eldon, his words hitting me hard in the chest. Slowly, I start to shake my head.

"He's right, Raven. I may not know you, but I don't have to. I can see the person you are by looking at the men around you. I've been warned that you refuse to be labeled as a hero, that saving the realm, or anything else, isn't in your plan, and that's what makes you different, not just from anyone else, but from any necromancer that has ever lived." I rub my lips together as I stare at Brax's mother. Her smile only widens and she stands, coming around to stand beside me as she offers me her hand. "Hi, Raven. I'm Marieta, and I pledge to help with all that I am, all that I could be, and all I wish to be."

I peer at Brax, completely overwhelmed, and he offers a subtle nod in response. Turning back to Marieta, I place my hand in hers and a sudden golden swirl sweeps over our joined hands, dancing for the briefest moment before settling against our skin and disappearing a second later.

"What was that?"

"That was a pledged oath," Brax's father answers, coming to stand beside his wife. "It's the kind of promise we give to The Monarchy, to a cause, a belief. And that's what you are to us, Raven. Belief. Hope." I don't know how to respond as he offers his hand to me. "Hi, Raven. I'm Peta, and I pledge to help with all that I am, all that I could be, and all I wish to be."

What is actually happening right now?

I place my hand in his and the same thing happens.

"Why?" I manage to croak. "What don't I know that you guys seem to?"

"What makes you think that's the case?" Creed asks, and I cock a brow at him.

"I just show up here and suddenly I'm learning about

pledged oaths? *To* me? I don't understand why, and I'm not saying that because I'm looking for someone to shower me with praise, quite the opposite."

Brax grins. Actually fucking grins. Marieta circles around the table to come to a stop behind him, gently placing her hand on his shoulder. "Stop looking so smug, Son. It suits you far too well."

"What does that mean?"

Marieta winks at me as Peta chuckles, taking his seat casually like the pair of them haven't just pledged themselves to me. What the fuck?

"It means my son has been here for a little over an hour and has already taken charge of everything. Right down to predicting how you would respond to the pledged oaths," she explains with a chuckle.

I glare at him but he doesn't falter under my stare. I exhale, a calmness settling over me as I look around the table. "Has Brax got everyone up to date on our end?" I ask, redirecting the conversation, and Marieta sinks her teeth into her bottom lip, trying and failing to stifle her chuckle.

I look at Eldon and Zane, helplessly confused, but they only smirk back at me too. "We said you would immediately try to distract the conversation away from yourself too."

Fuckers.

Of course they did.

Rolling my eyes, I turn my attention to Peta, hoping someone here is focused on something else. "Help me out, Peta. What do I need to know?"

"What don't you need to know would probably be the easier question, but that's not useful, is it?" He winks, leaving me no wiser.

Despite the stress and anxiety that insists on following me everywhere right now, I can't help but appreciate the moment. Surrounded by Eldon, Creed, Zane, and Brax, with his parents casting a calming environment around us with their mere presence, is something to appreciate. Especially when we don't know how many more moments we may get like this going forward.

Gulping down the remainder of my hot cocoa, I lean back in my seat, letting the tension ease from my shoulders.

"Is there anything we can be doing from the other side?" I ask. "I want us all together as soon as possible. Whatever it takes, I don't care. I can't continue like this." Creed's hand falls to my lap, squeezing in comfort as Eldon's arm drapes over the back of my chair.

"We need you to investigate some things."

My eyebrows rise to my hairline. "More things to investigate?"

Creed nods, his face falling solemn. "Erikel wasn't a skinwalker, Raven. Burton was, or is. I don't know." I freeze, letting his words settle in my mind as I try and fail to process them. "I know it sounds insane, but that's why we need to figure it out." My gaze travels to Brax and I can see in his eyes that they've already told him this, but it doesn't stop the furrow between his brows from growing stronger.

"What are you dealing with out there, Raven? Is there anything we can help with?" Marieta asks. "Our main focus right now is trying to communicate with the shadows in your absence, to convince them to help us. Now they'll acknowledge our pledged oath to you, so we may see more assistance from them. I can't explain how much that helps us, but I meant the pledge wholeheartedly. If there's anything I can offer, just ask."

Taking a deep breath, I think about all of the thoughts keeping me up at night, tearing them apart and piecing them back together.

"Are you able to help with wards or familiars? I think I'm going to need to get to Ari to be able to stabilize things on the other side. I don't know how much longer we'll be able to hide the fact that the guys are here. Erikel is going insane over the Potens Ruby and the guys' disappearance. I need to strengthen my defenses, and Ari is my key to that. I feel it."

"Ari?"

"He's her familiar, a griffin," Brax explains, and both Marieta and Peta stare at me with wide eyes.

"A griffin as a familiar is a true blessing, Raven." Their words warm my heart but don't ease the growing pain at the distance I'm feeling from him. "I think I can help with the wards. Come."

TEN

Raven

I don't want to leave. I really don't want to go. I'm completely overwhelmed with information, along with a stack of questions that are still unanswered. I want to stay forever. Above all that, I don't want to leave my men. Even if this is a dream and not my true form, I could stay forever and easily pretend the outside world doesn't exist.

Despite what I want, I know I can't. It seems I'm meant for bigger things. Things I'm not sure I care about, but I'm here nonetheless. Maybe once everything is said and done, if I succeed in whatever needs to be achieved, then I can just be. Me, with my men. Nothing else matters.

Brax grabs my hand, his fingers flexing around mine as he pulls me out onto the wraparound porch. My chest aches, disappointment seeping into my bones as the others follow behind us.

Once I'm at the bottom of the steps, I turn back to look at the pieces of my soul I'm going to have to leave behind. Sadness weaves its way between us, drawing us closer while making the distance that's about to follow even more prominent.

"I don't want to go," I admit, emotion clogging my throat.

Eldon reaches for me first, tugging me from Brax's hold to wrap me in his arms. "I don't want you to go either," he whispers against the shell of my ear. "It won't be for long, though, Little Bird. And it'll never be forever. I won't allow it," he adds, warming my bleak heart.

I cling to him, making sure to take a deep breath of his t-shirt so he lingers with me when I'm gone. Looking up at him, he strokes his hand over my hair, a lazy smile on his lips.

He doesn't utter a word and neither do I. Instead, his lips descend on mine, claiming me delicately as I fist the back of his t-shirt.

All too soon, we're parting, the distance growing between us once again, and Zane spins me to face him before my emotions get the better of me. "What we need more than anything else, Dove, is for you to behave," he says with a grin and a cock of his brow. I gape at him, which only makes a chuckle vibrate from his chest. *Ass.* "But for real, you can't be getting hot-headed right now, either of you." He lifts his gaze, glancing over my shoulder to find Brax, who doesn't verbalize his agreement. Zane rolls his eyes, turning back to me with one hand at my waist and the other cupping my cheek. "I'll see you real soon, Dove."

The softness of his voice leaves me weak as he presses his lips firmly against mine. I drink him in, eager for every ounce of him as I cling to his shoulders.

My eyes fall closed and remain that way until he takes a step back. A breeze flutters around me and I sense the moment it's Creed before me this time. I want to draw it out. Once I say goodbye to him, there's no reason to stay, which means we must leave, and the thought alone pains me.

"Look at me, Raven." I gulp, exhaling softly before I do as he asks. The moment my eyes clash with his deep onyx pools, my heart races. "You're stronger than the rest of us put together. Not just with your magic, in here too." He presses his palm against my chest, the beat of my heart beneath his touch. "We were meant for you because we each offer a part of ourselves that completes you, but you, my sweet fucking Raven, *you* offer yourself wholly to all of us because you have the heart, the resilience, and the fight deep in your soul to hold us together while shattering the world at the same time."

I'm rendered speechless as I stare at him with a soft

smile ghosting my lips. I don't know how to respond to that, but it sure as hell feels like he's showering me with praise I can't handle or fathom. Before I can refute anything he's said, he kisses both corners of my mouth, dragging out the tension until his lips claim mine.

I thank him with my mouth, portray my feelings with my lips, and show how much strength I actually take from them, too, with my fingers clinging to his arms.

Breathless, he tears his lips from mine, his eyes dark with desire as he takes a step back, not missing the opportunity to tuck a loose tendril of hair behind my ear before slipping his hands into his pockets.

A large hand engulfs mine and I don't need to look to know it's Brax. Turning to him, he lifts his hand to wave toward his parents, who quietly stand in the open doorway. I should be embarrassed over all the PDA they're having to witness, but I can't bring myself to care. Not when I'm basking in my men for the first time in what feels like an eternity. Every second away from them is just too long.

He drops his free hand, turning to me with a nod that I return, even though I'm not ready to go.

Looking back at Eldon, Zane, and Creed, I take a deep breath.

"I lov—"

The wind rushes from my lungs, cutting off my words as I find myself tumbling backward through the never-ending darkness. Nausea pools in my gut as my hand slips from Brax's, leaving me free floating on my own. It feels longer than it did on the way here, but I eventually hit the ground with a thud, and when I open my eyes, it's the familiar four walls of my bedroom that greet me.

Panting, my palm flattens against my chest as I lurch forward in bed, catching my breath as I take stock of my surroundings.

Fuck.

My body aches, and although I've technically been asleep, my eyes feel as heavy as they did when I was lying here staring into the twilight abyss. Dragging my hand down my face, I glance at the time and groan. Of course, we need to start getting ready for classes now.

"It feels like I'm living a double life," I grumble, shifting to swing my legs over the side of the bed.

"You're not wrong there, but we don't have time to dwell on it. We have things to do. A purpose," Brax states, shuffling to the other side of the bed. Rising to my feet, I move around to where he sits, and before I go into the bathroom to get ready, I slip between his parted thighs and drape my arms around his neck.

"Before we do that, we need to decide on a word."

"A word?" He quirks a brow at me, tired but intrigued. I nod. "Why?"

"So we know we are who we say we are."

His eyebrows furrow for a moment before understanding seems to wash over him and he nods. "That makes sense. It's easier than throwing random questions at each other like I did with Leila yesterday."

Silence descends over us for a moment as we think. I know it's the one as soon as it crosses my mind, and the moment I call it out, Brax smirks, the only agreement I need.

"Handbook."

My hair is twisted into a messy bun on top of my head, revealing more of the black strands of hair that intertwine between the pink. I almost considered turning it all black in the mirror this morning but decided I will likely live like that forever once I reach a certain point with my magic, and I'm all for prolonging the inevitable.

With my hand firmly in Brax's grasp, we're marching toward the main academy building with one thing on our minds: find Professor Figgins.

I'm hopeful that with the information Marieta gave us, we can control the ward that protects the compound. Working our way through that is one step closer to Ari, and I'm desperate for us to get it done.

We need a win, and after last night, getting to see Eldon,

Creed, and Zane like that, I believe anything is possible.

Leila wasn't waiting outside of the house this morning, and I can't decide whether it's a good thing or a bad thing. Once I've convinced Figgins about the compound, I can go in search of her.

After settling on our safe word, Brax and I agreed that it would just be for the two of us for now. Everyone else either needs an alternative word or to face our questioning. There are so many people here that I would love the opportunity to question, to demand answers from, the truth and only the truth, but it's not as easy as I wish it were.

The list continues to grow; the people we can trust are depleting, but one person in this place whose magic could be forever valuable is Lyra's. She's high on my visit list too. Even if I could figure out a way to get her to let me mirror her magic instead of draining her and exposing her to the enemy, I would be forever grateful.

"How deep in your mind are you right now?" Brax's question startles me, and the way his eyebrows rise tells me I've accidentally given him my answer. Deep. I'm fucking deep in there.

"It's hard not to be," I admit, making sure to keep my voice low. "We might have a bit of a plan of action, but that doesn't ease the obstacles we're facing, the what-ifs that surround us. My mind is going so fast, zipping from one thought to another, and it's a never-ending cycle."

He hums in understanding, but I still see the tic of his jaw, and I know what's going through his mind. He wants to fix everything for me, and the reality is he can't, not that I would ever ask him to. The feeling of helplessness that comes with that, though, is incomparable.

I squeeze his hand three times, silently conveying the emotion swarming inside of me. He doesn't respond to it, not that I need him to, but his focus is dead ahead as his steps slow. Following his line of sight, my back stiffens when I see Erikel standing by the main entrance to the building. Some students mill around, avoiding walking past him with their chins resting against their chest as they look anywhere but at him, while others slip past him, offering as much room as possible as they move with haste.

Fuck.

Of course, he has to be the first real obstacle we face today. I shouldn't be surprised.

There's not long before the first class starts, and if we want a chance to catch Figgins then we can't hang around avoiding him.

"I feel like this is one of those moments that Zane was referring to," I murmur, and my eyes follow my brother as he approaches Erikel.

"I agree. We can walk past him and hope it doesn't cause a scene, or we can cut through the grounds to the left and enter through the back doors, which are technically closer to her office anyway," he offers, running his thumb over my knuckles.

Dammit. I don't want to shy away from Erikel. Giving him that taste of delight doesn't sit well with me. But my ego can't distract us from the job at hand. Right now, I need to not seek trouble and take the path of least resistance.

"Let's go to the left," I mutter, nudging his shoulder with mine.

We move through the growing crowd, seemingly unnoticed, as we take the grassy trail around the exterior of the building.

"That's also why Zane told you to behave and not me. He knows you can assess a situation better without turning into an asshole," Brax grunts, making me smirk.

"Oh, I wanted to cause a scene with that fucker. I wanted to summon my sword and watch him bleed out as I danced in the crimson liquid, refusing to bring him back to life, but really, I want answers and a plan for Ari first. The former will have to wait just a little while longer," I admit with a sigh.

"Fuck, Shadow. You're crazier than I give you credit for."

I peer up at him with a smirk. "You don't give me nearly enough credit as it is." I wag my finger at him, avoiding his mouth when he attempts to snap his teeth at me, and I laugh.

"May I ask what it is the two of you are doing out here?"

We pause mid-chuckle as we turn to stare at the interrupter of our amusing moment, only to come face to face with Professor Figgins. She peers between us, arms folded over her chest, but there's no real authority to her stare, just a tingling of intrigue.

"Looking for you, actually." I turn to face her, a tight smile placed on my face for show, and without a word, she waves us inside.

We follow her through the doors and down the quiet hallway before slipping into her classroom. She doesn't utter a word at all until we're secured in her office and the lock is in place behind us.

"I have a class in a few moments. How can I help?" She rounds her desk but doesn't take a seat as she braces her fingertips on the wood top instead.

"We need to try and get to the compound. I have a plan for the wards."

"What plan?"

I shrug. "Due to extreme bullshit that keeps happening, I'm going to keep that tidbit to myself for now. Brax is still having no luck getting to the compound via a gateway, but we've been offered a vague direction without one."

"From whom?"

I shake my head. She's focusing on the wrong details.

"I can do this without you, Professor. I'm here, offering you an in because a part of me feels like you deserve a chance to help save us all."

My words hang in the air, floating like dust as she blinks at me.

"You're asking me to trust in you," she finally offers, folding her arms nervously around her waist, and I nod.

"I am. You don't have to, that's your choice, but I think we all know nothing is going to end well here. The decision we have to make is whether we're going to fall freely with whatever comes our way or take fate into our own hands and ride the storm."

My breaths come in short bursts, my emotions flooding my veins as they rise to the surface, and she continues to stare at me like I've got something on my face.

I haven't even question-checked her or made sure she is who I think she is, and that only makes me more annoyed at myself. I haven't said too much, but I'm quite firmly placing myself on the other side of the war to the one who believes himself to be my master.

Clearing my throat, I'm ready to leave when she strides purposefully back around the desk to stand in front of me. Brax shifts protectively at my side, placing himself between us, but I pat his arm, letting him know that I'm okay.

"You're right. This isn't going to end well. I wasn't

raised a quitter but I've been foolish enough to act like one since the day that man arrived. I knew there was something wrong then, but every day that I spend apart from my familiar is another painful reminder of what my future could look like, and I refuse." There's a tremble to her shoulders, revealing her nerves, but she still stands tall, adding strength to her words. "I refuse," she repeats, and I nod. "Tell me where to meet you once classes are done for the day, and I'm at your service."

157

ELEVEN

Raven

Seconds twist into minutes, which meld into hours. All the while, I'm ready to tear my hair out, eager for the end of the day to come. Yet it laughs at me, forever in the distance as the day drags into the longest ever recorded in history.

My ink scratches along my parchment, taking all of the notes as I gaze off into the distance, even less present now than I was in the first class of the day.

Leila has breezed in and out of my self-made bubble throughout the day with Grave on her arm. On one hand, it's a relief she's not quite under her father's thumb right now. Although, I'm sure he's got plenty of watchful eyes on her, making Fitch even more unpredictable than ever, in my opinion. Yet it's Grave's recent dedication to Leila that causes the smallest stutter in my thoughts.

We may not know Fitch's motives or what side of the faint line he stands on, but I feel like I have a better understanding of him than Grave. Maybe it's because I'm untrusting. I don't know. But an icky feeling twists in my gut when I glance at him out of the corner of my eye. He's older than us, so he's not in our classes, but he seems to be waiting at every door when time is called by the professors.

Sighing, I roll out my tightening shoulders and shake him from my thoughts. As much as he's making me question him, his presence doesn't rank high enough on my list of to-dos, and I really have to prioritize what I let myself get stressed out about. He's not one of them. Yet.

Professor Trigwell mutters about the plant in her hand, drawing me a little more to the present, but the information continues to go straight over my head. Nothing has stuck in my mind all day. Not a single class, and now, as we edge toward the end of the academy day, I'm getting antsier to get out of here.

As if sensing my thoughts, Trigwell plops the plant pot down on her desk, mumbling under her breath before tilting her head up to look at us. "Class is dismissed."

I don't need to be told twice. I'm on my feet and out of the door with Brax hot on my heels in less than five seconds. There were a few grumbles along the way, complaints of my barging past people in my mission to get out of there, but I don't give a fuck.

Brax nods at me as we head down the hallway, reaching for my hand as we make our way outside. Instead of taking the path toward the house like we usually would, following the rest of the students, we veer to the right, heading for the one spot that's been calling out to me all day.

The Gauntlet.

Anticipation swirls in my veins, quickening my pace until the arena comes into view. Once at the main entrance, we stop, glancing back to see if Professor Figgins is on her way. It's no surprise that she's not here yet, it will likely take her a few more minutes to not look suspicious, and I don't mind waiting a minute or two.

Turning to look through the open archway into the Gauntlet, a shiver runs down my spine. The first time we were led here feels like yesterday and a million years ago, all at once.

"Do you remember the first time we were brought here?" I murmur, still clinging to Brax's hand. "It doesn't feel that long ago," I add, the taste of worry still lingering along my skin from then as I stare down into the depths of the arena.

"It wasn't," Brax states, and I hum.

"So much has happened since then. Damn, so much happened that day." I shake my head in disbelief as I try to remember everything we faced so early on in the year, but it's completely dwarfed by the bigger problems we now face. I would much rather be selfish and go back to then, though, when I was worried more about myself and not the entire fucking realm. "Can you believe you, of all people, helped me survive the Gauntlet?" I muse, glancing up to meet narrowed eyes as he grunts at me. "I bet that's not something you ever thought you would do." It seems I'm in a pushy mood, wanting more than the simple grunt he offered.

He shrugs. "Maybe not, but everything changed when I met you."

"You didn't like me," I point out with a scoff, refusing to believe he's going to admit that so easily after fighting against the pull between us for so long. Things have changed drastically between us, but that doesn't mean he's going to be all hearts, flowers, and rainbows now, where he tells me all his thoughts and feelings. Not this guy.

"I was instantly drawn to you. That was the issue."

I gape at him, waiting for some smart comment or dig in my direction to counterbalance his statement, but nothing comes. Clearing my throat, I glance back at the Gauntlet. "Seems like a tough issue you were dealing with."

"It was. I let Eldon in because he was my friend, and he literally took me in with his family. When we became friends with Zane and Creed, that was all him, too. I was much slower to let my guard down, and that was a long time ago. I thought I had forgotten how to do it until you waltzed in with your crazy pink hair, big personality, and no-bullshit attitude."

Oh, he's on a roll. "Those are some pretty big compliments."

He cocks a brow at me, staring deep into my eyes. "Compliments?"

"From you? Definitely." A grin tips the corner of my lips playfully, but before a full smile can spread across my face, he leans down, crushing my mouth with his in a fierce kiss that leaves me breathless.

Clinging to his tie, I hold him closer, refusing to let go until the sound of someone clearing their throat breaks through my thoughts.

"I thought we had things to do."

We break apart, the interruption well and truly ruining our moment, but one glance at Professor Figgins as she stands awkwardly beside us with her arms folded over her chest reminds me exactly why we're here.

"Tell me something that only you would say and not someone impersonating you." Brax's demand makes her eyebrow quirk in challenge, but when he doesn't back down, she sighs, inching closer.

"Neither of our gateways worked that day in my office because of the drill siren. I will forever wish we were five minutes earlier."

Her words ring true and my lips press together, knowing

she is exactly herself. Brax must agree because he doesn't miss a beat.

"That will do. And you're right, We do have things to do," Brax grunts, taking a step back as I use the moment to catch my breath. "But don't question what we do while waiting for you to get here. Raven is the one out of all of us with the weight of the world on her shoulders. Don't trample her for having five seconds of a reprieve from that."

Gaping at him, I feel my cheeks heat. I'm prepared for Figgins to throw a retort back at him, but to my surprise, she nods. "You're right." *He is?* "Let's get on with it now, shall we?" Without waiting for confirmation, she steps around Brax and me and heads through the archway, hovering on the top step of the stairs. "What are we doing here anyway?"

"Getting to the compound," I explain, rushing past her to get to the bottom where the dome usually is.

"But I tried before I left. The gateways still aren't working," Figgins calls out, hurrying to keep up with us.

"We know. That's why we're here," Brax adds.

There's a coolness in the air that I don't seem to feel anywhere but here. It's not eerie and doesn't leave me on edge, but it's not soothing either. I don't know what it is, but it lingers, that's for sure.

Reaching the bottom, I place my hands on my hips and

survey the center of the arena.

"What are you looking for?" Figgins asks, and I decide to come right out with it, hoping she knows where to find it. It's an irritation to my ego, asking someone for help, but I'll get over it.

"We're trying to find the gateway that brings the magical creatures here when called upon to fight in the Gauntlet."

Her eyes widen as uncertainty flashes across her face. She stares at me for a moment and I'm sure she's going to bombard me with questions or refute it altogether, but after a few moments, she steps into the arena. I follow her to the center of the platform, where she reaches down, pulling at a small latch to reveal a swirling golden gateway beneath it.

"Holy fuck," I blurt, excitement fluttering through my veins as I beam at Brax.

"How is it still here? I hadn't even considered it to be an option," Professor Figgins murmurs, glancing between the two of us, and I shrug.

"I was told that for security measures, it's always generated under different wards."

"Who told you that?" Her eyebrows are pinched slightly, almost as though she's irritated she didn't know the information herself.

"Does it matter, or are we going before someone finds

us?" I distract, not wanting to give away too much given all the obstacles we're trying to maneuver.

She assesses me for a brief second before nodding, reconfirming her trust in me.

"Lead the way."

My academy-issued shoes squelch beneath me, the sodden ground shaded by huge trees, as a soft glow filters through the leaves, lighting the surrounding area. Relief floods my brain as I take a deep breath, letting the reality of where I am settle in.

"Uh, slight issue," Figgins murmurs, lifting the hem of her long, black cloak off the ground as she frowns. "This gateway has put us inside the compound, which is exactly what we didn't want to happen. Especially if there's no way of getting out."

"I know."

Her eyes ping to mine with surprise. "Don't you think that's the kind of heads-up I deserve?"

I shrug. "Maybe. But if I'm honest, I hadn't even considered it would be an issue. You said you wanted to help. I wasn't aware that it came with stipulations. No one is forcing you to be here or help. You can leave of your own free will once I've done what needs to be done."

There's no time for me to consider if it's shitty of me to not mention that fact ahead of time, but surely she should have realized where it would put us before we stepped through the gateway. If she's expecting an apology, she should prepare to be disappointed. Right now, I have one thing on my mind.

Trudging through the grounds, I take a deep breath and call out to my familiar in my mind. It's not a surprise that I'm greeted with nothing, but it still causes a deeper stir in my gut. Instead of letting the worry weigh me down, I try again. Only this time, I speak out loud.

"Ari." Nothing but the sound of our shoes beating against the hardening soil can be heard around us. "Ari," I repeat, making sure to be louder this time, but still, there's nothing back from him.

Leaves rustle to my right, making me pause as I glance over to where the shrubbery is thick. I'm almost certain it's in my head when I don't see or hear anything else, but just as I'm about to carry on moving, I see them.

"Gia? Gia, is that you?" I call out, immediately moving in her direction. She remains mostly hidden in the shadows, head lowered as she peers at me.

"Stay back." It's a whisper, dancing in the wind, and I frown but keep on moving.

"Gia. What's going on? What's wrong?"

"Stay back." The warning comes again, high-pitched

and barely audible above the breeze.

It doesn't make sense. If I can just get to her, then—

"Heed the warning before I force you back myself." My head snaps to the left of Gia, where a tall griffin steps from the shadows, a mountain of golds and creams emerging from the depths of darkness to reveal my familiar.

"Oh my goodness," I say with a gasp, my heart racing in my chest as I quicken my pace, only now he's my target.

"Stop," he bites, his front claws sinking into the ground as he stands protectively in front of Gia. His defensive snarl aimed my way.

I freeze, finally letting the warning sink in, but none of it makes sense. I can hear the footsteps of Brax and Figgins behind me, but I don't turn to check on them as I focus on Ari.

"I don't know what's going on, Ari. I'm here to help. I've been worried about you." He circles me, not offering a single word as a deathly silence clings to the air. I can feel his gaze tearing at me, ripping me apart and piecing me together again, but why? For what? "Ari?"

He comes to stand in front of me, head now high with a snarl still lifting his lip. "Of all the men you could have brought, you chose the one I trust the least. How foolish of you to think you could play tricks with me twice."

"Trust the least? What's that supposed to mean?" Brax grumbles from behind me, and I startle.

"You can hear him?" I ask, glancing back to see him, and he nods.

What the fuck? It's on the tip of my tongue to ask him about it, but he continues on with his tongue-lashing before I can beat him to it.

"I won't fall for your foolishness again, skinwalker, I—"

"Woah… skinwalker? Ari, it's me, Raven. I'm not a skinwalker."

My chest tightens with worry as I take a tentative step forward, only to yield again a moment later when he shakes his head vigorously, anger vibrating from him.

"I said—"

"How can I prove it? Please, Ari, tell me how," I interject, lifting my hands in his direction while somehow keeping my feet glued to the ground. All I want to do is feel his feathers, fall into his embrace, and drown in the connection I have with him and only him. My familiar.

He stands tall, looking down his beak at me as he cocks his head to the side. A sudden tug in my gut makes me yelp, dropping me to my knees with a gasp as my hands clutch my stomach. I can't explain it. The pull is right where my connection to him always is, where his emotions swirl inside of me, but there's never been anything like that before.

I don't get a chance to question it before it happens

again, my palms slamming into the ground as the wind is blown from my lungs.

"Whatever the fuck you're doing to her, stop. Now," Brax snaps, his hand landing on my back as he stands protectively over me. It won't do any good, though, not if he can cause me pain like this. But why?

"Raven?" My name on his tongue settles everything inside me as I peer up at him. The harshness to his gaze vanishes as he takes a step toward me.

"Ari," I rasp, and he cuts the remaining distance between us.

Crouching before me, he tucks his beak under my chin, forcing me to stand as I place my hand against his feathers. "It's you."

His words hang heavily between us and I feel the emotion in his eyes. Now isn't the time to be vulnerable. Forcing a smirk to my lips, I give him a pointed look. "I said it was. What makes you think it wasn't?"

He draws me closer, so I'm pressed in a warm embrace against his feathers, and sighs. "The skinwalker."

"A skinwalker showed up here… as me?" I clarify, disbelief rippling through me.

"Yes."

"When?"

"It doesn't matter. I didn't trust our mind bond after that and blocked my thoughts from yours," he offers, making complete sense of the total disconnect I've felt from him, but the reality doesn't ease the pain that it's caused me.

"And apparently, you've now decided to start talking out loud instead," I grumble, leaning back so I can see him properly. I sense Gia moving closer to us, but I keep my gaze locked on my familiar, too scared to let him out of my sight.

"I always could."

My jaw falls slack as I blink up at him. Fucker. Wasn't he the one to say he couldn't? Asshole. With a shake of my head, I sigh. "Of course you could. Here I am, panicked and worried because I can't reach out to you, and here you are, causing mayhem."

"You're welcome." I'm certain he's smiling, but the beak makes it impossible to know.

"Raven," Gia murmurs, calling out my name as she leans into her love, and Ari nuzzles against her.

"Gia," I breathe, relieved to see that she's still okay.

"If it really is you, why are you on the inside of the compound?" she asks, and I sense Ari stiffen with worry as I smile brightly.

"To get you out," I explain, taking a step back to intertwine my fingers with Brax's while Figgins gapes at all of us with a sad longing in her eyes. Her need for her own familiar must be driving her insane. I can't even imagine.

"You know that's not possible," Ari states, pulling me from my concerns, and I wag my eyebrows at him.

"Are you underestimating me?" Before he has the chance to lecture me on it, I take another step back. "Where is the closest barrier to the compound from here?"

He glances over me for a moment before reluctantly nodding behind him. I take off in that direction, Brax right beside me and Figgins trying her best to keep up as I hurry over the fallen trees and protruding roots sticking out of the ground.

"Where are you going?" Ari asks, the ground vibrating slightly with his steps. I ignore him, remaining focused on getting to the edge of the compound. "Raven, where are we going?" he prods again, but I continue to ignore him. I feel it the second he's no longer on the ground, and a moment later, he lands in front of me, blocking my path with his wings flung out wide at his sides. "Raven."

I ignore the warning tone of his words as I beam at him. "The silent treatment isn't so nice now, is it?" I snark, cocking a brow at him before I practically skip around him. I'm certain I hear what almost sounds like a chuckle from Gia, but I'm too fixated on the compound wards to double-check.

"You've made your point," Ari grumbles, turning to keep beside me, and I look up at him with another pointed look.

"Have I? I'm not sure."

Thankfully, I avoid another lecture when the area grows lighter and I spot the perimeter of the compound. Brax starts running before I do and I cling to him as we eliminate the distance, coming to a stop beside the barely visible ward that shimmers ever so slightly from the glow falling from the sky.

"Raven, before you attempt whatever you think you know here, I think we need to catch each other up to speed, don't you?" Ari asks, making a valid point, but uncertainty wars inside of me. Sinking my teeth into my bottom lip, I turn to face him.

"Honestly, Ari, I trust you with my life, but I don't know who or what may lurk in our surroundings and I refuse to give anyone the upper hand on us right now when everything is crumbling to the ground."

I pray like hell that he understands that we'll be able to do all of the catching up, but now just isn't the time. Even with Figgins in our proximity, it's too much.

"We could discuss it like this, in here," he offers, speaking directly into my thoughts again, and I make a mental note to ask him to help me block my mind off from others as soon as possible.

"I don't trust anything, Ari, and if something has you this spooked, I don't want to risk it. Once I'm done, we'll have all the time to catch up."

He stares at me for what feels like forever until he nods. "Yeah, you're definitely my Raven."

I smile at him as Brax's hand tightens around mine.

"*My* Raven," he bites, making me press my lips together to hold back my grin as both Ari and Brax glare at each other.

"Shall we get to the point?" Figgins asks, looking at me pleadingly, and I nod in agreement.

Turning to face the barrier that separates us from the real world, I suddenly feel a bout of nerves. This has to go right. I can't mess it up.

With a long and heavy breath, I stand mere inches from the ward, my skin tingling with nerves as I stretch my hand toward the barrier. I gasp when my fingertips connect with it, the magic coursing from it almost overwhelming, but as I twist my hand into the magic, I latch on to what I'm searching for.

"I can feel it." Hope blossoms in my gut as I tilt my head to glance at Brax.

His eyes are wide, arms slack at his sides as he stares at me. "You can?"

"Yeah."

I see the same hope reflecting from him as I feel in my veins. The magic dances over my skin, encouraging me to take control.

"What can you feel? What are you doing?" Figgins

asks tentatively, and I turn to face her. It seems it was never meant to stay a secret, and I don't know why, but I trust her enough to be honest.

"I can use my mirror magic to take control of the ward. Whoever placed it here left tendrils of their magic for me to harness. I believe it's on top of yours, so possibly, together, we could work through it. I wasn't sure it would be possible when someone offered the advice, but if I tug at it, I think it will fall down."

Wait until the guys hear about this. Wait until Brax can fill Marieta with hope that her guidance was perfect. I know the compound being opened doesn't directly impact them, but it feels like the first step in the right direction, and we all need that.

"Fall down? That would unleash all of the magical creatures," Figgins states, eyebrows pinching in concern.

"Well, yeah. I'm not just going to free Ari and leave everyone else to suffer here."

"But doing that would also include those from the Basilica Realm," she explains slowly, horror washing over her features.

"We can't," Ari grinds out, taking a step toward me, but the sound of a twig snapping underfoot doesn't come from him; it comes from the shadows to the right.

My gaze snatches to the Drake looming in the darkness and my spine stiffens.

Fuck. They're right.

"You can set us free from here?" The Drake asks, and Ari snarls.

"You can speak?" my familiar shouts, but the Drake ignores him, keeping his focus on me as he takes a step forward.

Wrong move.

Both Ari and Brax move to protect me, but the Drake manages to keep his eyes locked with mine. "Can you set us free from here?" he repeats.

"I could, but I don't believe that to be a safe or wise choice when you have familiars on the wrong side of the war on the other side of this barrier." Being honest makes sense. There's no point sugarcoating this shit with him, either.

He shakes his head. "We are fake familiars. That was just a ploy to get us on the property, nothing else," he explains, making my heart race. That does make sense, especially since no one has been going crazy over the fact that some of the Drakes have been dying at the hands of Ari.

"And then?" Ari snaps, dragging his claw through the compact soil at his feet.

"And then what?"

"What are you supposed to do? What are you here to destroy?" Ari pushes, and the Drake huffs, eyes returning back to mine, but not before he takes a moment to stare at my hair.

"You are the necromancer," he points out, redirecting the conversation and ignoring Ari's questions.

"What makes you say that?"

"Your hair."

Of course, he's familiar with the fact that my hair darkening in certain spots is linked to my magic.

"What does my magical ability have to do with anything?" I ask, irritated with the distraction the Drake is causing.

"If you're the necromancer, that means your name is… Raven, correct?"

I still, my mouth going dry, but tamp everything down and focus on remaining unfazed. "Correct."

With the confirmation from me, a sudden movement behind him catches my attention as more and more Drakes appear.

"Raven," Brax warns as Ari growls, ready to attack, while Gia and Figgins inch closer to me.

Before anyone can make the first attacking move, the Drake standing front and center lowers to the ground, knees pressing into the dirt with his head tipped. The second he's in position, the others follow.

I frown, staring at the group of Drakes kneeling before us as they shift before our eyes one by one.

They're not magical creatures.

They're men.

Shifters.

What the fuck?

"Raven, we are the Brotherhood of the Drakes. We pledge to help with all that we are, all that we could be, and all we wish to be."

They speak in sync, causing my throat to clog and my pulse to thump in my ears as I gape at them.

"They're pledging an oath to you," Brax mutters, stating the obvious as he stares in disbelief too.

"Why are they doing that?" Figgins asks, like I have any idea myself, but thankfully, the Drake, or the man who *was* the Drake, answers for me.

"We believe in the necromancer."

I shake my head. "Erikel may be trying to play me like a puppet, but I am not on his side or under his control. Pledging yourselves to me will not end how you envision."

"Oh, I believe it will." He rises, confirming that he doesn't, in fact, have a single stitch of clothing on. "Our agreement with Erikel was voided the moment he imprisoned us here and went back on his word."

"What was your agreement?" Ari grunts at the same time Brax speaks too.

"You can't go back on a pledged oath."

Silence descends over the forest as the Brotherhood of

Drakes all stand, revealing far too much limp dick for my preference. I hear Figgins splutter on her next breath, and I fight back a chuckle at the current turn of events.

"We have never pledged an oath before. We know the value of it," the original Drake states, planting his hands on his hips, all casual as hell.

"So, you didn't offer him the same," Brax clarifies, and the Drake shakes his head in confirmation.

"Why?" I ask, the question slipping from my mouth without thought.

"Because he won't join the realms and set us all free," he explains with a simple shrug.

"What realm are you from?" Ari asks, his tone a little less snappy now, and I'm hoping to take that as a good sign.

"We are from Torin Realm." Torin Realm? Where the fuck is that? As if hearing my thoughts or from reading all of our facial expressions, he explains further. "Our home is beneath Basilica Realm, but none of that matters right now. What matters is setting us free from here so you can work on joining the realms and aligning us all as one."

I shake my head in disbelief. "I don't even know of most realms, nevermind hold the capability to align them all."

"I know you will," he states, like his words are enough.

"How is that?" Brax grunts, clearly thinking the same

as me, and the Drake grins, his long black hair draping around his face.

"Because they saw it so."

They saw it so?

"Who?"

"So many questions, Raven, when your destiny is filled with actions."

He looks at me knowingly, as if he's seen this all unravel before, and there's something about it that fills me with strength beyond words, beyond my own thoughts. "What will it be, Raven?"

The Drake holds out his hand to me.

Everyone's eyes are aimed my way, warming me from head to toe as I mull over the answer. I already know it, and a peek at Brax confirms he does too. When he doesn't instantly object, I know he believes in me and my decision, so I exhale, and take the proffered palm in mine.

Light rises from every Drake present, drifting into the sky like a shimmering golden curtain before swirling around us in a vortex of power and settling between our joined hands with a gentle flash, cementing their oath and binding their magic to my own.

Taking my time, I turn back to the barrier and let my magic do the work. Professor Figgins moves to stand beside me, understanding without a word, her fingers grazing the ward with me.

Wetting my lips, I turn to Ari before settling my gaze on the Brotherhood of the Drakes, my new-found followers, and with all that I am, I tug at the ward.

TWELVE
Raven

Waves lap against the rocky cliffs, the sound floating around us effortlessly as we stare off into the distance. Ari lies next to me with my face mushed into his feathers as I lean against him, completely in awe of today's turn of events.

I know without looking that Brax is watching us from inside the house. He offered us some time and space the moment we landed. I'm not sure if it was the surprise flight from Ari that had him silenced or because he was trying to be understanding of me reuniting with my familiar.

Either way, I appreciate him now more than ever. His efforts to not be a constant grumpy asshole haven't gone unnoticed.

Figgins is safely back in her office, or that's where she was heading when I last saw her, while Gia and the other griffins were searching for somewhere for them to lay low for a few days. The repeated thank yous and words of appreciation have become too much from all of the magical creatures no longer held captive, but those from the Brotherhood of Drakes still weigh heavy on me.

More people pledging oaths my way. What are they now? My followers, my flock, my… what? I don't fucking know. I feel like a name is required to collectively think of every crazy person who has pledged themselves to me, but it sounds way too obnoxious to commit to one.

"Your greatness knows no bounds, Raven. You should be proud of yourself today," Ari murmurs, his voice gravelly yet content.

"Don't say shit like that," I grumble, sitting forward so I'm not leaning against him. Irritation courses through me at his words.

"How are you going to harness the power to do what everyone believes you can do when you can't even take a compliment?"

I glare at him, but his pointed stare doesn't falter. "It's not the same thing and you know it. Besides, I'm rocking the whole fake it till you make it, so if I have to wing the hell out of all of… this, then I will," I state, cocking a brow at him in challenge. He can push me all he likes, make me feel awkward, and everything else in between, but I sure as hell will push right back.

Silence descends over us for a moment and I'm thankful that he leaves it there, but now the topic is on the tip of my tongue; I need to air the stress building in my chest.

"I don't know why the mess I'm dealing with continues to grow. Whenever I think I've overcome an obstacle, a bigger one stands in my way."

"What do you mean?"

I think he knows exactly what I mean and he just wants to hear me break it all down. I'm getting wiser to his ways now.

"When I first arrived here, it was all about surviving an academy that will happily let you die in the process of learning. Then my magic awakened and everything went even more to shit. I was accustomed to being a Void, and sometimes I wonder if life would be easier if I still were."

"Of course it would be, but you were never destined for ordinary, Raven," Ari interjects, and I roll my eyes at him.

"Then Erikel arrives, and my problems go from surviving him to saving the academy from him. Which isn't even the peak of the damn mountain I'm facing, it seems, because now I have to figure out how to bring people back from the Realm of Shadows who aren't dead. I'm overwhelmed today, thinking I'm catching a win by releasing you from the compound, but it suddenly seems like I'm aligning realms and accepting pledged oaths for things I know nothing about." I'm practically panting, trying to catch my breath as

I summarize the shit I'm handling, and I'm only scratching the surface. This isn't even getting into the nitty-gritty of it all.

"Yeah, the Brotherhood of Drakes surprised me too."

I gape at him. That's all he has to take from that? I should have known. "I'm glad," I grumble, swiping a hand down my face.

"Their words were true. They might have saved some casualties if they had spoken to me earlier, but there's nothing I can do about that now."

"I'm sure what they're saying means something, but right now, I need to figure some things out before someone discovers that the compound has been unleashed on the academy. I probably should have thought that part through before tearing down the ward."

Ari stands, shaking out his feathers and fur. "Maybe, but you lead with your heart, Raven. As much as you don't think you have one, you do. It's apparent in all of your decisions."

I can't decide if that's a compliment or a dig, but before I can decipher it, a thud interrupts my train of thought and I turn to find Gia stalking toward us.

Her head tips down as Ari approaches her and they share a moment, nuzzling each other before Ari turns to face me. "They've found refuge. A shelter while we gather ourselves without being too far from you," he explains, tipping his beak out to the shoreline in the distance.

It's not far, and not a part of the academy either. Good choice.

Standing, I smile. "Go, make sure they stay safe. I don't want anyone getting trapped or detained by Erikel, or anyone else for that matter."

"We'll be ready to take action when you need us, Raven."

I shake my head. "I won't—"

"I won't pledge an oath to you. It's unnecessary. I am your familiar. Any war of yours is a war of mine. You once said that we could all be on the same side, you and I, magical beings of all designs. I would like to prove those words to be true."

I vaguely recall saying something along those lines, and I definitely believe it, but I don't remember who I spoke them to.

"And if I don't want a war?" I offer the truth heavy on my tongue.

"I don't believe we have a choice in that anymore."

I sigh, knowing that his truth outweighs my own. I'm along for the ride whether I like it or not.

"Don't shut your mind off from me," I murmur, walking closer to where they stand.

Ari lowers his head and my hand instinctively presses to his beak. A warmth floods my veins, tangling with my magic before settling in my mind.

"Channel this and you will be sure not to let anyone

intrude on your mind," he explains as my hand falls away.

I blink up at him in shock, sensing the magical barrier surrounding my mind that somehow uses my own magic and not his. "How can I show this to Brax?"

"You'll figure it out," he hollers before taking flight, Gia right beside him.

I watch in awe as they glide through the sky, wings spread wide as they dance through the air together. I remain rooted to the spot until they are tiny dots on the horizon, taking a moment to appreciate the calmness that surrounds me. I know it's not going to last much longer, not with the twists and turns inevitably finding their way into my path.

Turning to the house, I find Brax standing at the floor-length windows. My heart swells as I take him in, cutting the distance between us as the wind picks up around me. Shutting the patio door, I head toward him, but before I get too close, he's moving toward the dining table, where I find a spread of food laid out for us.

"Thank you," I breathe as I take my seat, and he nods in response. Instead of taking his usual spot across the table, he fills the chair to my left instead. His closeness is like a warm blanket, protective and safe against the bitter world that snaps at our heels.

Digging into the array of food, I sense his eyes on me, but focus on eating because I know how grumpy he can get about that. The silence almost starts to feel antsy, so I turn to him, only to find him staring at me already.

"Is something the matter?"

"No," he grumbles, taking a forkful of his food as he glances away from me.

It doesn't seem like there's nothing, but the last thing I want to do is push at him if he's not ready to talk. I've pushed too hard with him before, I can't have that distance between us now.

The uneasy feeling continues to thicken between us, and just when I'm ready to approach him again, he clears his throat.

"Raven."

"Yeah?"

He shakes his head. "Hi, Raven, I am Brax—"

Understanding quickly dawns on me, and I shake my head. "No! No fucking way," I interject, eyes wide with horror. "You do not get to do that," I ramble, my body vibrating with surprise.

"Do what?" he snaps, hands fisted on the table as he stares at me.

Taking a deep breath, I lean back in my seat. "Brax, I love you, wholeheartedly, and I believe you love me too. That's enough, *more* than enough. But when the time comes, if I need you to run, then I need you to run."

His brows furrow as he tilts his head. "Like, run as in *leave* you?"

"Yes, like that because—"

"Because what, Raven?" he snaps, anger exuding from him.

I search his eyes, hoping he can understand what I'm trying to say, but it's clear we're not on the same page. "Because I didn't decide this, Brax, but you decided it even less and—"

"Do you hear yourself?" he interjects again, frustrating me.

I'm on my feet before I realize it, hands slamming down on the table, making the cutlery rattle.

"Brax," I bite through clenched teeth, desperate to explain myself properly.

He looks me dead in the eyes, anger deepening his pupils. "If you ever ask me to run, Raven, I won't." His voice is low, gravelly, and full of warning.

"You should," I push back, angry that he doesn't see my side of the situation. Irritated, my head sags forward, my chin falling to my chest as I exhale slowly, but it does nothing to calm me down. Instead, I lift my hands and slam my palms into the table once more, trying to get the frustration out of my system.

Fingers wrap around my wrist, jolting me back, but I wasn't anticipating the move, so I have no room to fight as Brax encloses both of my wrists in his grasp and pins my upper half to the table. Thankfully, he seems to move the dishes and my cheek presses against the solid wood beneath me.

Anger coils from his body, intertwining with my own, leaving me breathless as I wriggle in his hold. His presence behind me, looming over me with his wide frame, does nothing to calm my racing heart.

Attempting another deep breath, I lift my head to glance back at him. His chest rises and falls harshly as he looks down at me, but his gaze is dipped down and I can't meet his eyes. It takes me far too long to recognize what has his attention, though, and I only truly grasp it when his free hand dances over the hem of my academy skirt.

The move sends a shiver of apprehension down my spine and I find myself rubbing my thighs together, desperate for any form of friction, but nothing calms the tension radiating from me.

"Brax," I rasp, eager to figure out this mess with him, but he doesn't hear me, or if he does, he doesn't acknowledge his name on my lips.

Instead, I feel a cool breeze as my skirt is removed and my panties are no longer covering my pussy. Not a second ticks by before the tip of his cock is pressing against my entrance.

I'm helpless against him as his thick length spears into my core with total disregard for comfort, not offering a single moment of reprieve to allow me to adjust. It doesn't help that I'm already slick for him, beckoning him deeper as a moan parts my lips.

Fuck.

"Brax," I repeat, unsure what I need his attention for, but his eyes remain glued on where we are joined.

His hips sling back until only the tip remains before he thrusts forward again, harder and faster this time. His moves are punishing, his force breaking, making the clench of my pussy around his cock breathtaking as I cling to him in every way possible.

Fuck. Fuck. Fuck.

"Tell me again what I should be running from?" he bites, fingers tightening around my wrists as he continues to slam into me over and over again.

"Brax—"

"Tell. Me," he grinds out, interrupting my plea.

"From me. You should run from me," I admit, my words barely audible among the moans he's drawing from my tongue.

"Fuck you, Raven," he snaps, his hips connecting with mine even more brutally than before.

"No, fuck you," I groan back, desperate for him to understand that what I'm saying comes from love. I don't get to add any of that on, though, to express how I'm feeling and why I want him to be free of me if necessary because I'm hurtling over the cliff of pleasure, drowning in the depths of my climax as my veins burn with ecstasy.

Wave after wave washes over me and I feel him lean closer, his lips at my ear as he continues to fuck me through my climax.

"Raven Hendrix, I am Brax Carlsen. I pledge to help with all that I am, all that I could be, and all I wish to be."

Each word is enunciated with a thrust of his cock, claiming me there and then while pledging himself to me.

That fucker. That absolute fucking fucker.

His hips jut slower as he presses his lips to my cheek, the pulsing of his cock fluttering in my core as he comes inside of me.

I'm breathless, shocked, and still completely at his mercy. I didn't want him to say those words, but he said them anyway. I want to be mad, angry, and given a moment to tear his fucking head off with rage, but deep down, something stirs inside of me. A truth I can't bring myself to admit.

Hearing those words from him means more than from his parents or the Brotherhood of Drakes. They mean something else entirely.

They scream forever and always, until death do we part, and he somehow managed to scrawl out the words, close the envelope, and seal it shut with his release.

THIRTEEN

Eldon

Darkness melds around me as I drift. Terror, panic, and uncertainty war inside of me as I fail to ground myself. Short, sharp bursts of cries echo in my ears, coming and going too quickly for me to pinpoint the direction or cause behind them. All I know is it's not good. Not good at all.

A familiar bird flies in the distance, slowly nearing with every flap of its broad wings.

A pink-feathered raven.

It circles above me as the cries turn into screams, and the world is no longer black. Dripping in blood, my feet filthy in the boggy ground beneath me, I stare at the horrors.

Death. Death. And more death.

A battle cry roars from above as the raven darts toward us. Instinctively, I reach my hand out toward the bright pink feathers, but it doesn't reach my palm before the bellow becomes too much and the world goes black once more.

Panting, a small flicker of fire burns in my hand, trying to light the space around me. A flash of stone, a blink of onyx, and the breeze from an invisible move confirm my brothers are around me. But where is my love? My heart? My raven?

My body strains, my magic weak as I try to expand the ember in my palm, but the effort produces very little result. I'm already at my limit, strung tight, but I need to find her.

"Raven!" My voice is hoarse, clogged with pain and heartache I know is coming. "Little Bird!"

Silence rings in my ears, offering me no solace as a hand lands on my shoulder. I turn to see Zane at my side, but it's Brax who speaks.

"That's enough, El."

I frown, confused by whatever the hell is going on, when Creed waves me closer. I don't know where I'm stepping or where we are, but that's not my concern. My priority is Raven.

As I near Creed, he crouches on the ground and my heart stops.

Gone is the familiar pink hair I've tangled around my fist so many times, and in its place are sheer black locks from root to tip. That's not the problem, though. No. It's the way it all cascades around her face as she lies completely still on the dried grass. It's the way her eyelids are closed, and I know in my soul they're not going to open.

Not now.

Not in a minute.

Not in an hour.

Not ever.

Dropping to my knees, my life ends there with hers.

I gasp awake, sweat clinging to my chest as I scramble to sit up. My feet hit the floor and my face falls into my hands as I try to calm my erratic breathing. Nausea swirls in my gut as my pulse pounds in my ears.

"Nightmare or a vision?"

I startle at Creed's voice, quickly remembering where I am, and I turn to see him sitting on the other sofa across from me. Sighing, I wipe a hand down my face. "Both."

"Want to talk about it?" he offers as I scrub a hand through my hair.

Do I want to talk about it? Fuck no, that feels like I'm going manifest the vision to reality if I speak it into the world, but shit, do I need to tell him about it? Fuck, yeah.

"She was dead, Creed. Dead," I croak, my palms pressing into my eye sockets as I will the words not to be true. Fuck manifesting, I'll do everything I can to make sure that isn't the case.

"We won't let it happen, Eldon," Zane murmurs,

appearing in the open doorway. He likely hasn't slept, not that I'm surprised, and after seeing what I just saw, I don't think I ever will again.

"It felt so real. It always does," I admit, prying my eyes open to stop the repeat from happening on the back of my eyelids again. "It started as the raven vision always does," I add, leaning back in my seat and rubbing my hands together. I need to get it all off my chest before I bottle it all up, which won't be useful to anyone.

"But the ending was different?" Creed summarizes, and I shake my head.

"There wasn't ever really an ending before. This time, there were screams of pain, visions of bloodshed, horror coating my limbs, and then her, Raven, with jet-black hair sprawled out on the ground."

"Fuck," the pair of them murmur in unison.

My chest grows tight. That can't be our end. It can't be. My lips part, but no words come out as I try to find the right thing to say. Thankfully, the alarm echoes through the house, just as it did last night and the night before, and the telltale sound of Marieta and Peta rushing down the stairs follows a moment later.

"They should be here soon," Marieta says with a tired smile as she peeks her head around the doorframe. I nod in agreement as I push up onto my feet.

My shirt clings to me slightly as I put it on, but the hope

and excitement to see Raven alive and breathing, even if only in her dream form, has me rushing toward the door.

"How do we know we can trust the shadows?" Zane asks, stepping out onto the porch first.

"We don't," I admit, another dose of reality tightening my throat.

"That's not unnerving or anything," he remarks with a lifeless chuckle.

"When you've lost hope in everything else, you're willing to believe in anything. It's a sad and harsh reality that we instinctively doubt anyone's actions. One day, we can only hope to create a safer realm for everyone to live in," Peta states, the strength in his words lifting me up, too.

Rolling my shoulders back, I stare at the bleakness that surrounds us until movement ahead comes into view. I would recognize those pretty pink strands anywhere.

I'm rushing toward her before anyone else can move, and no one tries to beat me to her. I silently thank my brothers for giving me this moment as I capture my little bird in my hands, pinning her tight against my chest.

Her arms circle around my neck as her legs coil around my waist. I don't move for a second, content to stand here and breathe her in.

"Is everything okay?"

I hum into her hair, not ready to let go of her. She must sense it because her hand trails down my back, consoling me with her touch until I'm able to lighten my hold on her.

"I'm good," I murmur when her eyes reach mine. There's a hint of worry to her smile, and her eyebrows pinch slightly, but she doesn't push. "I should let you greet the others, too, huh?"

Lowering her to her feet, she smiles up at me, but the determination in her eyes confirms I'm not completely off the hook; she's just going to give me a moment to get a handle on myself.

I press a kiss against her forehead before letting her run to embrace Creed and Zane while taking a second to just watch her. Her presence alone is uplifting, and I offer another silent thank you, only this time it's to the shadows. They brought her here, seemingly without Brax, so they held up their agreement with our shadow-seeing gargoyle even without his presence. That has to count for something… I hope.

"No Brax?" Marieta asks as I follow the others back to the house and Raven glances around to confirm he's not here, worrying her bottom lip as she does.

"I was actually asleep this time. It was weird as hell for the shadows to infiltrate my dream and pull me here, but I have no clue if Brax was sleeping."

"Not to worry," Peta says with a wry smile. "I can't imagine how disorienting all this is for you."

I stand tall with a sense of pride. The fact that Marieta

and Peta care for Raven as much as Zane's father seems to step up and shelter her is heartwarming. She deserves this unwavering appreciation from all of us. Even if she is hesitant to accept it.

"Is it safe to say he's not being an asshole while we're not there?" Zane questions, diverting the conversation as we take the steps up the porch. Raven pauses at the top, not ready to head inside yet, and I know it's because she's hoping he might appear any moment.

"Oh, he's definitely still an asshole, but he's also nothing shy of a saint right now," she admits, tucking a loose tendril of hair behind her ear as she smiles at Marieta. "This is hard for him, trying to hold down the fort without being able to lean on any of you guys. It's not easy having to handle me and all the drama that follows me by himself, and he's trying to be everything for me all at once. He's trying to understand, not be harsh, and to lighten a souring mood when and wherever necessary. All of it." Her gaze drifts back out to the bleakness surrounding us. "Maybe he deserves to sleep for a while without having to worry."

"Am I going to have to fight him when I get back because he suddenly thinks he's funnier than me?" Zane asks with a smirk, and she grins at him but shakes her head.

"He's not trying to replace anyone. He's just…"

My heart aches for the pair of them as much as it does for the three of us stuck here without them. It's not the norm to be trapped in the Realm of Shadows, but it's not easy to take on the academy as a duo instead of a five-person team.

"We know what you mean, Little Bird. We can see it too, and we appreciate it," I finish, reaching out to stroke her arm in comfort.

"Appreciate what?"

Everybody's head whips around to see Brax standing a few steps away with his arms folded over his chest and his eyebrow raised in question.

"You," I answer, giving him a challenging look that makes him roll his eyes as he steps around us and casually heads inside.

"Come on, we have a lot to talk about, and fuck knows how much time I have until I wake up," he grumbles. Marieta and Peta gape at him as the rest of us grin. At least when the five of us are all here together, he gets to be his usual grizzly self.

Raven beams at the back of his head as she follows after him and Marieta turns to me with wide eyes. "Is he always so…"

"He's an asshole, Marieta. Your son is a grumpy asshole, but we love him anyway," I say with a grin, making Peta smirk as Marieta shakes her head in disbelief.

It is a little amusing to see how calm and collected Marieta and Peta are compared to Brax, but I guess they haven't lived the life he has, endured the pain and heartache of losing his parents, only to find them again. No one can prepare for that, and no one can be mad about how he deals with it. Unless it affects Raven, then I'll handle the gargoyle myself.

Heading inside with everyone, we find Brax sitting at the dining table, stretching his arms over his head as he yawns. Fucker's asleep and still has the ability to be tired. Crazy as hell.

"Would you like some cocoa?" Marieta asks, and Raven nods eagerly in response before I take her hand and lead her to the table.

I take a seat, pulling my little bird into my lap, and Brax silently stands to help both Marieta and Peta at the stove. I expect Raven to clamber out of my lap and claim her own seat, but instead, she settles against me, cupping my cheek to stare into my eyes.

"What's going on? I could feel your heart racing like crazy out there," she asks, keeping her voice low as I gape at her.

I want to tell her. I know I should. I've told her about all my the other visions that have involved her, but how the fuck do I explain this one?

She cocks a brow, the challenge clear in her eyes, and I sigh. "I had a vision."

Her tongue runs over her bottom lip as she waits as

patiently as she can for me to explain more, but the words fail me.

"His vision wasn't the happiest of dreams," Zane interjects, a tight smile on his face, which only seems to leave Raven even more curious.

"You died," Creed mutters, grimacing at Raven. His words were likely harsher than he intended as he tried to take the burden from my shoulders.

"Oh."

I blink at her and blink again. She remains cozied in my lap, her palm still pressed against my cheek. Oh…

Just, oh?

"Raven, any luck with Ari?" Marieta asks, interrupting the conversation as she places two mugs of hot cocoa down in front of Raven and me while Peta carries his own and one for Zane beside him. Brax takes his seat with a mug in his hands, and Creed glances around to see his still resting by the stove.

"Get it yourself. I'm not your maid," Brax grunts, earning an eye roll from everyone.

"Everything you said about Ari, about the compound… it all worked," Raven breathes, circling back to Marieta's question.

It takes a second for her words to register properly in my mind, but when they do, excitement jolts me in my seat, pulling her in closer to my chest.

"It worked?" I repeat in complete awe, and she smiles wide at me as she nods eagerly.

"The portal was still open in the Gauntlet arena, and it led us straight into the compound. Finding Ari wasn't too hard. Well, he didn't hear me, but that's because he was purposely blocking me from his mind."

"Why?" Creed asks, distaste and irritation clear on his face.

Raven waves her hand with disregard but Brax catches us up to speed. "Someone, one guess who, showed up in the compound pretending to be her, which instantly sent him into lockdown. Dick move for sure, but I get it."

It must be genuine for Brax to accept it, but he's right, that was a dick move.

"Why would they be trying to impersonate Raven to her familiar?" I ask, confused by the attempt, and my little bird shrugs.

"I don't really know. I may need to speak to Ari about what happened, but we were slightly distracted by other things when dropping the ward to the compound."

"What does that mean?" Zane questions with a shake of his head. Raven and Brax share a glance before they nod subtly between one another and get into it.

Every new piece of information tossed our way sends me into a spin until I'm gaping between the two of them.

"Wait, okay, let me get this straight. The Drakes, like

the one we saw Ari destroy, are all shifters, actual men, from the Torin Realm. Which is apparently a realm that exists beneath Basilica, all of which have pledged an oath to you in exchange for releasing them from the compound. The compound that Erikel lured them into as fake familiars when, in fact, they are indeed men. Men?"

Did I mention that lethal thing in the woods was a man? Damn.

"That pretty much sums it up, yeah," Raven says with a nod, biting back a smile.

"Can we trust them? Now that they're not in the compound?" Creed's words echo my own thoughts, and Brax is quick to answer.

"They pledged an oath to her, without prompt, their only hope in doing so being their freedom. They're not going to bring harm to someone they pledged an oath to, right?" He turns to look at his mother, who is nodding in agreement.

"Pledging an oath not only offers yourself as a resource to that person but also confirms loyalty and safety. They cannot and will not attack or undermine Raven in any way. By proxy, that protects everyone she cares about too, as it is known that any harm to those she cares for would cause her unnecessary pain."

"And if they were to break their pledge?" I don't want to ask, but somebody has to.

Peta shakes his head. "Death. Breaking their oath will have them succumb to their own magical abilities, and death will follow."

His words are still a little cryptic for my mind right now, but I accept it.

"So we've overcome the first hurdle; what do we address next?" Brax ponders, tapping his fingertips on the table. "More specifically, how do we bring Erikel, or Burton, down? What the fuck are we calling them now?" He scrubs at the back of his neck, and as much as I want to chuckle at the fact that we don't know what to call the ruthless, conniving fucker wreaking havoc on our lives, it's a valid question.

"I think we stick with Erikel. Then we don't slip up in front of him," Raven offers, and I happily agree. We have to remain logical and make sure we don't fuck up any of the facts we have that we're not supposed to know.

"Erikel it is. How do we take him down?" Brax repeats, looking between his parents, but it's Creed who answers.

"I think we need to consider the other things we're facing as well. Like my father, Sebastian, Fitch, and The Monarchy."

Peta's head sags slightly as he nods in agreement. "I think he's right. We need to break down everything we're facing here, both out there and in the Realm of Shadows, before we have a complete view of the war we're on the brink of."

He's right. It's overwhelming as hell, but not wrong.

"You're going to have to talk us through some of the issues we're unaware of. We will offer any insight we may have without question," Marieta adds as the rest of us glance around the table at one another. Where to begin? I feel like I've asked myself that same question one hundred times already. As if sensing the uncertainty in all of us, Marieta continues. "Sebastian, who is that?"

"That would be my brother," Raven explains, eyes downcast as she looks at her hands.

"Tell me about him. Why is he a concern?"

Raven takes a moment to gather herself before looking at Marieta. A warm smile curves her lips, breaking down all of the barriers keeping Raven trapped in her head as she spills everything to her.

"I don't have many memories of my brother from when I was a child. I remember him being the big brother who never wanted me around, and then when my mother took me away, I didn't think much of him. Arriving at Silvercrest Academy, though, I was startled when he was the first person I met, and he was just as horrid as I remembered. If not worse." I stroke a hand down her back, offering her the same level of comfort she gave me as she pushes on. "He's made attempts on my life since I arrived, worked his way up the hit list we seem to have created, and I believed he was a willing accomplice of Erikel's. He assisted him getting onto campus and has proceeded to do his dirty work as and when called upon." Although, if Erikel has always been Burton then that doesn't really make sense, so I really don't know anything.

"You say you believed?" Peta asks, tilting his head at Raven, and she nods in response.

"The day we learned the golden table in the Nightmare's Guild had magical abilities was also the same day we saw Erikel shift to Burton or the other way around," she rambles, waving her hand. "During that snippet, we also had to watch Sebastian receive lashings to an already marked back, and since then, I don't know what to think."

"I vaguely remember you as a child. I wasn't as close with your mother and father as I was with others, but I still remember. The reality is, there's only one direction we should take next because, whether we like it or not, family is important," Marieta declares, taking a deep breath. "The next step is for you to speak with your mother."

FOURTEEN

Raven

"**H**ow the fuck do we work this thing?"

I sit at the foot of the bed, dressed in my uniform, with my hair loose around my shoulders as I turn the shell over in my hand. I can't for the life of me understand what I'm supposed to do with the damn thing.

"You don't know?" Brax asks, his brows furrowed as he steps out of the bathroom with a towel loosely draped around his waist. It's instinctive to linger on his impressive crotch, hoping the material hiding one of my favorite parts of him will disappear, but we really do need to focus on this.

Sweeping my tongue over my bottom lip, my magic flickers beneath the surface, eager to be used to eliminate the towel, but I turn back to the shell instead. I can behave for a little while.

"I've never seen one before Zane's," I admit, slowly turning the shell once again, hoping to see something new this time, but I fall just as short as the time before.

"But your father works for The Ministry, didn't he… shit, shut up, Brax," he grumbles, swiping a hand down his face as he recalls the excellent relationship I don't have with my father. I smirk at him and he sighs, planting his hands on his hips. "My parents were gone before I needed one, so I have no clue either. Isn't there a button or something?"

I spin it in my grasp again, but no magical button appears. "No," I admit. Finally able to look at him without fixating on the outline of his cock, I purse my lips. "I think our only option is to find Lyra and see if we can use her secret little room to reach out instead."

Brax nods, glancing at the time before swiftly using his magic to get dressed. My pursed lips tighten to a pout as his uniform now hides his body.

"We've got a little time if we leave now," he offers, and I nod, feeling reluctant to go anywhere at all.

Placing the shell in my backpack, I swing it onto my shoulder as I step out into the lounge behind Brax.

His hands move, and I watch with hope that a gateway will appear, but it seems the suppression on that simple mode of transport is still in place.

"Walking it is," I sing, heading for the front door. He

grumbles under his breath, but I don't catch it. "It will give us a moment to get our heads in the game anyway," I offer, smiling wide and positively at him, highly aware that it was me getting distracted.

"I don't think that's ever going to happen with all of the mess we're wading through," he grunts, and I can't help but hum in agreement. He's not wrong, that's for sure. But I'm focusing on one challenge at a time, or trying to at least.

The pathway is quiet since we're earlier than usual, and I use the reprieve to lace my fingers with his, enjoying the peace around us while we have it. Last night was another information overload. We're going to go from one mini-quest to another until all that remains is enemy number one. Once they're out of the equation, maybe we'll be able to actually take a minute to breathe and appreciate being young and somewhat free.

Maybe.

Hopefully.

We're stepping through the arched doorway into the academy building in no time, heading straight for Lyra's office. We don't come across anyone, which is a relief as her office door comes into view. Brax knocks without missing a beat, and I rock back on my heels as we wait patiently.

A few moments pass and I start to worry that I should

have reached out sooner. I haven't seen her since we were all taken to the cave in Ashdale, and I don't even know if she's been present.

Fuck.

Taking a step closer, I lift my fist to knock again, but before I can connect with the wood, the sound of the door unlocking echoes around us and Lyra appears in the gap. Her eyebrows pinch together when her gaze locks with mine, but she quickly shakes it off.

"Hey, is everything okay?" she asks. Her cheeks are a little pink and her hair isn't quite as smooth as usual.

"Is everything okay with you?" I redirect, watching as she straightens, running her hands over her silk blouse as she forces a wide smile onto her lips.

"I'm fine. How can I help you guys?"

"We need to use your…" My words trail off, not wanting to say it out loud, and she instantly nods in understanding.

"Oh, right, of course. Give me two seconds." The door slams shut before I can reply.

Brax clears his throat as he glances at me out of the corner of his eye. "Does she seem… odd to you?"

I try to bite back my smile, but it's not as easy as I hope. "She's acting like there's someone in there that she doesn't want us to see," I remark, watching the confusion gloss over his eyes.

"Why would…"

His mouth pauses as I wiggle my eyebrows and understanding dawns on him.

"Oh, like we're bothered about that shit. We're already pressed for time," he grumbles, scrubbing a hand over his cropped hair.

I shrug. "Girls are skittish with this stuff. Besides, she's doing us a favor, not the other way around. She doesn't owe us anything, yet she helps anyway."

A moment later, the door swings open and a much more put-together Lyra appears, waving us inside. Peering around the room, I don't see anyone, so I decide to put it to the back of my mind as we head into the private room. The layout is exactly the same as it was and we take a seat on the sofa like we always have.

"Is it Rhys you want to speak to?"

"Please," I murmur, looking up at Lyra, who smiles.

"Sure. I'll get it set up."

The door shuts behind her, hiding us away from the rest of the academy. Brax leans back in his seat, running his hands over his thighs before tapping his fingertips on his knees.

"What do you do while you wait?" he asks, already impatient, and my cheeks heat at the reminder that flickers in my mind. "Wait, did you and Zane..." He doesn't finish his sentence as I turn to face him, and his eyes widen in surprise before morphing into something else. The memory of being fucked by thin air ripples through me.

"I don't know what you're talking about," I say with a shrug, turning away as Brax splutters.

"Sure you don't."

Right on cue, Rhys appears, and my cheeks heat even more. Thankfully, he seems more concerned with our appearance than my actual state.

"Is everything okay?"

Gulping, I smile, nodding like a fool, but the exhaustion on his face is noticeable, and concern quickly gets the better of me. "Is everything with you okay?" I brace my elbows on my knees, inching closer, and the sigh that parts his lips feels weighted.

"Honestly, it's not going the best. I'm coming up against some blockers," he mutters, wiping a hand down his face.

"How?" Brax asks. "What is it?" he rapidly fires at him.

Rhys glances between the two of us before looking down at his hands. "I think there are connections aligning The Monarchy with Erikel. I don't know who to talk to, who to trust, or who to rely on, but I'm trying everything I can. I swear it."

I know that feeling deep down in my fucking soul.

"How are we going to get around it?" Brax asks, and Rhys shakes his head.

"No. That's for me to worry about. You have enough going on. Tell me what you're facing." He laces his fingers together as he peers from Brax to me and back again.

I glance at Brax, who nods at me subtly, and I take a deep breath, but it's my gargoyle who answers.

"My parents believe Erikel isn't Erikel."

Rhys's eyes crinkle as he processes the words. "How so?"

"Because my father killed him years ago."

Zane's father wipes a hand over his mouth. "He could have been on the brink of death before he was brought back," he offers, trying to see the situation from every angle, and Brax shakes his head.

"They're both certain that he doesn't have skinwalker abilities either."

Rhys seems stumped for a moment, and I decide to spell it out to him.

"They believe Erikel is Burton, not the other way around."

Rhys narrows his eyes, trying to comprehend what I'm saying, while completely understanding how ridiculous it sounds.

"How? Why?" His face falls to his hands for a moment, as if his simple questions are overwhelming him, too.

"We honestly don't know. I'm not familiar with Professor Burton, other than what he's portrayed himself as and what the golden table showed us, which made him look a hell of a lot shadier. As much as it initially seems impossible, it isn't."

"What do you know of Burton, Rhys?" Brax asks, eyes narrowing. "My parents said he's one of the few people to have ever been a skinwalker. You didn't mention that when we told you what we saw in the Nightmare's Guild."

My heart practically stops in my chest as I gape at Rhys, coming to the same realization as Brax. If this guy has been pulling the wool over my eyes the entire time, I really will explode. We've trusted him more than anyone.

Don't let that be for nothing.

"Tiran Burton's powers have never been shared with me. He falls under a different department at The Monarchy, so I've never been privy to his details, just as he wouldn't be aware of mine either." I search his eyes, seeking what I'm not entirely sure of, but all I find is sincerity. "I can't understand how he would make any of this happen or why he would stab himself the night we were all there. We all saw it ourselves."

"I know, but there is the consideration that Raven bringing him back from the dead allows him to visit the Realm of Shadows now… like me," Brax admits, seeming to accept Rhys's words too.

"We're getting closer to figuring this all out. I know we are," he murmurs, shaking his head as he remains slightly dazed by the facts.

Clearing my throat, his gaze finds mine. "That's actually why we're calling."

"Anything."

"Marieta believes I should speak to my mother."

He nods, rising to his feet immediately without question. "Of course, give me a few moments."

The room falls quiet as he leaves and I fall back in my seat, chancing a glance at Brax to find him already staring at me.

"Do we trust him?"

My teeth sink into my bottom lip as I think it over, but ultimately, I nod. "He's either a phenomenal liar or telling the truth. As much as my mind wants to believe the worst in everyone, he's never done anything to make me believe he's anything other than genuine."

"I hate that I can only agree with you. I just hope we're right."

I nod nervously, but before we can say anymore, Rhys reappears, only this time my mother is beside him. My heart races at the sight of her as she rushes closer, her hand reaching out toward me before she quickly retracts it, remembering she's not actually here.

"Oh, Raven," she whispers, falling to her knees before me, and I shift awkwardly in my seat.

I want to reach out to her, too, and offer her some kind

of comfort, but I don't want to drift my hand through her projection.

Her hair is pulled back tight into a ponytail, her eyes heavy as she tries to smile. We've all clearly got a lot going on. It feels insane to comprehend that there are more problems out there when I'm already dealing with a lot.

I don't know what I expect from her, but just as quickly as she dropped to the floor, she gathers herself, stiffening her spine as she takes a deep breath and meets my gaze with determination vibrating from her.

"What do you need from me? Anything, I'm here."

I exhale slowly, her words pushing me forward as I smile at her, and it's not forced. "I spoke with Marieta, Brax's mother," I state, pointing to my gargoyle without glancing in his direction. My mother follows my finger, offering him a smile. "I have some concerns over Sebastian and she thinks I need to speak to you about it."

"Of course." She nods for me to proceed, and I do.

I tell her about the hostility I received from him as soon as I got here, the attacks I received at his hands, the attempts on my life, everything. With every instance, her eyes widen, her jaw falls more slack, and a combination of disappointment and heartache washes over her.

"I'm sorry, Raven," she apologizes as if it's her fault, and I shake my head, but Brax speaks before I can soothe her.

"I wanted to kill him," he grunts, and I watch as my mother gulps nervously. Silence stretches out, filling the air as Rhys remains quiet. "But—" Brax breathes, shaking his head like he can't believe where the conversation is leading.

Placing my hand on his thigh, I take over again. "But, we've seen some things that have left us questioning if his decisions were his own." My mother leans back, stiff, as she waits for me to proceed. "We saw his back, it's covered in scars from lashings, watched what he… endured, and we heard the threats aimed his way." I know it's vague, but my stomach curls with the thought of repeating it. It doesn't matter, though; I'm familiar with the twinkling of knowledge in her eyes and it's my turn to go rigid. "Mama?"

She glances at Rhys, who is an image of pity as he nods at her. "Your father is the same." Her words hang in the air for a moment as I try to process them, but before I can question her further, she offers the information freely. "Your father is currently under protective magic to ensure he isn't a harm to himself… or others." She clears her throat, trying to tamp down her emotions, but it's clear it's not easy. "We found the same lashing marks on his back. We're not certain who they're from, but magic is controlling him and it looks like it's been going on for a long time. Whoever is controlling your father could be doing the same to Sebastian."

Fuck.

Rubbing my lips together, I let that knowledge settle over me for a moment while Brax speaks. "It was Erikel or Burton, along with Fitch, who we saw giving Sebastian the lashings."

My mother wipes her hands down her face, an action we're all seemingly familiar with at this stage as we try to brush off the issues that continue to weigh us down. We're not dealing with anything easy, which means every new piece of information leads us further down another bumpy path.

"We believe it's someone in The Monarchy who has done this to your father." Damn. Tears track down my mother's face now, but she wipes at them swiftly. "I should never have run, Raven. Not for your father's sake, not for Sebastian's sake, but especially not for yours."

I shake my head. "We can't change the past. We can only pursue the future. What ifs and the endless possibilities are out of our hands now, but we can make a difference in what comes next." I believe the words so deeply that my chest warms, and Mama smiles at me.

"I know, but I feel like taking you away only worsened an already bad situation."

"We can't turn back time to determine if that would result in a different outcome or not, so we have to let it go.

The world is crumbling around us and we need to decide if we're going to control where the pieces fall or not."

"Raven is right, Evangeline," Rhys murmurs, planting a hand on her shoulder. "I'm not sure why Marieta referred you to your mother for this, but it only strengthens my belief that her inkling links back to your father, and The Monarchy, too," he states, and I nod in understanding. "Now that we're aware of it on both sides, we need to tread carefully. Sebastian may not be of his own mind, but that doesn't make him any less dangerous," he admits, a solemn atmosphere casting over us. A bell rings from their side of the communication and Rhys glances off in the distance. "I'm sorry, guys, I have a meeting, an important one," he states, eyebrows raised. "Is there anything else before l leave?"

"No. We should go, too. We've got classes to get to," I mumble, in no way ready to be surrounded by people who have no clue what's truly happening around them, all while trying to play the dumb girl who is just as clueless.

"Okay. Oh, wait. Is there anyone there with the last name Richardson?"

I frown, thinking, but my mind is blank.

"Yes," Brax confirms. "There's a Grave Richardson. Why?"

Rhys shakes his head as my mother looks at him, her eyes filled with concern. "Keep an eye on him. It's his grandfather causing me the most concern within The Monarchy."

Fuck.

"Okay," I mumble, my mind in overload.

"I love you, Raven. This will all be over soon," my mother promises, arms folded tightly around her.

"I love you too," I rasp, the words razor-sharp in my throat, but I can't get caught up in emotions right now. Just as they're about to disappear from view, I call out Rhys's name one last time.

"Yes?"

"How do I work this thing?" I ask, digging my hand into my backpack to find Zane's shell.

He smirks at me as he points to the smaller end. "Blow in it."

I gape at him before rolling my eyes. "Of course, it's something dramatic," I state as they disappear from view, leaving just Brax and I in here.

"Are you okay?" Brax asks, and I nod, not really giving myself a moment to consider the true answer, and the knowing glint in his eyes tells me he knows it too, but he accepts it for now.

Heading to where the door should be, I rap my knuckles softly against the wall to alert Lyra that we're ready to leave. A few moments pass before I hear the click of the door as it appears before us, but as I push it open, I'm halted in my tracks.

"Sister, we have a lot to discuss."

FIFTEEN
Raven

I gape at Sebastian as he stands before me, arms folded and feet planted firmly, shoulder-width apart. He holds his head high, looking down his nose at me as anger boils deep inside.

My nostrils flare before I can bottle my emotions, revealing the effect of his presence on me. Brax shifts discreetly at my side to place his arm in front of mine, ready to block whatever he deems necessary. His other hand is already balled at his side, ready to swing at any given moment.

"Back the fuck up. Now," my gargoyle bites out as I keep one hand on my backpack slung over my shoulder.

"Raven, please, give him a chance." My jaw tics and my eyes widen as I glance past my brother to see Lyra leaning back against her desk, nervously tapping her fingers on her arms.

"You," I snap, pointing a finger at her as I glance at my brother. "Is this…" My words trail off as I connect the dots. Lyra's sheepish face as she ducks her head confirms it.

The reason she was disheveled earlier is because she was messing around with Sebastian. Wonderful. Pressing my fingers against my temple, it does little to alleviate the building pressure.

"Please, hear him out, I swear. Use my magic." She stands, offering out her hand as wisps of magic swirl in her palm.

Flicking my gaze back to my brother, I find his eyes narrowed as he glances between Lyra and me until he settles on me and nods.

"You killed Genie. I should have known," he states casually, as if he's reporting on the weather, leaving me to sputter.

"Excuse me," I start, but he quickly interjects.

"No excusing necessary. I should probably thank you, but we're past that."

It's my turn to frown now as I try to read between the lines of what he's saying, but it's too much to break down coming from him. With a sigh, I give him a pointed look. "What could you possibly want, Sebastian?"

He shifts slightly, surprised I'm asking the question.

Clearing his throat, he answers. "Your word."

"My word?" I feel the crease between my eyes deepen, but if he's aware of how confused I am, he doesn't show it.

"Yes, and in return, I will help you."

Brax scoffs, disbelief coming off him in waves as I tilt my head at my brother.

"What could you possibly aid us with? You're lucky I don't just kill you right now," Brax grunts, and Sebastian smirks, rocking back on his heels as he sinks his hands into his pockets.

"Always so grizzly, Brax," he remarks, earning himself a growl, which makes Sebastian realize just how serious Brax is with his threat. Clearing his throat, he looks back to me. "Is there any point in me speaking if you're not channeling Lyra's magic yet? Repeating myself is pointless."

I purse my lips. He forgets the fact that my mirroring Lyra's magic is for me to hear him out. It's for his benefit, not mine. I want to cuss him out and tell him to get fucked, but then the reminder of the lashings he endured filter through my mind, exposing the smallest crack in my walls.

Lyra must sense the leniency in me because she steps closer, coming to my right side with her hand extended. She mouths her thanks, but I ignore her as I grasp at the tendrils of magic I can see.

"So it's true… you can mirror magic."

I cock a brow at him. He just heard Lyra mention it, and that's if she hasn't already told him before today. What else has she shared with my brother? Fuck. Tamping down my wandering thoughts, I focus on Sebastian again.

"What do you want?"

His gaze shifts between Brax and me as he wets his lips. "What can you do with your magic? What have you learned so far?"

Irritation bubbles in my veins as my gaze narrows at my brother. "That's not answering my question, Sebastian."

He rolls his eyes at me, rubbing at the back of his neck. "I'm going to continue with my assumption that you killed Genie. I'm not saying it was on purpose," he quickly reassures as I open my mouth to speak, but he quiets me once more. "But if you've been working on mirror magic, then there is an opportunity to take someone's magic completely, and my gut tells me that's why you couldn't bring Genie back. Necromancers tend to latch on to magic. That's how this all works for you. You can touch it, take it, claim it. You can do all of that, including snippets."

"Snippets?" I murmur in confusion, and he nods.

"The power you could have had with my help will forever be wasted," he murmurs with a sigh, making Brax growl again. "Snippets are like blossoming flowers, so to speak. The magic is the flower in full bloom, and just like with flowers, you can take small parts of it to regrow elsewhere. That's what you have the ability to do as well."

I frown, confused with his analogy, until he lifts his hand to reveal his magic floating around his palm. "Grasp it."

I don't move at first, rendered completely immobile as I consider if he could make this backfire on me. Finally, curiosity gets the better of me and I slip the strands between my fingers.

"Now, from what I've read, mirror magic can be performed while you're touching it. If you completely yank at it, the magic would leave my body entirely with no way to return. However, if you lightly tug, you can pull away the smallest branch for yourself without causing any permanent damage and no longer need the source of the magical presence to use it."

I blink, and blink again.

That definitely does sound helpful, really fucking helpful, but shit, what is it he wants in response?

Wetting my lips, I keep my hand where it is and meet his stare. "What is it you're expecting for giving me this information?"

He shakes his head. "This isn't the information I'm making a deal on. I'm just making you aware."

"Why?" He waves me off with his free hand, glancing away, but my heart is racing too fast for me to let it go. "*Why*, Sebastian?"

"You're going to need somewhere to store all of the

tendrils of magic you take a snippet from." He digs around in his pocket, and a moment later, he reveals a long gold chain with a locket on the end of it. "Tug slightly at my magic first, then you can do Lyra's and Brax's if you want, just to be sure you have it right."

"Why, Sebastian?" I repeat, louder this time so I can hear the words over the pounding of my pulse in my ears.

"Because you're going to save us. All of us. If you want any chance of that happening, the more magical abilities you have access to, the better."

Gulping, I layer his words on top of the others he's already unloaded on me.

"Why are you offering me this now? What's changed?"

He shakes me off again, his gaze latched onto the locket. "I need you to tug lightly and see what happens. Once you have a little piece of it, you can store it in here." He opens the clasp on the intricate golden locket to reveal two children's faces on the inside. Two I'm more than familiar with. It's me and him.

"Where did you get that?"

"Does she always ask so many questions?" Sebastian asks, glancing at Brax, who grunts in response. I can't look at him right now to decipher his thoughts on the situation. I need to handle this for myself and I don't want my feelings to get muddled with his if they're not aligned quite yet. "It was mother's," he finally explains, twisting back to me.

"It was one of the few things she left behind after she took you away."

I roll my eyes at him. "You were more than happy about that fact."

He raises an eyebrow at me. "Was I?"

"I remember your anger," I state, nodding.

"I was angry that you were leaving, Raven. What did you expect me to feel?"

He stumps me for a moment, which only irritates me more. "You were an asshole then, too," I grumble, refusing to accept his words that offer a completely different perspective to the one I've clung to all this time.

It feels like he observes me forever, his eyes digging deep into mine, searching for fuck knows what before he sighs, looking down at his hand. "Tug, Raven. Let's see if this works."

"And if it doesn't? If I pull too hard?"

He shrugs. "I'm trusting you not to."

Well, he's hopeful. More than me, that's for sure.

Taking a deep breath, I try to remain as relaxed as possible, which is hard to do when I have Brax, Sebastian, and Lyra watching me at the same time. Keeping my movements light, I avoid the desire to pull as hard as I can like I did to Genie, and after a few soft attempts, a small strand detaches from Sebastian, making me gasp.

"Have you done it?" Brax asks, and I nod without

turning to look at him.

Sebastian inches the locket closer and I slowly drop the tendril of magic into it before it snaps shut.

Holy fuck.

I take a step back, completely bewildered with what I've just done, as Sebastian looks at me with something that could almost be considered pride, but I quickly dismiss it.

"Did it hurt?" Lyra asks, looking at Sebastian, and he shakes his head.

"I didn't feel a thing."

Lyra offers her hand out in response, her magic vining around her fingers as I tentatively inch forward to do the same. It's easier this time, although the desire to rip the magic from her still remains.

Sebastian helps me store the magic in the locket again before offering it out to me.

"Is this a trap?" Brax asks, and Sebastian offers him a tight smile.

"Not this time," he mutters in response, and Brax takes the locket from him. My gargoyle drapes the gold chain around my neck, securing the clasp so that I can let the little prison of magic rest against my chest.

I glance back at him with a thankful smile as Sebastian clears his throat. He waits until my gaze is locked on his before he speaks. "I don't know what it must feel like to be attacked by your own flesh and blood, and I only recall

any of it because Lyra uses her magic to help me. I just…
I haven't… I'm…"

My senses tingle, understanding what it is he's trying to say, but it seems showing any form of vulnerability is a Hendrix issue across the board. "I know, Sebastian."

"What?" His brows crinkle as he stares at me and I'm suddenly at a loss for words. How do I explain or delve into this without making the situation worse?

"Well, I only think I know," I start, rubbing my lips together nervously. "But I believe someone is controlling you, which makes me even more concerned that you're under their influence right now," I admit.

A darkness casts over his gaze but he quickly shakes it off. "I am. But not now, not in here. Lyra has made this my safe space. Even though she interrupts our time together to let my little sister into her secret room without explaining why," he adds, giving Lyra a pointed look, and she shrugs.

"I told you, Raven is not a topic I'm willing to discuss. I trust her, and she trusts me. I won't change that."

My eyes widen and I hope her words are true, but now isn't the time to delve into it. Turning back to Sebastian, I want to question him about who may be controlling him, but he seems to have other plans.

"The deal I want to make is to offer to help you with the realms."

What does that mean?

"And what do you expect in return?" Brax asks, the chords in his neck tightening as he assesses my brother.

Sebastian glances between the two of us before settling his eyes on mine. "The deal is for you to promise to bring me back."

Bring him back? What does that mean? Just as quickly as I ask myself, I understand. "Why?" *I mean, I get why. I'm sure anyone and everyone would want to be saved from certain death, but this seems more specific.*

"I know I'm going to die before the week is out," Sebastian admits, rubbing nervously at the back of his neck.

"How?" This time the question comes from Brax instead.

"I just know."

Brax shakes his head, clearly not happy with that answer, and Sebastian must sense it too because he's suddenly pulling out a thick binder from thin air. He nervously hovers for a moment, the binder hanging between us as he thinks, but a moment later, he's lowering it into my hands.

"What is this?" I ask, my fingers trembling slightly as I stare down at the blank cover.

Sebastian's hands find their way into his pockets again as his chin lowers. "The reason I know I'm going to die. It contains everything you need to know to combine the realms. Everything you need to help put a stop to all of this."

"Wait, what do you mean combine the realms?" I meet his gaze to find nothing but sincerity staring back at me.

"I mean, in the right hands, it offers insights into merging the realms. Merging us and… the Realm of Shadows."

SIXTEEN

Brax

What in the backwards Basilica Realm, shifting Drakes, and family drama is today? Because it sure as hell has me fucked over a barrel with no lube and a spiked dick. I don't think I've ever been so mentally drained in my entire life, and I've been through some shit. I don't even have the brain function to eat the food laid out before me.

I'm not usually an emotional eater. I see food and shove it in my mouth. Not today, though. My head is firmly lodged up my ass, and I can't even comprehend what Raven must be going through.

Glancing in her direction, I catch the smallest glimpse of the new chain that hangs around her neck that she's slipped beneath her blouse. It rests firmly against her chest, just above the valley between her breasts. If anyone else saw it, they would assume it's just a piece of fashion jewelry, but in actual fact, it's far more significant than that.

Not only does it harbor magical abilities that my fucking woman somehow snipped from Sebastian and Lyra, but the two pictures inside, those children, hold sentimental value too. It feels like a peace offering from Sebastian to Raven in some ways. I don't know how to feel about that, and I know that ultimately, as much as I want to steamroll the entire situation, I can't. So until she talks about it first, I'm going to keep my lips firmly shut.

Or try to, at least.

More than that, it's not the biggest piece of information he gave her.

No.

If I thought the surprises were going to stop at the locket, I was truly mistaken.

Picking up the fork in front of me, I use it to nudge the food around on my plate, still unable to lift anything to my mouth as I remain deep in my thoughts.

How are we always the last to know things like this are possible? The snippets of magic, the merging of realms? Where the fuck do people find this information, and where do we go to join them?

I don't like the fact that the important information we keep stumbling over is coming from others. It's not easily accessible to us, and being reliant on other people pisses me off more than anything else.

Glancing at Raven's plate to my right, I watch her play with her food like me. I instantly want to demand she eats, she's going to fucking need it, but I'm not a hypocrite, not today at least, so I can't call her out on it unless I get a grip on myself too. Which isn't proving likely right now.

Instead, I opt to keep down the train of thoughts that have consumed me since we were in Lyra's office this morning. Lunchtime or not, the hours since everything happened have done nothing to dull my racing mind.

Raven's father being controlled isn't a surprise, but I'm not going to broach that subject with her until she's ready. Not when she has Sebastian on top of that, along with a new ability to comprehend. Fuck, I really need her to take the lead with this conversation shit. I won't be able to keep everything bottled up forever.

Acutely aware that my thoughts are all awry, I take a deep breath and circle my contemplation back to that fucker of a brother she can't seem to shake.

She shook his hand.

Shook. His. Hand.

Sealed the fucking deal.

His life is in her hands now, and if it's true that he dies for the binder going missing, then I'll be more than happy for Raven to bring him back to life so that I can get the chance to send him all the way to the Realm of Shadows. Although, I'm not sure he'll stay there for long if what he says about the binder is true.

Fuck.

I hate that these facts are coming from Sebastian. Hate it. Hate it. Hate it. My hold on the fork tightens so hard I feel it bend under my grip.

I let it clatter to the plate before wiping a hand down my face.

"I still can't understand why he would hand it over," Raven murmurs, purposely keeping her voice low even though it's only the two of us at the lunch table. I have no idea where Leila is but I'm glad she's not here. We need a moment, just the two of us.

Sighing, I admit the truth that grates on me the most. "Because despite the control, he knows you're the savior of the Elevin realm and everything else that comes with it." I watch as she grimaces, not appreciating my honesty. "Not to give you any more pressure or anything," I ramble, hating that one of the other guys isn't here to soothe her after my words.

To my surprise, she shrugs. "I said from day one I'm not a hero. I'm selfish and defensive with a mean-ass resting bitch face. That's not going to change, no matter what anyone expects of me. The only reason I'm doing anything at all is because it's affecting me and those I love.

Otherwise, I'd happily live under a rock with my head buried in the sand, hiding away from it all."

I can't help but smirk at her. That's not true and she knows it. Yes, she can be selfish, rightly so. Yes, she can be defensive, which is another well-earned trait. And that resting bitch face gets me hard, so I can't even deny it, but she also can't just sit around and watch injustice. Not after living in Shadowmoor, suffering at the hands of The Monarchy's choice to use Shadowmoor as a poor barrier between Haven Court and the Basilica Realm. She's faced enough to demand better, not for her, but for us. Eventually, she'll see that, too, but for now, I'll let her keep pretending that her actions don't speak so much louder than her words.

She pinches the bridge of her nose, exhaling slowly. "How are we going to get through afternoon classes when all I want to do is rip into the damn thing?" she grumbles, referring to the binder just as she has in every class we've had so far today. It's burning a hole in her bag, desperate for her attention, and she can't seem to shy away from it. "And if you say some shit joke about delayed gratification, I'll kick you in the shins," she adds, giving me a pointed look as I lift my hands up in the air defensively.

Fuck. This woman has me on point.

Still smirking, I decide to go easy on her as I place my hand on her thigh in a gesture of comfort. "I'm more intrigued to know if we can get this to the Realm of

Shadows with us so there's more of us who can dive into it or whether we're going to have to sift through the pages ourselves."

Her eyes widen as she nods. "Damn, that's a good idea. Who knew you had those?" She winks, making me glare at her poor joke, but she proceeds before I can throw anything back at her. "Maybe we should take the rest of the afternoon to figure it out." There's hope in her voice, hope I can completely relate to. The thought of continuing classes for the rest of the day has me ready to scratch my eyeballs out, too.

"Maybe you're right," I offer, and she gapes at me in surprise.

"I am?"

I don't bother answering. Instead, I shrug before standing, leaving a full plate of food to go to waste. Raven grabs her bag and rises, and as we push our chairs back, Leila suddenly appears with Grave at her side.

My back stiffens at the sight of him after Rhys mentioned his name earlier. My instinctive reaction is to cut the distance between us and slaughter the motherfucker here and now. I've had enough information today to last a lifetime, and if I can relieve us of one issue, then I will. Despite my knee-jerk reaction, Raven's hand on my shoulder seems to keep me rooted to the spot.

"Hey, aren't you guys eating?" Leila asks, her gaze

flicking between the two of us and the plates on the table.

I lift my hand, my lips parting, but Shadow squeezes my shoulder and speaks before I have a chance. "I'm not feeling too good." Frowning, I glance at her, catching on a little too late to the white lie that falls from her mouth. "Brax was just taking me back to the house before the nausea gets any worse."

Leila's face is an instant mirror of concern, while Grave's lips purse just the slightest bit, setting me even more on edge.

Clearing my throat, I wrap my arm around Raven's waist, pulling her against my side as her fingers stroke from my shoulder to my neck. "We should go," I murmur, speaking into her hair, and she nods.

"I'll catch up with you later, okay? When I'm not feeling like this," Raven states, and Leila nods.

"Of course. I'll make sure the professors know why you're not there if you don't make it back," she offers, and Raven mutters her thanks before we turn and head for the door.

I sense them still tracking us, their eyes burning holes into our heads until we exit the dining hall and walk toward the main exit. This would be a lot easier if I were able to create a gateway, but luck still isn't on our side with that.

The hallways are quite empty since it's lunchtime and we manage to make our way toward the large double doors with ease. Raven glances around us before turning to look up at me as we walk.

"We probably should stick around them more to spy on him."

"Nope," I grumble, not agreeing with her in the slightest.

"No? Why not?" she argues, and I give her a pointed look.

"You're in enough danger with everything else. We're not adding that on top, as well. Rhys said to keep an eye out for him, not actively seek him and his bullshit out."

She rolls her eyes at me but I let it go over my head. I'm going to stand by my point, and the fact that she declines to argue any further tells me she knows it's going to be a losing battle.

Stepping out into the cool afternoon air, I glance up at the sky, wishing I could feel the sun on my skin again. The sky has been like this since Erikel arrived, a weird mirage of colors intertwining that lightens in the day and darkens at night. Another mark of his presence that pisses me off.

We barely make it to the bottom of the steps when six Shadowgrim students appear out of nowhere, creating a wall in front of us.

I really don't have the time or patience for these fuckers right now. "Move out of the way," I grunt, a bored hint to my tone as we come to a stop in front of them. They smirk, each shaking their head, making my tolerance of their presence fall even lower. "I. Said. Move."

Footsteps echo from behind us and I recognize the clanging of the metal on the floor in time to turn and find the golden warrior approaching, with his treacherous leader a step behind him. It's clear the Shadowgrim barrier was to hold us in place in anticipation of Erikel's arrival, and I'm already over whatever bullshit is going to come out of his mouth.

His floor-length fur cape drapes around him like a protective shield, the jagged scar seeming even more prominent today as he takes a step toward my woman.

My nostrils flare as my hands ball at my sides. I want to stand between her and this fucker, but he's the last person I want her to seem weak in front of, so I use all of my pent-up energy to remain as still as possible.

"Why is my Potens Ruby in the Realm of Shadows?" he snarls, his lip curling as he bares his teeth.

"I don't know what you're talking about," Raven grumbles with irritation, which only seems to piss him off.

"Don't try me, Shadow Dancer." He inches closer and it takes everything in me to stay still.

"I. Don't. Know. What. You're. Talking. About," Raven bites, holding her ground when he moves rapidly, backhanding her across the face.

That motherfucker.

I lurch forward, ready to pummel him into the ground. Shifting from flesh to stone as I travel through the air, I'm held back by the golden warrior before I can connect with Erikel's skull.

My body tenses, adrenaline coursing through my veins as I try to break free of his hold, but it's impossible, even in my gargoyle form.

"Let me the fuck down. Now," I spit, barely able to breathe properly as I rage with every gasp.

Neither the golden warrior nor Erikel pay me any mind as Erikel wags his finger in Raven's face. "You have two choices. Tell me why it's there, or take me to it."

My jaw aches from grinding my teeth, unable to bottle up the anger building inside me. If this is Burton, he should be able to visit the Realm of Shadows like me. Why doesn't he fucking go there and find it for himself?

I'd rather he didn't, not wanting to put my parents in danger, but surely that should be a tactic instead of pushing harder on Raven.

Fuck.

Raven sighs, lifting her fingers tentatively to the red mark deepening on her cheek. *He's going to fucking pay for that.* "I can't do either, you fucking fool, because I don't know why and I don't know how to get there," she grinds out, eyes blazing as she glares at him.

Erikel tuts, shaking his head in disapproval. "You're

a necromancer; communicating with the shadows is your primary ability." Raven rears her head back slightly as I continue to wriggle in the warrior's hold to no avail. Erikel's eyes narrow as he assesses my Shadow before a flash of surprise burns deep in his irises. "You haven't communicated with them."

He inches closer, lifting his hand toward her, but she slaps him away. "Keep your fucking hands away from her," I boom, frustrated beyond words with being restrained.

Erikel continues to ignore me as he leans closer to Raven, but he doesn't try to touch her again. "Why?" he bites, peering deep into her eyes, but she doesn't falter under his proximity. "Why?" he repeats, and I watch Raven's face scrunch in distaste before she answers him.

"I don't know how."

Erikel stands back to his full height, sneering at Raven. "If I hadn't seen you bring people back from the dead, I wouldn't even believe you were a necromancer," he snaps, making his disapproval more than known.

Raven gapes at him, unsure what she's expected to say or do, but before Erikel can continue his tyrannical display of belittling her, Fitch appears.

"Erikel, there's an important call awaiting your attention. I've been sent with great urgency to collect you," he explains, not looking at Raven or me as he speaks to the fucker holding everyone's attention.

He growls, irritated with the interruption, but before he steps away, he makes sure to glare at Raven once more. "This isn't over," he promises, turning away with his fucking cloak fluttering in the wind.

"No, but it will be soon enough," Raven promises, her words too quiet for him to hear, but the warrior holding me back catches them and his hold on me loosens.

In a swift move, I break out of his grasp, spinning to connect my stone fist with his face, even though I know he can deflect everything we throw at him. To my surprise, my move connects with force and he tumbles back, landing with a crash on the ground.

Raven gasps beside me and the Shadowgrim audience that is still here watching chuckles before sauntering inside without a backward glance.

"I deserved that," the golden warrior mutters, making no effort to get back up.

"You deserve more than you'll ever receive," I bite, towering over him, and when his dark eyes collide with mine, I deliver my promise. "If you ever get in the way of me defending Raven again, the woman I love, the woman *your son* loves. I'll kill you with my bare hands, whether Creed cares or not."

SEVENTEEN

Zane

I don't know what time of day it is. I never fucking do. Everything is starting to merge together. I'm pretty certain we're now sleeping during the day and focusing on being awake in the dead of night so we're alert and ready in hopes that Raven and Brax appear.

It's not ideal—none of it is—which is probably why I'm barely managing to get more than a few hours of sleep, but we're rolling with it. It's all we can do.

I leave Creed and Eldon in the information room, which is my new name for the space filled with all of the attempts Marieta and Peta have made to get the fuck out of here, and head upstairs. Closing the bathroom door behind me, I methodically turn the shower on and grab a towel from the closet. As the water warms up, I brace my knuckles on the vanity, staring down at the porcelain while I get lost in my cluttered mind.

Sometimes, there's just too much going on and it's hard to focus. Without Raven's guidance, knowing which path to follow or which thought to center on is hard. That puts a lot of weight on her shoulders without me trying to, but I would follow my dove to the end of the realms and back without question if she asked me to.

Attempting to do anything without her near to me is hard, but knowing that everything we're doing here is as much for her as it is for us keeps me going.

Steam begins to billow around me, fogging up the mirror, so I quickly undress and step under the spray. It's hot as it hits my skin and I relish it. I don't know why, but no matter how much I wash myself, I don't feel any cleaner. It likely has something to do with where we are, but I still go through the motions anyway.

It's as if the Realm of Shadows clings to me in every way possible and I'm struggling to remember what it felt like on the other side.

The other side with my girl.

Fuck. I miss my dove.

The flash of her pink hair, the soft curve to her lips, the feel of her nails pressing into my skin, all of it. I should have made it clear in the handbook that we couldn't be separated like this, but it's too late now.

My eyelids fall closed and the beauty that is my dove

comes to life before me as the water continues to pound against my body and I quickly blink them back open. Thoughts of her stir my cock to life, and I squeeze it tight, willing the desire to go away, but my need for her is relentless. So is the pulsing hardness that refuses to go untouched.

Tugging once, hard and fast, I exhale while internally berating myself.

I shouldn't.

I should save every last drop for her, let her feel the weight of how much I've missed her when I finally get the chance, but I can't help it. Today has been another cluster fuck with no success and the only thing I can cling to is my want for her.

My hand moves of its own accord, tugging harshly at my stiff cock, and I give in, closing my eyes as I let the flutters of ecstasy float along my skin. The vision of her, my dove, only intensifies. Her pink and black hair splayed out, fanning her angelic face as she forms the perfect *O* with her mouth. Ruffled sheets frame her, her knuckles white as she holds on for the ride.

I can see the flush of pink that travels over her skin, hear her breathy moans as she chants through her release, and feel her nails piercing my skin.

That's all it takes.

All I need.

My release paints the tiles as I blink my eyes open, instantly coming down from the high I was riding seconds earlier. It's anticlimactic, to say the least. My hand slackens on my cock that still stands hard, desperate for the real thing, but that's not going to happen anytime soon. There is no feeling in the world quite like coming inside of her. The feel of her pussy clenching around me is a craving I'll never be able to sate, and I'll never want to.

I'll hear her cries soon enough. I have to.

Mindlessly running through the motions, I finish my shower and step out. Water droplets cling to my skin as I reach for the towel, running it over my damp hair when a blaring sound echoes from the other side of the door.

Frowning, I head for the door, but as I grab the handle, I quickly remember I need to put clothes on. I rush to get dressed, refusing to use my magic. Every ounce of my magic is being saved for when it matters most. Not that I'm certain it will make a difference, but I'm not willing to chance it.

I can hear the others talking, confusion and a sense of panic in the air as I clamber down the stairs to find them gathered at the front door.

"It feels too early for them to be here," I state, joining them to earn a pointed look from Creed.

"It is," he grumbles, and the impending worry that was simmering inside of me roars to life.

Eldon's brows are furrowed as he pulls the front door open and peers outside. Marieta and Peta are just as tense as the three of us, which doesn't calm the situation.

Something isn't right.

Fuck.

We're not going to get any answers if we just stand here, though. No matter what it is, I'm sure we've faced worse, and if not, it will be good practice.

Slipping between Creed and Eldon, I move out onto the porch, ignoring Marieta whispering my name. I'm not trying to be rude, but I'm not waiting around for trouble to come to us when we could have acted first. It's exactly what Raven or Brax would have done, but neither of them is here.

Brax has held up everything on our end in the Elevin Realm; it's only fair I channel his fearlessness here too.

"What's happening?" Eldon asks, and I shrug, not turning to check in with him.

"I'm not sure."

All I can see is the same blank space around us. An array of grays coloring the area, all except Brax's family home. Closing my eyes, I focus on my other senses, hoping to hear something or feel the hairs on the back of my neck rise in anticipation, but nothing comes.

Turning back to the house, I find Eldon and Creed slowly making their way toward me as Peta appears in the doorway with a sword, Marieta a step behind him. He spins the handle, the glint of the silver-tipped blade dancing at his side.

The second they're all off the porch, the house disappears. My eyes widen along with my stance as I blindly prepare for whatever is about to come next.

"What the fuck is going on?" Eldon bites, hands fisted at his sides as movement flickers out of the corner of my eye.

I twist in a rush to see a shadow forming beside me.

Holy fuck.

The silhouette shows a head, arms, legs, and torso, just like my shadow would appear. But this is different… completely different.

Another appears, followed by another, until six stand in a line beside me.

"Zane," Marieta warns, panic clear in her voice. I lift my hand slowly, signaling for them to remain calm and not act yet. Something's going on; we just need a second to understand what.

The shadow moves toward me and I take a step back, not in fear of them, almost as though I'm instinctively following their guidance. A few more steps and I'm standing between Creed and Eldon with Marieta and Peta right behind them. Before there's time to act, the shadows circle us. Hands joined, they grow, stretching out longer and longer until they rise, covering us.

Everything goes black, but the desire to fight doesn't come. They don't feel aggressive or malicious, but I don't know why I feel that way.

The darkness only lasts a few moments before they move again, but this time, we're not standing in a blank space; we're in a cave. Not just any cave, the one we were in before we stepped through the emerald gate leading to the Realm of Shadows.

The black silhouettes remain spread on the floor at our feet, making me frown. When I glance at the others, I find them just as confused as I am.

"What are we doing here?" Marieta asks, gripping Peta's arm.

"This is where the emerald gate was. This is where we were with Erikel, searching for the ruby," Creed states, and her eyes widen, but she nods in understanding.

"Are we—"

"No," Peta interjects, cutting Eldon off. "We're still in the Realm of Shadows." I want to ask how he knows that, but before I can question him, he points down at the shadows. "I think they want to show us something… listen."

Pressing my lips together, I keep my mouth shut, doing as he says. It takes a few seconds, but I hear something in the distance. I can't piece together what's being said, but can sense them getting closer.

A moment later, a familiar fur cloak drags along the floor as a man trudges across the rocks and damp ground toward the gemstone-covered wall where we found the Potens Ruby.

"The Potens Ruby is here somewhere," Erikel snarls, throwing his arms out wide. "I know it is," he insists, continuing to talk to himself. "Whether that bitch knows how to speak with the shadows or not, I know she knows where the ruby is."

His rambling makes my breath catch. I know he's referring to Raven. He has to be.

Fucker.

I want to cut the distance between us and beat the shit out of him, but the shadows seem to be blocking us from moving. I can't take a step over them.

"I want to pummel the fuck out of him," Creed grinds out, his voice raspy as he keeps it low.

Erikel's gaze whirls around in our direction and I freeze, thinking he heard my friend. But it's as if he sees right through us—like we're not here at all.

"Whatever he's doing, the shadows want us to see," Peta offers, sheathing the long blade he brought with him.

"But why?" Eldon asks, but no one can answer him because we're all as clueless as one another.

"That scar," Peta murmurs, pointing to Erikel's side

profile. I gave Erikel that scar."

"Does that mean it's him?" I ask, watching as the asshole continues to survey the wall of rubies.

"No," Marieta answers. "We're still in the Realm of Shadows here, remember?"

"How do you know?" I push, swiping a hand through my hair.

"The shadows are showing us this. They can only access the real world through a necromancer, and that's only when summoned."

I shake my head. "But Raven has mentioned before that she sees them in bed without having called for them."

Marieta's eyebrows rise, but she shrugs. "She's calling for them somehow, even if subconsciously."

I don't have an answer for that, so I turn to focus on Erikel but instantly freeze. "So if he's here, he's either a necromancer or someone who has died and been brought back."

"Yes," Peta says with a heavy sigh.

My mind races, trying to put the final piece in place, but it's as if I can't speak it.

"They're helping us," Creed states, distracting me as he points down at the shadows on the ground. "They're helping us see what they believe we need to see within the Realm of Shadows."

How? Why?

"So if we're able to see this, inside the Realm of Shadows, it's like Zane said. He's either a necromancer or someone brought back from the dead," Eldon repeats as if his brain is short circuiting too.

It's staring us straight in the face. We just have to speak it.

"It means our assumptions were correct and Erikel is…" Marieta's words trail off as we gape at the scene before us, watching as the scarred face and long nose morph into another set of familiar features we know.

The fur cloak frames the shoulders of our true enemy.

Burton.

He bellows before we can take the information in, anger echoing around us as the rocks shake. One little move from him and the shadows seem to panic, and a moment later, we're being transported again. Darkness swarms us for a brief second before Marieta and Peta's home comes into view.

I feel breathless without even doing anything.

Spinning, I try to garner the attention of one of the shadows, but they disappear before I can even try, leaving me frustrated and helpless once again.

"What now?" Creed asks, planting his hands on his hips as his head hangs with the same deflation I feel.

"I think the Potens Ruby could help break us free from here," Marieta thinks out loud, and Peta drapes his arm around her.

"Maybe," he offers, guiding her back toward the house. Without a word, the three of us follow after them.

"All we can do is wait for Raven and Brax to get here. They're our hope," Eldon states, and I nod in agreement. The countdown continues to tick down.

Hurry, Dove. The end seems to be drawing near, and I have to be by your side when it comes.

EIGHTEEN

Raven

I barely make it over the threshold before Brax kicks the door shut with a bang, effectively blocking us off from the rest of the campus. I drop my backpack on the closest sofa and heave a heavy sigh as I plant my hands on my hips.

Today has been a whirlwind, and it's barely lunchtime.

"We need to act sooner rather than later," Brax states, speaking my thoughts out loud, and I nod. "We can't keep waiting around."

"I agree. After today, fuck, this morning, we need to get this moving along. Now."

Glancing in his direction, I catch his nod, his stance a replica of mine. Silence descends over us as we stare at one another, chests rising and falling rapidly from the comedown of another run-in with Erikel. Or whoever the fuck he is.

I'm exhausted from trying to figure that out, nevermind any of the actual physical strain we're under. Refusing to weaken or lose sight of what's important, I give myself one second longer to gather myself before I set into motion.

Digging into my bag, I find the binder Sebastian gave me earlier this morning. It's weighed down my backpack since the moment it came into my possession. Now, with the opportunity to actually delve inside the pages, it's lighter. Like knowing of its presence added to its weight when I couldn't actually get my hands on it.

"Let's see if this has anything to offer."

Brax eliminates the distance between us, engulfing my waist with his huge hands. I'm off my feet before I can process it, clutching the binder to my chest. My back ends up pressed against his chest as he lowers to sit on the sofa. "If not, I get full permission to off Sebastian with no repercussions," he breathes against the shell of my ear.

A shiver runs down my spine as I glance over my shoulder at him with a quirked eyebrow. It takes everything in me to ignore the feel of his steel thighs beneath me, the outline of his cock that sits prominently between my ass cheeks. All the while, the smirk on his face doesn't falter.

"And if I say no?"

The darkness deepens in his eyes as his smirk grows. "You're assuming I'm asking for permission."

My jaw grows slack as I gape at him, too stunned to find any kind of response before he reaches for the binder, perusing the pages without another word.

Fucker.

Our attention is quickly drawn to the sheets of paper and the cursive text that awaits us. Shuffling in Brax's lap, we both gain a better view of the text. I reach out, glossing my fingertip over the aged pages.

It's overwhelming at first, and to add to that, it's as though the language is… different. Everything makes sense but with an extra *E* here and there or an unnecessary *ST* at the end of a word.

The first four sheets mean nothing at all. I can't even decipher what the words are referring to. The frown on Brax's face makes me assume he feels the same. Turning to the next page, I still when all that greets us is a charcoal handprint.

No words.

No gibberish.

Nothing but the hand.

Every detail is noted in the press of fingerprints and the crook to the middle finger. Somehow filling the image with… pain.

I can't help but run my finger over it, and the first slither of contact makes me gasp.

"Raven?" Brax murmurs, concern echoing in my ears.

"I'm okay," I whisper, my gaze locked on the image that's causing a stir inside me.

Creeping more of my hand over the image, I can feel every callous and imperfect inch of the paper. I hover, my fingertips aligned with those marked, my heart racing with the urge to press my palm against it.

It's like the decision is taken from me as my hand falls flat against the parchment. Anguish consumes me, and my eyelids fall closed as my lips part.

"What once was mine was taken as yours. What once was pure was tainted with pain. What once was the heavenly divine of the afterlife was broken, tattered, and torn. What once was the Realm of Eternity became the Realm of Shadows. What once was broken will be no more."

I gasp, yanking my hand back as I blink at Brax.

"Did—"

"I heard it," he murmurs, and my shoulders relax with relief while my body still trembles from the surprise of the woman's voice that played in the air.

"I can't... I... what?" I ramble, pinching the bridge of my nose.

"I'm not going to lie, that sounds like the kind of prophecy shit Eldon would tell me about from one of his visions."

I nod in agreement before taking a deep breath. "What

are we supposed to make of it?" I ask, repeating the words in my head.

"I think it's a promise of exactly what Sebastian mentioned, it just doesn't tell us how to make it happen," Brax offers, reaching around me to turn the page.

The handwriting turns from cursive and elegant to jagged and sharp.

When green arches hold delicate reds, all that is needed is a touch of darkness, a promise of change, and an unwavering belief.

I read it again, and again, and again, before flipping the page, but there's nothing except blank sheets. One after another, after another.

"What does that mean?" I grumble, flipping back to the start of the binder with no success.

"When green arches hold delicate reds, all that is needed is a touch of darkness, a promise of change, and an unwavering belief." He reads the passage out loud, offering no bright moment of realization.

"I need a drink," I murmur, tapping on his arm to release his hold on me. I head to the kitchen with a stomp, swinging the fridge open to grab two bottles of water before turning back toward the couch.

"It's still amusing that you don't just use your magic," Brax states as I throw a bottle toward him. He catches it with ease and I shrug.

"Sometimes, I like the simplicity of doing something mundane. It can help me clear my mind," I explain, and he looks as bewildered as before, a smirk quirking the corner of his mouth at my expense.

Rolling my eyes, I turn away from him and look out at the afternoon views. The water looks still in the distance, even though the trees on the coast move with the wind.

Maybe stepping outside, getting some fresh air, and soaking in the earth beneath me might help me think. With my mind made up, I move toward the patio doors but pause after taking only two steps.

Backtracking, I frown at Creed's bedroom door. The confusion only deepens the longer I look.

"Brax?"

"Shadow."

"Has there always been a green glow coming from Creed's room?"

I can feel his eyes roll even though my back is to him. "No, why?"

"Because there is now."

Moving toward the beacon shimmering beneath the door, I hear Brax's footsteps rushing toward me.

"What the fuck?" he whispers as I reach for the door handle, but before I can grasp it, Brax kicks the wood with his heavy boot, splintering the door frame in the process.

It's on the tip of my tongue to berate him, spew some

shit about not being such a brute, but it falls short when the reason for the green glow comes into view.

"Raven," Brax says, not turning to look at me, and I step in beside him, lacing my fingers through his.

"Is that…"

"Yeah," Brax answers, pulling me a step closer to the shimmering green jewels of the emerald gate. The emerald gate that leads to the Realm of Shadows. The same gate that disappeared back in the caves. Now it stands before us.

"I guess it's found a better place," I breathe, still in complete disbelief.

"I guess so."

"What do we do now?" I ask, knowing the answer but wanting to hear him say it.

His thumb runs over my knuckles as he exhales slowly. A flicker of understanding and excitement dances in his eyes when his gaze meets mine.

"It's time we figured out how to do exactly what the prophecy declared."

A shiver runs through me as I step through the emerald gate, still completely stunned by the fact that it appeared in our home. I'm taking it as a sign that the Realm of Shadows trusts us to be what it needs. Or is it the Realm of Eternity? I'm still all tangled up on the prophecy; the intricacies of it leave me confused.

The dim light from Creed's room is quickly replaced with the marbled effect of grays, from almost white to coal black. My hand remains engulfed in Brax's as his childhood home comes into view. However, the clear path that we usually have to the wraparound porch is obscured by silhouettes and shadows.

Gulping, I feel the energy shift around us. "What's going on?" I ask Brax, not pulling my eyes from the obstruction.

"Ask them," he mutters, instantly reminding me of Erikel's bullshit comment about me not being able to speak with the shadows even though I'm a necromancer.

"I don't know how," I remind him, my body tingling with anticipation from the vulnerability I know they will likely sense.

Brax's thumb caresses my knuckles again. "You just have to take your time, Raven. Feel it inside."

I recall the fact that he has been able to do this. I don't know how, but it worked. He managed to get the shadows to bring me here in my sleep. I want to give him some smart remark about thinking he's a pro now, but compared to me, he just might be, so I keep my mouth shut instead.

As much as I need Brax's comfort and touch right now

to keep me grounded, I need to focus on my magic and the shadows before me, so I release his hand and take a step toward them. I instantly want to lace my hands together, twiddle my thumbs, and sink my teeth into my lip. The need to fidget is overwhelming as fuck. But that only reveals more weaknesses I don't want to expose. Apparently, being out of Shadowmoor for this long has softened me inside. A fact that I'm more than happy with, but for now, it's the old me that's needed when it comes to this war. The version of me that didn't lower her walls for anyone. That swung her fists first and asked questions later. That's what I need, no matter who it is I'm communicating with.

Rolling my shoulders back, I relax my hands at my sides and tilt my chin up, oozing the effortless confidence I used to own, even though it doesn't quite sit with me the same as it once did.

"I want to understand the prophecy, the intricacies of the situation, and I feel the pain that runs deeply throughout this realm. I want to help you as much as I want to bring my family home." The words pour from my mouth without thought, and I find each and every one of them to be true.

I mean it.

I do want to help.

That pain I felt from the binder resonates inside of me.

One shadow moves, inching toward me as it grows in size. I stand tall, refusing to falter as it drifts perfectly so the silhouette of a hand ghosts over mine.

"Darkness. Promise. Change."

The words echo in my mind, reiterating three words from the guidance written in the binder on how to fulfill the prophecy. It feels like words of promise, words of confirmation that it's me they believe can do it. My darkness, my desire for change.

"Raven." I tilt my face to see Eldon step onto the porch first, and I smile, but quickly look back to the shadows as they dissipate, no longer standing between us and the house.

With a clear path, I rush toward him, leaping when I'm close enough and he catches me seamlessly. Wrapping my arms around his neck, his hands splay against my back as I breathe him in.

"Hey, Little Bird," he murmurs against my ear, and I sink into him further.

"Hey, El," I reply, clinging even tighter.

"Don't hog her all to yourself," Zane grumbles, making me grin as I lean back just enough to kiss Eldon before he lowers me back down. I'm quickly lifted off my feet again, spinning in a circle as Zane holds me just as tight. "I miss you, Dove."

My heart aches. "I miss you too."

If the prophecy in the binder is true, we may not have to miss each other for too much longer and that thought encourages me. As much as I want to sink into his warmth, I press my lips to his before leaning back, and he lowers me to the ground.

I need to see Creed, let his hold ground me even further, then we've got work to do.

Turning out of Zane's arms I find the man I'm looking for. He smiles softly at me as he inches closer, draping his arms over me as he pins me against his chest. He's quieter than the others, he always is, not offering a single word as he feeds me his touch just as effortlessly as he consumes me.

Lifting my chin up, I rest it against his chest before kissing his soft, full lips. Excitement zings through me, hope blossoming beyond control in my chest.

Reluctantly stepping back, I find Peta and Marieta standing on either side of Brax as they smile lovingly at him. Their gazes find mine and Marieta takes a step toward me.

"It seems they've seen something in you, Raven," she says, pointing to where the shadows were a few moments ago. "Their help has been unprecedented today," she adds, causing questions to tumble over one another on the tip of my tongue, but it's Brax who speaks first.

"What does that mean?"

She turns back to him as Peta pats him on the back. "Cocoa?" she offers, glancing around at each of us, and I shake my head.

"Not today, thank you. We have a lot to do."

"It sounds like you have big news too, and I noticed you came through the emerald gate," Peta states, waving for us to enter the house, indicating that the help they're alluding to from the shadows has led to something big as well.

"Yeah, it reappeared for us," I manage. Creed laces his fingers with mine, encouraging me inside as everyone else does the same. Despite the lack of hot cocoa, we find ourselves seated around the dining table anyway. Creed on my left, Eldon on my right, with a grumpy Zane on the other side of him. Brax occupies the spot after him while Marieta and Peta fill the remaining seats.

Everyone glances at each other; Creed to Zane, Zane to Marieta, Marieta to Eldon, Eldon to Peta. It's like they're silently trying to decide who should speak first.

Marieta clears her throat. "Burton was here."

"Burton? How?" Brax grunts, sitting tall.

"The shadows showed us," Peta explains as I soak in the knowledge that he said Burton and not Erikel.

"So it's really him," I state, needing the confirmation, and they all nod simultaneously at Brax and me.

"It's really him," Creed confirms, squeezing my thigh. *Fuck.*

"What happened with you guys?" Eldon asks, glancing

between us, and Brax scoffs.

"That's a loaded question if I ever heard one," he admits, and as true as it is, his grumbling makes me smile. "Where do we even start?"

We should probably start at this morning, when we went to Lyra's office, but I think the direction we're heading seems more necessary.

"We're going to combine the realms," I blurt, almost amused by the surprise in everyone's eyes.

"How?" Peta asks, reaching for Marieta's hand on the table.

I look at Brax, who places the binder on the table and nudges it toward his mother. She tentatively reaches for it, dragging it along the wood between her and Peta. Opening the leather, they delve inside and Brax quickly flicks the pages to the end. I watch their eyes scan the text once, then again, and a third time for good measure.

"Where did you get this from?" Marieta asks, passing the binder to Creed to read.

Taking a deep breath, I answer her. "Sebastian."

"Since when can we trust him?" Zane grunts, instantly defensive.

"I'm not sure he *can* be trusted, but if this works…" My words trail off, the hope lingering in the air, saying all that needs to be spoken.

Creed passes the binder along for Eldon and Zane to

read, and once everyone has memorized the text, Brax explains the prophecy we heard when my palm touched the hand.

"What once was mine was taken as yours. What once was pure was tainted with pain. What once was the heavenly divine of the afterlife was broken, tattered, and torn. What once was the Realm of Eternity became the Realm of Shadows. What once was broken will be no more."

"It kind of makes sense, in the cryptic way that prophecies do, but there's still a lot of guessing here," Eldon states, rubbing at his forehead.

"I agree, but we have to start somewhere," I answer, and he turns to me with a soft smile. His lips part, but no words come out as a shrill sound echoes around the house.

"What's that?" I ask with a gasp, adrenaline instantly coursing through my veins as I lurch to my feet.

"Someone or something is here," Marieta mutters, rushing for the front door with Peta hot on her heels, sword in hand.

Holy fuck.

Turning to Eldon, my eyes still wide, I find him on edge but nowhere near as startled as I am. He must sense the confusion in my gaze because he quickly smirks, stroking a finger down my cheek.

"It sounds every time someone is near, which isn't

often, but it's usually an indicator that *you* are close."

I nod in understanding, but the uncertainty of who it may be still gets the better of me and I hurry to my feet to see what or who it is. I'm halfway down the hallway when Marieta opens the front door wide, and all that's visible on the other side is shadow after shadow.

Rushing out onto the porch, my eyes grow wider with every passing moment, moving from one silhouette to another. If I thought there were a lot here before, that's nothing compared to now. They must have doubled, possibly tripled. At least.

"I think they want to show us something else," Peta says from behind me. I quickly realize that he can see them now, just as Marieta seemed to know where they had been earlier.

"You can see them?" I ask, needing the clarification to calm my racing heart, and he nods.

"It seems that when they want to reveal themselves, they will," he offers as an explanation.

My Bishops appear behind Marieta and Peta, as intrigued as I am. I turn to the silhouettes again, feeling their energy drawing me closer. I hear the creak of the steps down the porch under my feet as I swallow down the worry threatening to rise.

One shadow stands out from the rest, just like it has before in my bedroom on more than one occasion. I don't stop moving until I'm right in front of it, dropping to one knee.

I can't explain what I'm doing or why, but it feels right. Placing a hand on the ground where their shadow falls, my head dips as pain emits from the touch, just like in the binder.

"Show me the way. Show me the way, and I will help you the best I can. I just want my family together again," I promise, despite hating the heroic tinge that dances over every word.

A warmth travels up my arm, almost as if it's consoling me before it inches away.

Standing, I understand. Turning to the house, I find Marieta, Peta, Eldon, Creed, Zane, and Brax all waiting as patiently as possible for me to explain. "They're going to show us."

I'm not sure how, where, or even why. All I know is when; now.

"Is this a good idea?" Brax asks, furrowing his brows as he glances from me to the shadows dancing across the ground behind me. "Freeing them, I mean."

"The shadows are just that, in this realm or another, that's not going to change. And if they weren't, the pain I feel for them… they want to rest, to dissolve the restlessness that consumes them. They've been through enough. I can't explain it, but we have to consider the fact that they've chosen us to do this, to have darkness but hope for change and an unwavering belief of more, of better. They trust us to do this because we don't want them for our own needs or cause. I just want you guys home." My chest tightens and I tilt my face to look back at the shadows. "Returning to our world leaves them completely powerless."

"Except at your command," Creed states, and my nose wrinkles.

"Except that," I grumble, aware that all necromancers before me have tried to control the shadows and create an army for a selfish war.

"And what is your command?" Marieta asks, teetering closer.

I shake my head. "I haven't figured that part out yet. I've been focused on the hope that we can all be together again. The rest of the world doesn't matter, just us."

Eldon moves first, holding my hands in his as he peers down at me.

"Just us it is."

My heart warms, faith almost haunting me.

Taking a deep breath, everyone steps up to the shadows with me. I kneel before them once more. "When green arches hold delicate reds, all that is needed is a touch of darkness, a promise of change, and an unwavering belief." The words pound in my ears as I feel their weight. I know it, but I don't understand.

"Green arches, delicate reds," Creed murmurs from behind me, and Eldon stumbles back a step.

"Wait here. I think I might have it."

I frown in confusion, not wanting to allow this hope to grow anymore, as I watch my fireball rush back into the house. A quick glance at everyone else tells me they have no clue either, but there isn't much time for us to sit and consider the situation because he's racing back to us a moment later.

He comes to a halt beside me with his fist clenched as he holds it out in my direction, slowly uncurling to reveal the Potens Ruby.

"When green arches—the emerald gates—hold delicate reds—the Potens Ruby—all that is needed is a touch of darkness—a necromancer—a promise of change—still you—and an unwavering belief—us. All of us."

I blink at him, heat tingling along my skin from head to toe as his words click together in my head.

"But she's been in the Realm of Shadows along with the Potens Ruby before and it hasn't made a difference," Peta murmurs, wincing at the dampener he threatens to put on the mood, but Brax waves his hand, interjecting.

"But the delicate red hasn't had a touch of darkness through the green arches." My eyebrows pinch again as I glance at him, confused as hell, and he sighs. "You've never touched the Potens Ruby, Raven. Not in the Elevin

Realm, and certainly not in here."

My palms instantly feel clammy as I swipe my tongue over my bottom lip, turning back to Eldon, who holds the ruby between us.

"It can't be as simple as just touching it… can it?"

"We won't know unless we try," Zane murmurs, hope twinkling in his eyes.

"Hold your hand out, Little Bird," Eldon directs, and I slowly turn my hand over to reveal my palm, lifting it toward him.

His eyes lock on mine and I can feel everyone staring at me, the attention making me falter as I exhale slowly. He poises his hand above mine, ready to drop it into my open palm but waiting for my signal.

Clearing my throat, I look him dead in the eyes. "I love you. I love all of you," I state, words firm as I turn to look at Creed, then Zane, and finally Brax.

Emotion rises inside of me as the rest of the realm drifts into the darkness. All that exists is me and the glistening red ruby in Eldon's hand.

"Do it."

NINETEEN

Raven

The weight imprints against my palm, slamming my eyes shut and wobbling the ground beneath my feet. Colors flicker on the back of my eyelids as I open my mouth to gasp, but it lodges in my throat.

My pulse whirls in my ears, leaving me lightheaded as I try to blink my eyes open.

Everything is bright, *too* bright, and I have to shield my eyes with my free hand as color dances around us, banishing the gray hues that have haunted us for so long.

I see Eldon first, still standing right in front of me, but his gaze is taking in our surroundings. Looking for the others, I find them in the exact spots they were in moments earlier, only the ground beneath their feet isn't filled with emptiness. It's rich green grass with perfectly trimmed blades. The smell of lavender engulfs my senses as birds chirping in the distance register in my ears.

Turning, I put my back to the beaming sun so I can see without worrying that my retinas are going to fry. Everything feels the same, yet bursting with color and… happiness.

Shadows swarm us, dancing and twirling against every surface until they disappear from sight.

Confusion and self-doubt overwhelm any hope or faith until I'm suddenly swept off my feet. The arms aren't familiar and my back stiffens defensively until I hear their voice.

"Raven. Oh, Raven! Thank you. Thank you. Thank you."

I glance over my shoulder to see Peta holding me tight as he bounces with blissful joy.

"Oh my gosh. I can't believe it. I can't," Marieta bawls, launching herself at Brax, who returns his mother's embrace just as tightly.

"We did it?" My voice trembles, stunned with disbelief as Peta lowers me to the floor.

"*You* fucking did it," Zane corrects, scooping me up in his arms, forcing me to the tips of my toes as he crushes his mouth to mine in a blistering kiss.

The ruby is still in my right palm, but I tug at his hair with my other hand, basking in his delight as my own bursts inside of me.

Marieta isn't the only one who can't believe it. I'm still unsure if this is really happening too.

Zane releases me, my lips swollen from his touch. I stumble as I try to look around, but he catches my waist, stopping me from falling. A moment later, Eldon appears in front of me and I nervously hold out the ruby to him. Initially, he starts to shake his head, but he must see the certainty or panic in my eyes because he relents, taking the magical item from my hand.

"Where are we?" I rasp as Brax appears at my side.

If I looked deep enough, I'm certain I would find unshed tears in his eyes, but he quickly blinks it all away as he settles his gaze on me.

"We're home."

Turning, I see the same home I've visited a few times now, only this time, it's in full color. Soft yellow covers most surfaces, with white trim around the windows and doors. The wraparound porch sits proudly in a bed of soft oak.

"It's real? It happened?" I reiterate, locked in a somewhat trance.

"Yeah."

Excitement buzzes inside me as I take a deep breath, exhaling long and hard as one of the heavy weights on my shoulders melts away.

"What now?" I ask, glancing at Creed, who stares at

the house with the same wonder as I do.

He steps closer, wrapping his arm around my shoulders as he leads me toward the house, which Marieta and Peta are already nearing.

"Now we rest before the world demands your brilliance once more."

Damp hair clings to my neck and back and I don't bother to use my magic to dry it. It somehow makes me feel grounded and present, and I like it. Stepping out of the bathroom in an oversized t-shirt one of the guys offered me, I find myself in a new version of Brax's bedroom.

When I stepped into the bathroom to take a shower, there was a single bed and childish trinkets everywhere, untouched and still holding memories from when he was younger. Now, a large bed, just like the one back at the academy, sits in the center of the room. Natural light filters in through the window, growing darker with every moment as dusk creeps upon us.

When the sun rises again, we'll be back on target, refocused, and drenched in the mess that still requires our attention. For now, tonight is ours.

Eldon lounges on the bed with his back against the headboard, crooking his finger for me to come closer as

Zane presses a kiss against my temple before slipping into the bathroom. I follow Eldon's sultry order, sauntering over to him as Creed sits in a navy-blue chair that is now located in the corner by the window. His eyes are closed, but I know he's not asleep. Not yet at least.

As I crawl up the bed, Eldon parts his legs to accommodate me and I lean back against his chest, basking in the warmth emitting from him as he bands his arms around my body.

"You smell like Heaven," he murmurs against my ear, making me shiver, and Creed grunts, not bothering to open his eyes.

"She smells like home," he corrects, and I feel Eldon's lips curl against my skin as he peppers kisses along my neck.

"That too."

I feel delirious, finally being in his arms for real. This is no dream, no alternate realm. We're all here in the flesh. We can't be separated like that ever again.

Zane steps out of the bathroom with a flourish, steam billowing around him as Creed stands from the chair and wordlessly trades places with him.

"You don't know how good that feels," he states, running a towel over his hair as another clings to his hips, offering a spectacular view of his magical *V* leading down to his even more spectacular length.

It feels euphoric, that's the best explanation I have, to be here with them in such a mundane scenario. I love it. I *love* them.

As if sensing my joy, my brain taints the happy moment and my gaze drops to my hands.

"We're going to have to head back eventually," I murmur, letting my magic ripple from my fingertips as I run them through my hair, drying the ends.

"We know, but that's not for us to worry about tonight," Eldon replies, stroking his hand over my arm.

"How are we even going to get back there?" I ask, and Zane shrugs.

"I don't know, but that feels like a problem for tomorrow. For tonight, there's something more important than that for us to handle," he states, dropping the towel in his hands before letting the one at his waist crumple to the floor too.

My heart races, my eyes widening as I take him in. Eldon's lips return to my neck, pressing firmer this time as he uses his feet to spread my legs wide.

I gasp, fully aware that I'm not wearing any panties right now, and Zane groans with delight as he gets the perfect view of my pussy. His cock is hard, needy, and demanding as he places his palms and knees on the bed and slowly climbs over the sheets as I had done earlier.

His palms drag over my thighs slowly, no urgency in

his moves as he takes his time teasing me. His fingertips stop at the apex of my thighs, a breath away from where I want him most, and the smirk on his face tells me he knows the exact feelings he's conjuring in me.

I can't find the words to encourage him, my body begging for him desperately, and he doesn't disappoint as his tongue presses against my folds, dragging from my entrance to my clit. I moan, unabashed, and instantly panic when I remember Brax's parents are here somewhere.

Attempting to slam my legs shut, Zane looks up at me with a frown. "Give me my pussy right now, Dove," he growls, and I shake my head.

"Marieta. Peta," I stammer, and he shakes his head back at me.

"I soundproofed the room. Besides, they're in the kitchen with Brax. If you're nervous about it, then you can try to be quiet, but I'm having this pussy either way."

Gaping at him, my body trembles, and despite my concern, I let my legs fall open when he pries at them. A devilish grin spreads across his face as he repeats the motion, his tongue making me dance between him and Eldon as ecstasy coats my skin.

Fuck. I can be quiet. I think. But he did say he had soundproofed the room.

Eldon's hands swipe under my oversized tee, caressing my skin as he teases my hips and works his way to my breasts, feeling their weight in his palms as he nips at my neck.

"Fuck," I rasp, my vision blurring at their combined touch.

The sound of a door clicking shut freezes me as panic zaps through my veins, and I turn to find Brax leaning against the door, eyes fixed on where his brothers are touching me.

"Don't stop on my account," he grunts, making a show of adjusting himself as his eyes meet mine. "In fact, I insist," he adds with a nod.

Zane takes the opportunity to tease two fingers at my core while lapping at my clit, and I buck up off the bed as he thrusts them deep inside of me. My moan is muted, lodged in my throat as need dances over my skin, illuminating every touch from him and Eldon as Brax's gaze only adds fuel to the fire.

"Make her come for us, Zane. I want your face painted in her release," Brax orders, taking control as he usually does, and I shiver with anticipation.

"With pleasure," he replies, doubling his efforts as he finger fucks me with precision, swirling around in my core as he rakes his teeth over my clit.

Eldon twists my nipples, lapping at my neck as my eyes fall to half mast just in time to see Creed open the bathroom door.

"Fuck. I leave you alone for two minutes and you've already got her on the brink of coming," he grunts, dropping his towel while his onyx eyes remain fixed on mine. He reaches for his cock, tugging slowly at his length as he watches me come apart between his friends. A grunt sounds from Brax and I tilt my face in his direction to find him in the exact same position.

With Brax and Creed's eyes on me, Zane's tongue, Eldon's lips, and both of their fingers, I'm a goner. The climax builds with haste, tingling from my toes all the way through my body as pleasure ripples through me in crashing waves.

My hips buck, my head falling back against Eldon as I moan low and raw while Zane's movements don't falter, dragging out every inch of my climax.

"How's that?" he finally asks, lifting his face from my pussy to reveal glistening lips and remnants on his chin.

Fuck.

I should be embarrassed. *Should* being the keyword, because, really, that is hot as fuck.

"It looks like she's ready for more," Brax replies, his gaze fixating on mine as he grins. "Would you agree?" he asks, but deep down, I know it's not a question, not a question at all. This is him making it clear his plans aren't done with yet.

"What do you have in mind?" I ask, my core clenching

with desire.

The corner of his mouth tips up, but he doesn't offer an explanation. He just uses his magic to remove the clothes from his body and takes a step toward the bed.

His gaze leaves mine, locking with each of the guys as they hold a silent conversation. They must decide on something, fuck knows what, but they each nod in agreement before Eldon's hands move to my waist.

"This is for me, Little Bird," he murmurs, lifting me off the bed slightly, and his cock nudges against my ass, confirming what he means.

Fuck.

"You're going to want me in here first, though, Dove," Zane adds, grabbing my thighs and banding them around his waist as he lines his length up with my entrance.

My hands fall to the sheet on either side of Zane's waist as I cling on for dear life, both excited and nervous for what's to follow. There's no warning before he slams his cock deep into my core, making me moan louder than before as my pussy stretches around his girth.

His thrusts don't pause to offer me a chance at acclimating to him, and a moment later, I feel Eldon's fingers teasing at my ass, eager to fill me completely.

Gasping, I let them take my weight, focusing on thrusting between them as they both stretch me out in the most blissful way possible. I can barely see straight as I feel the weight shift beneath me, and a cock presses against my lips.

I look up to find Creed peering down at me with his length, eager for more of me. I part my lips, tasting him on my tongue at the same time Eldon's fingers are replaced with his lubed-dick.

Holy fuck.

Holy fuck. Holy fuck. Holy fuck.

Zane stills, allowing Eldon to take control of the pace between my thighs while Creed fucks my mouth, slamming to the back of my throat in one swift move.

My moans become garbled, and my body stiffens at Eldon filling me so much, but after a few seconds, I melt into him.

One thrust, two thrusts, three.

Eldon.

Zane.

Creed.

One after the other, they dominate me, seeking their own pleasure while showering me with my own. I feel full, fuller than full. It's on the brink of too much while being perfectly everything I need all at once.

Someone is missing, though.

Forcing my eyes open, I glance at Brax as Creed continues to fuck my mouth.

"I'm here, Shadow. Right where I want to be," he

states, seemingly feeling my urgency to find him too.

I settle once more, grinding my hips along with Zane and Eldon's thrusts.

"Come for us, Little Bird. Show us how much you've missed us," Eldon murmurs against my ear, making the hairs on the back of my neck stand on end.

I want to tell him to paint me with his release, fill me with his seed, show *me* how much they've missed me too, but something tells me that order won't be necessary.

Leaning one hand behind me, I grab on to Eldon's hair while lifting the other to Creed's thigh, digging my nails into his skin as he fucks my mouth relentlessly.

Zane presses his thumb against my clit, making me gasp, and I can't take any more. With his cock filling my core, Eldon's stretching my tight muscles, and Creed hitting the back of my throat, all while Brax's gaze burns me, I come apart.

I moan around Creed's length, succumbing to the pleasure as I explode.

The tang of Creed's release hits my tongue first, heightening the pleasure running through me as he groans low and deep. Eldon's moves stutter next, his fingers gripping my waist in a bruising hold as he mutters my name against my ear.

"Fuck, Dove. Fuck," Zane bites, baring his teeth as his neck flares red and he comes inside of me.

My chest rises and falls harshly as exhaustion clings to me, and I manage to catch a full breath when Creed leans back, releasing his cock from my mouth. The second he does, I feel the warm splutter of cum against my chest and find Brax hovering over me with blazing eyes and desire ticking at his jaw.

I feel raw and emotional, on the verge of tears for some reason, and I can't explain why. Before I can even try to verbalize anything, Creed, Zane, and Eldon all say my name in sync.

"Raven." I blink up in a daze, releasing my hold on Eldon and Creed as they continue to speak as one, making my heart stutter.

"Raven Hendrix, I am Zane Denver. I pledge to help with all that I am, all that I could be, and all I wish to be."

"Raven Hendrix, I am Creed Wylder. I pledge to help with all that I am, all that I could be, and all I wish to be."

"Raven Hendrix, I am Eldon Rhodes. I pledge to help with all that I am, all that I could be, and all I wish to be."

Tears prick the back of my eyes, rendering me speechless as I feel their gaze on mine. After a moment, my chest still heaving with every breath, I hear Eldon growl Brax's name. "Pledge your oath to her," he insists, and despite the emotion bubbling inside of me, I chuckle as Brax responds.

"I already have."

TWENTY

Zane

Warmth cascades over my right side and my fingers splay out over soft skin. Peeling my eyes open, I find a mess of pink and black hair draped over my shoulder, an arm sprawled over my chest, and a delicate thigh hooked over me.

Raven.

Fucking, Raven.

Peace at last. A feeling I wasn't sure I would ever experience again, and now here it is. Reality rears its ugly head, reminding me that the battle isn't over. The war technically hasn't even begun.

Glancing across the rest of the ridiculously big bed, I spot Eldon pressed against Raven's back and Creed stretched out on the other side of him. Brax, however, is nowhere to be seen. He could possibly be with his parents, but for now, while I'm reaping the rewards of Raven's slumber, I'm going to assume that he's okay.

As if sensing my thoughts, the bedroom door swings open and the grumpy gargoyle fills the open space. His eyes fall on Raven first, tracing over her from head to toe before they settle on me.

"Come," he grunts, waving me toward him, but I shake my head.

"Why would I want to leave my spot?" I ask, raising my eyebrows. I'm sure he would be asking the same thing if our roles were reversed, but the situation isn't the other way around, so all I get is one of his signature deathly glares.

It seems time hasn't changed this asshole's consistent rough demeanor, but I try to give him the benefit of the doubt since he's taken such good care of our girl.

"Just move your lazy ass," he snips, and I shake my head.

Fucker.

"Listen, I don't give a shit what you want or need me for. I'm not leaving—"

"I'll come too," Raven murmurs, interrupting what would surely have led to an argument. Any irritation with the asshole is quickly forgotten as I turn to glance down at her with a smile.

Pressing my lips against her temple, I tighten my arm

around her shoulders and bask in her presence for a second longer.

"We can just pretend to be asleep and he might leave us alone," I offer, earning a chuckle from my dove as Eldon and Creed stir awake.

"The look on his face tells me we're not getting out of this one. Let's go," she states, kissing my cheek before shuffling to the end of the bed.

I fold my arms behind my head, happy to watch her as she prances across the room, heading for the bathroom. The door closes behind her with an effective thud, leaving me to pout.

"What's up, man?" I ask, and Brax just rolls his eyes at me.

It seems I'm going to have to go and see for myself.

Standing, I use my magic to dress in a pair of sweatpants and a fitted tee, just in time for Raven to step back out in a similar outfit, but she looks way fucking hotter.

I watch her in awe, from the loose tendrils of hair that frame her face to the cuffs of her sweatpants. This woman. This *fucking* woman.

"You're wasting time," Brax grumbles, opening the bedroom door wide, interrupting my appreciation of her again.

I sigh, slapping my hands at my sides. I'm aware I probably look like a cranky toddler, but I don't care. "What time? You're not sharing anything."

"Zane?"

I still, the familiar voice traveling up the stairs, catching me by surprise. I glance at Raven first, and the small lilt to the corner of her mouth confirms it belongs to who I think it does.

Rushing down the stairs, my heart hammers in my chest as my father comes into view. The peppered hair at his temples looks more gray than usual, and the bags under his eyes weren't there the last time I saw him.

Fuck.

"Pops," I breathe, launching myself at him.

He envelops me in his arms and I squeeze him back, thankful to be able to see my father in the flesh again. We rock from side to side for what feels like forever until I finally lean back.

"It's so good to see you again, son. It's so good to see all of you," he breathes, patting my shoulder as he glances at the others too.

Everybody joins us at the bottom of the stairs, where we're then led into the kitchen and hot cocoa awaits us. My father's hand remains on my shoulder as we take our seats. His presence makes up for the fact that Creed and Brax bundle Raven between them.

"There's so much to discuss," Marieta says, getting comfortable in her chair.

My father nods in agreement. "I've missed you both dearly. You're right. There's a lot for us to go over, but for now, let's focus on the main points before I'm called away," he insists, patting my shoulder one final time before reaching for his mug.

Raven and my father, both with me, completing me in a way I can't explain. It's everything.

"What have I missed with you?" I ask, intrigued.

The disappointment flares in his eyes as he turns to me. "We believe Erikel has a connection within The Monarchy. I'm trying to root them out."

"Burton," I correct, and his eyes widen.

"It's confirmed? We know it's Burton?" he asks, sitting taller.

Burton, Erikel…

Erikel, Burton…

It's giving me a fucking headache.

"Yes."

"It's definitely intertwined," he insists. "Everyone I'm in close contact with is trying to act on the students' behalf, desperate to bring them to safety, but something or someone is holding back on pulling the trigger."

My hands clench in my lap, anger creeping up my spine. Of course there is. Nothing is ever easy or simple in this damn life.

"We need to figure it out. I want nothing more than

for this bullshit to be over. I'm done with this war and it hasn't even started yet," I grumble, and my father nods knowingly.

"I agree. I did mention my concern about someone to Brax and Raven the other day, but I'm sure you guys have been through a lot. I want you to be cautious of Grave Richardson."

As we take in the information, my eyes widen along with Creed's and Eldon's.

"Sorry," Raven murmurs, wincing at the fact that she hadn't passed the information on. But my father was right; we've had enough going on already. I'm sure there are other things we haven't discussed yet.

I shake my head at her, the apology not necessary, as a beeping sound comes from my father's suit jacket. He frowns as he digs it out, instantly rising to his feet after he's glanced over the words.

"What's going on?" I ask, following suit.

My father's eyes fall to Raven's instead of mine. "I have to leave. I've just received word that your father has managed to break free."

Raven's hand falls to her chest as she gapes at him, nodding dumbly while panic dances in her pretty eyes. "Of course," she murmurs, wiping her hands nervously down her thighs as she stands.

"I'm sorry I can't stay," he continues, looking at me.

He takes my hand, pulling me in for a half hug as he pats my back, swiftly moving around the table to embrace the others, including Marieta and Peta.

"Thank you for coming, Rhys. I can't wait to catch each other up to speed," Peta says with a tired smile before my father comes to a stop in front of Raven.

"I'm sorry you're having to deal with this," she breathes.

"Don't apologize. Especially when you brought my boy back to me," he replies, bundling her in his arms for a beat longer than the others. "Are you going to return to the academy?" he asks, glancing over each of us.

"I think we have to," Raven states, wriggling her fingers at her sides. "He's only going to hunt me down otherwise. It's the *how* we need to figure out, along with explaining where these guys have been," she adds, tension rising in the room.

"If you need me, you know how to reach me. Stay in contact," he insists, heading toward the door, but he doesn't step over the threshold before he spins, pointing a finger at Brax and Eldon. "Oh, and you two better be prepared for Eldon's mother's wrath. I've kept her up to date, so she knows you're safe, but she said that's only until she gets her hands on you." He winks before sauntering out the door as the pair of them groan in sync.

"Ah, shit."

The familiar setting of the Gauntlet arena comes into view as I dust off my pants. It feels odd as fuck to be back here, of all places, but not as weird as slipping through the gateway that leads here. The compound was derelict, with no magical creatures in sight, but it feels more eerily quiet here.

The dim sky outside reminds me of how tainted Silvercrest Academy is becoming. Strange colors loom above, reminding us of the darkness that threatens to destroy us. The gloomy vibe only worsens in here, shadows casting over the stone steps as tiny dust particles float in the air.

"Let's get the fuck out of here. It's giving me the creeps," Eldon grumbles like we haven't just been surviving in the fucking Realm of Shadows.

I smirk, rolling my eyes, but the smart comment on the tip of my tongue is cut short when Raven slips through the gateway, quickly followed by Brax. Everywhere she goes, she takes my attention with her. There was no denying it before. Now, it's even worse.

Being here again, not just at the academy but at the Gauntlet specifically, resonates deep inside of me. It's like we're here for the first time again, facing the sirens. My heart clenched when she was in there, leaving me helpless and rendered useless. It was in that moment, though, in what feels like forever ago, that I saw her transition before my eyes, revealing the survivor beneath the harsh exterior she put out as a defense to hide behind.

That was then. Her survival instincts have only increased since, as much as I wish they hadn't. But along with that has come more confidence, more power, and a truer understanding of what she's capable of and what she's destined to achieve.

Being at her side through all of this is the greatest honor.

"Are you okay?" she asks, waving her hand in front of my face, and I shake my head, quickly realizing that I zoned out.

"I'll be better with you under my arm," I reply with a wink. Even though she rolls her eyes at me, she relents and slips beneath my arm with a contented sigh.

Eldon is already waiting at the steps, ready to get the fuck out of here, and once I start toward him with Raven at my side, Creed and Brax follow.

It doesn't seem to get any brighter as we step outside, taking the path back to our house. We're more alert, that's for sure, but as we bypass the academy building and head down the quieter walkways to the houses, we don't come across anyone.

Odd.

Although, it's been a minute since I've been here. This could be the new normal now, I don't know, but the frown pinching between Raven's eyebrows tells me she seems surprised too.

"How are we going to explain how you got out and the five of us returned?" Creed asks when we don't come across anyone, and Raven shrugs.

"I'm just going to go with the shadows."

Brax's pace quickens and he appears a moment later on her other side. "Then he'll think you can control them."

Apparently, that's not something we want.

"I can't think of another reason, can you?" Raven replies, lips twisting in thought, and the grumpy asshole shakes his head.

"There's potential that the three of us could hide out at the house," I offer, glancing down at my dove to see her frown even deeper.

"We are not hiding," Eldon states, glancing back over his shoulder. "Raven needs all of us around her at all times. If that means we have to come up with some bullshit reasoning, then so be it." There's not a single ounce of doubt or question in his tone. He means every word, and hearing them solidifies my agreement.

At least I put an alternative offer out there.

"Besides, we're not unseen," Creed mutters from

behind, but I don't turn back. My gaze whips up and I see three people in the distance, one of whom is Sebastian.

My spine stiffens, my anger bubbling to the surface.

He may have helped Raven free us, but the promise she had to offer in response pisses me off.

To my surprise, he seems to lock eyes with each of us for a split second before settling on Raven. A look passes between them and he nods, as if confirming he held up his end of the bargain. Then he distracts the other two students with him and they continue in the direction they were heading.

We move the rest of the way in silence, Sebasitan's presence seemingly leaving us all to fester in our thoughts until we turn down the path to our home. The familiarity of it doesn't offer any sense of comfort, not that it ever truly did, but it feels even more foreign now.

Eldon unlocks the door and swings it open with a grunt but comes to a stop before stepping over the threshold. Tension heightens around us as we peer over his shoulder and understanding quickly takes over.

The place is trashed.

T-R-A-S-H-E-D.

I drop my arm from around Raven and step past Eldon to enter the lounge. The sofas are tipped, the coffee table is upended in the kitchen area, and the dining table and chairs are scattered across the garden with broken glass from the patio cascaded over them.

Someone seems to have had a good time at our expense.

"I'm going to assume you didn't leave it like this," I murmur, glancing over my shoulder to see everyone else stepping inside.

Brax and Raven can't even summon a response that reconfirms my thoughts.

"Shit," Raven gasps, hand flying to her chest as her eyes grow wider. My veins pulse with adrenaline, ready to act on whatever has her worked up. "The emerald gate," she chokes out, and Brax is bounding across the mess toward Creed's room before she can move.

The door slams against the wall as he whirls inside, but a moment later he's in the doorway shaking his head. "Gone."

"Would it still remain if…" My words trail off and Raven's jaw falls slack.

"It's likely gone, but do you think they could have found it?" she asks, and Creed steps up beside her shaking his head.

"It disappeared between us at the cave because it didn't feel safe. If someone was coming here with bad intentions, I don't believe the gate would have stayed here," he insists.

"Someone is going to pay for this," Brax bites, hands fisted at his sides.

There's a lot of shit that needs repaying at this stage,

and I'm more than eager to get started on that list.

"What do we do now?" Eldon asks, waving his hands around, and I take a deep breath, my mind, body, and soul settling on what's to come next.

"We tidy this place up, rest, eat, and prepare, because come tomorrow, mayhem begins."

TWENTY ONE

Raven

Every layer of my uniform feels heavier than the last, the weight of our future seemingly stitched into every tier. I can feel the buttons of my blouse against my chest, the hem of my skirt at my waist, and the padding of my blazer at my shoulders.

I know it's all in my head, but as we walk toward the main academy building, the five of us all together, it feels like it restricts every step I take. So much has happened here on campus. The good, the bad, the ugly. There's no shying away from it, but it hasn't brought me to my knees yet, so it's not starting now.

Brax is up front, no longer occupying the spot by my side now that the others have returned. Eldon is on my left, his arm slinked around my back, while Zane is to my right, my hand encased in his. Peering over my shoulder, I find

Creed, but his gaze isn't on me. He's alert and aware of everyone and everything around us.

The relief I feel at us being reunited feels tainted by the fact that we're back here, choosing to put ourselves in danger. I may question the decision for the rest of my life.

I didn't want Burton to bring his self-proclaimed war to the rest of the Elevin Realm in search of me. Especially with the remnants of our house last night, and that's just what he did here. I don't have the proof he was behind it, but my gut knows. Outside of the academy grounds, the mass destruction would have found undeserving casualties, just as he did with the civilians that lost their lives in Pinebrook. I refuse for that to be on my hands. That kind of bloodshed is unfathomable, and as much as I believe I'm not a hero in all of this, I'm certainly not going to willingly offer up innocent people to be sacrificed to him for no worthy reason at all.

Above all of that, the pain I have felt at the hands of this man is endless, and I want the satisfaction of bringing him down once and for all. I want the smell of copper in the air, the visual of his lifeless body sprawled at my feet. I want it all. I don't know what that makes me, but I don't care either.

I remind myself of that fact as we near the academy building, coming across larger groups of students who watch our every move. Conversations simmer down to a whisper, murmurs swirling around us about the three Bishops that have suddenly reappeared before them.

It feels odd not anticipating Genie's unwanted attention like we would usually get, but I can't say I miss it. My gaze searches for the uniforms among the masses that don't match ours and it doesn't take long for Ruben to step forward, flanked by a guy on either side of him.

Brax doesn't stop until he's standing toe to toe with him, looming over the assumed enemy by an extra couple of inches.

"Oh my gosh, Raven," Leila whisper-shouts, taking a few hurried steps toward us as she gapes at my men, relief flashing in her eyes. I shake my head subtly and she draws to a halt, Grave a step behind her.

His hand falls to her shoulder, surprise consuming his features along with many others around us, but it's not relief that resonates in his eyes. It's something else. Something I can't put my finger on, and that only intensifies my wariness of him.

Wetting my lips, I turn my attention back to Ruben to see a few more guys standing closer to him now, all dressed in the same uniform as they sneer at Brax. Eldon's arm drops from my side while Zane's hand flexes tighter around mine.

I half consider asking him to use his magic to turn us invisible so I don't have to deal with this shit, but there's no point in delaying the inevitable. Releasing Zane's hand, I take control of the situation.

"Are you going to get him or not?" I ask, cutting the remaining steps toward Brax, but instead of slowing to a stop, I brush past the Shadowgrim students with ease. "It would save me the time if you did," I add, glancing over my shoulder to see Ruben glaring at me. "We'll be in the courtyard."

I don't wait for a response, absorbing the sound of my shoes hitting the marble floor beneath my feet. Anger fills my thoughts as I consider whether it was Ruben and his asshole friends who ransacked our home and damaged our belongings. *Fuckers.* It took ages to reorganize everything last night, and that was *with* magic.

They'll have retribution to face if I find out it was.

By the end of the hallway, Creed has managed to outpace me, placing him a step in front while Zane and Eldon reappear at my sides. The opposite way around. The grumbles and heavy footsteps behind me confirm Brax is still with us too. He's probably not happy with me for disrupting his preferred formation with which he likes to protect me, but I won't falter under these fuckers. He knows that. Deep down, I know he trusts my judgment on it too, but that doesn't make it any easier for him to swallow.

Stepping into the courtyard, there are a few groups

huddled together waiting for classes to begin, but one snarl from Brax has everyone scampering without another word. I roll my eyes at their lack of backbone, but appreciate the empty courtyard at the same time.

The back of Zane's hand ghosts against mine, and as much as I want to reach for him and feel his warmth against my palm, I refrain. It's already clear to Burton, even in his Erikel fur cloak, that these men are my weakness; I don't need to offer him the reminder of it, too.

As if sensing my thoughts, hurried footsteps echo from the marbled hallway and a moment later, a sword-wielding golden warrior appears. He eyes us frantically, his pupils dilating just a smidge, but it's enough for me to notice. His gaze settles on Creed, eyeing him from head to toe before he tucks his sword into his sheath.

"Clear," he calls, and a second later, Fitch steps out with Burton behind him. It's weird to call him that when he looks every inch like Erikel. A wolf in sheep's clothing. But we'll call him what he is, even if that's not who he resembles right now.

The sneer over Burton's face accentuates the scar down his eye as he storms toward me with barely contained fury. His hand rests on the hilt of his sword at his waist, like he's tempted to use it, but before he can get within arm's reach, we all summon our swords, just as planned.

Weighted silver hangs from our grasp, the golden hilts shimmering enough to make his steps slow as he snarls in my direction. "You were called upon yesterday. Where were you?"

That's where we're going to start? I thought for sure it would be more around the three men that are now back at my side.

Shrugging, I keep my mouth shut, silently enjoying the irritation that brims in his dark eyes.

"Your lack of attendance hasn't gone unnoticed for the entirety of the day yesterday and half of the day before; consequences will come," he promises, and I roll my eyes before I can stop myself. His knuckles turn white as he grips the hilt at his waist tighter, but he still doesn't pull the weapon. "Are you going to tell me where you were, or are we going to have to interrogate you?" he snaps, turning his attention to Zane, Creed, and Eldon. He may seem done with me, but I know it won't last. That's the one and only certainty in this whole situation.

"You left us in the cave system," Zane replies, twirling the tip of his sword against the grass at his side.

"Don't lie to me, boy. We returned, and you were nowhere to be found," he sneers, clearly enjoying baring his teeth at us a little too much.

"Well, we obviously weren't going to stay there, and our magic doesn't allow for us to re-enter the academy, so we took shelter elsewhere," Eldon states, his tone bored as he sighs heavily.

"I had men search your homes. You. Weren't. There. So try again," he pushes, and I feel the anger thrum among Creed, Zane, and Eldon.

Rhys didn't mention that? Would he have told us, or would he have considered that something for him to worry about and not us? Fuck, I don't know. Either way, fucking with their families is not in his best interests, that much is clear.

"The closest home to the cave system was Brax's. We took refuge there," Creed bites, clearly feeling anger on behalf of his mother. We haven't had any contact with her, but if she's been left vulnerable at the hands of this man, my onyx-eyed love is not going to be happy.

Burton shakes his head, anger burning deeper from within him. "Of course, you'll tell me somewhere that no one can bear witness to you since his parents are dead." He spits the last word with purpose, aiming them like spears at Brax, who doesn't move an inch.

He knows differently, and we know differently now, which only makes it sweeter. This man is out of his depth. Minute by minute, hour by hour, nothing is going his way, and now he's floundering, leaving us with the opportunity to get the upper hand.

When it's clear he's not going to get the response he

wants from Brax, his glare turns back to me. "How did you reconnect?"

"The shadows."

His gaze narrows. "How?"

"I asked, and they showed me."

He dismisses my answer with a shake of his head. "That's not how it works."

"What would *you* know?" I ask, acutely aware that I'm the necromancer here, not him. I might not know what I'm doing with the shadows, but I surely know more than him.

"They always want something in return," he presses, taking a step toward me, and my hand tightens around my blade. I peer at Fitch over his shoulder for a second, still confused about how this man so openly stands at his side now.

"We didn't have negotiations." I sigh, shrugging, and Burton's sword whirls toward Eldon, the tip of his blade stopping mere inches from his face.

My spine stiffens, panic thrumming through my veins as I use all of my strength to remain still and not react too quickly.

"Did you bring back what belongs to me? What's rightfully mine?"

"I don't know what you're talking about," Eldon states, cocking a brow at him, which increases the fury radiating from him.

"Don't play dumb with me. The ruby. Give me the ruby!" he snaps, jabbing the blade an inch closer to Eldon's face, and I lift my own, aiming it in his direction.

"We. Don't. Have. It." The words burn my throat as my pulse pounds in my ears.

"Read her. I want the truth," he snaps, nodding in my direction, and the golden warrior inches toward me. He's remained silent this entire time, his gaze locked on his son, and I can't tell if it's relief he feels at having to read me instead of him, but I would take it this way every time.

I can block him. Ari taught me.

Exhaling, I build my walls up, letting the golden glove press against my temple as he tries to penetrate my thoughts. It's a gamble whether he's going to reveal my ability to shield him or not, but my instinct tells me he's desperate to separate his son from this mess. Most of that time has been getting him away from me, but reality clearly shows that's never going to happen.

At this moment, we're either his enemy or he's slowly becoming our ally. There's no in-between.

My gaze doesn't falter as I stare deep into his eyes, and a moment later he steps back, drawing his hand away as he turns to his leader.

"She's telling the truth."

Fuck.

I sag with relief inside. I had refused to consider what the alternative may have brought, unwilling to deal with any more possibilities, and now I don't have to.

"You're playing games you can't win," Burton promises, withdrawing his sword despite the murderous desire flickering in his eyes. "Getting on the wrong side of me puts you on the wrong side of the war."

"What war? The one you expect us to blindly follow you into when we want nothing to do with it?" I snap, eager to get the fuck out of here without injury, but the part of me that wants to continue to rile him up is prominent. "You may have coaxed some members of the academy to your side," I push, glancing back at Fitch again. "But I believed in Burton, in what he stood for. What did you do to him, huh? He would never leave the academy in such disarray. He gave us strength, fortified our alliances, and encouraged us with hope. None of what you have to offer puts the war in a good light for us. There's no gain for us, just for you."

Nausea swirls in my stomach as the words slip from my lips. I fucking know it's him underneath this façade, but he doesn't know that. I want him to think he's winning despite my desire to argue. Let him think he's got the upper hand, but it's only a matter of time before it's all going to come crumbling down.

The flash in his eyes confirms who he truly is, the sense of pride still cascading over him, and I have to bite back the smirk threatening to spread across my face.

Burton flicks the fur coat at his sides, turning away from us as he heads back toward Fitch. It's not until he's by the doorway that he turns back to us, determination shimmering in his eyes. "Burton was weak. The time has come for stronger and wiser leadership. You would do well to learn that, and learn it fast because the realms are changing around us." His lips purse for a second as he assesses me before the corner of his mouth tips up and my stomach sinks, bracing for whatever is about to come next. "You will fall in line, or all of your current leniences will be taken away."

It's not a threat; it's a promise.

"What the fuck does that mean?" I snap, nostrils flaring as I glare at him.

"I have a pretty little cage with your name on it ready and waiting. Give me one excuse to use it, just one. I dare you."

TWENTY TWO

Creed

The day passes in a blur, leaving me to feel as though we've never been away. It's crazy how that works. I was certain we may spend the rest of our lives lost to the Realm of Shadows, yet it feels more like Hell being back here.

We once sought solace from these guarded wards. I believed we would come to Silvercrest Academy to hone our magic and defeat the challenges all other students would face before finding our place in the Elevin Realm. As a soldier, maybe, I don't know, I hadn't really thought that far ahead. I wanted to walk in my father's footsteps with honor, but that's all tainted now.

We've had the pleasure of the Shadowgrim students following our every move all day, irritating the fuck out of me, and I'm ready to brawl. Maybe it would expel some of this energy I'm struggling to disperse.

My head is all over the place. I haven't been able to focus on a single thing all day. Nothing except the presence of my woman. I squeeze her hand instinctively, reconfirming she's right there, and she peers up at me with a smile reserved only for the four of us.

Nobody bothers us as we head down the pathway to our house while I bask in being at her side. Zane can take one for the team this time and trail behind. Not that I really gave him a choice, but I've missed Raven just as much as he has. To be fair, it's not a bad view, watching her sweet ass sway from side to side, but shit, feeling her palm against mine is something else entirely.

"Raven, wait up."

I stiffen at the sound of Leila calling out Raven's name, who comes to a stop, making Brax grunt. He's in his usual spot up front, turning with a huff and his arms folded over his chest. His glare deepens, and I know that she's not alone.

"Don't say a word," Brax rumbles under his breath, earning an eye roll from our woman.

"I know," she snips back before her friend rushes to a stop in front of her, Grave two steps behind her.

I want to pummel him into the ground. I don't know what for, we haven't figured out that part yet, but if Rhys is telling us not to trust him, it's for some pretty epic reason.

Only time will reveal the truth to us. The quicker, the better.

"Are you all okay?" Leila asks, her gaze flicking over each of us, but it lingers a hint longer on Eldon, Zane, and me. "I've been worried."

My eyes narrow at the added concern, but as much as her words make me want to scoff and call bullshit, her pupils only shimmer with worry. There's no double meaning there that I can detect, but I could be completely off base.

"They're fine. We're all doing okay," Raven answers for all of us, and Leila takes a step closer. That on its own is fine, but it means Grave inches closer too, and that instantly pisses me off.

"Are you sure?" Her eyes land back on mine, her eyebrows pinching. "Have I pissed you all off in some way since I last saw you? Because I'm definitely getting that vibe."

I sigh. I need this to be over, and I need Grave to be as far away from Raven as possible. "Unfortunately, we're stuck in our thoughts, Leila, sorting through shit that's taking its toll," I grunt, unable to keep the annoyance from my voice. "We need to find an end to this madness that has Raven locked under Erikel's sights. Anything you could have done to piss us off doesn't reach the same level as that. Sorry."

She gulps, nodding lightly as she takes a step back.

"I'm sorry," she murmurs, and any other time, I'm sure I may have cringed at my tone, but fuck if I give a shit right now.

"That's harsh, man," Grave states, slinging his arm around Leila, who leans into him. I don't respond to him. I can't. My thoughts and desire to question this fucker are too close to the tip of my tongue. So instead, I glare at him.

"Nobody asked you," Zane hollers from behind me, showing less control than me when it comes to this guy, but before anything can be said, Leila quickly waves her hand in surrender.

"No. No, it's fine. You're right. Is there anything I can do to help?"

Keep that fucker away from my woman. Thankfully it's only a thought and not blurting from my lips.

"No, but if there is, I'll ask," Raven promises, a smile on her face that doesn't quite meet her eyes as she flicks her stare to Grave's hand on Leila's shoulder.

"Okay. I chased you down to confirm there's a meeting tonight," Leila adds, taking a step back.

"Nightmares Guild?" Raven clarifies with a frown, and Leila nods. "Why now? It's been forever."

"I don't know. My contact with my father is minimal, but he managed to snap the words at me in passing earlier, and this is the first chance I've had to tell you," she explains, and Raven nods in understanding.

"Usual time?" Eldon confirms, and Leila nods again. "Thanks for the heads-up. We'll meet you there."

Without another word, he steers Raven away from her friend and continues down the pathway to our house. Brax keeps his strides long as he keeps upfront and my hand remains in hers as we leave Leila and Grave without a backward glance.

"None of that makes sense," I murmur when I'm sure we're far enough away.

"What?" Raven asks, peering up at me.

"That Fitch is suddenly happy for her to waltz around with Grave and not be under his thumb. Especially after the confrontation they seemed to have before Erikel summoned everyone to the cave system."

Raven sighs, lips twisting in thought. "Not much makes sense these days."

"Agreed. We're going to have to start wielding some extra special magic to piece this fucked up puzzle together because I sure as shit am confused with all of it," Zane states, remaining a step behind us, and I hum in agreement.

Eventually, some of this might make sense. I'd love for all of the information to fall into place, but I'd take just some at this stage too.

We remain in our thoughts as we turn down our path, a comfortable silence clinging to us until a glint of gold shimmers by our front door and my steps halt.

My breath hitches despite my best efforts to remain unaffected. I saw him earlier with Burton, playing the dutiful warrior he is, and the memories of when I last saw him came flooding back to me. I've tried to keep them tamped down, but it's harder than I had hoped.

Betrayal. That's all I see right now when I look at this man.

He had delved into my mind without my consent, taking information that wasn't for him to feed his fucking master. That call, that move from him, was the pinnacle that led us to the caves and me and my friends into the Realm of Shadows with no way back.

Does he regret it?

Does it hurt him to know the amount of pain he's caused?

Not just now, but all these years since he supposedly died.

He clears his throat as Raven and the guys shift on their feet. They surround me, waiting for me to decide how this will proceed.

"Father," I grunt before he can speak first, and his onyx eyes bore into mine for a beat before he finds his voice.

"We need to talk."

"I don't believe we do," I retort, and his gaze hardens.

"I'm not asking, Creed."

My teeth grind together with anger, but despite the fury

rising inside of me, I see the pleading in his eyes.

Fuck.

"Who knows that you're here?"

"No one." His response is quick, but not so quick that I can feel a lie. "You can check my mind if needed," he offers, and it irritates me even more.

It's on the tip of my tongue to throw some back-handed retort at him since he never gave me the chance to offer when the roles were reversed, but that's not what right now is about. Glancing at Raven, I notice the uncertainty in her eyes as she instantly sees the wavering inside of me. Rising up on her tiptoes, she presses her lips to my ear as she whispers.

Each word holds power and strength, and my eyes fall closed as I absorb each one of them. Each syllable resonates inside of me as I take action, doing as she says, only blinking my eyes open when I feel the walls in my mind are firmly in place.

I don't know who taught her this but thank fuck they did. Shit, I'm sure it's something I should have known since mind power is my thing, but classes haven't touched on the subject of warding our minds, and I've never figured it out for myself, either.

I can stand here and face this man without worrying he's going to get in my head.

He can't.

She takes a step back, slowly releasing my hand as I stand taller.

"I shouldn't be more than five minutes. If it gets to ten, come get me."

Locked in a stare-off with my father, I'm certain I've wasted the first five minutes already, neither one of us starting the much-needed conversation. But I'm standing here for him, not me. So if he wants to waste the entire time, then that's on him.

As if sensing the mental step back I'm about to take, he swipes a hand down his face. "I'm sorry."

His words hang heavily in the air, but he's going to have to be a little more precise than that, and we both know it.

"What for?"

His head dips, his eyes unable to remain fixed on mine.

"For taking your thoughts without your permission," he clarifies, and my eyebrows rise in surprise.

I wasn't expecting him to acknowledge that he fucked up. It's a start, I guess, but it doesn't fill me with the confidence I wish I felt when I look at my father. The man who had been such an important part of my life as a child.

"Why are you here?" I ask, not wanting to let myself get distracted by his presence like I have every other time he's spoken with me at the academy.

His gaze finds mine again and the despair is clear this time. "When you didn't come back with Raven and Brax…" His words trail off, unable to finish that thought, and I snicker.

"Did you think I was dead just like we assumed you have been all this time?" I bite, beyond infuriated with this man, and he shakes his head. I don't know whether it's with disappointment or disbelief, but I push on before he can voice his feelings, desperate to drive the nail home on his actions and the damage they caused. "I don't think you'll ever understand what you did to us, to mother and me, the pain and terror you left in your wake. And for what? What do you gain from this?" I'm eager to fucking know, but once again, he shakes his head.

"Nothing." He taps his armored foot on the ground, the noise grinding through my veins as my jaw falls slack.

"Nothing?" I call bullshit.

"I gain nothing from this. Nothing at all. I lost everything for you to gain an exemption from Erikel's wrath."

I stare at him, waiting for the lie to reveal itself, but all I see is heartache in his eyes. I'm not buying it, though. It's not possible.

"Bullshit. If that was the case, then why did he target me the night you arrived? Make me the one you had to kill unless the necromancer revealed themselves? Made *Raven* reveal herself," I snap, anger coiling tightly as my eyes narrow.

He shrugs, his movement subtle given the weight of the armor. "I don't know why he does what he does. I just follow orders. But in that instance, I think that was more of a power move over me, reminding me of the bargain I agreed to."

"And if she hadn't revealed herself?"

"I don't know."

"You don't know?" Unbelievable. "My death would have been on your hands. Then what would all of this have been for?"

He looks away, still unable to accept that whatever heroic move he thought he was making all those years ago, it didn't make a fucking difference because I was still a pawn in that man's games.

"What don't I know?" I ask, refusing to dwell any further on a situation that could have been, on all of the things that could have been different. Fuck knows we have enough of those.

"I don't know what you mean," he murmurs, brows furrowing.

"What makes you stay with him? What makes you stand before me as half the man I knew? What is it that has you still trying to help me if you're doing all of this for that purpose?" I know I'm throwing too many questions at him at once, but I can't stop it. The urgency to know is overwhelming.

"You're my son, Creed. I'm stuck in a lonely place doing what I believed to be the right thing to protect my family."

What the fuck does that have to do with anything?

"And you were my father, my hero, yet here we are," I bite, unable to keep the dejection from my voice as he looks down at the ground with an air of resentment. Not for me, but for himself. When he still doesn't answer, I take a step back, clenching my hands at my sides. "If you want to help me like you claim that you do, tell me something that will save us all from that man's damnation."

He straightens, eyes burning into mine again as he sighs. "He's not who you think he is. His connections run deep. There's no stopping him. I'll regret being by his side every day, but I will never regret believing I was saving you. Not a day has passed where I haven't thought of you and your mother, but with this…" He stops, pointing at the chest of his armor like it means something. "I'll forever be his weapon."

What the fuck does that mean? Could we have been right about him, his armor, when we had read through the parchments about magical objects? If that's what this falls down to, surely I can…

"Tell me how you get rid of it. Tell me how to—"

"How to what? Save me?" he interjects, a sad smile playing across his lips. "There is no saving me. When the time comes, I won't be able to stop, I have to follow his commands."

"What does that mean?" I ask, my voice hoarse as I see the pain in my father's eyes.

"It means that if there's a piece of information I can offer you that can stop him, it's this." I part my lips, ready to ask what he means, but he drives the words home before I get a chance. "The most valuable information I can offer you is how to kill me."

TWENTY THREE

Raven

Worry gnaws at me as I stand impatiently waiting for Creed to join us. It's almost been ten minutes, and I'm ready to act on his word the second it ticks past.

Zane was gifted with amazing parents. Well, father at least. I haven't met his mother, but Rhys is enough to make a decision. Eldon's mother has done nothing but be supportive, not only to her own child, but Brax too. Brax's family dynamic is even more complex, but now that we know they're not dead, they have done nothing but show up for all of us.

That leaves Creed and me.

Both with caring mothers who seem to have complex counterparts, and our fathers leave a lot to be desired. The reminder that Rhys had to leave us early the other day because my father has escaped their confines tightens my chest with concern, but I quickly push it aside. Creed's father is on the other side of the door, wearing his flaws, and as much as I sometimes see past the golden warrior to the father he is, it doesn't stick long enough for me to trust any of his actions.

Not that I would admit that to Creed. It's his father, and it has to be his call.

When my mother ran from my father and brother, condemning us to life in Shadowmoor, I didn't go under the illusion that my father was a hero, a god among men. I went remembering the stern look on his face, the bite in his words, and the pain that whatever happened was irreparable.

Creed didn't have that. He loved the man who raised him and idolized him in every way. All for it not to matter the moment he stepped through the doors of Silvercrest Academy in his golden armor.

"Why don't any of us have enhanced hearing?" I grouch, glancing at the time again.

Brax, Eldon, and Zane are all casually sitting around the dining table like this isn't a fucking mess while I'm one step away from pacing in front of the door. How the hell are they all so calm and collected?

"Why don't you get a glass and press it against the door, amplify their sound?" Zane asks with a grin, earning a laugh from Eldon.

Wetting my lips, I consider my options and decide it's worth a try. I don't even bother trying it the mundane way like I'm used to; instead, I use my magic to produce a slim glass in my hand.

"Fuck, Raven. I was joking," Zane says with a splutter, and I shrug, frowning down at the glass with uncertainty.

Would it be rude of me?

Suddenly, the door swings open and slams shut behind a storming Creed. His hands are balled into fists at his sides as his chest heaves with every breath.

I'll kill him. Whatever his father did to make him look like this, I'll kill him for it.

The glass almost topples out of my grasp, so I use my magic to make it disappear before I inch closer to him. The distress is evident on his face, from the tic of his jaw to the pinch around his eyes.

Twisting my fingers together, I force myself not to move any closer. "The need to ask you if everything is okay is overwhelming me, even though I can tell it's clearly not," I rasp, and he sighs, his gaze fixated on the floor.

"It's okay."

"It's not," I insist, my foot starting to tap on the wooden floor as I fight the urge to move.

"What did he say?" Eldon asks, cutting to the question that has me sinking my teeth into my tongue.

Creed runs his fingers through his hair, a heavy sigh

falling from his lips before he finally lifts his head. "Not enough? Too much?" He shakes his head, aware it makes even less sense to us than it does to him.

I just want to help him, and that means giving him what he needs and not what I want.

Fuck.

Clearing my throat, I force a smile to my face. "I feel like you want to hide away in your room and I'm stopping you."

Guilt swirls in his onyx eyes as his gaze meets mine. "You would be correct," he admits hoarsely, and as much as it's not what I want to hear, the fact that he's being truthful with me in this moment means everything.

"If you need space, I want to give that to you, even if it goes against my better judgment." I take an instinctive step forward, my fingers twitching to touch him, embrace him, and bask in his warmth while offering him mine.

He shakes his head. "No. The last time I did that, I was a dick and earned myself a face full of Brax's fist," he grumbles, earning a chuckle from the guys at the table.

I cringe at the memory, eager for it to not get to that stage again.

"It's whatever you need, Creed," I breathe, while defying my actual words and taking another step toward him.

"No, it's always what you need, Raven. That's how I

need it. That's what keeps me grounded."

His statement makes me frown, the words tightening my chest as I peer up at him. He's within arm's reach now, but I focus on keeping my hands at my sides.

"You can't lose yourself in me like that."

He scoffs. "Like you haven't done the exact same with us." His eyebrow rises in challenge, firmly putting me in my place and he knows it.

I pout despite the truth. Not liking him using it against me, but he has me there, and even I can admit to that.

The need to offer him something is on the verge of consuming me. The intense care I feel in my soul for them is unwavering, and I can barely breathe. It's in these moments with my men that I truly realize I'm a fixer. The undeniable desire that radiates through me to solve problems and make things better is glaringly obvious.

"She's right, Creed. We need you to handle this whichever way avoids you getting another beating," Zane states, the grin on his face noted in his voice. "If you need to be alone, say the word. If you need some Raven time to yourself, I'll begrudgingly agree to that too," he adds, and I note the smallest shift in Creed's shoulders as the tension eases just a smidge.

"Raven," he rasps, eyes fixed on mine, and I smile at him. Softly and genuine this time.

I feel like he's letting me in, past the final hurdle, and

despite the circumstances being terrible, it's one of the best feelings I've experienced.

The chairs scrape along the floor as the guys start to rise from the table, but Creed quickly shakes his head, darting his eyes at them. "Outside."

Zane, Eldon, and Brax pause, which kicks Creed into action. He reaches for my hand, tugging me to his side, and I lean into him as he heads for the patio doors. I can practically feel him vibrate with anger from his thoughts, but as we step outside into the late afternoon air, I sense another small shift in him.

The door closes behind us and he cuts across the grass until he's happy with the view it offers. The horizon settles in the distance. The sky sits awkwardly and heavy on the waterline, and I desperately wish to see the sun setting, bask in the feeling it gives me to watch something so natural and exquisite. But until Burton is dealt with, I don't think that's going to change.

Creed's hold on my hand tightens as he lowers to the ground, sitting on the grass with another heavy sigh, and I follow suit. I settle in beside him, looking over the shoreline where I know Ari and the other creatures are.

I can't hear him or talk to him, it seems, but I sense him there, in my soul. A warmth I've never felt from him before, and it fills me with a dose of hope I long to soak in forever.

Time passes us by, and with every minute, I feel another level of calmness wash over the man beside me. I don't want to overstep a line I can't see, but I want him to know I'm here in whatever capacity he needs me.

Turning to glance at him, I startle when I find his eyes already aimed in my direction. His lip curls, barely, but it's there, and I take that as my opening to speak.

"If you can't find the words but want me to know, you can always use…" I trail off, using my free hand to tap at my temple, and his brows furrow.

"I wouldn't do that to you."

"Even when I'm asking you to?" I push back, and his lips part. I think I may have finally stunned him into silence, even if only for a few moments.

When he doesn't protest, I take a chance, raising my hand that is enveloped in his and bringing it to my face. His hold loosens as I keep my eyes locked on his, slowly splaying his fingers to feel his palm press against my cheek.

My eyes flutter closed at the contact, and I feel his magic dance along mine in a heated caress. A moan slips from my lips despite my best efforts to contain it, and I hear him curse under his breath.

"You're not supposed to moan like that."

"I can't help it," I admit, unable to pry my eyes open. I feel like I'm panting. I've felt his magic before. I've felt *all* of their magic before, but there's just something in this moment that makes me weak to the touch.

"It's like I can feel you caressing me. It's hard to ignore," I explain, running my hand over his, and he takes a deep breath before my vision is filled with four onyx eyes. A replay of everything spoken between them filters into my mind, and when he's done, I'm left gasping at the revelation he ends with.

I don't know what to make of it, and when I finally manage to open my eyes, I can tell Creed feels the exact same way. Nothing about this is okay and we both know it. My lips part to ease his worry. With what words… I don't fucking know, but they quickly slam shut again when I realize he's in no position to analyze any of this.

I don't know how to help, how to take his pain away, but before I can figure out a way to verbalize any of that, he presses his palm firmer against my cheek, sending a stronger ripple of his magic over my body.

Holy fuck.

I shiver, the move involuntary and pointless when it does nothing to expel the thrum of magic flooding my veins. I gasp, lips parting as my eyes fall closed again. It's like he's dancing along the edge of my mind without actually playing with anything.

It's like he's riling up all of my nerve endings, and I'm lost to the feeling as another moan tumbles from my lips.

"Fuck, Raven."

"You're doing it on purpose," I murmur, panting with every word. I can't deny how much I like it.

"You're the most beautiful distraction sometimes. Especially when I'm supposed to be focused," he states, and as desperate as I am to see his face, wanting to read into his eyes, I can't pry mine open. It's too intoxicating.

"Sometimes a distraction is exactly what we need," I reply, my nipples pebbling beneath my uniform.

"You sound sure."

"I know from experience," I promise, unable to stop the sultry tone of my voice.

I'd tried to block out distracting myself like this, but that doesn't mean I can't offer it to him.

Whatever he needs. That's what I promised.

Grasping the locket around my neck, I let the essence of his magic run along my skin. Not long after we were all properly reunited and had fucked ourselves back together again, Brax had explained its purpose. One by one, the rest of the Bishops poured tendrils of their magic into my pendant, and I've never been more thankful for it.

I slip my hand from his, where he keeps it pressed against my cheek, and I return the motion, cupping his face as I let his magic dance between us.

"Fuck," he curses, his head falling back slightly with a groan.

I let the visions that consume me drift along his

thoughts. The touch of his fingertips running up my thigh, the press of his lips at my collarbone, the weight of him above me before he claims my core with his length. I give him everything, every ounce of desire as it plays out in my mind.

We're moving before I realize it, my back pressed against the blades of grass as I look up into deep, swirling eyes. A distraction is definitely what he needs, and I'm more than happy to be a part of it.

He uses one hand to hold both of my wrists, pinning them to the ground above my head. My back arches on instinct as I peer up at him, and in the next breath, every layer of clothing between us is gone.

A chill coats my skin, and I look down the length of our bodies, eyeing where his cock juts toward me, precariously close to my core. My necklace hangs between my breasts as his eyes feast upon me, his intention clear.

"It's hot when you use my magic on me, Raven," he mutters, his dark hair falling around his face as he inches closer to me.

My teeth sink into my bottom lip, trying to bite back the moan eager to echo around us.

"It's hot when you let me."

He presses a kiss to my jaw, slowly repeating the motion as he trails down my throat and over my collarbone, just like my vision had shown him.

"I could get lost in you forever," he murmurs against my skin, making me shiver as his fingers caress my taut nipples.

We should probably be cautious with the fact that we're outside, but I enjoy the thrill of it too much. Besides, I can't break this moment. It's palpable, and I want to ride it out to the very end.

"Do it. Lose yourself. Consume me," I whisper, and his onyx eyes cling to mine as he pauses.

No words pass between us, but whatever was holding us back is obliterated in that moment and all I'm left with is the carnal side of him.

His cock nudges at my pussy, which is already slick with desire, but he doesn't thrust inside me straight away. No. He teases me. The most purposeful tease I've ever felt before he slams inside of me without warning.

I cry out with pleasure as he fills me to the hilt, stretching me completely to mold perfectly around his length. Clinging to his shoulders, I hold on as his movements immediately turn feral. His grip shifts to my thighs, pinning me wide as he pounds into me with a strength and fury I've never felt from him before.

There's a sense of urgency, a need to fuck it all away while never wanting it to stop.

My skin is electric, the friction between my thighs leaving me gasping for air until he stops suddenly and spins so my knees fall on either side of his waist.

Blinking at him, it takes me a second to reorient. I relax my hands on his shoulders, acutely aware of the marks from my nails that remain in his skin, but if he notices, he doesn't show it.

"Fuck me, Raven. Take it all away." He leans back, bracing his weight on his palms as he tilts his hips up, rocking his cock deeper into my core, and my head lulls back with ecstasy.

Digging my knees into the ground, I flex my hips, testing the movement as his jaw ticks and his fingers grip the blades of grass. Giving up control isn't something that comes naturally to him, but I can promise to make it worth his while.

I slip my hand to his face, running my thumb over his bottom lip as I rise higher on my knees this time, slamming back down on his cock with more purpose, and he groans. I repeat the motion again and again, watching in delight as his eyelids fall to half-mast and he loses himself between us. I let myself do the same, eager to bring him the heavy dose of euphoria he deserves.

My clit grinds perfectly against him with the angle of my moves, and I trail my hands down his abs, watching his muscles flex beneath my touch. On my trail back up, my hand ghosts over the locket and I feel a zap of Eldon's magic against my skin.

Fuck.

Wetting my lips, I let the burning impulse take flight inside of me. My magic intertwines with Eldon's, shimmering heat through my veins, but it quickly travels to my core and Creed groans.

"Fuck, Raven. Fuck," he grunts, flexing his hips to meet my movement, eager to feel more.

I grin with triumph, raw need taking over as the heat continues to rise but stops before it becomes unbearable.

He leans forward, grabbing at my thighs as he takes control of each slam of my pussy on his cock, chasing the high that dances between us.

"Give it to me, Raven. Come for me. Come for me now," he bites, his nose brushing mine, and like the desperate and eager bitch I am, I detonate around him, his words sending me over the edge without care.

We're moving again, his cock still inside me as I ride out every wave of my orgasm. My back hits the grass as his hand presses against the side of my face, holding me in place as he fucks me with a ferocity I didn't think was possible.

I know the moment he comes, and even though I can feel him pulse between my legs, it's the almighty roar that burns from his lungs that confirms it.

His hold on me slackens, but the punishing thrusts of his cock take longer to wane. I blink up at him, aware of the dirt pressed against the side of my face from his hold, and I grin. The uncertainty and doubt in his eyes are immediate, and I shake my head, desperate to dispel it.

"Thank you," I croak, not sure which part I'm most thankful for. The fact that he was open with me, the fact that he shared, or the fact that he used me just as I had imagined. All of it. I'm thankful for all of it in equal measure.

His thumb strokes over my cheek, his eyes swirling with words he doesn't know how to process, but they're left unspoken when a voice sounds from behind us.

"That was great and all, but we're going to be late for the meeting."

TWENTY FOUR

Raven

My fingers are intertwined with Creed's, his scent still enveloping me as we take the steps leading down to where the rest of the Nightmares Guild gathers. I would have rather stayed at the house, continuing to get lost in my men, but it seems there are more pressing matters than stacking up my orgasms for the day.

I can't seem to shake the unnerving sense of dread that clings to me. There haven't been any meetings called since Erikel pulled us all out to the cave system at Ashdale, and now, all of a sudden, the guys come back and they're summoning us to meet.

Brax leads the way, his frame seeming wider than usual as he trudges down the stairs, making the few lingering people hurry out of his way. Zane and Eldon keep a step behind us in the narrow hallway until we enter the open space, the golden table a beacon in the center of the room.

Does it hold any more truths that are yet to be told?

Maybe we should consider sneaking back in here again when no one else is around. Maybe I should make it come to life with everyone in here so they all know what we know, too. But that would just reveal the upper hand we have, and I'm not ready for Burton to be clued in yet.

I spot Leila immediately, looking up at Grave with a softness reserved for someone you have feelings for, and my gut clenches. She's either blissfully unaware of the dangers that lurk with that guy, or she loves him despite it all. I'm praying it's not the latter because I really don't want to add her to my growing list of enemies. I need to learn the truth before I pass judgment again. She doesn't deserve that. Not if she's completely unaware of what she's tangled up in.

"We need to keep our distance," Brax grumbles, slowing to a stop before reaching Leila. I see the crinkle around her eyes, confusion getting the better of her.

Shaking my head, I tighten my hold on Creed's hand and continue past the grumpy gargoyle, but not without murmuring to him first. "We also need to make sure we don't act so obvious about it."

He grunts, but a second later his back is in front of me, coming to a stop closer to my friend, but he doesn't acknowledge either of them.

I fight back the eye roll, aware his intentions are good, but his execution leaves a lot to be desired.

"Hey, you guys okay?" Leila asks, and I nod.

"Yeah, you?"

"I'm okay," she breathes, a softness to her eyes that only solidifies to me that she's as pure as she was the day I met her.

We fall into a comfortable silence as the crowd grows around us, and I listen in on their conversations, intrigued to note that they seem just as suspicious and confused as I do.

"Why are we even here? All our missions and tasks drew to a halt the day Erikel arrived. We were supposed to stand for something more, yet we're being led to follow under the enemy's orders. Where's the rebellion in that? Where's the burning need and fight to take on the dangers that threaten our realm?"

I peer at the guy, trying not to draw attention to the fact that he has piqued my interest, and I notice it's one of the fourth years.

"I know what you mean. What use has Burton been? I was almost certain he had found a way out for himself and left the rest of us to rot," his friend retorts. "Especially since Fitch is hanging off Erikel's every word," he adds, and my gaze shifts to Leila, but she seems lost in a quiet conversation with Grave.

As I turn back to the fourth year, the room falls quiet, and the source of that becomes clear a second later when Burton appears. I feel like it's been forever since I've seen him. Technically, I saw him earlier, but not in this skin.

It's strange to say, to believe the extent of the magic some people wield, but I know it to be true. I've seen it with my own eyes. I'm sure if I called him out for it, right here and now, the gathered crowd wouldn't believe me so easily.

His eyes are tired, his jaw tight, and his gaze lingering in my direction for a brief moment before he comes to a stop, leaning back on the golden table with a sigh as he intertwines his fingers in his lap.

I get the sense he's gathering his thoughts, considering where to start or pausing for a sense of sympathy, but before he can compose himself enough to speak, questions are fired in his direction.

"Where have you been?"

I'm not surprised it's the fourth year from earlier; I'm more impressed that he has the balls to call him out to his face.

Burton's jaw tightens as he glares at the guy. "Trying to find any kind of information that may aid us," he snaps, sitting taller as if to stoke fear into his audience, but it falls a little flat.

It seems we're not the only ones bored of his bullshit.

"Aid us in what?" The question comes from the fourth-year's friend, who folds his arms over his chest and quirks a brow in question. "We've been left vulnerable at their hands," he adds, refusing to falter under Burton's growing death stare.

"Do you want to run this academy? Do you want to run this guild? Do you want to consider all of the pieces of this situation that must be balanced to ensure the safety of not just us, not just the remaining students here at Silvercrest, but the entire Elevin Realm?" Burton vibrates with rage and I spot a few students taking a step back, lowering their heads and falling under his control just as he hoped we would.

"We're doing nothing," the guy continues to push, not backing down, and my admiration for this stranger is only growing.

"We're doing all we can. There are many layers at play here. We have to bide our time, wait out the storm," Burton snaps, although it's clear he's trying to hold back the burning anger from moments ago.

"What storm?"

"What is it Erikel wants?"

Both of the fourth years buzz him for more answers at the same time, and it takes everything in me to keep a smile from my face. Burton, however, isn't pleased. His eyes turn toward me, ignoring both of them as he sneers.

"Why don't we just give it to him? He'll leave as soon as you do, surely." My heart stutters as I feel every set of eyes in the room turn my way. "I think our necromancer knows what he wants, and she's unwilling to hand it over."

Is this for real right now? Surely not.

Clearing my throat, I feel Brax, Zane, and Eldon take a protective step closer to me while Creed's hold on my hand tightens. "I don't know what you're talking about."

"Erikel believes you know where the Potens Ruby is. Does he not?"

"I don't know where it is," I retort, keeping my voice even, and I'm technically not lying either.

I know who last had possession of it, but I specifically made a point of none of us knowing where it would be stored or destroyed so that we wouldn't find ourselves backed into a corner. I'm aware magic like Lyra's is possible. We couldn't reveal a truth against our will if we didn't know where it was.

"Are you sure?" he presses, coiling my muscles tight with frustration.

Is this why he called a meeting? So he can try and gain the information from me as himself instead of the second skin of Erikel he has taken on? Joke's on him, but it's good to know he isn't aware we know his secret.

He's going to be sorely disappointed if he thinks he's going to break me today. That's not how this is going to go. But the few glares I feel aimed in my direction confirm that he may have other students pitting against me if they believe his words.

Fuck.

"If you have the ruby, just hand it over," someone hollers, but I don't manage to see who.

Still, I sigh, refraining from showing my irritation with any other movement.

"I don't have it," I repeat. "I don't know where it is. But you're right; if I did, I wouldn't give it to him. Too much power in the wrong hands is a dangerous thing. I think that's clear to everyone."

Magic tingles across my skin and the need to protect myself is growing, but I'm not going to deny the facts. Burton frowns at me, tongue sweeping over his teeth. My magic is eager to narrow down a target on his head. Recalling what happened to Genie, it's eager to sink its claws into him in the exact same way.

If I was one thousand percent certain that it would bring a definitive end to this mess, I would do it in a heartbeat. But we have to be sure first. I don't care if my moves may make me look like the bad guy here. I'll do whatever is necessary.

"What is Erikel's plan, anyway? Handing things over to a madman doesn't sound like the logical answer," Leila blurts out, and Burton's stare turns her way.

"Yeah. That's true. We don't even know what the meaning of all this is," the fourth year adds, nodding in agreement.

Burton glances around the room, folding his arms over his chest as he speaks. "Vengeance."

One word. Two syllables. Yet the weight of a thousand.

"Vengeance? Why?" Someone from the crowd calls out, and Burton sighs in frustration.

"Because…" He stops, mouth open as he gapes at me. His hands fall to fists at his sides as he shakes his head dismissively. Clearly, whatever he was going to say wouldn't have played into his hands right now. Whatever he was about to say may have led us to believe he's closer to Erikel than anyone else is aware of.

Watching him slip up would have been spectacular.

Maybe if we keep pissing him off, it just might happen.

Burton straightens the lapels of his suit jacket and addresses the entire gathering. "If we don't hand over the ruby, we'll be forced into battle."

Nice transition back to pinpointing this on me. Asshole.

"If he gets the ruby, we will be forced to fight then too. Regardless, we're being left bending the knee to his will," I bite, and Burton bares his teeth for the briefest second before gaining control of himself.

"Are you going to summon us all to our deaths?"

This fucking man. He's rocked up here without caring

about anything but his own intentions. One slip and his layers of secrecy and betrayal will all come tumbling down.

"This isn't on me. It's on Erikel. I can say it until I'm blue in the face but it doesn't stop the fact that you're not hearing me. I don't have it. I don't want it. And I don't know where it is. If that's the only thing saving us all, then give us a mission, set us a task, and we will perform for the safety and security of our academy and the realm."

My words are firm, and my attempt to redirect the situation back to him is pretty successful, but he still inches toward me.

He's either going to back off or expose himself, and I'm willing to watch either unravel before my eyes.

"Does nobody else find it strange that Genie was found dead in the caves, exactly where the ruby was believed to be? Her magic no longer lingered, and she couldn't be saved from the darkness. That's something only the ruby can do. Someone must have it, someone with fury aimed in Genie's direction, wouldn't you agree?"

My teeth grind together in anger, but I manage to keep my face neutral as I shrug. "I don't know anything about that."

Did I kill her? Yes. Did I take her magic? Yes. Did I use the ruby? No. And I don't want him to know what I'm capable of either, so he isn't going to find out right now.

Hurried footsteps stumble into the room, drawing

everyone's attention to the hallway where Professor Fitch steps in.

"And why is this guy hanging off Erikel's every word all of a sudden?" the fourth year bellows, aiming his finger at the new arrival. This time, I have to lift my hand to cover my grin.

"How do you think I'm getting the information," Burton snaps back, his face reddening.

He looks crazier than ever, completely unhinged.

A total madman, not the smooth, polished leader he was before. I'm not even sure how or why any of us are listening to him.

Fitch doesn't pay the comment any mind, not even glancing in Leila's direction as he leans in to murmur in Burton's ear. He stands abruptly as Fitch takes a step back.

"This meeting is dismissed. Think about what I've said." His eyes land on mine.

All he's actually said is that I have to hand the ruby over, and I really don't fucking have it.

Muttered annoyance echoes around the room as everyone shuffles toward the hallway. I hang back a step, hoping to catch any glimpse of information, but there's no luck. Reluctantly, I take Creed's tug on my hand and fall into step with him, surrounded by the rest of my Bishops as we go.

My steps falter when I make it to the bottom of the

staircase, watching as my brother trudges down the steps with an unwavering aura of fear oozing from him.

His eyes lock on mine, pinning me in place as he mouths one word to me.

Now.

TWENTY FIVE

Raven

My heart stutters as the word continues to revolve in my head.

Now.

Now.

Now.

Fuck.

My fingers tremble, my breaths coming in short, sharp bursts as I gawk at my guys.

Brax glares at the spot where Sebastian passed us moments ago while Eldon frowns, uncertainty flitting through his eyes. Creed stands with his hands in his pockets and an impassive look on his face, which is the stark opposite of Zane's slack jaw and wide eyes as he glances back to the room we just left. The room Sebastian just entered. The room where he believes he's about to meet his death.

There's no time to wait, no time to consider my next move. I already know it.

I made a deal, an agreement, a promise.

Fixing my gaze on Zane's, I exhale slowly. "Hide us. Please."

I know I could do it myself, grab the locket still hanging around my neck and make myself invisible, but I'm still learning how to use the magic Zane gifted me. His abilities are more honed, practiced, and better executed. I don't feel like being caught because of mistakes this evening.

He schools his features, his jaw setting in a hard line as he looks deep into my eyes. Uncertainty swarms inside of me, worry mounting more and more with each passing second that he's going to decline my plea, but to my relief, he reaches for my hand before I can work myself up to a full meltdown.

His touch is warm against my palm, fueling me with determination as each of my men holds on to Zane or me to join us. I can tell by the flare of Brax's nostrils that he's not happy about it, but he's with me no matter what. They all are.

Eldon is the closest to the drama we're expecting to unfold, so he leads us with slow, precise steps. Thankfully, no one is around us, since we were the last to leave, and as we step back into the room, it's only the three of them.

Sebastian, Professor Fitch, and Burton, only now, he's dressed as Erikel.

My gut clenches as we keep to the edge of the room, watching as Erikel shakes out the fur cloak around him. He glares at Sebastian, who stands before him with his head bowed. Professor Fitch hovers at his side, tongue swiping over his teeth as he assesses my brother.

"You know why you're here," Erikel/Burton states, distaste clear in his voice. The sneer that curls his top lip only reinforces it.

"I do?" Sebastian questions, peering up through his lashes.

"You do," Fitch bites, hands balling into fists at his side. "And the price for your punishment is going to cost you more than lashings this time." A grin flashes across his face, revealing the excitement he's taking from the scenario.

Sick fuck.

This isn't the man I first met when I arrived at Silvercrest Academy, the father who worried over his daughter and moved with an air of honor. None of the men before me are the same as they were then.

Those I thought I could trust are now at the polar opposite end of the spectrum. They're my enemy, the other end of the war that's coming. And the guy I swore was my nemesis is… fuck, I still don't know what he is.

Despite how I feel about my brother, one thing is certain: he's here because of the information he gave us. He knows it, I know it. If our agreement is anything to go by, he knew helping me would come to this, so why help at all? It doesn't seem to fit the character I've become accustomed to, but I don't truly know him; that's the reality.

"Where is it?" Burton bites, the telltale scar down his face standing out more prominently with the growing anger emitting from him.

"Where's what?" Sebastian's snark and clear attempt at playing dumb only fuels Burton's rising temper.

"Don't play dumb with me, boy. The binder! Where is it?"

Before Sebastian can form a thought, let alone an answer, Fitch steps forward and backhands him across the face, the sound reverberating around the room. Sebastian falls to his knees, a low hiss slipping from his lips, but otherwise, he remains unaffected.

"Such a willing puppet," Burton muses, trailing around Sebastian, his cloak dragging along the floor with every measured step. "It's a shame your sister doesn't fall so easily."

I stiffen at the mention of me, as do my men beside me. Anger tingles among us but we focus on keeping our emotions in check. Sebastian hangs his head, not willing to respond, and I can't tell whether the comparison pisses him off or embarrasses him.

"Is that where you took the binder? Did you give her the information she needed to shatter the Realm of Shadows?" Burton asks as he pauses, looking at Fitch for a moment as they silently communicate with one another.

"I don't know what you're talking about," Sebastian repeats, but it does nothing to convince Burton.

"You don't think I can feel the shift in the realm? I can tell something has changed, and I know I didn't do it. Offering your help to her is too little too late after everything you've done, don't you think?" Burton's jibes are greeted with silence, which seems to bring him joy. He crouches beside Sebastian, a wicked grin tilting his lips. "You're alone, boy. Alone with a scrambled mind, just like your father. You were easy to manipulate. Not as easy as him, but still, Abel was always a fool. Too loving, too caring, too giving. I put a stop to that."

My chest tightens at the admission falling effortlessly from Burton's lips, while the actual words he uses to describe the man I call my father confuse me. Loving, caring, giving? My father? I think not.

I don't remember anything but a dismissive man who was hard and cold toward his family. The stormy night I left with my mother will forever be etched into my mind. Not a single hint of care, love, or selflessness present.

Zane squeezes my hand and I turn to glance at him.

I can sense his need to make sure I'm okay, so I offer a simple nod, trying to focus on anything else these fuckers might reveal.

Burton stands, swiping a hand down his face before he comes to a stop in front of Sebastian again. "The second I learned what powers your sister could wield, the fear your father had, the good he wanted for her, I laid all that to rest before he even left my presence. I've bided my time, waited, and now everything is mine except the ruby and the necromancer under my thumb."

What does he mean by "the good he wanted for her"? For me? What good could have come my way?

"You're boring me with talk of a girl I don't care for and a time I don't recall. Why don't you just kill me already?" Sebastian grumbles, and to my surprise, his words don't cut me in any way. I can see them for what they are—a deflection.

It earns him another strike from Fitch, a fist to the nose, and I hear the telltale sound of bone crunching from the force. He manages to catch himself on his palms, avoiding face planting on the floor as he falls sideways, and the urge to reach out to him heightens.

Fuck.

Clearly, I'm soft as hell. Softer than I care to admit, and I don't like that quality in myself right now.

Burton throws his head back with a haunting laugh,

bracing his hands on his hips as he speaks down to Sebastian. "I want an audience, someone to hear my greatness before I send you to your death." This man is delusional. Completely and undeniably. "Don't you wonder what all this is for?" he pushes, throwing his arms out wide. "Especially since you seem to be able to deflect my powers all of a sudden," he hisses, that tidbit of information causing him more rage.

"You're a crazed man with a vision no one but you understands. Trying would only be a waste of my time," Sebastian states, and Burton swoops in, gripping my brother's chin as he forces him to look up into his deathly stare.

"I *will* get vengeance for my wife, for my daughter, and I will rule as I always deserved to rule. Every realm will be mine, every civilian my soldier. I will be undefeatable, undeniable. *I* will be victorious," he snarls, his voice gravelly. "The realms are already merging, and I didn't have to move a hand to do it. I will rule, I will lead, I will conquer. And *you*... you will rot in Hell as I do so. Your insignificant role in my plan is no longer worth the trouble you cause."

Burton bares his teeth with a sneer before lifting his free hand to Sebastian's throat, and in one swift move, he snaps his neck.

TWENTY SIX

Raven

Despite how much I thought I was prepared for this moment, I was truly mistaken. My hand claps over my mouth as my teeth sink into my tongue, reining back my gasp.

I've seen death, even before I came to Silvercrest Academy—it was everywhere in Shadowmoor—but this somehow feels different. Sure, he's my brother, my blood, but he's an asshole; yet he still matters.

Sure, I can't forgive the shit he's put me through, but the ability to stand back and watch him collapse to the floor in a heap of limbs proves far more difficult than I initially anticipated.

One of my guys squeezes my shoulder in an attempt to comfort me, but it does little to quell the nausea swarming in my gut and the panic rising in my chest. I can't turn to see who it is, either. My gaze is locked on the three men, desperate for an opening to heal Sebastian like I promised.

I have to help him. I know I do. My magic thrums through my veins so strongly that even if I were unwilling, it would still force me to my knees to aid him. My magic and I are one, but sometimes it almost feels like it has its own mind and it's different to mine. It's like a compulsion to heal others, to activate to save lives. It sounds dumb, but at this moment, I know we are aligned.

Burton moves first, sweeping the fur cloak dramatically as he takes a step back from Sebastian's lifeless body. "Come, Fitch. We have much to prepare. Everything has been approved from inside The Monarchy. We're moving faster now. With or without the ruby, we can't stop all that is in motion."

"The body?" Fitch asks, casting an inconvenienced glance Sebastian's way, and my blood boils.

"Send for one of the Institute boys to get rid of him," Burton orders with a wave of his hand, effectively dismissing the mess he's made as he heads to the stairway without a backward glance.

Fitch follows after him like the well-trained puppet he is, but I don't immediately move when they're out of sight. It takes everything inside of me to fight against my magic, which pleads for me to move now, but even if I did relent, the hand on my shoulder tightens as if sensing the battle inside of me.

"We have to think this through before we move from here," Creed states, his voice barely more than a whisper. When I turn to glance at him, I find it's his hand on my shoulder.

"I need to heal him," I grind out, my chest tightening with every second I remain in place. My magic has a different plan altogether.

"I know, and you will, but are you doing it here, or are we going to move to a more secure location before someone from Shadowgrim Institute arrives to get rid of him?"

Fuck. He does have a point.

Swiping my free hand down my face, I sigh, trying to ground myself so I can think clearly, but the magic pulsing through my body makes it more difficult than usual.

"We should move him," Eldon recommends, giving me a soft smile as Brax nods, and their willingness to help me aid him calms the storm brewing in my chest.

Maybe one of my worries was that one or more of the Bishops would intercept what I needed to do, and hearing them confirm the opposite allows my magic to settle. Not much, but enough to think a little clearer.

"Where?" Zane asks, straightening his shoulders as

his brows crinkle.

"Are you okay? If you need to drop your magic, you—"

"I'm good. For now. Once we're outside, the fresh air might help me too," he explains with a tight smile, and I know he's pushing himself. For me. Again.

Maybe if I could use my mirror magic to conceal myself, that may help. Although, taking directly from him will only drain him the same.

My lips twist, indecision rippling through me, but the pointed stare he gives me confirms there's no room for me to argue. I reach for the pendant around my neck, holding it tight and focusing on his magic concealed in there before releasing our connection. Taking a deep breath, I let my concern simmer down as I feel the magic drift over me. I don't move away from the group, eager to stay close in case something goes wrong, and when it doesn't immediately go to shit, I turn my attention back to the dead body that requires my assistance.

"You're a goddamn menace, Dove," he rasps, and I bite back the pleased smile on my face.

"Let's head to the Gauntlet." The second I say it, I'm certain it's the right place to go.

The Bishops must agree with me because no one argues as we move as one toward Sebastian.

Coming to a stop before him, my knees buckle, the

need to fall at his side and get to work overwhelming, but my men manage to keep me up without a word needed between us.

"I think I can use my telekinesis to hold him off the ground while projecting my invisibility through the connection," Zane starts, and Brax grunts, cutting him off.

"Or I can just carry the fucker."

My eyebrows rise at his offer, but before I can say a word, he swoops Sebastian over his shoulder with one hand while the other holds onto Zane to allow him to remain invisible.

"Can we trust you with him?" Eldon asks, quirking a brow at his friend. Under any other circumstance, I may have chuckled at the question and the entire scenario, but right now, the clock is ticking and we need to move as fast as possible.

"He's almost irrelevant when he's dead. It's a shame Raven's going to bring him back and piss me the fuck off, but I pledged an oath. Here's me following through on that."

I gulp, his words growing softer and more weighted as he speaks.

Nodding, I can't find the words to show my appreciation, but Brax turns away anyway, not needing the recognition. He starts to move, each one of us remaining connected as we shuffle as quickly as we can toward the exit. The stairs take longer than usual with our measured steps, but we have to remain pressed against the wall and out of the way in case someone appears.

I don't know whether we're lucky or destined to make it out of here unscathed, but as we step out into the night air, we manage to miss any obstacles. Once we're through the treeline, with a clear view of the Gauntlet, Brax releases his hold on the group, letting Zane's magic wash off him as he marches toward the looming building ahead.

Glancing at Zane, I see the relief in his eyes, although the flash of worry at us being exposed is still prominent. It's worth the risk, though. He needs to rest, and since we can't head back to the house to recharge, this will have to suffice.

The rest of us follow suit, releasing Zane from the need to shield us all with his ability, and his footsteps instantly quicken as he directs his energy elsewhere.

As we reach the top of the Gauntlet, the cool air and stone steps come into view and I exhale slowly, eager to get to the center of the arena at the bottom so I can finally get to work.

"In here or through the gateway?" Brax asks, marching down the steps two at a time, and I race to be at his side.

"Through the gateway."

The farther away from the academy we can get, the better. The compound isn't nearly as far enough away as I would like, but for now, it will have to suffice.

Brax moves through the gateway without a backward glance, and if he hadn't just reminded me of his pledged oath and promise to help me, I would be worried he was up to no good, but the moment I follow him, I find my gargoyle laying my brother down on the grass.

Gently? No.

Carefully? Definitely not.

Disregarding? Absolutely.

I don't argue or complain as I finally get the relief of dropping to my knees beside Sebastian's graying body. I sense Creed, Zane, and Eldon around me, making me feel whole, but I don't turn to look at them as my magic takes over.

A chill runs down my spine, stiffening my bones as my hand presses against his chest. The need to touch someone while healing them has never crossed my mind before, but for some reason, with Sebastian, I can't help it.

Darkness seeps into my veins, twisting and coiling with precision as I clench every muscle in my body, fighting against the pain that threatens to crush me in its grasp. My eyes flutter beneath my eyelids as my magic focuses on my brother.

The longing for warmth, brightness, and joy pounds through me, unrelenting as I feel my magic wash over him. Panic starts to kick in when I continue searching for him, leaving me certain that I waited too long.

A frustrated groan escapes from my lips at the same time and I feel the softest caress of warmth run up my arms. My head lolls forward, my mouth falling open as I let the feeling rush through me. It feels like I'm held in a warm embrace, the sun shining down on me on a late afternoon as butterflies dance in the sky around me.

It's overwhelming, a complete contrast to where I was moments ago, and it's all quickly taken away from me again as I blink my eyes open to look down at Sebastian.

My chest rises and falls rapidly as I stare at him, fingers tingling from where they rest against his academy-issued uniform. With my pulse ringing in my ears, doubt starts to take over when nothing instantly changes.

Don't do this. Don't do this to me. Don't make me break my promise. My word is everything, even to assholes I don't trust.

"You can get off me now." The rasp of Sebastian's voice startles me and I'm quick to retract my hands as Brax grunts from my side. I don't need to look at my grumpy gargoyle to know he's already regretting bringing my brother back.

"Are you okay, Dove?" Zane asks, crouching beside

me as he soothes a hand down my back, and I nod.

"I'm okay. It felt harder than before but I don't know why," I admit, tucking a loose tendril of hair behind my ear.

"That would explain it," Eldon mutters, making me frown.

"Explain what?"

He clears his throat, glancing at the others as the growing uncertainty inside of me makes itself known. "Your hair is completely black."

Completely black? Fuck.

Bye-bye pink and girly, hello dark and dangerous.

"Where are we?" Sebastian asks, and I compartmentalize my hair to address it at a different time. He sits upright and my heart calms, seeing him in front of me once more. It's a pity he pisses me off the second he opens his mouth, but that's never going to change.

"We're still on campus, but it's not shielded by the wards here," I explain, glancing around the tall, thick tree line and lush green shrubs.

It doesn't seem to hold the same magic and wonder as it did the first time I came here to speak with Gia. So much more has happened since then, and their absence is truly noticeable now. Gone is the whimsical sense of adventure, and in its place remain plants and trees that are no longer filled with life.

The ground is scattered with brown, crunchy leaves, twigs, and branches falling around us. Even the lush green shrubs that first caught my attention seem darker and dimmer the more I look.

"Lyra," Sebastian croaks, pulling my attention back to him, and my eyes widen. Before I can try to understand what he's asking for, he continues, "He's going to know it was her that aided me in being able to see through his magic."

Fuck.

I don't know what I'm supposed to say or do, but Lyra has helped me too. She can't die at the hands of the enemy. I refuse.

Settling my gaze on my brother, I open my mouth to speak, but he cuts me off before I get a chance. "I can't leave without her. I promised. You have to help me."

"She doesn't have to do shit," Brax grunts, folding his arms over his chest as he looms over my brother. I can sense the desire to step between us if needed, but I shake my head gently as I look up at him. "Your deal was to bring him back from the dead. Nothing more," he states, giving me a pointed look.

"Raven, please," Sebastian rasps, ignoring Brax's truthful statement.

"You realize it makes no sense for her to continue to help you after everything you've done," Creed adds, and my eyes fall closed.

My magic battles inside me, reconfirming the worry from earlier. I have to follow my own heart and mind, not those of others. Even if they are my men, the missing pieces of my heart and soul—pieces I never would have imagined having the luxury of—I have to make this decision for myself.

"I'm not asking for forgiveness, Raven. I'm not even asking you to do this for me," Sebastian pleads, emotion clogging his voice as his words thicken. "I'm asking you to help an innocent person who has clearly helped when you needed them to," he pushes, stating the thoughts that were running in my mind.

I open my eyes. There's no point in shielding myself from the world I already know I can't hide from. I know my answer, whether I like it or not. Hiding from the moment is only delaying the inevitable.

"Where can I find her?"

Sebastian's shoulders sag with relief as my men remain quiet around us. Slowly, he shakes his head, swiping a hand down his face. "You won't be able to reach her until morning."

"I could find her now," I retort, not wanting to drag the situation out any longer than necessary. Waiting until morning only gives Burton more time to act.

"The professors' quarters are impossible to access.

You won't be able to get there. If you're willing to help, it will have to be in the morning, just like the other day when she helped you."

I pinch the bridge of my nose, exhaustion threatening to claim me as the mess around us continues to grow. I haven't forgotten the words Burton stated earlier, either. Whoever he's working with in The Monarchy is allowing them access to push forward with their plans.

That's another hurdle we're going to have to face sooner rather than later, but maybe for tonight at least, it will keep him occupied.

"You're going to have to hide out here for the night." I look into my brother's eyes and he nods, unfazed by a night in the forest. It feels like a stark contrast to the boy I met when I arrived here; one full of demands, selfishness, and a pompous attitude. "I'll bring her to you, then you're on your own," I add, meaning every word, and that seems to be more than enough for him.

"I won't go quietly," he croaks, scrubbing the back of his neck as he exhales, eyes still locked on mine. Brax inches closer to him in a defensive manner, but I raise my hand, wanting my brother to explain further. He must sense the question without me saying it because he slowly rises to his feet, standing tall as he offers me his hand. Indecision flickers through my thoughts for a split second, but despite the uncertainty, I place my palm in his and he pulls me to my feet. "Whatever you need, whatever this battle requires, I'll be there."

"No," I state with a shake of my head, and he completely ignores me as he glances at each of my men before boring his eyes into mine once more.

"I deserve to die, but not in that room. I deserve to die for a purpose greater than me. Raven Hendrix, I am Sebastian Hendrix, and I pledge to help with all that I am, all that I could be, and all I wish to be."

TWENTY SEVEN

Raven

The echo of our front door closing behind us solidifies the fact that we're home and hidden from the rest of the world. My eyes dart around the open-plan space, making sure there haven't been any more surprise intrusions, and when everything appears to be untouched, I sag back against the door with a sigh.

We haven't spoken. Not a single word. I've been trapped in my head the entire time, trying to figure out where my mind is at. I'm exhausted. Bone-dead exhaustion from the constant shit we find ourselves in.

Burton's confirmation that his plan proceeds, Sebastian's assholey face back to normal as he breathes pleas for Lyra, my new jet-black hair.

I'll look at it later. It's not high enough on my priority list right now.

Creed takes my hand, silently tugging me from my spiral as he walks me toward the sofas. I flop against the cushions just as dramatically as I had leaned against the door. My eyes fall closed, and I try to calm my breathing.

Hands touch my arms and legs, shifting me into place so that my feet are propped up on the coffee table and my head is nestled against the back cushions. I wiggle in deeper, my eyes heavy, until lips press against my cheek, bringing me back to the present.

"How are you feeling?" Zane asks, running his thumb over the spot he just kissed. I sense someone on my other side, too, but I don't turn to look. Instead, I try to answer his question as honestly as possible.

"Confused." The word feels heavy on my tongue, weighing me down as if admitting the truth only adds to the confusion.

Despite my growing inner conflict, Zane smiles softly at me, shifting his hand to hold my chin in place, forcing my eyes to lock on his.

"Confused because you're glad you helped your brother despite him being the biggest cunt that ever existed? Or, confused because you're still going out of your way to help him? Even though you're technically telling yourself you're doing it for Lyra." He quirks a brow at me, the knowledge and challenge clear, while all I can do is gape at him like a damn fool.

Frowning, my lips purse, unsure if I like his reading of me or not. "I thought Creed was the one with the mind reading abilities…" My gaze seeks out my onyx love at the mention of his name, and I find him sitting at the dining table with Brax, his head in his hands as he tries to smirk at me, but it falls flat.

It seems I'm not the only one drained and exhausted by all of this.

"Mind abilities aren't needed," Eldon states from my left, his hand falling to my thigh as Zane hums in agreement.

"When you came to the academy, Raven, a complete whirlwind of attitude and anger, you kept everyone at arm's length, us included. But with every layer you've peeled away, the more you've revealed yourself." A lightness dances in his eyes.

"So you think you know me, huh?" I grumble with a pout, slightly impressed that he knows me as well as this but irritated by it at the same time. How am I supposed to dwell and stress if it can be explained away so easily?

"I don't *think*, I know," he retorts, earning an eye roll from me. I should have expected a response like that.

"How so?" I push, intrigue getting the better of me. I can't deny the fact that hearing him read me so effortlessly both warms my heart and sets my soul on fire.

He tucks a loose tendril of hair behind my ear, letting

his fingertip stroke over my cheek before he finds the words to answer. "Shadowmoor made you a tough bitch, Dove. A badass in her own right, but being here with us has allowed you to find the inner Raven you always were. The little girl you kept tucked away inside, hiding from the rest of the world; she gets to find herself too."

I feel like I can't breathe, my throat clogged with emotion. "And who is she?" I ask, barely able to hear the words over the pounding of my pulse in my ears.

"She's just as fucking ruthless, let's start with that," he states, holding up a finger to count, and a small snicker burns through my chest, escaping from my lips. "But that ruthless girl? She cares more deeply than anyone I've ever known. Still selfish, sure, but not for her own safety. *Never* for her own safety, annoyingly enough. But for the ones she loves, and I'll forever be honored to be on that list."

The words hit home, eliciting raw pleasure and emotion in my heart as I let them hang between us. Each one reinforced the young girl I was and the strength that I now have—that *she* now has.

"I've heard you repeatedly say that you're not a hero," he continues, seemingly on a roll now that he's letting it all out. "And you're not trying to be one. No hero complex in sight. But you believe in doing the right thing, you believe in protecting the innocent, and you believe in the villains getting what they're due. I don't know what that makes you to the rest of the academy, the realm, the whole fucking world, for that matter. But to me… that makes you my Dove. Always."

All I can do is gape at him. My heart races so fast I know he's triggered my fight or flight mode, yet for the first time in my life, I'm stuck in freeze. The words swirl in my mind, finding me, seeking me desperately as they solidify who I am. Branding me without offering a label, declaring who I am and what matters most to me.

He says them so easily, defining me without effort, and all I can do is blink at him.

My limbs remain stiff even as he grabs my waist and hoists me in the air before ungracefully lowering me to his lap. I cling to his shoulders for balance, my heart lurching in my chest as I struggle to breathe, but the moment he envelops me in his arms, pulling me tight against his chest, I succumb to the warmth.

Wrapping my arms around his neck, I nestle my forehead against his throat, breathing him in as he strokes his hand up and down my spine in the most blissfully lulling way ever.

"I fucking love you, Raven. We all do, just as fiercely as you love us. We'll follow you blindly into whatever draws you close without question. But if I can start to see it wearing you down, like now, then we're going to have to have a system in place that allows us to take control.

You're my everything, and I refuse to watch you struggle under the weight of the world that's been thrown on your shoulders. You're strong as fuck, and one-thousand percent I know you can handle it, but if you don't have to, I'd rather you didn't."

I bury my face even deeper into the crook of his neck. I am strong, I know I can handle it, but there are so many layers to everything now that I don't even know where to begin.

"I think what Zane is trying to say, Little Bird, is that we're here to shoulder the strain too. If that means we have to help Sebastian, then that's what we do. If we have to spend the rest of the night going over what Burton said to Fitch, then so be it. Whatever it takes. I think we can all agree that we want a future that is more than this. Fuck, you deserve a hell of a lot more than this, but we'll weather this storm if there's a glimpse of sun on the other side." Eldor's voice is soft as his words wash over me, grounding me even further.

What would I do without them? How would I handle any of this shit?

It's a pointless question, really. The only way I wouldn't be here handling this shit is if I never left Shadowmoor, and the truth has revealed that it was never my destiny to remain there.

They were my fate—all four of them—just as much as

the damn visions and prophecies that seem to put me at the helm of bringing the realm back from the brink of chaos.

My knees press into Zane's sides, my body desperate to wrap around him like a new shadow as I lift my head enough to meet Eldon's heartfelt gaze. Finding the words I need to say is harder than I expected, but in my defense, I wasn't expecting tonight to turn into such a deep moment.

I swipe my tongue over my bottom lip as they part, but Eldon presses a finger to his lip, pausing me before I can speak.

"Don't say anything, Little Bird. I think you might just need a moment to feel."

His raspy voice makes my body stiffen once more, but it's not with panic or fear this time. No. It's exactly what his words suggest.

Zane's hands shift to my waist, squeezing me just right so that my hips move, and I find myself grinding along his length. He repeats the move again, but this time, he tilts his hips up to meet the motion. I stifle a groan.

Leaning forward, I feel the brush of his lips over the shell of my ear. "I should be a gentleman and break you in, but feeling your pussy stretch around my cock is like stepping into Heaven for a split second. I can't seem to deny myself that feeling right now," he groans, making me shiver. The tremble elongates down my spine a split second later when he lifts the hem of my skirt and uses his magic to remove my panties.

Everything else remains in place; my blazer, my shirt, my bra, and my skirt. Only the barrier to my pussy is removed, and the grin spreading across his face confirms he's more than happy with the fact.

His fingers caress up my thigh, inching higher and higher until he swipes his thumb over my clit. The thrumming explodes through my veins, heightening the desire they create in me as my jaw falls slack.

"So fucking beautiful, Dove," he murmurs, hitching my skirt around my waist as he grabs my hips, lifting me just enough to press the tip of his cock against my core. That second, those milliseconds of pressure at my entrance are the only warning I get before he drives deep inside of me with one powerful thrust.

Pleasure mixes with pain as I adjust to the length of him, a deep, guttural groan tumbling from my mouth.

"Definitely not a gentleman," Eldon states, humor in his voice, but I can't focus on him. My eyelids refuse to remain open as Zane controls my movements. There's no moment to adjust to his length, no breath to catch before he claims me completely. Nothing.

The second he fills me, he retreats to the tip before repeating the motion, setting my body on fire with coursing need.

"Don't stop," I croak, my head tilting back as I press

my fingernails into his blazer, holding on for dear life.

All I can feel is him, all I can hear is our panting breaths, and all I can see are the fireworks imprinting on the back of my eyelids. Nothing else in the world matters right now.

Just us.

It may be a short reprieve from the madness around us, but I'll take it.

"Look at Eldon watching you, Dove. He's jealous. Jealous of the sounds I'm getting from you, jealous of the way he knows you're making my cock feel right now, and jealous that you're putty in my hands."

I shake my head, not even bothering to look as Zane tries to goad his friend. "He isn't," I grumble, and a scoff sounds from my right a moment later.

"I definitely fucking am," Eldon bites, and my eyes whirl around to him. His pants are unzipped, his dick in hand, and there's a dark desire swirling in his eyes.

"Then you can fill me next," I breathe, making his pupils dilate as he nods.

"He's not the only jealous one, Raven," Zane pushes, and my eyebrows pinch in confusion.

"Oh, don't mind us, we're more than happy enjoying the view," Creed rasps, spiking the ecstasy coursing through me.

Zane grins, his hold on my waist tightening as he moves me harder, faster, all while thrusting up into me like his life depends on it.

Fuck. Fuck. Fuck.

I can feel the impending release inching closer, my eyelids falling to half-mast once again, so I startle when I feel a gentle breeze brush over my nipples, making them pebble instantly.

Eldon smirks up at me before his lips wrap around my taut skin, sucking sharply, making my gasp echo louder around us. I'm certain my nails have pierced holes in the shoulder pads of Zane's blazer by now; I'm clinging that tightly.

The combination of Zane's unrelenting control and Eldon's warmth around my hard nipples is impossible not to succumb to. As if sensing how close to the edge I am, Eldon sinks his teeth into my flesh, and I fall apart like it's a life or death command.

Wave after wave of euphoria tingles through my body as I shatter. Zane's hold on my waist pinches closer to pain as his movements falter, and he roars, exploding inside me. He doesn't release me until he's completely spent and I'm like liquid in his lap, moldable at his whim and desire.

"Eldon's turn, Dove," he whispers against my ear, his voice so soft I swear it sounds like a lullaby.

"I'm already so close for you," Eldon bites out, effortlessly lifting me from Zane's lap. A second later, I cling to him just as harshly. "You happy there, Little Bird, or do you want me to shift us around?" he asks, stroking his thumbs over the spots I'm sure are starting to bruise from Zane's hold.

My tongue peeks out as I think, and it doesn't take long for my mind to be made up. "I want to stay exactly where I am," I mutter, trying to muster more strength than I have as I rise up on my knees, desperate to feel the same sense of fullness I had moments ago.

Eldon grips my chin, holding my gaze as he presses his length against my aching core. His hold on my chin grows tighter, making my pulse ring in my ears as I gape at him, liking the harsh hold far too much as he speaks.

"Feeling someone else's release inside of you is too fucking much." My pussy clenches around him, the remnants of my own release mingling with Zane's as I take Eldon deeper, inch by inch. "Holy shit, Raven," he rasps, eyes rolling to the back of his head as I'm completely seated on his cock. "You're going to have to move so it doesn't look like I'm about to come from one stroke of your pussy, Little Bird," he adds, his pupils completely blown as he peers up at me.

There's something in that look right there that fills me with a confidence beyond anything I've ever felt. I can wield power, we all know that at this point, but nothing compares to the intense strength of bringing my men to their knees like this.

He's just as wanting as I am, and just as eager to surrender to the unwavering desire.

My body moves at his command as he leans forward, sinking his teeth into my breasts again. Not just the nipple this time, but anywhere and everywhere he can reach. Each bite gets fiercer, but every swipe of his tongue becomes more languid over the top, soothing the pain away before he reignites it somewhere else.

I grind along his length, groaning with every stretch of his hard cock inside of me as my clit dances expertly over him, bringing me to the brink of another orgasm in a matter of seconds.

"Eldon. Eldon. Eldon," I chant, unable to calm the rising pleasure in me.

He buries his face in my breasts as he squeezes my ass cheeks, filling me with his release, and the pulsing of his length has me tumbling into the wave of another climax.

Panting, I feel like I'm floating. Perspiration clings to me like a second skin as I try to catch my breath. It takes a few seconds to find the strength to push up, and the second I do, panic kicks in.

"Eldon? Eldon?" I repeat, nudging his shoulder with urgency.

His head is back against the cushions, his face tilted up to the ceiling, but his eyes are glossed over. I turn my attention to Zane beside us, my mouth opening but nothing coming out as he eliminates the distance between us to cup my cheek.

"It's okay, Raven. I think he's having a vision."

A vision? A fucking *vision*?

With his dick still inside of me?

I feel like I'm violating him or something.

Shifting in his lap so that's no longer the case, I feel Creed and Brax silently move closer, the concern thickening in the air as what feels like an eternity passes. I run my hand over his cheek, my lips pressed together in a thin line, when his eyes suddenly ping open and he gasps.

I sag with relief, my heart still thundering with worry as his gaze shifts around erratically before landing on mine.

"A vision?" I ask, trying to smile, but the way his brows furrow doesn't fill me with hope.

"Yeah."

I don't want to ask it, but I have to. "Everything okay?"

A sad smile takes over his face as his eyes fall closed. A long moment passes before he looks at me again, and I can see the dread in his eyes.

"It was the academy, drenched in blood."

TWENTY EIGHT

Raven

My sleep is broken. Twisted and dark. Shaped by words spoken over the past twenty-four hours, with a few from the past sprinkled on top for good measure. The main two looping on repeat come from Eldon and my brother.

If Eldon had a vision of the academy drenched in blood, then nothing good can be heading our way. Not that I'm not already aware of that, but shit, he's solidifying it for sure. Sebastian, however, believes he deserves to die, but for a purpose greater than himself.

Something about it doesn't sit right in my chest.

Sure, none of us would like to die. The natural fear of the afterlife stokes terror in all of us, and imagining it's for an almighty cause, something more than our lives, is to be expected. But the way he said it… the determination in his dark, sunken eyes, is something I can't get out of my head.

My men sleep around me, all tossing and turning in their own way as the looming doom lingers around us. But I do manage to find another kind of solace, more than one if I'm being specific. Shadows.

Everywhere.

Silhouettes outline every inch of the bedroom. I'm certain there are more in here than there ever has been before, but that's not the part that soothes me. No. It's the way they seem to be standing guard protectively around me.

I haven't dared utter a word to them. I refuse to disturb my men from their already restless sleep, so instead, I just watch. Not a single shadow leaves me unnerved. If anything, I feel closer to them now than I ever have before, and I can't truly explain the how or why.

Maybe it's the way I can see the outline of some holding hands, the way it's clear some are bigger and older than others, or maybe it's the way hands run over the bed sheet that covers me as if trying to soothe the uncertainty away.

It's as fucked up as everything else in my life, so I'm opting to roll with it. Especially since this is the first time they've reappeared since I merged the realms. I thought they were gone for good. Where would they have gone? I don't fucking know, but to see that they're still here fills me with joy and a sense of doubt at the same time.

Why aren't they somewhere safer, calmer, happier? Why are they still here?

Swiping a hand down my face, I sigh, peering at the time. We've still got a little over an hour before we can hunt down Lyra, and lying here is officially doing nothing to calm the adrenaline building beneath my skin.

I need an outlet, something to shut my brain off.

Slipping from between Brax and Eldon's sleeping limbs, I crawl to the end of the bed and tiptoe to the door as quietly as I can. I breathe a sigh of relief when I manage to close the door behind me without disturbing anyone, and the second I do, I get a tugging sensation in my gut.

It's familiar, and I immediately know where it's coming from.

Heading toward the patio doors, I can't see anything beyond the first few yards outside, but I know there's someone watching and waiting. Keeping all the lights off, I unlock the door and slip outside. The cool air is a blessing, sweeping over my body as I shiver.

"Ari," I murmur, squinting up at the huge griffin waiting patiently for me.

"You've had your walls up," he grumbles, giving me the griffin equivalent of a death stare.

I shake my head at him as I near, mindlessly running my hands over his feathers as I peer out over the water crashing below.

"You told me to do that, literally taught me, remember?"

"I didn't mean toward me as well. I haven't been able to reach out," he retorts, clearly irritated, but I'm unsure if it's because I seem to be doing it so well or because he taught me to begin with. I don't focus on that, though. Instead, worry creeps up my spine about what he may have been dealing with.

"Is everything okay? Is Gia alright?" I blurt, tilting my face to look up at him.

He relaxes, lowering to the ground as he brings me in closer against his chest, sheltering me from the wind that continues to pick up.

"I'm fine, Gia is fine, everything is fine. It's *you* that's had me concerned."

My eyes widen at his statement and I think about everything that has continued to unravel since he stopped avoiding me. Shit, I've been feeling a lot of things, big and small, but everything is definitely heightened.

I forget that the feelings can be so strong between us, and guilt instantly gets the better of me. "I'm sor—"

"Don't give me that bullshit, Raven. Don't apologize for fighting and surviving." His words feel familiar, reminding me of what Zane said last night. It felt completely out of left field, just as this does now, but it must be the madness in the air that's encouraging them to express it. I've never needed anyone to boost me up to spike my confidence, but

I can't deny the effect it continues to have on me. "So, are you going to talk to me about it?"

I clear my throat, toying with the feathers on his chest as I try to piece the words together. I'm honestly sick of living in this stress. Feeling it is enough, having to discuss it is even harder and it makes me want to bury my head in the sand and not come up for air until it's well and truly passed us by.

Unfortunately, that isn't our reality. Well, it's certainly not mine.

So I explain it. My deal with Sebastian, officially bringing him back from the dead; Burton's confirmation that The Monarchy is aiding him; everything in between; and I top it all off with the details of Eldon's vision. I feel spent and exhausted by the time I'm done, and this time, I feel the trembling, frustration, and anger reverberating from him because of it.

"I think you should just let me tear their heads off," he bites, shaking his head from side to side. I brace for impact, but somehow, his beak doesn't actually hit me as I expected.

"Who?" I ask with a snicker, trying to make light of the situation.

"Every single one of them."

It sounds enticing, like the best idea I've heard, but it's not as simple as that, and neither is putting him in so much danger. Not that I can tell him that. It would just earn me another griffin death stare, and one is more than enough to last a lifetime.

All I seem to be doing is adding people to my protection list, piling more weight on my shoulders, which is the complete opposite of what the guys asked me to do last night, yet I can't help but feel responsible for everyone's safety.

"I wish it was as simple as that, but I can't risk you in that way. Not for your sake, not for mine, and I certainly couldn't do that to Gia." I risk speaking the truth that resonates inside me despite the impending death stare, but to my surprise, he nuzzles against my neck.

"Raven, you have an army around you. We're here at your command. All you have to do is say the word and we'll be there to aid you. Not just me and mine, but the drakes too. I heard their pledge, and despite my dislike for them, I believe they'll keep it."

I hum in agreement, a new sensation flitting through my veins as I take his words in. *Really* take them in. Maybe everyone is right, much to my dismay at having to agree with them, but maybe I need to take stock of who is at my side and who is willing to remain there to the very end.

All those pledges toward me.

Fuck.

Instead of being unable to do anything because I don't

know where to begin, maybe I need to be considering the fact that there are people around me with different strengths and weaknesses to mine. Imagine what could be possible if we worked off that, bringing us all together to finally lay this evil to rest.

"I can feel it."

"Feel what?" I ask, but the stubborn griffin shifts, rising to stand before offering me a response.

"Your brain whirring to life."

"What do you mean?" I push, frowning up at him as the sky starts to lighten around us.

"I mean, you're finally getting it."

I roll my eyes. This griffin is going to be the fucking death of me. "Getting what?"

He doesn't offer me an explanation, though. That would be too easy. Instead, he moves toward the edge of the cliff, only glancing over his shoulder at me at the last second.

"Tug on our connection as I did to you. That's all I will need to know you require us."

Before I can pester the fuck out of him to understand what he means by that as well, he's gone.

TWENTY NINE
Raven

Lips press against my neck as my eyelids fall closed, and I lean back into the hard chest behind me. Last night may not have left me the most rested, but officially starting the day with all of my men at my side definitely makes up for it.

Peering through my lashes, I find Creed looking at us in the reflection of the bathroom mirror with a soft smile on his face, which I return.

"Are you ready to head out?" he asks, trailing another kiss beneath the collar of my academy-issued blouse, and I hum in agreement.

"Yeah. The quicker we get this moving, the quicker we can move on to everything else." Speaking the words out loud fuels my determination. After my impromptu talk with Ari this morning, I feel somewhat rejuvenated and a lot more focused on the giant task at hand.

It seems breaking the issues down in my mind and considering who would be best suited to the task works wonders, as opposed to the opposite. Which was figuring out how to bend myself at will to achieve everything with little help.

I practically pranced back into the bedroom after my familiar took off with a knowing look in his eye, waking my men with my rambling, but thankfully, it had them all intrigued, too. I already feel lighter from getting it off my chest, all we have to do now is start putting things into action. We just have to get over this hurdle first.

"Agreed. Then we can come up with the longest fucking vacation that ever existed."

I lift my hand to my chest, soaking in his words as I nod eagerly. "*That* I can sign up for," I insist, taking one last look at my new hair in the mirror before I follow his lead.

The pink is completely gone, and there's no chance it's coming back. I was expecting the black hair to be a drastic shift, but it weirdly highlights my eyes, even if it does leave my skin looking a little more porcelain than before.

I don't mind, though. I can take it all in my stride if I'm here, still kicking, and that's what grounds me more than anything. We've faced a lot over the past few months, *I've* faced a lot over the past few months, but I'm still fucking here, and there's a reason for that.

The moment we step into the lounge, I'm yanked from Creed's hold, and I don't miss the grumbling under his breath as Zane grins down at me.

"How's my dove doing this morning?"

"The same as I was doing five minutes ago when you last asked me," I retort with my eyebrow raised at him, but he waves me off, guiding me toward the front door with his arm around my shoulders.

"It was seven minutes ago, but who's keeping count?"

I roll my eyes at him, which only makes him smirk more, and I'm certain there's a huffed chuckle that comes from Brax's lips, too, but it's gone before I can confirm it.

The air outside is warmer compared to earlier as we make our way toward the main academy building. The pathways are quiet, not a single person around since it's well ahead of classes being due to start.

We walk in comfortable silence, and when the building comes into view, our pace quickens. The faster we can slip inside and get to Lyra, the faster it will be done with. Not that I'm trying to wash my hands of her; I possibly am with Sebastian, but there's really no time to waste worrying over that with everything else going on.

We've played one step behind this entire time and I'm done being on the defensive with Burton. It's time moves were made and lines were drawn.

The double doors stand wide open, enticing us in, and we hightail it to Lyra's office, but I still two steps back from her door when I see it standing slightly ajar. My eyebrows pinch and panic tingles down my spine as I peer at Brax, Creed, Eldon, and Zane to see the same hint of uncertainty and confusion on their faces.

Inching closer, Zane's hand slips from my shoulders to grasp my palm, refusing to leave my side, and I freeze once again when I lift my hand to push against the door, not actually connecting with the wood.

"I can feel something," I breathe, resisting the urge to swing the door open.

"In what way?" Eldon asks, and it takes me a moment to find the right words to describe it.

"It's magic, but it's not like anything else I've felt before," I admit. "I can't actually feel it with my fingertips, but it's in the air. I can sense it."

"Then someone else steps in first," Brax grunts, squeezing by me so I have to back up a step, and I glare at his head. "Don't give me that look, we've talked about this shit," he adds, making my jaw fall slack.

How does he know exactly how I'm looking at him right now when he isn't even looking at me? Fucker.

It's on the tip of my tongue to blurt the question at him, but he's nudging the door open before I get a chance, distracting me from my thoughts.

He scans the room, and I try to catch a glimpse around him but his broad frame fills the open doorway, giving nothing away. Growing impatient, I tap on his shoulder blade, and a moment later, he takes a step into the room. I'm right behind him, trying to step to his left as I slip my hand from Zane's, but between the pair of them, I don't stand a chance.

Brax's arm swings out wide, blocking me from passing him, while Zane's hold slips from my hand to my wrist. I'm not about these good reflexes outside of the bedroom. Assholes. Clearly, I'm cranky this morning with my lack of sleep. Swiping a hand down my face, I try to compose myself, but my words still come out harsher than necessary.

"Can you two not?"

Brax glares daggers at me, but I match them right back. His glare deepens, and my neck muscles jump. "I can do this all day. Can you?"

He rolls his eyes at me, muttering the word *dramatic* under his breath before he sighs, dropping his arm to his side. "I can't see anything," he grumbles, but I don't take his word for it. Something isn't right here, I know it.

Zane releases his hold on me, and as I move, it feels as though the magic is dancing around me like thin fabric draped from the ceiling. Her desk area is set, her chair twisted out, but there's no sign that she's already been here.

It's not until I turn toward the far left that I see the

secret entry to her private area of the office is also slightly open. My feet carry me toward the little hole in the wall before I can consider my options and the magic seems to thicken around me.

"I feel like it's hard to breathe," I state, my hand lifting to my chest as I struggle to take a deep breath. Glancing back at the others, I find them frowning.

"It seems fine to me," Eldon offers, concern flitting in his eyes as the others nod in agreement with him.

Forcing the strongest inhale I can, my lungs almost feel like they're burning. I push against the door tentatively, my vision blurring as the magic becomes unbearable, and it only takes one second of peering inside for me to realize why.

"Oh my gosh," I rasp, falling to my knees. The magic around us becomes dizzying, but I fight through it, crawling on my hands and knees to where the body lies.

Not just any body… Lyra's.

Hands grab my waist before I can get to her, hoisting me into the air, and I all but collapse in their hold as they shift me around to carry me.

Colors flash around me as we move until everything seems to calm down, but that's when I realize I'm no longer in Lyra's secret room. I'm slowly lowered to Lyra's desk, and I manage a deep breath, my body trembling with relief as a hand brushes down my back comfortingly.

"I need to help her," I state when I can focus properly, my eyes landing on Brax's, and he grimaces.

"I don't think that's going to be possible, Shadow."

"Why?" I bark, trying to scramble to my feet again, but he pins me in place.

"Because only you can sense or feel the effects of the magic swirling in the room, which is conveniently keeping you away from her," he grinds out, the anger not aimed at me, but it still sends a shiver down my spine.

Who would do this?

"Is she…"

His eyes darken as he nods once, and a strangled sob parts my lips as my heart races so fast, I'm certain I'm going to pass out.

"How… I… There must be something I can do," I say with a gasp, my eyes darting back to the room just as Zane steps out, followed swiftly by Eldon and Creed, who carry Lyra's body between them.

I shuffle off the desk, moving everything with me as they lay her down on the glass top, and I'm relieved to find that I'm not overcome with the same disorientation I had been when I stepped into the room a moment ago.

"I'm okay here with her; I can help," I state, running my hand down her arm as the others take a step back, but it's just like Genie; my magic finds nothing to cling to.

Lyra's eyes are still open, glossed over, and void of any

life, making my gut twist with pain.

"How did this happen?" I ask, hoping someone can piece this together better than I can, and it's Creed who speaks.

"I think the room was coated in some kind of ward or spell that would only have the ability to affect you and no one else. I don't know what or how, but it clearly took hold of you while leaving us unscathed," he explains, but that doesn't really get to the reason why Lyra is lying lifeless like this.

"And her?" I push, sweeping a hand over her hair before closing her eyelids, unshed tears filling my eyes.

Fuck, I hate how emotional I can be. I've seen death enough times for it not to hurt like this, or it didn't used to, at least.

"I don't know, Raven. There's no physical sign of pain, and I can't access her mind."

"I can't find a single piece of her to hold on to, to try and bring her back," I admit, pressing my lips together as I try to stop the tears from falling down my face.

"What do we do now?" Zane asks, the room growing quiet for a moment as we realize everything that was planned for this morning isn't going to happen.

"Whoever did this did it to impact you, Shadow," Brax bites, hands clenched at his sides, and I nod in agreement.

"Which means they likely know about Sebastian, "

Eldon adds, and I curse under my breath.

This is exactly why we should have moved yesterday, then we could have saved her.

"We have to tell him," I say with a sigh, and Zane offers me a sad smile.

"Do we take her with us or not?" he asks, and my stomach clenches.

The alternative is to leave her here, and she doesn't deserve that. She's already been put through more pain than necessary.

"With us," I murmur, placing my hand on her one last time to make sure I'm not missing something, and in doing so, I spot a black mark on her chest. "What is that?" I ask, not wanting to snoop on a dead woman's body, but surely it means something.

Eldon steps closer to get a better look, and the way his face pales tells me it's not a good sign. "That's magic at play. Whoever did that marked her with death. It could have happened at any time. I've heard my parents talk about it, but I've never seen it for myself," he explains, swiping a hand down his face. "It's a special kind of magic, one that leaves an invisible imprint on the person without them even knowing, and with a simple snap of the power-wielders fingers, the magic can take effect."

"So, you're saying someone marked her with this and pulled the trigger when they wanted to without even being present?" I clarify, and Eldon nods.

Fuck. I didn't even know something like this could exist.

"Let's get her out of here. If this was aimed at me, then I'm certain we don't have much time before Burton decides to make his next move. We need to be as prepared as possible."

"I'll carry her and hide myself with my magic until we get to the Gauntlet. Is that okay?" Zane asks, and I nod, mouthing my thanks as we head for the door.

My body is a scrambled mess. I'm not ready to proceed to the next step, whatever or wherever that may fucking be. I need a minute to deal with this heartache first, but our enemies don't care about that. This just plays to their advantage. Which means I need to get my shit together and fast.

I expect someone to jump out at us as we exit into the hallway then leave the academy building, but to my disbelief, nobody does. It doesn't fill me with a single ounce of confidence, though. It leaves me even more unnerved, which is exactly what Burton will be going for.

This has to be him. This has to be his move, and now he has me on high alert, looking over my shoulder at every turn, yet I know he's still going to have the ability to catch me off-guard.

I take the stone steps into the Gauntlet arena two at

a time and find Zane already waiting at the bottom with Lyra's body. He must have run ahead, which is weird as fuck because I had assumed he was at my side the entire time.

Seeing her like this again pours another bucket of sadness over me. I clench my hands tight, my nails digging into my palms as I hold my emotions at bay. I can fall apart later and drown in my feelings then, but for now, I have to power through.

As I reach his side, he drapes an arm around me, pressing his lips to my temple as Eldon silently picks Lyra up. Brax moves through the gateway first and I follow after him, aware the others will be hot on our heels.

A moment later, the familiar forest that was once the compound of the magical creatures comes into view. Yesterday, it was a glimpse at a fresh start, a symbol of hope for Sebastian, whether he deserved it or not. Today, however, it feels like torture.

Stepping over a fallen log, I hear movement from my right, and a moment later, Sebastian's face comes into view.

His jaw falls slack before he rushes toward me as fast as he can. "Where is she?"

I stare at him bleakly, wiping a hand down my face as my eyebrows pinch and my jaw wobbles.

"What have they done?" he snaps, his eyes searching

mine before he glances over my shoulder. I see it the moment he has his answer. The color drains from his face, his jaw hits the floor, and his pupils turn to pinpricks in his eyes.

I'm uncertain whether he's going to fall to the ground, swarmed with pain, or charge into battle, especially as his nostrils flare and his hands curl into fists.

"I'm sorry," I whisper, not really apologizing to him, but to her. "She was… I couldn't…"

"This isn't your fault, Raven. Don't put the weight of this on your shoulders as well," Creed says, eyes glued on my brother as he awaits his response.

Sebastian peers at me, then at Lyra, then back at me. Clearing his throat, his mouth opens, but nothing comes out as he moves toward her instead. He takes her from Eldon's hold, lowering her to the soft earth beneath us as his head hangs between his shoulders.

Silence cascades over us as emotions rise, leaving my heart racing wildly in my chest once again.

"This wasn't on you, Raven," Sebastian finally states, stroking a hand down her face before rising to his feet. "*None* of this is on you," he repeats, and I feel the tension gripping my men ease, but there's still an edge that surrounds them. One that I don't think will ever go away when it comes to my brother. "I will die in her honor, Raven. I swear it. I pledged an oath to you, and I need you to know that this includes her, too. I will right my wrongs in her name. Tell me you understand."

"She doesn't have to tell you shi—" Brax's grunt is cut off when I nod, looking my brother square in the eyes.

"I understand."

If this was the other way around, if this was one of my men lying on the ground like this, I would be doing the same. The least I can do is understand.

"What now?" he asks, his gaze glancing to Eldon, Creed, Zane, and Brax, as well as mine.

"They knew Raven would go to her. Am I to assume you played a part in that?" Creed questions, cocking a brow at Sebastian, who gapes at him in horror.

I clutch my necklace, feeling Lyra's magic still thrumming inside of the locket as Sebastian speaks. "Are you fucking serious right now? I wanted her safe. I didn't think they would do this and cause…" His words trail off as he looks down at Lyra, and I know every word he said is true.

I nod subtly at my men, confirming the fact that he isn't giving us some covered bullshit.

"If that's the case, then I think they know Raven helped you. Which means—"

"They know I'm still alive," Sebastian admits, finishing Zane's sentence, and I sigh. "There's no point hiding then. They're gearing up for war; I'm better at your side than hidden away here," he adds, and I purse my lips, trying to decide if that's the best option or not.

"Oh, you better believe your ass is coming back with us," Brax grunts and my eyes widen in surprise.

"Let me say goodbye first," Sebastian mutters, dropping to his knees beside Lyra. He whispers words to her so softly that I can't hear them, and I instantly start to feel like I'm imposing on a private moment, so I take a step back.

My men follow and we wait beside the gateway until Sebastian stands, using his magic to bury her, placing a single flower where she was moments ago. He walks toward us with a new-found purpose.

Brax steps through the gateway first, as always, and I follow after him, but I stumble to a halt when the Gauntlet arena comes into view.

It's nowhere near as empty as it was before. Every possible seat is filled with students, both Silvercrest and Shadowgrim alike, but it's the fact that my father has Brax on his knees, arms pinned behind his back and head slung low, that freezes me in place.

A cackle rings in my ears as I hear Sebastian curse under his breath beside me a moment later. My eyes lock on the source of the harrowing cackle: Burton, dressed in his Erikel get-up again.

His gaze travels from mine to Sebastian's then to my

father's before coming full sweep back to me again.
"Ah, what a family reunion this is."

THIRTY

Raven

I can feel every pair of eyes on me as my gaze remains fixed on Burton's. His Erikel fur cloak and scar down his cheek is pissing me off now. Everything that continues to transpire at the hands of this man is too much, too far, and I'm damn well over it.

"You told me he was dead," my father bites, and I spy him in my peripheral vision, wagging a finger at Sebastian.

"He was. It seems someone took pity on him," Burton sneers, eyes glaring daggers at me.

He's too fucking childish and easily disgruntled to lead a war and cause a revolution or whatever the fuck this is. I can deal with him in a minute, but first, I need my father's other hand to move.

"Get your hands off him," I snap, my eyes flicking between my father and Brax, who remains on his knees, head dipped as he's restrained by some kind of magic at my father's hands. My father's eyes meet mine, but they're void of any significant presence, a reminder that this man is at the command of someone else, and the reality pisses me off even more. "I said, get. Your. Hands. Off. Him."

My magic vibrates through my veins, ready to take action in whatever way necessary to protect my grumpy gargoyle. When he still doesn't listen, I take a step toward him, but before I can attack, my hand grips the pendant around my neck.

I expect to feel some kind of stronger attack at my fingertips, like Brax's gargoyle strength or Zane's fire, but to my surprise, it's Lyra's magic that coils around my hand as I press my palm against Abel's chest.

He startles at the contact, his hold on Brax shifting. I sense my man move, but I don't turn to look. I can't. My eyes are locked on my father's as I physically watch his clouded vision disappear. It seems the tendrils of Lyra's magic reveal your truth just as much as the truth around you. He falls to his knees before I can catch him, but Sebastian swiftly moves him to the side so nothing stands between me and Burton.

I crack my neck, releasing the necklace from my grasp as I glare at the fucker who has caused so much damage.

"What are you doing? Why is everyone here?"

My questions go ignored as he shakes his head at me.

"I'm the one who asks the questions around here." I roll my eyes. I really should be more prepared for his bullshit by now, but he's not as easy to predict as it seems. "And you will address me appropriately," he adds, peering down his nose at me as a sneer spreads across his lips.

Fucker.

If that's the game he wants to play, then I'm more than willing to pretend to follow his lead. It will make bringing him down that much sweeter. "Oh, great one," I say regally, dramatically bowing as I throw my arms out wide. His sneer sways into a triumphant grin as I stand back at full height. "What is everyone doing here?" I repeat, anger and adrenaline consuming me.

"Waiting for your return, of course," he retorts, like it really is as simple as that.

Of course he was watching us; I was foolish to believe he wasn't. He's sly, conniving, and the biggest fucking snake I've come across. And that's saying something after surviving Shadowmoor. But that feels like a sliver of Heaven in comparison to all of the darkness I've endured at Silvercrest Academy.

I'm still rolling my thoughts around in my head when he turns to address the gathered students who look confused as fuck in their seats surrounding the Gauntlet podium. Fear is visible on paler faces with every second that ticks by, while some flex their muscles, getting ready for battle.

"The time for war is now. The time for strengthening our community is here. The time to reveal the final steps in our plan has come," Burton announces, arms flung wide as he tries to rally the students.

I'm pretty sure it's not *our* plan, more his, but I manage to keep my mouth shut. Semantics aren't what's needed right now. It's action, and I get the feeling that the beginning of the end is upon us.

A flash of gold catches my attention, trudging down the steps as he pulls along a man with chains wrapped around his wrists and ankles. The clunking of the golden warrior's armor on the stone steps pulls everyone's attention a moment later, sending a wave of murmurs around the space.

"Who is that?" Sebastian asks, standing to my left with our father at his side.

I squint for a moment, taking in the man, and despite his current state, I know exactly who it is.

"It's Monarch Dutton. The man I revived," I mutter, my teeth clenching as the memory of that day comes to the forefront of my mind. The day Creed was taken to attack the village, he instead had his memory tampered with by his father. It's a relief to know he was kept safe now, but at the time, it was another layer of strain we really didn't fucking need.

"He doesn't look to be in the best shape," Eldon states, and I can't deny the truth in his words.

"May I present to you, Monarch Dutton, the head of the Elevin army," Burton declares, swinging a hand in his direction. "It makes sense for us to use the realm's own army against them, don't you agree?" he adds, earning a cheer from the Shadowgrim students, but there are a few Silvercrest Academy pupils joining in too.

I survey the crowd, and it takes a few moments, but I find who I'm looking for. Four rows back, right at the end, beside the guy who has been on my radar, is Leila. I can see her eyebrows practically touching her hairline from here as she continues to skim her eyes over everyone. It's not lost on me that her father isn't here yet, but it's more the smirk on Grave's face that holds me captive.

I'm going to fucking kill him for whatever connection he has to this.

Shaking my head, I turn my attention back to Burton. "None of this makes sense. You know that, right? Not a single ounce of it," I bite, fingers flexing at my side as he stares me down.

"That's because you're a dumb, foolish girl with only one use. It's no surprise that things here don't make sense to you." His lip lifts with a sneer and I want to wipe it from his face with my fist, but it would take too long to cut the distance between us, so I opt to use words instead.

"What doesn't make sense to me is why you're still in that skin," I holler, loud enough to garner everyone's attention, but of course, no one understands what I mean.

His sneer turns into a deathly glare before he shakes his head and waves his hand dismissively at me. "You're talking nonsense again, Miss Hendrix. Do I need to remind you what I'm capable of if you don't fall in line?" he threatens, and I grin. This, I can handle. The sly shit is what fucks with my head, but threatening me in any way, shape, or form, including those I love, is something I know how to react to and handle.

"I think we're beyond that now, don't you?" I taunt back, taking a small step toward him, and I immediately feel my men shift around me. I know they'll be wanting to protect me, shield me from this man and his fucked up shit, but it's too late for all of that, and I think we all know it.

"I know your weak spots," he pushes, and I laugh. A wholehearted chuckle straight from my stomach.

"I know you are Burton." Gasps echo around the Gauntlet at my admission, but uncertainty around the truth of my words only thickens.

"How educated of you, but whatever you think you know, however you think you see this going, you're wrong. I'm going to break down how it's actually going to happen." He takes two measured steps toward me, fingers splayed in the air as he points to each one. "You will fall in line. You will play the perfect puppet. You will stand at my side as we take down the realm. Or… I will start to kill off your men."

The excitement at that thought flashes with wonder in his eyes, but I don't falter under his intense stare.

"What then? Once you've done that, you'll have lost all of your leverage," I retort, still goading him, and I'm pretty pleased with myself when I watch his face turn red, along with his telltale sneer scrunching his face.

"Warrior," he bellows, waving his hand for the golden warrior to approach him without actually turning to find where he is.

The warrior pauses for a moment, his gaze flicking to Creed's before he releases his hold on Monarch Dutton and begins to approach. The second the man in the golden armor is on the platform with the rest of us, Burton turns to us with a twisted smile, and I know what his next words will be before he even says them.

"I want you to kill… him."

I'm not shocked to find his finger aimed in Creed's direction, but the finality of it still makes my heart skip a beat with panic.

Creed's father looks torn, glancing from Burton to his son and back twice before he reluctantly nods and slowly heads our way. We knew this would happen. If anything, we half-banked on it, but that doesn't make it any easier from this point. It just signifies the point of no return.

Golden metal-clad fingers reach for the hilt of the same colored sword at the warrior's waist. His onyx eyes are fixated on matching ones as he gets closer and closer. I don't move, keeping my feet rooted to the spot, as Creed shifts enough to be two steps ahead of me.

I instantly feel what it's like to be in their position, anger and distress clouding my thoughts as I desperately hold myself back from reacting.

The sword is half unsheathed when the movement is halted, and he jerks when the weapon tumbles from his grasp, clattering to the floor with an overwhelming echo.

"Kill him!" Burton yells as the golden warrior stares down at the weapon before peering back at his son. I follow his line of sight, but the next time I glance down at the shimmering weapon, it's nowhere to be seen. "Where is it?" Burton cries out, clearly searching for the missing blade, but the uncertainty doesn't last long as the weapon appears a moment later in Zane's grasp, at Creed's side.

My heart races as I look at the triumphant grin on Zane's face as he hands the sword off to Creed, but the look of elation doesn't travel to him as well. He knows what he must do.

Creed takes a step forward at the same time as his father does, eliminating most of the distance between them in one swift second, and it's instinctive for me to follow suit, but I startle when I feel an arm band around my waist, halting me from going any further.

Glaring over my shoulder, I'm surprised to find it's my father. "Don't you dare," I hiss, prepared to beat the hell out of him if necessary, but he relents, his eyebrows furrowed as he relaxes his hold.

I take another step toward Creed, but he throws his left arm out, warning me not to go any further without taking his eyes off the sword. He twirls it in his hand, the onyx gem standing tall and proud in the handle.

"Allow me," Brax grunts, moving to Creed's other side. Everything happens so fast, the world seeming to slow around us as my gargoyle grabs the blade in his hand and snaps it in two.

The murmurs around the room grow louder, nobody is willing to take action in any way until Burton fucking says so, and it makes me want to get this over and done with even quicker. The strength of Brax alone doesn't release the onyx stone as he intended, but Eldon is right beside him in a flash, pressing a heated hand to the metal, and a moment later, it pops free and Creed catches it before it hits the ground.

I can hear Burton still yelling in the background, his voice getting angrier with every syllable, but none of it registers as I watch Creed stare his father down. My heart aches, my limbs pleading to take a step toward my love and cradle him from the storm that's coming. But this is it. This is exactly what his father said.

A look passes between two sets of onyx eyes as the golden warrior exhales slowly, his arms hanging loose at his sides. "I love you, Creed. Do it, son. Do it now."

The onyx stone twirls through Creed's fingers for a split second before he takes the command. He launches it at his father, the stone aimed at his head, and as the gem touches the warrior's forehead, he collapses to his knees in pain.

My chest clenches, pain etching its way through my veins as members of the crowd scream, watching as a black cloud billows from the connection between stone and armor, swelling outward in an ominous, twisting explosion of darkness that surrounds the golden warrior, confining him within its inky shadow, until it suddenly collapses in on itself, leaving nothing in its wake.

Not even a sliver of golden armor.

Creed stares down at the empty spot, eyes wide as the world swirls in turmoil around him. The cries from the crowd grow louder and I tilt my face to look at them. Hysteria is real, and I can't help but laugh. Burton truly believes he's going to take these people to war. What a fucking fool.

"You won't get away with this. Where is he? Tell me where he is right now. Bring him back," he snaps, not actually giving anyone a chance to respond to the shit he's spouting.

At least he can't ask me to heal him if he's not here. Not that I wouldn't if that's what Creed wanted and needed, but after the conversation he had with his father at our front door the other day, we know this is a blessing for him more than anything. It's the only way he was ever going to truly have freedom from the shackles holding him in place, and my heart bleeds for the honorable-yet-pained decision he had to make.

Zane wraps his arm around his friend, pulling him back in line with the rest of us when a fresh shadow falls over the entryway into the Gauntlet.

I don't recognize the man, or the men and women that follow after him, and it makes my stomach clench to see Grave step out onto the staircase with his arms open wide. The two embrace before the new arrival turns his attention to my father.

"Fall in line, Abel. Bring your children with you or face the consequences." Leila gapes at Grave, horror coating her vision, but I turn my attention to my father. When my eyes lock with his, he remains clear-minded, and I hope like hell that it's enough to keep him out of their grasp. "If you won't take the warning from Erikel, then take it from The Monarchy," he adds, his voice thundering around the space, and I spy a few students shudder in their seats.

Burton claps his hands together, grinning at me with joy in his eyes like he still believes he has the upper hand. "You've taken down my golden warrior, but I have the Amayans, and I believe you've already met my army of Drakes."

My heart stills as their shadows come into view first, moments before claws appear and they begin to ascend the staircase together. One by one, the Drakes surround the podium where we stand, their teeth bared in our direction, and my stomach sinks.

Motherfuckers.

THIRTY ONE

Creed

The feelings coursing through me are overwhelming my senses, leaving me at a complete loss as to what to do next. I just killed someone in front of the entire academy. No, not just someone, my own fucking father.

Agony, relief, and determination for it to not be in vain vibrate through me. I can't dwell on it. I have to use it to push myself forward and bring all of this shit to an end.

My father died for a purpose, despite the treacherous years that have led to this moment. This was exactly what we'd discussed. I can only hope and pray that he finds solace wherever he is.

I can't stay in my head, drowning in my thoughts when the Drakes surround us. Not with the way Burton is sneering, like everything is falling perfectly into place for him.

Over my dead body.

I brush off the growing ache in my chest and focus on the most important thing that matters right now: keeping Raven alive.

Wiggling my hand behind me, it takes two short breaths before I feel her delicate fingertips run over mine, giving me the strength I need, just as I hope to fuel her.

I keep my eyes fixed on the Drakes as I insert myself in Raven's mind as politely as possible. She shivers at the initial contact, spiking my own adrenaline, but I can't get lost in our connection like I did last time. Instead, I focus on what I want to say to her.

"Take him now. Just like you did to Genie. You can do this."

I spy her subtle nod out of the corner of my eye as her father argues with the member of The Monarchy that has just arrived. I'm going to assume it's Grave's grandfather by the way they embraced. Rhys had been right: Grave is a part of whatever fucked up shit Burton is fighting for, which only places him higher on my kill list.

Burton is too interested in watching the Monarch and Raven's father argue to see us coming, which almost makes it a whole hell of a lot less fun to bring him to his knees. But his death will do, however we get it.

Raven releases my hand when she gets a few feet away from the man still dressed as the "Lord of Basilica", and it takes everything inside of me to let her lead. The hardest thing in the world isn't protecting those you love, it's learning to know that they can handle themselves. To stand back and let them protect themselves.

I watch in awe as she lifts her hand in Burton's direction before she yanks as hard as she can. I don't physically see anything happen except Burton stumble a few steps to the side. His glare is instantly focused on Raven as she stares at him with wide eyes.

Before he can snap his teeth in anger at her, she does it again, and I watch with disbelief as his magic becomes visible around him. She grunts, using all of her strength and magic to pull as hard as she can, but when her gaze collides with mine, I know it's not going as seamlessly as we had hoped.

"It's not working," she grinds out, nostrils flared in anger as her knuckles start to turn white.

"You think you can come for me as you did my daughter? Your magic won't work on my abilities. Only the Potens Ruby could bring me to my knees in that way, and it seems you don't have it," he snarls, inching closer, but as the rest of us encircle Raven, her father, and Sebastian included, it's no surprise that he falters, calling out to the Drakes instead.

"Take down her men."

The crowd is on their feet, gaping in a mixture of terror

and delight as everything continues to unfold between them, but it's the swift movement to my left that has my muscles tensing as I go to defend Raven. The knee-jerk reaction isn't warranted, though. It's Leila who comes into view, standing tall beside us as she holds her hands out, ready to fight.

Satisfied she's not going to cause us any trouble, I draw my attention back to the Drakes, who continue to circle us like we're their next meal. I'll kill every last one of them for lying to Raven, and if they even think of causing her harm, I'll make it even more painful.

Finally, the Drakes pause as one of them climbs the steps, pressing us into defensive stances as his claws scratch against the wood beneath us. His eyes lock on Burton's.

"We don't fight for you. We fight for her."

My jaw falls slack as I gape in surprise, beyond shocked because I was certain they had double-crossed us.

"What have you done?" Burton growls, dark, hooded eyes aimed in Raven's direction as he moves toward her. I move to protect her, instinct taking over, but at the same time, a Drake lands beside us, taking the same stance and knocking me off my feet.

Fuck. Clambering to stand back up, I startle when I see Grave and his grandfather marching toward us. Moving feels…slow and heavy, each muscle in my body weighing more than the last. I can see Zane, Eldon, and Brax struggling just as much as I am, but I don't waste time or unnecessary effort trying to check on them when it's taking so much out of me. Raven requires every ounce of my strength.

The world slows around me, but not because I'm hyper-focused. No. Because the Monarch himself has his hands raised in our direction, holding us in a delayed sense of time.

I can't fight past it, break through the surface and breathe. It's all-consuming, suffocating, and affecting each and every one of us. Fighting back with everything that I am, success slips through my fingers as my gaze finds Grave's and his intent is made clear.

"Nooo," I snarl, my throat burning from the force when only the smallest sound breaks past my lips.

Horror sets me alight as he calls upon his golden sword, wielding it with precision as he spins the hilt in his hand before slamming the tip against his target.

Raven.

THIRTY TWO

Brax

I thought I knew what it felt like when your body turned to stone; unmoveable, restricted, and heavier than you can fathom. I know nothing. Nothing in comparison to the horror that burns through my body as I remain locked in place, watching my world shatter around me.

I'm helpless.

I'm worthless.

I'm broken.

Inexplicable pain ricochets through my body as I powerlessly watch Grave drive a sword through Raven's chest. The crimson-dipped gold pokes out of her back as he pushes all the way to the hilt, and there's nothing I can do about it.

A harrowing cry echoes in my ears as I fall in slow motion, crumbling to my knees. I don't feel the bite from my kneecaps hitting the harsh floor, but the thud from Raven's body hitting the wood will forever haunt me. Even over the gut-wrenching cry that continues to ring in the air around us, the sound is undeniable.

Take me now. Take that blade and drive it through my heart because I refuse to spend a moment in this realm without my woman beside me.

Blinking up at Grave, who wears a triumphant grin from ear to ear, I snarl.

No.

He doesn't get to add my name to his death toll, not when there is vengeance due. He won't get away with this. He won't take what's mine and live long enough to reap any kind of reward.

Consequences. That is all that is coming his way.

I swear it.

The fucker presses his palm against Raven's chest, blood coating his fingers as he does, before he wrenches the sword from her dying body.

Magic still clings to my limbs, rendering me useless as I scramble to find my feet again. The cry filling the air turns gargled, making me frown, and I glance away from Raven for a split second to see if I can find the source of the awful sound.

Of all the people around us, my eyes lock on Leila, who is gaping at me with tears streaking down her face.

My nostrils flare. I don't need to worry over her right now. I keep searching. It's when my eyes find Eldon's that I understand.

Lifting a hand to my throat, I feel the vibration, and with a sharp gasp, the noise stops.

It's me.

The shrill cry was coming from me.

My throat instantly clogs, the emotion unable to escape past my lips as it had been, and I channel that energy into my limbs instead. Adrenaline floods my veins and a snarl snaps from my mouth before I push to my feet.

Objective one: kill this motherfucker. Objective two: kill everyone else in the vicinity that poses a threat. Objective three: find a way to save Raven, no matter the cost or sacrifice.

Glancing down at Raven, I bite back the growing ache at the sight of her closed eyelids, along with the growing spread of blood pooling around her. I let the reality of it wash over me, though, fueling me. I want to see Burton's face, whether as himself or as Erikel. I want to see if this was a part of his plan all along because I sure as fuck can't piece together how this works in his favor, but before I can lock eyes with the fucker, everything begins to shift around me.

My hands whip out to my sides, trying to remain

balanced as colors blur, and a moment later, the view around us changes, too.

"Raven. No, fuck, Raven," Zane cries out, rushing to her side. I frown, noting the speed behind his move, and I quickly realize the magic holding us back is no longer pinning us in place.

Eldon and Creed fall to their knees beside Raven, running their hands over her body as they call out her name, but my instincts take over, my protective nature taking the lead as I piece together what the fuck is happening right now.

Blades of grass crush under my boots, the field rolling out in every direction, but it's not somewhere I'm familiar with. Trees are dotted sporadically around us, not really shielding us from view, but I'm not sure we're anywhere near Burton right now.

"Brax."

The sound of my mother's voice threatens to drop me to my knees once more, the need for her to take all of my worry and pain away overwhelming. But more than that, the pounding in my head calms when I comprehend the fact that we're safer than we were moments ago.

Spinning to lock eyes on her, I'm relieved to see my father at her side. Rhys and a woman, who I now know as Raven's mother, stand with them, and I get the unfortunate pleasure of reliving the horrors of Raven's attack through her eyes, too.

"Somebody has to help her. Now," Creed bites, desperation thick in his voice as he sweeps a bloodied hand down her face in panic.

"Evangeline." Raven's mother responds immediately while my brain stutters over the fact that it's Raven's father's voice I heard call her name. Turning to my left, I find him and Sebastian still with us.

If it was left to me, saving them wouldn't have been high up the priority list, but right now, that doesn't matter. All that matters is Raven and vengeance.

"What happened?" Rhys asks, approaching with my parents a step behind him. "We worked as fast as we could, I swear. I didn't… I'm so sorry," he rambles, coming to a stop behind Zane, planting a hand on his shoulder in comfort.

My parents approach me, but I refuse to let them touch me. Touching me will only confirm the pain consuming me, and I can't accept that this is real. Not yet.

Slipping away from my mother's hand, I crouch by Raven's head, stroking my fingers through her new jet-black hair, and my chest clenches unbearably tight.

"Save her. Save her *now*. Someone here must be able to," I order, first looking to my parents before turning my glare on Rhys and her parents. Sebastian hovers a step back, his brows pinched together as he looks at his sister, and anger burns up my spine. "Get him the fuck out of here before I do. She saved you. Risked everything to save Lyra, and you can't offer her the same," I snarl, and I feel like I can't breathe because I know it applies to me too.

She saved me, brought me back from the dead, and I can't offer the same in return.

Fuck. Fuck. Fuck.

"I-I'll take him," Raven's mother says with a sob, hand pressed to her mouth before she places her hand on Sebastian's arm, guiding him farther away. "Abel, take care of her," she adds, looking deep into his soul, and he nods in agreement.

"Excuse me," he mutters, and it takes a second for us to realize he's talking to the four of us crowding around our love. Our central point. Our universe.

"If you think I'm going to let you touch her after everything you've done, you're fucking insane," I bite, eyes burning with challenge.

He swipes a hand down his face, nodding in understanding before he meets my gaze. "I can heal her."

My jaw clenches, my nostrils flaring, and the desire to tell him to go fuck himself is strong.

"Let him in, Brax," Zane murmurs before rising to his feet, and the others follow after him.

I still can't bring myself to move. Her father must

sense it, too, because after a few moments, he drops to his knees on her other side and presses his hands to her chest. His eyes fall closed and his fingers twitch as the red stains covering her body grow smaller, but something doesn't seem right.

"It's not happening fast enough," I grunt, and he shivers, the cords in his neck tensing as his breaths grow heavy.

"It's draining me. I'm trying, but it's taking everything," he rasps, making my heart thunder in my chest.

"Then fucking give it to her," I snap, desperation taking over. I don't truly understand what it is I'm demanding, the consequences of my order, but when his eyes meet mine, it all makes sense.

"Abel," Evangeline hollers. Hurried footsteps approach, but I don't look away from the solemn look in this man's eyes.

"Tell her I love her. Tell her I'm sorry. Tell her to stay strong. Please."

A lump lodges in my throat at the rawness in his words, but despite the pain I can hear, I do what I have to. I nod.

"Abel, wait!"

He doesn't hear her as he takes a deep breath and closes his eyes, lifting both hands to cover her open wound. He cries out, the sound is pained and tortured, before he collapses with a thud, lying side by side with his daughter.

One heartbeat.

One breath.

One life.

But whose?

THIRTY THREE

Raven

Excruciating pain burns in my chest as I try to pry my eyes open. It's harder than I expect and I struggle to wade through the confusion clogging my mind.

"Raven? Raven!"

I try to rush toward the sound, but I feel delirious. My mind is whirling, yet my body remains lax, which does nothing to calm the panic starting to take hold.

Get it together, Raven.

My brain finally wakes up enough to redirect my frustration, stopping it from blocking me from doing what I want, instead, using it to power me forward, and a moment later, I'm blinded by the light that surrounds me.

"Holy fuck, Raven."

"Shit."

"Thank fuck."

"He did it. He fucking did it."

My heart lurches at the strained emotion in my men's voices, and after a second, I can focus on their faces. Brax's eyes are wide, one brown, one green, taking in every inch of me as I gasp each breath into my lungs. Creed swipes a bloodstained hand down his face as he smiles at me softly. Eldon runs his thumb over my knuckles as he grips my hand, a single tear falling down his cheek, while Zane clears his throat, wagging a finger at me.

"Adjustments are being made to the housemate handbook because I swear to all that is holy, you can't put me through that again," he rasps, revealing his true feelings beneath his attempt at making light of the situation.

I frown, rubbing my dry lips together as I try to understand what he's talking about. The second I try to search in my mind for the last thing I remember, it all comes crashing back to the forefront.

My eyelids slam shut, but it does nothing to eradicate the vision that plays out before me as I helplessly stand frozen in position while Grave plunges a sword through my chest.

"That motherfucker stabbed me," I blurt as my eyes reopen, and a chuckle from my left catches my attention.

Sebastian.

He looks away quickly, not wanting to anger me, but I can't say I'm mad. I find my mother beside him, and that's when I start to get confused again because I'm completely certain that she wasn't with us when Grave stabbed me. Neither was Rhys, Peta, or Marieta, but here they are, along with…

"Why is papa…"

My words trail off just as quickly as my thoughts and I try to rise enough to shift closer to him, but it takes two attempts before I can make it happen. No one offers me a hint of explanation in that time, which doesn't sit well with me.

I sense it the moment I press a hand to his chest and I gasp, digging deep into my magic to set it to work, but nothing happens. I try again, and again, and again, to no avail, and when I feel a hand clamp down on my shoulder, dread fills my limbs.

"Raven, your hair is black." I glance back, surprised to find it's Rhys attempting to offer me comfort.

"I'm aware," I state, likely harsher than is needed. The man has done nothing wrong, but the emotions bubbling inside of me make it impossible for me to control my tone.

He thankfully doesn't take it personally as he offers me a weak smile. "I'm sure you are, but I'm getting the sense you're not aware of what that means." I gulp, shaking my head. He's right. I don't have a fucking clue, and I get the feeling I'm not going to like what he has to say next, either. He glances at his son before clearing his throat and looking back at me. The discomfort is evident enough to have unease rippling through me. "Research shows that when a necromancer brings someone back from the dead, it leaves an imprint in some way, a marker of the power used and measurement of what's left. In your case; your hair. Which is why your hair has progressed in segments with each time your magic has been used."

I nod in understanding, still not able to shake the weariness coating my skin. "What does it mean when it's all black, Rhys?" I ask, my gut knowing where this is going, but I need to hear someone say it. Unfortunately for him, it's his unwanted responsibility.

"It means you can no longer harness the power to bring someone back from the dead."

My heart seizes, my body freezing as I gape at him. I knew he was going to say it, but it doesn't stop the surprise from taking over.

I don't know how I feel about it. The only person I truly wanted to bring back from the dead was Brax. Everyone else has been at someone else's demand or in honor of a deal I made. My gaze shifts to my brother for a moment, but his face is downcast. He knows. He knows I can't bring back our father because I brought him back first, staining the rest of my hair black for an eternity.

Pursing my lips, I look back down at my father. "What happened?"

I shouldn't care, I shouldn't be bothered that my father, that Abel, is dead, but the younger version of myself, the one who didn't have to question and second guess everyone's intentions, feels every ounce of pain.

"He healed you," my mother croaks, her bottom lip wobbling as she tries to smile, but it falls flat.

"You were on the brink of death," Brax adds, rolling his shoulders back as he clears his throat. "He told us it would drain him, that it would take everything, and I told him to do it." My eyes widen, but I don't see an ounce of regret in his eyes. "He said he loves you, he's sorry, and that you have to stay strong." He nods, more to himself than me, confirming that he relayed a message.

"I don't know how to feel," I murmur, refusing to look at my mother or brother.

"It's okay, Raven. You're not supposed to know right now. You haven't had the easiest relationship with him, a lot of which has unfortunately been outside of his control, but the pain has been everlasting. Let's just make sure he didn't die in vain. You don't have to love him back or even forgive him, but I think you can honor his wish of remaining strong. Then you can process everything else later." My mother swipes at her face, ridding her cheeks of the tears as she smiles at me. It's stronger this time, and one which I manage to return.

Rhys squeezes my shoulder, but he looks around the

group as he speaks. "I know dads are dropping like flies to save their children, but I think I speak on both my and Peta's behalf when I say I hope we've reached the limit of that today. Not that I wouldn't die for my son, or any of you for that matter, but they don't get to take any more lives from us. Agreed?"

I gulp, my throat burning from the ache as I nod. Rising to my feet, I cringe at the blood still staining my clothes. "You're right. They've taken enough. They don't get anything else."

"What do we do now?" Marieta asks, reaching for Brax's arm, and he steps into her half embrace. I watch as her eyes fall closed, relief washing over her. I have no idea what that's about, but the smile on her face calms something inside of me.

"We have to end this war before it leaves the academy. We have about an hour before they leave and descend on Haven's Court," Rhys states, fixing the lapels of his suit as if he's talking about a business meeting instead of a freaking battle.

"Will they really need to battle if they have the aid of The Monarchy? Why not just organize a coup and save on the bloodshed?" Zane scrubs the back of his neck, looking to his father for an answer, but it's Sebastian who clears his throat to speak.

"Because they will want to make a statement. The more

blood and death there is, the more fear he creates. Besides, they don't have the backing of the entire Monarchy, so it's going to be a battle either way."

Peta nods in agreement with Sebastian's assessment. "Their numbers are growing, with or without the other students. We need to throw everything we have at them. Even if it's only those of us here who do it. We need the realm to see that their actions will not be tolerated."

"Not that we have much to work with, but everyone at The Monarchy is now aware of the situation and the fact that some members stand beside this tyrant. Those who disagree will fight on our side. They await our arrival at the gates."

"The gates? Where even are we now?" I ask, suddenly realizing that I'm not actually still in the Gauntlet and the surrounding area isn't familiar.

"We are on one of the surrounding islands near the cliffs of Silvercrest. We managed to attack their wards just long enough to get you out of there with my magic, but I'll have to do it again to try and get them in. And us back there, of course," he adds quickly.

"So it's us and them?" Sebastian clarifies, and Rhys nods.

"Yes. Unless we can remove the control magic from The Monarchy's army."

Taking a deep breath, I know this is it. This is the

moment he was talking about and I waste no time tugging at my core, at my pool of magic, just like he said. Wetting my lips, I take a step back from everyone, making sure I'm not blocked by the tree line as I look up at the grim sky.

"What are you doing, Dove?" Zane asks, moving toward me, but I shake my head.

"I don't really fucking know if I'm honest," I reply, huffing a laugh as I let my eyes fall closed.

Silence descends around us as I focus on my magic, calling out with everything I have, which isn't fucking easy when you've never done it before. It definitely doesn't help that I'm so fucking stubborn and independent. My heart and head don't like the idea of it, but my soul knows better.

I'm ready to give up, drop my arms, dust off my uniform, and get to the academy to battle alone when the subtle sound in the distance rings in my ears.

I open my eyes as the sound of flapping wings gets louder and take in what exactly it is I've done. A smile spreads across my face as allies converge on us from above and below in a deafening flurry. Hope pools in my stomach as familiar faces land with a thud around us, eyeing my family and friends with an air of superiority that makes me want to roll my eyes.

"What is this?" My mother asks, eyes wide with her palm pressed against her chest. Her gaze flits from the griffins to the Drakes before gaping at the growing shadows that surround us.

Creed, Brax, Eldon, and Zane grin at me, making the hope blossoming inside of me burst into a shit-eating grin across my face.

"You said we need everything we've got. This is exactly that."

"You really are incredible, Raven," Rhys murmurs, gaping at the allies that surround us. "Are we ready to put a plan together?"

I nod, surrounded by my familiar. My family. My Drakes. My shadows. My Bishops.

This is everything that I am, and *so* much more than I ever hoped to be. With them at my side, I'm ready to conquer it all.

THIRTY FOUR

Raven

I spend a moment saying goodbye to my father. The words are stilted yet rushed, and I know when I have more time to process everything, I will have more to say, but for now, I surprise myself by leaning in to press a kiss to his forehead.

The second I stand, I'm hauled into a hard chest and the familiar scent that I know belongs to Brax surrounds me. More and more arms wrap around me from every angle and I know it's my men. It's weird being the one on the other side of death.

For me, it was all dark and bleak, but to them? Everything inside of me wants to apologize for putting them through that. Five seconds or five hours in the limbo of the unknown when a loved one is hurt equals the same amount of despair, and I hate that I put them through it.

"I'm sorry," I mutter, and Brax rears back instantly with his usual frown in place.

"Don't fucking apologize. Just be ready for us to slaughter that motherfucker on sight," he grunts, and I have to bite back a smile at his fury.

"He's going down. They're *all* going down," Creed adds, promise in every word, and I let his promise fuel my adrenaline.

"Are we ready?" Rhys asks. I find his gaze over Zane's shoulder and nod.

"Yes."

"And you?" His question is aimed at someone behind me, and as I slip from between my men, I find it's Sebastian who has his attention.

"I'm all in. For my father and for Lyra," he states, a darkness settling over his eyes like I've never seen before. I thought I had seen his dark side before, but this… this is something entirely new. And if it were aimed at me, I'd be terrified.

Mama grabs his hand and he stares down at it, his body stiffening, but he seems to accept her comfort despite his clear desire to not be touched. It's weird to let someone in when you've been programmed to believe they're the enemy. Even weirder when those people are family.

"Everyone, gather in close. We need to meet up with the others. Let the war begin," Rhys says with a heavy exhale, and we all move in before he raises his hands in the air.

My eyes widen as the world shifts around us and I quickly realize he's not using gateways. He's just… moving us.

Noise picks up around us, warped and distant at first, as the scenery changes and bodies come into view. There are more people here than I expected, but still not enough to compete with the entire realm's army.

"Zane!" The shriek comes from a girl who races toward us, bundling Zane in her arms before I can see her face, and my blood runs cold as jealousy coats my skin. My jaw clenches and my nostrils flare as they dance around in a circle, hugging each other.

"As much as green looks good on you, Little Bird. It's his sister," Eldon mutters, nudging me with his elbow, and embarrassment quickly prickles the hairs down my arm, replacing the jealousy that slipped over me so easily.

"I knew that," I grumble, clearing my throat, but I know I'm not fooling anyone.

As if sensing my inner turmoil, the girl releases Zane and her gaze immediately fixes on me. "Oh. My. Gosh. You must be Raven, sans the pink hair, of course." She smiles wide, and as I take in her facial features, it's beyond clear that they're definitely related. "I'm Sammi. The Denver who got the better genes, so I apologize for the shit you have to put up with from this one," she adds, her grin widening even more, and I can't stop my own grin from taking over my lips.

"I'm thankful you're a girl because if you had taken that department as well, I would—"

"Ew! Ew! Ew! Too much. Too fucking much," she squeals, covering her ears with her hands as Zane laughs before smothering my cheek with feather-light kisses. The air transforms around us, a solemn and eerie atmosphere reminding us of what we're about to walk into. "Are you guys ready?"

"I was born ready, Sammi," Zane retorts, puffing out his chest, and she rolls her eyes at him. "I mean it, Zane. I fight for a living. I need to know your head is on straight and you're not going to do something stupid the second we get in there."

"He definitely can't promise that," Brax mutters, earning a death glare from the man in question, but he doesn't respond to him, instead focusing on his sister.

"I've got this, Sammi. I promise."

"Perfect. I was worried I was going to have to make you drop and give me fifty push-ups." She winks at him as he shoves her away, then saunters off to join the others. That's when I actually pay attention to what she's wearing. She's dressed a lot like a student from the Shadowgrim Institute. She's geared up for war in tight attire, covered in sheathes with daggers attached to her in some way or another, and her hair is braided back off her face.

She looks ready for war and I look like I'm ready to… go to first class.

That needs to change, and fast.

"Any chance of getting our hands on some alternative gear to actually go to war in? I don't think this skirt is quite as versatile as I'd like it to be." I'm still looking down at myself as I ask the question, not realizing Rhys has rejoined us. It's all well and good using my magic, but I don't know where I'm at in relation to my closet so I can't quite pinpoint what I need.

"Once we get inside, you can do what you need. We're going to split up once we're in there. The Monarchy members and fighters are going to circle around from the back of the Gauntlet. I believe he is going to have everyone gathered near the main entry point, and we're hoping for the element of surprise. I'll transport you guys to your house so you can take a second, and we'll meet you here." He holds a map out, and we all nod in acknowledgment. "Are the shadows, Drakes, and griffins waiting like we said?"

A smirk tilts up my lip. "Fuck yeah, they are."

The stunning view from the cliff's edge swiftly fills my vision after Rhys gives his orders, and I can't deny that this feels like a final goodbye. This place lured me in, made me believe there was hope in a time when I thought there was none left in the world.

It's weird to consider how things carry on existing whether you do or don't.

Inhaling a deep breath, I take in the jagged edges, the crashing waves, and the birds in the distance one last time. No matter what happens from here, I'm never going to live in these walls again. Win or lose my things will be shipped out and I'm finding a better alternative.

Lips press against my temple, filling me with a calmness that feels out of place in the face of what awaits us around the corner. I lean into their side, peering up at Eldon a moment later.

"Let's gear up. It's about time we brought all of this to an end, don't you think?"

"I couldn't agree more," I murmur, despite the thoughts rattling around in my mind. I want to explain how much he means to me, how much they all mean to me, how this isn't what I wanted for any of us, how I've wondered what a normal, mundane life with them would look like, but none of it is relevant right now.

Maybe if we get through this…

No… *when* we get through this, I can say it all then.

"Why did Rhys send us to our house to change when we could have used our magic to do it?" Brax asks, and I frown, just as confused by it as he is.

"I think he wanted to give us a moment. Everything happened so fast back there, and even though we don't have much time, it's a moment just for us. To take a deep breath, feel gratitude for everything that has led us to this moment, both good and bad. Then we can charge out there, focused and aligned with what needs to be done," Zane explains, the words resonating deep inside of me.

A serene feeling settles over us and I know the rest of my men are letting his words settle in them too.

After a moment, I clear my throat before tugging at my magic to change. I watch the material change on my body, but I still feel the icky blood clinging to my skin, even though it's no longer there.

"Dove, you look hot as fuck," Zane blurts, eyes roaming over me.

"She's ready for battle, now isn't the time for you to start leading with your dick," Brax grumbles, earning a chuckle from Creed and Eldon.

"You're just jealous you don't look that hot ready for battle," Zane retorts, wetting his bottom lip, and I roll my eyes at him.

Black combat pants tucked into black combat boots with a skin-tight long-sleeved t-shirt slipped beneath the waistband. I opt to braid my hair too, taking inspiration from Zane's sister, but I try to pin the entire length to my head in an intricate design so it won't get in my way.

Calling upon my sword, it appears in my hand a moment later and I strap it to my waist. No other weapons, no other items of defense except for the necklace around my neck. I run my fingers over it and take another deep breath, then I tuck it away for safekeeping.

I may not be able to bring anyone back from the dead, but that doesn't mean I've lost my other abilities, and I can still wield the magic gathered in the locket too. Mirror magic is now my bitch if bringing people back from the dead isn't, and I can't deny that it feels right… more me. The version that has had to adapt to the ever-changing world around me.

I'm a force to be reckoned with, and Burton isn't prepared for what's about to come his way.

Looking over at my Bishops standing before me, it feels strange to call them that now. It was a nickname bestowed upon them before I arrived here, and now that they're my men, I don't find it fitting at all. They're more than Bishops, more than any other piece on a chessboard. They're not a game piece to be played at someone else's whim. They're strong, resilient, and the backbone keeping me up.

They're each wearing similar outfits to me, black from

top to bottom, with fitted long-sleeve t-shirts, combat pants, and boots. They have more weapons attached to their hips in comparison to me, but Zane is right: prepared for war is definitely a hot look.

I store that fact away for another time as I roll my shoulders back, stand tall, and exhale.

I'm ready.

I part my lips, about to say those exact words when a garbled cry softly echoes in the air. My eyebrows pinch and I glance at the others to see if they heard it too. Everyone's heads whip around when it sounds again, and we start to try and follow it to see what the source is.

Walking along the cliff's edge away from our house, the guys right beside me, it feels as though the noise is getting louder, and after a few moments, understanding comes into view.

"Holy fuck." I gasp, gaping at Leila, off the side of the cliff, her back pinned to the jagged rocks. Her arms are wrapped around herself as she sobs, confirming the source of the sound, and I hurry toward her.

"Raven, wait. It could be a trap," Creed calls out, but it's too late to question myself because I'm hovering above her, calling out her name.

She cranes her neck, staring up at me with tears streaming down her face. She blinks, and blinks again, her cries softening as she looks from me to my men and back again.

"Raven," she croaks, tears continuing to flow down her cheeks. "You're here. Y-you're not d-dead."

I try to smile, but I know it doesn't meet my eyes. "No, I'm not. What's going on here, Leila?" I ask, and she swipes her hands down her face, a choked snicker tumbling from her lips.

"My father wasn't too happy with how I used my magic on Grave the second his grandfather's abilities didn't render me useless. I didn't realize he could slow time for everyone in the vicinity."

"What do you mean?" Brax grunts, folding his arms over his chest.

She's the closest thing to a best friend I've ever had, so I hate that I do it, but I press my hand to my locket, seeking Lyra's magic to ensure she gives us nothing but the truth.

"I mean that motherfucker stabbed Raven. Rage coursed through me, and in the next breath you were all gone, and someone had to retaliate."

"So you decided that person should be you," Creed states, and she nods.

"Even if he hadn't hurt Raven, I would have done it. That fucker used me, or tried to at least. The entire time he was working with my father, with *him*. I'm pretty sure my father made a big fucking deal about me hanging out with him because he knew it would push me to go against his wishes anyway and throw me into the arms of the person he wanted me beside all along." The tears start again, her pain vibrating from her.

"Is Grave...?"

"No, I didn't get the opportunity to kill him. My father intercepted me before I could," she admits, hanging her head in shame, but I'm quite certain the fact that he's still breathing is a relief because I want to either do it myself or watch one of my men finish him. I deserve the satisfaction of watching him fall.

"Can we help her up?" I ask, unsure how to go about it, but the guys make it look simple as they hoist her up and place her on the grass beside me.

"Thank you," she murmurs, running her fingers through her hair before exhaling harshly.

"Why did he leave you here like this?"

Her gaze falls to her hands twisted in her lap. "He declared me unsuitable to fight because I refused to stand beside them." A hysterical chuckle breaks free from her throat as she shakes her head. "He muttered some shit about protecting me too, but felt I needed to be taught a lesson at the same time. Hence the cliff hanging." Her head sags further with disappointment. "I had been holding out hope that he was under someone else's control, Raven. Like, silently pleading every moment of every day, and to realize that this is all him…it's harder to swallow than I expected."

My chest clenches for her. All of this is hard, but at least on my end, both Sebastian and my father weren't truly themselves. It doesn't make their actions any less heinous, but it clouds my instinctive thoughts to rain Hell down upon them.

Standing, I offer her my hand, and she takes it.

"I can't believe you're here," she rasps, making my chest clench for an entirely different reason.

"Are you ready to fight?"

She nods before I even finish asking. "I'm ready to wreak havoc."

Determination flashes in her eyes as Eldon pats her on the shoulder. "Perfect," he mutters in approval.

"What's the plan?" Her hands clench at her sides and her sword appears a moment later, ready for whatever comes next.

Smiling, I'm sure I look feral, but I'm channeling it. "We'll walk and talk."

THIRTY FIVE

Raven

Rejoining Rhys and the small army we have gathered is easier than I expected. Zane's father leads the way, his sister a step behind him, with men and women he's explained are part of her battalion behind her.

His sister is a soldier. She's badass as fuck, and I'm in awe of her.

Brax's parents, along with my Mother and Sebastian, walk behind them, followed by another battalion, while we bring up the rear.

They're more practiced than us; that much is clear. They walk stealthily, not making a single sound. I assumed that's why they were going unnoticed as we made our way around the Gauntlet area, down toward where Rhys believes Burton is gathered, and although their ability to be so covert could definitely be adding to the fact, it's not the only reason why.

It seems we haven't truly seen the full extent of Burton's theatrics and how eccentric they can get when he's wearing the fur cloak and scar as Erikel.

They're gathered by the main gates, the exact ones where we met Zane's sister and everyone else on the other side. The entire student body from Shadowgrim Insititute stands around the perimeter, weapons raised and attack stances taken. They're watching for us, waiting for us to come charging at them from every direction except the one we're approaching from. They're expecting us to come from outside of the academy.

Dumb. As. Fuck.

"Is he…?"

"Yes, yes he is," I murmur, peering up at Eldon, who can't seem to finish the sentence even though the answer is staring us right in the face.

Zane snickers, shaking his head as the black throne floats in the sky, Burton perched on it with the furs drifting in the wind, still disguised as Erikel. A mass of Monarchs, soldiers, and students stand around him. Some with foggy eyes that don't seem all that present, while others tremble in fear. The ones doing neither of those are the most concerning, the ones eager for blood.

I tighten my grip on my sword, prepared for whatever comes next. I'm confused by the fact they haven't seen us yet until Rhys turns to face us all.

"In a few moments, Sammi is going to drop our invisibility cloak."

My jaw drops, my awe for Zane's sister only growing. I peer up at him and he grins. He has the same magic as his sister. Does anyone else in his family tree have it? Is he capable of keeping a large group like this hidden in plain sight in the future?

Holy. Fuck.

"Close your mouth, Dove," he whispers with a smirk, and I slam my lips closed, focusing back on his father.

"Once she does, I'm going to address them, give the students the chance to actually choose their side, but after that… it's all out of my control. I know we're all here for our own reasons, but above everything else, we know this isn't right. Not for this academy, not for the realm, not for our people. If I die today, which I would rather I didn't, I'll know it was for the purpose of the people." Cheers ring out through the crowd and my gaze darts toward Burton, but still, they are oblivious to us. "Any final words?" he adds, scanning over the crowd, but no one responds. He's said what needs to be said. We're not wasting our time on dramatics. "Sammi, release me from the magic first. I want Raven held off until the end."

I frown, instantly wanting to correct him, but Creed quickly whispers in my ear. "Element of surprise."

Gulping back the instinctive defenses that have risen in my chest, I nod.

Rhys produces a sword at his side, sheathing it as he starts down the grassy hill toward the gathered crowd. Burton doesn't notice him at first, his arms wide in the air as he speaks down to the crowd.

"Our first attack will be Shadowmoor. We'll lower the defenses at their weakest spot, show them the blood we can shed, and then we'll move up. Pinebrook isn't on the list; we already made a display there, caused a stir. Once we've hit their vulnerabilities, we will finally bring this to Haven Court. By which time, there will be nothing left for them to defend, and anyone remaining at The Monarchy who isn't on our side will face our wrath."

The army around him cheers, but there are many students among the crowd who remain silent, their faces growing paler as the reality of what they're getting into continues to unravel before them. This is exactly what we were being trained for, the whole reason we were here, but now that they're being put into action—on the enemy's side, no less—it's all becoming a lot more real.

"That's quite a speech, Burton, but I must say, I don't think you're the best person to lead anyone into anything, much less a war," Rhys commands, his voice carrying far and wide, gathering everyone's attention.

I instantly spot Grave and his grandfather, their eyes

widening at the sight of him, but they quickly brush it off as they turn to face him.

"The Monarchy isn't on your side, Denver; give up now," Burton orders with a sneer, not acknowledging the fact that he called him Burton instead of Erikel.

Rhys shakes his head as if he's disappointed to be dealing with this fool. I know the feeling. "We don't need The Monarchy on our side. We just need the power-hungry fuckers to be gone from this realm and the next."

"I think you're outnumbered for that," he remarks, the onyx throne slowly lowering to the ground. He really thinks he's worthy of leading our entire realm. That's not what we're made from. The Monarchy is already fucked; using Shadowmoor as it has, making moves for personal gain. We need a change, but this definitely isn't it.

Rhys doesn't respond to him. Instead, he turns to the crowd, specifically the students. "If you wish to fight for this man, please remain where you are. I will apologize now for your death in the near future. However, if you would like to fight for the greatness of our realm, now is your moment to decide. Unfortunately, your training hasn't been for the weak, so not fighting isn't an option. For those not wanting to sacrifice themselves for the greater good, you will find yourselves caught in the crossfires regardless." Gentle murmurs shift over the students, indecision flashing across their faces as they glance between the two men leading either side. One is erratic and full of theatrics, while the other is composed and calm. "There you have this man you barely know, with the corrupt members of The Monarchy, or you have me, Monarch Denver, still fighting for my realm until the end."

"They know me. They know who I am!" Burton snaps, the scar down his face turning redder with every passing moment.

"No, we don't." The outburst comes from the crowd of students, and I recognize the guy as the same one who had the balls to stand up to Burton in the Nightmares Guild.

"Yes. You. Do." The words echo around us like thunder and my body stiffens as if ready for the lightning I know will follow, and it does. But not in the way I would ever expect.

There's no flash, no chaos, just the transformation of the man holding everyone's attention.

Gasps ricochet around us as the scar disappears, the long hair retreats, but the fur cloak remains. Only now, it's draped over Burton's shoulders.

"He thinks revealing himself as Burton now is going to win some of them over? Why even bother to begin with?" Brax grunts from beside me, and I hum in agreement.

None of this man's actions make any fucking sense. It's pointless for us to try and understand it now.

"What I am doing *is* for the greater good. Things have

to change. Sacrifices need to be made. I've lost everything to The Monarchy, this academy, and now is the time for me to take everything back. With you at my side," he bellows, his jaw clenching tight with confined rage.

"And you expect us to follow you now that you've revealed another secret, another layer of doubt between you and us?" the same guy pushes back, and I can't deny it; I'm impressed.

Sammi doesn't seem to think the same, however. She shakes her head as she folds her arms over her chest. "He's going to get himse—" Her sentence is cut short by a thud, followed swiftly by a gargled grunt, and I blink down at the crowd to find him bleeding out on the grass. My chest clenches, horror dancing in my vision. "Dead," she mutters, her head hanging in disappointment, and my desire to kill this fucker only increases.

"Does anyone else want to question me? Stand against me? Do it. I promise you, it won't end well."

Silence descends over everyone as questioning gazes flicker from one person to another until, one by one, the members of the Nightmare Guild step out of the crowd and head toward Rhys.

Once they're all standing behind Rhys, I assess the remaining students, and it's clear they're staying out of fear, but I can't let the weight of that rest on my shoulders. It's their choice to let fear guide them. It's my choice to have strength lead me.

"You still don't have enough to go against us, and once we leave the academy, the realm won't stand a chance," Burton grinds out, and Rhys shrugs so casually that I have to bite back a snicker.

"You won't leave the academy, and you, of all people, should know that some things aren't always as they seem," Rhys retorts. Sammi takes that as her cue, briefly looking over her shoulder to lock eyes with Zane before dropping the magic from around us.

Burton's stare darkens as he takes in the larger group than what was present moments earlier, and I don't miss the curse under his breath. His gaze skims over me, though, making me pout, but I quickly realize why. There's a hand on my shoulder.

Not just any hand; Zane's.

He's shielding me.

"Hidden until the last minute, remember?" He quirks a brow at me and I roll my eyes but nod in agreement. Looking down the line of us, from Brax to Creed, Eldon, Leila, and Zane, I know this is the last moment of us like this, as these people. Whatever follows ends with us dead or tainted by our actions. Either way, I soak it in, this very moment, letting it spike my adrenaline as we move with the crowd.

"You think you can take me down with this group of…

nobodies? I have waited too long for this. I vowed to avenge my wife, my child, and you will not get in the way of that," Burton snarls, irritating me further because I still don't understand what he's avenging them for. Not that it really matters now when he's beyond reason. "Shadowgrim, do not let them advance any further," he snaps, and a moment later, the sound of bows being drawn rings in my ears. I look across the main crowd to see each student, Ruben included, with arrows aimed in our direction.

Rhys unsheaths his sword, twirling it in the air before aiming the tip at Burton. "There's no going back from this, Burton. What happened to Finnea never had to come to this, and I will not allow it to go any further," he promises, and my eyes narrow. He knows what this is about. Why the fuck don't we?

We're at war for a man's love of someone he believes is unfairly treated. If I had stumbled into this before meeting my men, it would have put me off love altogether, but now I can kind of understand the desire to protect those we love, no matter the cost. It doesn't mean his actions are right though, and we're going to have to prove that to him.

"Fire!"

The command is followed effortlessly by the whistle of arrows soaring through the air in our direction, a few grunts of pain echo around us as some hit their target, and I stumble to the side to avoid one aimed our way.

In doing so, I fall from Zane's grasp, and a moment later, I find eyes settled on mine. Death thunders in his vision as he loses the fur cloak and aims his finger in my direction.

"You."

THIRTY SIX

Raven

Calculating eyes and measured steps approach me as the rest of the world seems to drift away. The disbelief is evident. I shouldn't be alive. He didn't want me here, which is likely because I'm of no use to him now. I can't bring people back from the dead, but screw him for underestimating me once again. Or, more specifically, underestimating the love people have for me, which is matched only by my love for them.

When people like you and care for you, they actually want to be around you, a concept I'm quite sure he's unfamiliar with. My mind immediately goes to my men, who I know are around me somewhere, I just don't know where, exactly.

Burton, however, feeds on fear and power. A constant, eternal need for power. Even when he was just Burton and not the mirage of Erikel, he was always using power and talking down to everyone with a special level of finesse that only he could achieve.

I know there are people moving around us, but I can't take my eyes off him. As he continues to inch closer, I reach for my sword, tingling with the preemptive expectation of slicing this fucker open.

The vision becomes more vivid as he nears, and the taste of it on my tongue becomes more desirable until he's barreling toward the floor, tumbling to my right, and the sound of a riot bursts around me.

I don't see who does it because I'm too swept up in the battle cries that reverberate around us. A glint of gold shimmers as it flies toward my head, and I kick into action just before it can connect with its intended target: my throat.

The clang of metal on metal vibrates through me as I look up at a woman I don't know. That doesn't stop her from glaring at me, evil intent in her eyes as she tries to push her weight down on me.

I falter an inch, the blades coming closer to my face, and her sneer spreads into a triumphant grin. It lasts all of two seconds before I grunt, thrusting up and knocking her away. She stumbles over her own feet, clattering to the ground with a shriek.

Her eyes turn to pits of death as she looks back at me,

and fire appears in the palm of her hand. I know exactly where she's going with that heat, and I don't fucking want it. Before she can singe a single hair on my head, I wield my sword and slam it in her direction.

Blood pools at my feet, seeping around her as her eyelids pause at half-mast and her body goes limp. My pulse thunders in my ears, confirming exactly what I just did, but I brush it off and take a deep breath.

Right now, it's either kill or be killed, and I'm not down for the latter. I can figure out how to compartmentalize all of that until there's a moment to consider it, and even then, I may lock the door shut and keep it that way forever.

"Raven, you good?" I whirl around at the sound of Eldon's voice and smile when my eyes lock with his.

"Yeah," I breathe, earning a nod from him before he charges off to the left, battling with a student from Shadowgrim.

Fuck. I better do the same.

There's going to be a lot of blood on my hands by the time we're done here, and there isn't a spare moment for me to relax between engagements.

Inhaling, I search around me, watching as magic is thrown around and weapons launch through the air. I get the briefest fangirl moment, watching as Sammi slices someone's head off with ease, but a flicker of movement behind her has me pausing.

Wild blond hair drifts around in the air as a girl storms with purpose across the field. I try to look ahead to see where she's fixated, and it's not a surprise to see the same motherfucker I want dead caught in her line of sight.

Shoving through the crowd, my sword dragging through the dirt as I go, I startle when she raises her hands above her head. A scream pierces the air as she thrusts them down, and ice darts toward her target.

"Leila!" I holler, just as a sword is swung through the air, and I duck down, rolling through the dirt to avoid the blade before continuing toward her. "Leila," I repeat, not wanting to distract her, but the look on her target's face tells me he's completely unfazed by her attempt to hurt him.

Grave.

His lip is curled with a smirk as he watches her, effortlessly brushing off the ice that managed to touch him, but the second he sees me over her shoulder, the look drops from his face.

That's right, motherfucker, you didn't kill me like you thought.

I hope I'm a living nightmare as I make my way toward him with blood splattered up my dark clothes and across my face. I hope I'm what haunts him in Hell, where he'll never rest.

Leila follows his line of sight, catching a glimpse of

me, and it gives him the split second he needs to get the upper hand. His arms go around her neck as he hauls her back against him. She kicks and swings her arms around, but he doesn't falter.

I approach him, sauntering through the crowd with my predatory stare locked on my prey.

"Come any closer, and I'll kill her," he warns, making me scoff.

"Please, you're going to kill her whether I approach or not." His eyes darken, hating that I know his plays, but unfortunately for him, I don't have time to waste spreading out the torture for his long-overdue death. "Now, you're going to let her go because you've done enough damage to her, and you and I are going to fight this out. You owe me."

His jaw tics, irritation creeping up his cheeks, but his hold on Leila only tightens.

Fine, I guess we're going to have to do this the hard way.

"Leila," I call out calmly, and her gaze fixes on me as she goes still in his hold. "Aim low," I state, not wasting a moment before I eliminate the remaining space between us with my sword aimed high as she forces all of her weight to the ground.

Grave is too busy trying to keep his hold on Leila to brace for my attack, so it's completely satisfying and devastatingly swift when my blade spears into the flesh at his throat, digging deep as blood squirts everywhere. The nick of an important artery will do that to you.

His grip on Leila quickly relaxes and she stumbles from his grasp a moment later, catching herself at my side as she turns to watch the life drain from this asshole's face. I tug my sword from his throat for good measure as he drops to his knees, eyes rolling to the back of his head before he collapses in a heap.

Holy fuck.

I was hoping for something way more satisfying when it came to him, but I guess it will have to do. Instead, I grab the hilt of my sword with both hands and sweep the blade down on his lifeless body a few more times for good measure. As someone who didn't quite die at the hands of one of these swords, I want to be sure he definitely gets the pleasure.

"Are you okay?" I ask, peering at Leila, who nods distractedly for a moment before she shakes it off and turns to face me.

"Thank you."

"Where's your sword?" I ask, not acknowledging her appreciation when I definitely did it more for myself than anyone else.

"My father took it."

"Took it? Where is he?" My gaze is already sweeping around the crowd, but there's too much happening around us to see him.

"I don't fucking know," she grumbles, sweeping a bloody hand down her face.

"Why can't you just summon it back? Fuck him," I grunt, and she sighs.

"Because he snapped it in half, rendering it useless."

Professor Fitch will forever be an enigma to me. He's a self-centered, single-minded fool. I'd gladly see him dead too.

It's on the tip of my tongue to offer her mine before I remember that the swords choose us, so sharing isn't caring in this instance.

"Fuck, Raven," she murmurs, the tone heightening my adrenaline and drawing my focus back to our immediate surroundings, where I find Ruben approaching us with two of his henchman flanking his sides.

Perfect.

The three of them circle around us like we're the dainty little hunted, but I'm not afraid of them. Ruben makes a little show of twirling his sword around in the air and I yawn, absolutely fucking bored.

"Are you done? We actually have shit to do," I stare at my nails, picking at the blood that's already starting to dry, and Ruben laughs like I'm telling the world's best joke.

"Baby Girl, I'm just sad I won't get to pry those legs open before I kill you. Maybe I can keep your body out of sight so I can come back for you later," he says with a wink, making bile burn the back of my throat as Leila openly wretches.

"You're disgusting," she snaps.

"And you're dead," he retorts, slowing a few yards away from us, and I have to school my features for a whole five seconds before I get to throw his own words back at him.

"No… you are." I smile wide as three out of my four men come to a stop behind them, swords poised between their shoulder blades before they stab them with force, their blades erupting through the fronts of their chests. Wide eyes meet mine and I can't help but inch closer to Ruben as he falls forward, capturing his chin in between my finger and thumb.

"Don't worry, Baby Boy, I have no intentions of fucking your corpse, but I'm going to leave you in the perfect spot for the Drakes to feast on you." I look over his head, meeting Brax's stare, and nod. One motion from me, and he twists the sword inside him before snapping it back. He falls at my feet beside his comrades, death claiming each of them in turn.

"Blood should not look this good on you," Creed states with an assessing eye, and I gape at him for a moment, expecting that kind of comment to come from Zane, not him. Eldon pats his friend on the shoulder and Brax shakes his head gruffly while I try to figure out where the insane one is.

"Where's Zane?" I ask, glancing around to come up empty-handed.

"With Sammi," Eldon explains, pointing off to the left, and I see the siblings fighting side by side. This shit is intense, and I'm just standing here when there's more to be done.

Nodding, I turn to my right, where more danger lurks from the enemy, Burton at the back, manically laughing with blood splattered across his face. But right now, he seems intent on watching the battle unfold instead of partaking like everyone else.

"What have I missed?" A light voice startles me, and the sight of Professor Figgins at my side catches me even more off-guard. I haven't seen her since the day we broke down the compound wards together.

"Where have you been?" I ask, an accusatory glare on my face that I can't seem to conceal.

Her cheeks turn pink as she looks down at the ground for a moment before she clears her throat and meets my stare. "Honestly, I felt the magic shift in the air and ran."

"Doesn't seem like you got all that far," I state, quirking a brow as I acknowledge the fact that she's still somehow standing before me.

Scratching at her neck, I notice that she's in similar

attire as us instead of the usual cloak and professor-esque clothes she would normally wear.

"When I got to where I was going, I decided I was in search of my number one ally before I swiftly turned around and found you all here."

"Ally?" I ask, aware the chaos around us is getting closer. With a smirk, she points in the distance, confirming exactly why that is.

A huge monster prowls toward us with four legs, fur, and a snarly set of teeth. It's like a cat, only one hundred times bigger.

Holy. Fuck.

"Your familiar?"

"Uh-huh. Although, I must say, I was expecting to see yours," she pushes back, and I grin.

"He's been waiting for my call, and I agree, maybe now is the time," I murmur, taking a step back as I lift my hands up in the air, summoning him and the shadows, along with the Drakes, once again.

I feel the energy shift in the air as they draw near, and I barge my way through the crowd so I can have the perfect view of Burton when he sees them approach. His lip lifts in a sneer when he sees Ari leading the griffins, all together, before he fully bares his teeth at the sight of the Drakes.

That's right, motherfucker, they're still pledging themselves to me because I'm not dead.

But it's when the sky darkens, all of existence solemn as shadows consume every inch of the land that surrounds us, that Burton's stare finds mine. His hands clench at his sides as he struggles to contain the rage burning through his veins.

Come and get me, old man.

Slipping back into the throng of fighting soldiers, I block one attack from someone's short daggers and step into a blast of flames before sinking my sword to the hilt in some random soldier intent on bringing me down.

My limbs ache, my head is foggy, and my eyes are tired, but there's no time to rest. Not until everything is dealt with.

"Hey, Raven." I tilt my face to the left to see Sammi jogging toward me. Her face is practically covered in blood, her clothes drenched in it too, but she pays it no mind as she nods toward where Burton stands. "I think we're wasting time and energy taking down these men and women. They're nothing in the grand scheme of things, innocent lives, if anything. What we really need to be doing is taking down the man controlling them." Her stare locks on Burton, who is now flanked by Grave's grandfather and Professor Fitch.

Fuckers.

She's right. She's more than right. That's exactly where we need to be focusing all of our energy.

A hand lands on my shoulder and I glance back to see Zane staring down at me. More bodies inch closer, and I know it's not with dangerous intent, it's with love. I make eye contact with all of them.

Zane.

Eldon.

Creed.

Brax.

"Together?" Eldon calls before pressing a kiss to my crown, and I smile, content despite the circumstances.

"Together," I repeat, the word soothing me and encouraging me in one breath.

We move as one, Sammi, Leila, and Professor Figgins right there with us as the monsters on our side wreak havoc on the fodder of people that stand in our way. Fitch is the first to notice our approach, distaste filling his eyes as he sets his sight on his daughter. He shakes his head, but it doesn't falter her steps at all.

"Figgins, take Fitch with Sammi. Leila, stay by Raven, who is going straight for Burton. Zane will be right there with you while Creed, Eldon, and I charge Monarch Richardson. Use your familiar if necessary, Figgins. We end this all now," Brax commands, sending another thrill of adrenaline through my body.

I press my palm against my chest, feeling the necklace around my neck. They may know I can mirror magic, but they don't know I have it accessible like this.

Burton is more than aware that he's now our target and sends soldiers toward us in a bid to stop our ascent, but our path remains clear with the aid of the Drakes as they continue to interfere, slaughtering anyone who gets in our way. He stumbles back a step when we're within a few yards, but I don't quicken my pace to get to him. I want to see this play out in his eyes for as long as possible.

Second by second, minute by minute, I want this to be what he remembers when he realizes his efforts were no match for us, were no match for me.

"You think you can defeat me? You're nothing, no one. Your greatest attribute was used up before I could even make full use of you. I have no magic worth mirroring, unless you want to skin-walk as me for a moment, feel what greatness truly is before you meet your demise," he bites, his words thrumming from him as I simply smile.

Get close enough to hurt a man like this and he'll quickly shift the narrative to bring you down, twisting words to hurt you instead of letting you get close enough to see how truly weak and undesirable he is.

I won't be fooled by it, by him. I know my worth and my value, and it doesn't come from what magic I can or cannot do. It comes from within, from who I am and what I believe is right. None of which aligns with this man.

He's strung us along on a ride that has made no sense to

anyone but him, caused distress and heartache to everyone simply to further his agenda, and I'm done.

"I know I can't defeat you, Burton. Not alone. I've known it since the moment I got here, believing I was a Void. But you're fragile, exposed, wounded, and completely powerless. Whatever drives you doesn't seek purpose in me; that's never going to change. You should have killed me when you had the chance instead of playing me in a game I had no need to be in." My grip on my sword tightens as my left hand clasps tight, too.

"No? You don't think you would go to extreme lengths to protect those you love? Let's put that to the test, shall we?" He whistles before I have a chance to answer and a shrill cry echoes around me. Turning toward the sound, I find my mother lifted off the ground and my heart lurches, but I focus on keeping my features neutral. "What would you do if I killed her right now?"

I shrug. "You've already caused the death of my father today, what's one more?" I poke, hating the taste of the words on my tongue. Instead of faltering under the pressure of my family's lives in his hands, I move closer, much to his annoyance.

"Let's see, shall we?"

I rush toward him, only a few feet between us, hoping to catch him before he can make another move, but as I swing my blade at him, the shrill cry gets louder, raking my bones. I can't look. Instead, I swing again and again, hating that he dodges both moves.

His face isn't one of boasting, though; if anything, he looks angrier. Risking a glance behind me, I see why a moment later. The blood of my family is being spilled all over the grass in a horrific display, but not my mother's…

Sebastian.

I don't know what happened or how, but the way Mama cries and the placement of his body, I know in my heart he was defending her.

Fuck.

"That part of your bloodline won't cause you any pain," he grunts, and the words cascade over me in the strangest way, because there is definite pain twisting in my gut.

I've said it before, but now there is nothing between us. I am done with this man and his bullshit. It ends today, now, in this moment, written in the history books as nothing more than a battle at Silvercrest Academy.

I launch my sword at him but he manages to sidestep the onslaught just in time and it slams into the ground beside him. My blade is useless when it comes to this man. It's going to take everything to bring him down, and I'm going to make it happen.

Glancing to my left, Zane nods at me, silently confirming he's here for whatever I need, and a brief flick of my eyes to my right confirms Leila is on the same page.

"Throw everything at him. Everything," I breathe, not even truly sure if they can hear me or not, but in the next moment, I aim down my sights, clench my left hand as tightly as possible around the locket I snapped from my neck on my march over here, and throw Hell at him.

My emotions cling to the magic, erratically burning through my limbs as I scream, thrusting my hands in his direction.

Fire travels over my arms as they turn to stone. At the same time, Leila blasts him with ice and Zane uses his magic to launch a tree at him. My vision blurs, power rippling through my body as I continue to step closer, closing the gap to my final goal.

The moment I'm within arm's reach, I rear my arm back before slamming my gargoyle fist into his face, repeating the motion for a second time for good measure before I slam both hands against either side of his face. I expect to set him alight and watch him burn at my touch, but it's Creed's magic that flickers forward, and my mind is consumed with his memories and thoughts.

Darkness sweeps over me, pinning me in place as the image of a couple walking hand in hand swims to the forefront of my mind. A toddler waddles a step in front of them as they laugh. I can feel the warmth, the love, the family aura that surrounds them, and it's so sickly sweet it almost hurts. Then it does. Hurt.

The scene shifts before me. Only the woman is present now. The open area seems familiar and it takes a second for me to recognize we're at The Monarchy's big HQ in Haven Court, where I first met Rhys.

She scurries through the halls, panic clinging to her as she rushes into a small room and slams the door shut behind her.

My brain swirls with the fact that he has this memory even though he isn't present, and it makes my head pulse with a vigorous headache.

"Do you have the answer?"

The question startles her and she presses her hand to her chest as she tries to catch her breath. Slowly, she shakes her head. "M-My husband doesn't know what you speak of," she insists, the tremor running through her making me shiver too.

I can't see who she is speaking to; they're perfectly seated in the dark corner of the room, out of view. All I know is the voice belongs to a man.

"Does your husband understand the consequences of his lies?" She scrunches her face, shaking her head again, and the snarl from the corner takes my breath as it roars around the room. "Make sure he's aware that your death will forever stain his hands."

"Raven! Raven!"

The present slams back into view, but my breath is still

lodged in my throat back in that memory.

"Raven. He's gone. He's gone." I blink at Zane, his voice registering in my head, but the words don't make sense.

Slowly, my senses come back, one at a time, and an awful burning tingles at my fingers. I look down at my hands and gasp. Tendrils of flames dance at my fingertips as large embers burn beneath them.

What was there?

What was decimated at my touch?

I frown, glancing up at Zane once again as he speaks. "Raven. He's gone. Burton is gone, you can let go now."

Wrenching my hands back, I take in the burning remnants as understanding washes over me.

He's gone. He's fucking gone.

I drop to my knees, my body aching from the magic still storming through my body. Maybe using multiple tendrils of magic all at once isn't the best idea, even if it wasn't intentional.

"Raven?" Zane repeats, but his voice is softer, distant, as I fall to my back, blinking up at the sky with deep exhaustion consuming every inch of me.

I need to sleep for a minute, an hour, a day, a week; I don't know, but I don't have a choice, I just know I have to. My eyelids grow heavy, weighing me down, but I don't miss the first peek of the sun bursting through the clouded sky that has been cast over us for what feels like forever.

I smile.

A sense of relief washes over me as I willingly allow the darkness to take me while two mantras, filled with words that were once haunting, play in my mind before everything goes quiet.

Follow your heart, find solace in the shadows, and take down the dawn.

Follow the sun, destroy the shadows, and survive another dawn.

EPILOGUE
Raven

"The faster we get this done, the sooner you get your surprise." I quirk an eyebrow at Zane, who wiggles his back at me, and my eyes narrow. "I'm just saying. Tick tock. Tick tock."

Damn, it's a good thing he's handsome, because if he was this annoying without being so pretty to look at I think I may have throttled him by now.

"Maybe if you tell me what my incentive is it might make me speed up," I retort, which only earns me a chuckle from Eldon.

"That's not how surprises work, Little Bird," he mutters before pressing a kiss at my temple. The move softens the irritation that was rising in me and I relax. "But it's pretty good, so get a move on," he adds, spiking the annoying intrigue inside of me once again.

Turning away from the pair of them, Creed and Brax too, I look at the shimmering emerald gate that appeared this morning.

"Five days. Five damn days of hoping for peace since fighting in an actual battle and they give me trouble like this. I thought I was going to be able to rest," I grumble to myself, completely aware they can hear me.

"You had plenty of rest when you slept the first two days of that. Two days we, in fact, didn't get to rest because we were beside ourselves with worry over you," Creed points out, and I roll my eyes at him.

So dramatic.

I was fine. I just needed to recover from wielding too much magic all at once and finally bringing Burton down. It still doesn't feel real. Everything feels far too…serene. Right now, it's calmer than it was before Erikel appeared, more relaxing than when I was in Shadowmoor, and less stressful than any other moment I've ever experienced in my life.

It's not a feeling I'm familiar with, but apparently, it's one I need to get used to. Especially if my men have anything to say about it.

Burton is gone. Forever. But it still confuses me why he chose to impersonate Erikel. What connection does that have to anything? I don't understand. I've mentioned it to Rhys twice now, and there's something about the look in his eyes that tells me he knows, but he's not open to sharing. Maybe I don't need to know, but that doesn't mean I don't *want* to know. I fought a damn war for it.

The only other enigma I still face is the reappearance of the emerald gate before me. An addition which has had me rereading the scrolls about the magical items that make this world so damn messed up.

In my slumber, Rhys transported us back to his home, Zane's childhood home, for us to rest and recoup while I slept away my worries. I've enjoyed the past three days exploring the ridiculously large grounds, meeting with my mother, and indulging in my men in the entire fucking wing dedicated to Zane.

This morning, however, when I stepped out of our bedroom to slip down the hallway to the main bathroom with the clawfoot bath, I was stopped in my tracks by the shimmering green gems.

With the shadows still around, I knew we had missed something with the prophecy, but there was no time for me to consider anything with everything else unraveling around us. It seems the gate felt the same way, waiting until now to reappear.

The passage I came across earlier consumes my mind. As if sensing my thoughts, Brax speaks. "We just need to figure this out, Shadow. Then, the passage promised that the completion of the prophecy regarding the Realm of

Shadows would come to fruition."

"You say that like I'm going to have any confirmation once it's done," I grouch, huffing in irritation, even though I'm aware it's definitely not his fault.

"It states that once the prophecy is completed the correct Realm of the Afterlife will be restored. The shadows will be where they're supposed to be. They'll be safe. Will we have confirmation? No. But we will have done everything we can on our side, and if not, we'll know because they'll still be here. Which means we'll keep trying until they're fucking not."

Well… when he puts it like that.

"Say it to me one more time." I don't peer back over my shoulder to clarify who I'm talking to. He's read it to me far too many times already to know I mean him.

His heavy sigh echoes around me, but I know it's not frustration at me. It's at the fucking prophecy. "When green arches hold delicate reds, all that is needed is a touch of darkness, a promise of change, and an unwavering belief."

I purse my lips as my foot taps on the marble floor. Initially, we had assumed my stepping through the green arch into the Realm of Shadows and holding the Potens Ruby was what was needed, but clearly not.

Edging closer to the emerald arch, I let my fingers run over the gems. When I reach the top, hovering on my tiptoes, I pause. The familiar feel of sharp edges and smooth surfaces is absent, making me frown.

"Brax, can you—" My words are cut off when he stands before me a moment later, hands wrapping around my waist as he nuzzles his face in my neck. I hum in approval, still caught off-guard when he lets down his walls and embraces me like this.

"Whatever you need, Shadow," he breathes, and I smile.

"Can you lift me in the air? Just a little, please," I ask, and before I can finish saying please, I find myself in the air already.

I can see the top of the arch much better from here, and a gem-shaped space at the crown of the keystone sits empty, just like my fingers detected. "Do we have the ruby?"

A moment later, I feel the press of a jewel in my palm and glance down to see Eldon smirking up at me. He wraps my knuckles around it, pressing a feather-light kiss to them before releasing my hand.

Slowly prying my hand open, the Potens Ruby gleams, trying to draw the desire out of me to use it for my needs instead of getting rid of it. Its allure does nothing for me, and I waste no time holding it up to the empty spot.

It fits perfectly, and when I push it into place, a shiver runs down my spine. Brax pulls me back a step, lowering me to my feet as the jewels shine bright.

"What—" Creed's question is short-lived as the room falls dark.

One by one, shadows and silhouettes appear before us, dancing along the walls and stretching along the floor before embracing the darkness that falls inside the emerald arch. It feels like hundreds, if not thousands, appear, some taking their time while others rush through until, all at once, the room goes still again and the emerald gate shatters. Shielding my face, I brace for impact, but it's as if it implodes, all the shards drifting into the darkness just like the shadows did moments ago, taking the Potens Ruby along with them.

"When green arches hold delicate reds, all that is needed is a touch of darkness, a promise of change, and an unwavering belief. The Potens Ruby needed to go *in* the actual emerald arch. Even though you're technically not a necromancer anymore, your touch still counts as darkness. You've done more than promise change with an unwavering belief, Dove."

I take a deep breath, letting Zane's words wash over me. They're all true, all correct, but it's still weird as hell that he's referring to me when he says it.

"Do you want to summon those fuckers? Check if they respond, just to confirm?" Brax asks, cocking a brow at me, and despite his teasing tone, I do just that.

Connecting with my magic, I call for the shadows,

but nothing happens. My shoulders sag with relief, and it surprises me how much this was weighing down on me after everything else we've been through. Lips press against my temple, my hand, my crown, my neck. Each of my men reaches out for me as I happily embrace their touch.

"Now, are you ready for your surprise?"

"What does it involve? And is it a good surprise for me or a good surprise for you?" I quiz as Zane takes my hand and leads me down the stairs.

"It's good for all of us, and you'll see," he answers, a knowing smile at the corner of his mouth.

Fucker.

When we reach the bottom of the steps, I expect him to turn us to the communal areas where I've been catching up with my mother, Leila, and even Sammi a few times, but instead, he turns toward the front door.

The moment we step outside, I start to panic.

A gateway gleams ahead, enticing us forward, but I freeze on the spot. "Are we going somewhere?"

"Yes," Eldon answers with a grin, but my frown only deepens.

"Where to and for how long?" Brax gives me a deathly stare, not impressed with my questioning, but I can't help it. "It can't be for long. I promised to help the Drakes—"

"They're already on their way home. Guided, I might

add," he interjects with a sigh.

"Wait, what? Without saying goodbye?" My jaw falls slack. That's some shit right there.

"Of course not. Well, technically, yes, but we've made agreements to go and visit them in the next few weeks," Creed explains, tampering down the disappointment inside of me.

Clearing my throat, I nod. "Fine, but I also have to help Ari and Gia with the magical creatures from the—"

"Done."

I blink up at Eldon. One word. One word and another job on my to-do list seems to be completed.

"How?" I question, narrowing my eyes at him.

"They actually really love the island off from Silvercrest Academy. Figgins has helped put a new set of wards in place for them. Wards that allow them all to come and go as they please while keeping unwanted guests out," Eldon adds, and my heart clenches.

Damn, that's the best idea. I've been trying to tackle one thing at a time, and I hadn't gotten around to that particular issue yet, but it makes total sense.

"Thank you," I breathe, but my mind is still racing, trying to piece together something else I have to handle. "Well, we can't be gone long because..." My words trail off when I come up blank, but my heart continues to race.

"Raven, everything is going to remain exactly as it is

until we get back. Your mother is going to stay here with Leila, take a little R&R in a place they feel safe," Creed states, waving his hand at the huge mansion behind us. The mention of my friend hurts my heart a little. She lost her father in this battle too, and she's hurting. It's a feeling she can't quite comprehend since he was working with Burton. She's never going to have an explanation for his actions, understand his motives. Nothing. But she'll get through this, she's stronger than anyone else I know. "The Monarchy is in tatters and it's going to take more than a few days or weeks to recover. Rhys is heading all of that, and if he wants our input on anything, you know, we'll give it to him. The academy is not in service right now, or for the foreseeable future. Some big changes are going to have to happen, and I'm not trying to shock you or anything, but that's not our shit to deal with."

My eyelids fall closed as I take a deep breath. He's right, he's really fucking right. It's just hard for me to switch off when I've been alert and handling so much shit for what feels like an eternity. They've taken care of everything within their control while swiping things off our to-do list that didn't require my direct attention. Fuck, I love them.

Blinking open my eyes, I look up at them as a smile grows across my face. "Okay, so what's the plan?"

"Step through the gateway and you'll find out," Zane

answers, sweeping his arm dramatically in that direction.

A bubble of excitement rushes through me and I nod, moving toward it, but before I can step through, Brax beats me to it, always leading the way. I'm right behind him, and the second the new scenery comes into view, my chest clenches.

"Where is this?"

"This is paradise, Shadow," Brax breathes, slinking his arm around my shoulders and pulling me into his side as I stare out at a long stretch of sand and a little hut shack situated all alone. "And it's ours for the next five days."

The sun beams down, warming my soul along with my body, and I sigh contentedly. Relaxing isn't the norm for me and I don't know how I'll handle it, but remaining calm for five days doesn't sound too bad… I don't think.

"We're going to work your body so hard for those five days, Dove; I hope you're not planning too much relaxing in your head," Zane murmurs against the shell of my ear, and I shiver, excitement coursing through me.

"I would never." I can't keep the smile off my face.

"We'll let her relax a little, at least. Especially since we'll be heading to Shadowmoor before we go home," Creed states, and I frown in confusion as I look to him for further explanation. "Rhys agreed that it's time Shadowmoor wasn't suppressed anymore, and felt there was only one person suitable to oversee it be done properly."

I blink and blink again, in awe of his words.

Holy fuck.

"Does that sound okay to you, Little Bird?" Eldon asks, and I nod vigorously.

"That sounds more than okay," I admit. It's about time the realm wasn't subjected to this kind of shit. Everyone should be treated equally and given a chance to nurture their own abilities.

"Are you happy, Raven?" Creed asks, and I take a second to really think about it.

If my life has taught me anything so far, it's that happiness isn't a destination. I don't get to arrive there and stay there forever. It's an emotion, just like sadness, anger, and heartache.

Are there sad moments in my life? Memories I'll never be able to avoid, and pain that will come and go whether I like it or not? Yes. But is there also love in each embrace, heart in every encounter, and a reason to keep on living? Fuck yes.

There's only one answer to his question. There will always only be one answer to his question. Because if I ever feel anything other than happiness, I know I'll be able to ride out the storm and feel it warm my veins once again when I'm ready.

"With the four of you by my side, I will forever be happy."

AFTERWORDS

Well, well, fucking well.

What. A. Ride.

This story came out of left field, wrapped me up in all its feels and took me on a journey I didn't expect. Wrangling these Bishops into line wasn't always easy, but that's why we love them.

To be real for a moment, do I think there are still parts of this story to unravel? Yes. Do I think they're Raven's to tell? No.

That being said, it's either going to be explored in her box set or we're going to eventually get a novella for it. Another job added to the never ending to do list, which would be much easier to complete if I didn't get distracted by brand new series that hold me captive.

That's right, you heard me, a brand new series is already rolling into May for us.

It has me by the hooks, and I know I say that a lot, but this is intense. Like take my soul and give me all of the words intense.

It takes more time for me to write about than it once did. The giddiness of diving into my first book, Featherstone Academy, had me completing the first draft in three weeks.

I've never done that since. This new series however, has had me write the first twenty chapters in two weeks which feels so refreshing it has me ready to burst.

Thank you for always being here on this journey with me. You're the lifeline I love with all of my heart.

As a thank you, I thought I should give you a cheeky glimpse at the mysterious handbook. And I may even put chapter one of the new release in the back of the book too.

HOUSEMATES HANDBOOK

Welcome, chosen one. I'm going to use this book against you at all times. You're welcome.

These words are said with love. I swear. It didn't exist until you stepped through those doors, and now here we are. If anything, it's your fault not mine, so you should take a look in the mirror if it offends you.

Peace,

Zane

(And Creed, Brax, and Eldon… but more so me.)

Rule #1

There are no rules unless I call them. If necessary, this folder will be used to whack you around the head to knock some sense into you.

Rule #2

Okay, now there are rules. Look what you made me do. Hmm? I hope you're happy with yourself.

This handbook now declares it is necessary for everyone in this house to help and aid each other so we can be at our best. Which means luckily for you, we're going to make you stronger than ever. Again, you're welcome.

Rule #3

Housemates HAVE to show patience with one another. That includes these assholes. More them than anyone else. You, my sweet Dove, need to let us in.

Rule #4

No sneaking out. Or being a general menace, even though it suits you so well.

Rule #5

When one of us claims you, we all do. Get ready, Dove.

Rule #6

Surviving the Gauntlet is a necessity. No failure is allowed. We'll make sure of it.

Rule #7

No shielding or hiding away. It's hot as fuck, but I already told you that.

Rule #8

No more making me worry. I mean it.

Rule #9

No more doubting. Compliments may only be accepted with a smile or a blowjob. The choice is yours, Dove.

Rule #10

Morning orgasms have now been officially added to the handbook.

Rule #11

As experience decides, no separation. Ever. I can't breathe without you.

Rule #12

Don't ever fucking come that close to dying again.
I love you.

THANK YOU

Michael. What a man. I love you. Which is why this book is dedicated to you. Does this get me out of chores? I think it should.

To my babies, nothing fills my heart quite like my love for you. You make me proud every day, and nothing gives me more joy than making you proud too.

Nicole, Jeni, Tanya. You guys are my queens. Thank you for loving these words as much as I do. You give me all of the vibes.

Kirsty, mate. Thank you for coping with my head mash. You're a silent rock and a pillar of support, in more ways than one.

To my beta readers, your comments give me life. I love taking this journey with you guys.

Thank you to Sarah and Lily for making everything perfect. You gals are superior.

ABOUT KC KEAN

KC Kean began her writing journey in 2020 amidst the pandemic and homeschooling… yay! After reading all of the steam, from fade to black, to steamy reads, MM, and reverse harem, she decided to immerse herself in her own worlds too.

When KC isn't hiding away in the writing cave, she is playing Dreamlight Valley, enjoying the limited UK sunshine with her husband, children, and furbabies, or collecting vinyls like it's a competition.

Come and join me over at my Aceholes Reader Group, follow my author's Facebook page, and enjoy Instagram with me.

ALSO BY KC KEAN

Ruthless Brothers MC
(Reverse Harem MC Romance)
Ruthless Rage
Ruthless Rebel
Ruthless Riot

Featherstone Academy
(Reverse Harem Contemporary Romance)
My Bloodline
Your Bloodline
Our Bloodline
Red
Freedom
Redemption

All-Star Series
(Reverse Harem Contemporary Romance)
Toxic Creek
Tainted Creek
Twisted Creek

(Standalone MF)
Burn to Ash

Emerson U Series
(Reverse Harem Contemporary Romance)
Watch Me Fall
Watch Me Rise
Watch Me Reign

Saints Academy
(Reverse Harem Paranormal Romance)
Reckless Souls
Damaged Souls
Vicious Souls
Fearless Souls
Heartless Souls

Silvercrest Academy
(Reverse Harem Paranormal Romance)
Falling Shadows
Destined Shadows
Cursed Shadows
Unchained Shadows

Floodborn Academy
Kingdom of Ruin